The Sign of The Blood

The Sign of The Blood

LP O'Bryan

ARDUA PUBLISHING

Ardua Publishing
5 Dame Lane,
Dublin 2,
Ireland
http://arduapublishing.com

Ordering Information: Contact the publisher.

This novel is a work of fiction. Any resemblance to actual persons, living or long dead, is entirely deliberate.

Acknowledgements

I'd like to thank my editors, Alex McGilvery, Sheryl Lee, Helen Pryke & Catriona Troth, and beta readers, Tanja Slijepčević, Robin Levin, Cheryl Carpinello, Roy Foster, Dwayne Lara & Kelly Lenihan. All remaining errors are mine. Special thanks also to all BooksGoSocial supporters and my wife, Zeynep, and my children, who've had a lot to put up with.

Historical Background

The novel takes place between the years 297 A.D. and 306 A.D. The Roman Empire had numerous emperors in the preceding century and had recently entered a system of rule with four emperors, two in the west and two in the east. Below are the real historical figures we encounter in this fictional retelling of a crucial period in world history, when Christianity took a major step in its journey from being a marginal and persecuted religion to becoming the most powerful religion in the Roman Empire.

The **Emperor Galerius** was the junior emperor in the east at this time. As we first encounter him, he has been tasked with the defeat of the Sasanians, the last Persian Empire before the rise of Islam.

The **Emperor Chlorus** was the senior emperor in the west. He had given his son, Constantine, as a hostage to the eastern emperor, as was common practice at that time, as a sign of commitment to their power sharing agreement.

Constantine, later to become Constantine the Great, was a young man of twenty-five in 297 A.D. He was an officer in Galerius' campaign, learning the arts of war.

Helena, his mother, had separated from Constantine's father, the Emperor Chlorus. He needed to marry a more suitable wife for someone rising fast in Roman politics.

Theodora, a Roman aristocrat, and the **Emperor Chlorus'** new wife.

Juliana, a fictional character I created to help tell the story of Constantine's rapid rise to power.

Place Names Used At The Time (297-306 A.D.)

Bithynia - A Roman province in what is now western Turkey.

Britannia - A Roman province now comprising England & Wales.

Caledonia - Much of Scotland, outside of Roman control.

Eboracum - The Roman city, now York, in the north of Britannia.

Gaul - A Roman province, now largely France.

Germania - Germany, most of which was outside the empire.

Gesoriacum - The Roman port town, now Boulogne, in northern Gaul.

Italia - Italy, the home province of the Roman Empire.

Lindum - The Roman city, now Lincoln, in central Britannia.

Londinium - The Roman city, now London in southern Britannia.

Massilia - The Roman port city, now Marseilles, in southern Gaul.

Moesia - A Roman province, including most of modern Serbia.

Nicomedia - The Roman city, capital of the Eastern Roman Empire at the time, now the city of Izmit in Turkey, on the Sea of Marmara.

Palandoken - Mountains in the area between modern Turkey, Iran and Armenia.

Treveris - The Roman city, now Trier, in western Germany, on the River Moselle, inside the Roman Empire, capital of the western Roman Empire at that time.

"Praise be to the Lord my Rock, who trains my hands for war, my fingers for battle."
Psalm 144:1.

Prologue

The Roman City of Eboracum (York) - Northern Britannia, 306 A.D.

The slave girl raised her arms, spread them like an eagle about to take flight, then leaned towards him. Blue feather-tattoos covered her skin. Her eyes were rimmed with silver. She shook her soot black hair. Curls flickered in the light from the oil lamps.

The Emperor Constantius Chlorus waved her forward. "Are they all like you beyond Hadrian's Wall?"

She shook her head, bared her teeth. One on each side had been sharpened so she could suck blood from the necks of her enemies or from animals downed in a hunt.

A low and pleasant hum warmed his blood. This one had a spark in her, not like the other beaten curs they'd sent to his rooms every other time he'd been to Eboracum.

"Come here."

She moved towards him. With her large white breasts and long legs, she looked like the fresco of a painted savage he'd seen once in Rome.

He hardened fast, cupped one breast in his hand, then the other. The erect tips had flecks of blue on them. He pulled her to him. They tasted sweet.

He closed his eyes as she lowered herself on top of him.

"What do your people say about me?" he asked, when he was finished, and she was moving away from him, crawling backwards towards the door.

She stopped, leaned up, placed her hands together, as if in prayer.

"You will die before the moon rises."

I

Lower Armenia, 297 A.D., Nine Years Before.

Juliana had been warned often enough. "Beyond the Wolfe's Teeth Mountains lies the daemon world."

They'd been right too. Every half-dazed step confirmed it, as did her dreams filled with blood-smeared faces and strangled screams. And every morning when she woke it was to the knowledge that what had happened was even worse than all those dreams, and that her only hope was that some of them had survived, a friend, a cousin, her mother.

She shaded her eyes from the burning sun. A line of dust-streaked cavalry rode about an arrow's flight away on her right. Sun-whitened grass faded into the horizon beyond. Hot air eddied above it all, as if the land itself boiled.

An executioner's call rang out. Her ten-year-old body shook. An intake of breath passed along the line of shuffling captives.

"Look up, runts, children of our enemies! See how those who displease us find the end to their days."

The executioner threw a severed head towards the prisoners. The mouth gaped wide. Blood dripped from where the neck should have been. The head tumbled onto the grass near her, its blank eyes accusing.

She stared again at the bare back of the prisoner in front of her, willing herself not to care, pressing her hands into dusty fists. Glimpses of mutilated soldiers, one-handed thieves, and the leprous beggars who occasionally visited their village had not prepared her for any of this.

LP O'Bryan

But she lived, and for that she had to be grateful as another day headed towards its end and the longed-for watery gruel.

Juliana turned her grease-smeared wrists to examine the sores festering there. They were not healing. She looked up. The tiniest of breezes had stroked her cheek. It held a smell too, a memory of food. Roast lamb, spiced maybe, like her mother used to make, or was it something else?

A distant fanfare blared. Shouts rang out. The clamoring grew, spreading towards her along the ranks of the army. Then, as quickly as it had sprung up, it died away. The rustling of ten thousand cavalry, the clinking of their sun-emblazoned shields and breastplates, had terrified her at first, but as that summer wore on, the noise had faded in her mind, until now, she only heard them if she truly listened.

Another murmur passed along the column.

Every head turned.

The naked executioner gestured stiff-armed contempt at the captives passing by, as laughing soldiers dragged a boy clothed in a single rag, with a mane of charcoal hair, towards him.

The boy arched his back like a terrified goat which had smelled the block.

Dizziness blossomed inside Juliana and she stumbled, fell out of the line. The two girls who were roped to her flailed to a stop. She pulled them towards her, out of the way of the other captives trudging past; the women staring their pity at her, the young men's eyes drinking in her body visible through the tears in her thin woolen dress. She glared back at them, too tired to care about what they could see. Some men, the girls had whispered, could rip a loin cloth away with their teeth, even if their arms were cut off.

The two girls tied to Juliana were already cursing like cheated traders. One of them kicked Juliana's thigh, hard. Screams followed. Juliana looked up at them through dust-rimmed eyes. Another kick landed. But that was it. Both girls were distracted, glancing back and forth along the column, fear filling their eyes.

She let her breath out, relishing the momentary relief of not trudging forward. She closed her eyes. *When will it all be over?*

4

"You'll have plenty of time on your back in the years ahead, Roman," a eunuch's disdainful voice called out.

She opened her eyes. A horse's thigh shivered above her. Giant flies danced around it. A hoof pawed the whitened grass around her. She moved back swiftly, using her elbows. The horse stomped after her.

Her muscles tightened, expecting the crush of the hooves. She stopped moving, closed her eyes. *Let him stamp on me. I don't care.*

But all the eunuch did was curse her loudly in Persian. She breathed in the dust, held it as it tickled her throat. Trampling was not how the Persians killed disobedient captives. They had more entertaining ways to do that.

Her hands were yanked, her shoulders half wrenched from her body. The eunuch's whip snapped the air.

He leaned towards her. He knew how to finish off captives who couldn't stay the pace. The Persian army left bodies in its wake every day.

"Don't rest, little Roman, or I will send you to him." The eunuch pointed towards the ridge on the right. The executioner had the boy's head in the air on his sword tip, the face contorted with fright, the mouth so wide the back teeth glistened as blood dripped.

"Move, Roman, or you will be the next to die."

The eunuch turned and cantered off in a spray of dust. Juliana glared at him. Death held no fear for her. It would be more than welcome. She made a defiant face at his disappearing back. The other slave girls copied her. Then she stood, and they all started walking. She could not see them dead because of her.

Walking, walking, walking until, just when she knew for sure the day would never end, the horns wailed. The army spread out, winding into a circle, transforming that part of the grassy plain into a nomad city. Cooking fires were lit and, almost instantly, a patchwork of tents mushroomed around them. Juliana and the girls she was tethered to waited, huddled together, too far beyond exhaustion to talk.

Nearby, the nobles' tents were being set up. It was the first time the captured slave girls had been told to wait near these tents.

5

They had the same round shape as the tents that made up most of the camp, but these were not patched like the others, they were newer, cleaner. Whenever they stopped, she tried to spot Narses, the Persian King of Kings. She wanted to see the man they called the Grand Mage, the Keeper of the Sacred Fire. They'd been told they were his property now when they were captured, and that if they ran and were beheaded as a result, their villages would owe their price to him.

She saw something that made her almost call out. Two girls, about her age, sheathed in shimmering gold cloth, were running through the half-completed nobles' tents. They looked happy. And then they were gone.

She closed her mouth to stifle the cry of envy which rose like a blade inside her. She went back to dreaming of food and buckets of water. Enough to keep her tongue from swelling.

She bent, coughed, coughed again.

"You Romans should bury your shit." She looked up. A eunuch strutted towards her.

She straightened her back.

"Stupid, dirty Romans." He laughed to himself.

It made no difference that she wore her hair in the never-cut pony-tail style and that it was the right oil-black color and length for a young Persian girl. Her long bony face looked foreign, Roman, unmistakably so, and all Romans are the spawn of Ahriman, the great daemon, she'd heard them say often enough.

"Roman legions are near. Our scouts can smell their dirt," the girl beside her whispered. Juliana touched her lips for silence.

"Your chicken-hearted emperor will have to fight soon."

Since they'd found out that her father had been a smith attached to a Roman legion, they'd not let up with the jibes and insults. But she hadn't known her father and wouldn't recognize him if he lay dying in front of her. Though strangely, the idea that he might be near sent her gaze to the horizon.

"No talking," the eunuch roared. His bull whip cracked the air. This one was younger than the others. He'd spoken to her in a way that had sent peals of hope through her after she'd been captured, but now she'd learnt what all the eunuchs were like, it sparked only

6

wariness. Eunuchs, she'd learned from the whispers of the other girls, like to play games with captives destined for the slave market, especially the ones with ugly foreign faces, who were unlikely to make a good price.

"Well, my little Roman." He was standing near, his mustiness overpowering. "Did you see our little friend today? He was from a village near yours, wasn't he?" She kept her face still. The eunuch's lips cracked open and the folds of flesh above his ears creased, as if worms were arranging themselves beneath his skin.

He pointed a dirty finger at her. "Remember." He leaned closer. She could smell garlic on his breath. She stared back at him. "I can cut your heart out." He put his hand to the hilt of the knife in his belt. "And eat it in front of you, and all I will get is praise for removing another Roman daemon from this world."

A second eunuch had come over to see what was going on. This one stroked an amulet, an oversized phallus, which rested against his bloated stomach as he spoke.

"Did you tell her?"

"Not yet. Can't I have a little fun?" The first one laughed, his small bare belly gyrating.

"The priests require a volunteer, little ones." He walked around them all, his tone soft, mocking. "A volunteer who wishes to be freed from our daily toil." He looked into one tired girl's face, then the next.

"A volunteer, a little one who's right for this duty." He winked at Juliana.

She looked away. Loud squawking broke out above her head. A flock of silvery cranes flew past, oblivious of everything going on below, heading towards the forested slopes of the mountain. A deep longing filled her, sending trembles through her chest. She knew such forests well, the calls of chiffchaff, the cries of the secretive black-hooded crows her mother fed and talked to. They were a refuge, a place of safety, where her mother had taught her things, answered any question, and eased her fears with hugs and whispers.

"Look at me, little Roman." Her tied wrists were wrenched high.

She looked at him, her mouth clamped shut, staring directly into his eyes, daring him to kill her and get it all over with.

He shook the rope.

She swayed, closed her eyes.

Make it swift, please. I am lost. I am alone. I may as well be dead.

The whip cracked through the air.

II

Lower Armenia, 297 A.D.

Constantine looked up through a gap in the canopy of trees as a flock of birds flew past, silhouetted against an azure sky. They were hurrying, beating their wings as if, like the army he was attached to, they too were being chased by a Persian army.

He breathed in hard. Every action he took part in would be judged, he knew, and to a high standard, not only because he was a junior Tribune of the Jovian guard, the emperor of the east's personal legion, and had to be regularly assessed for his ability to lead, but also because he was Flavius Valerius Constantine, the son of the emperor of the west.

When he looked back down along the steep embankment, a dizziness almost overcame him. He had to close his eyes to steady himself. When he opened them, Persian horsemen had entered the narrow track below. He counted. There were ten of them.

The observation point he'd picked was a good one, behind a drift of fallen pine tree branches, on a bed of quills, where he could peer through gaps in the brush to see the track below.

"Awooooooooooooo." A distant wolf howl cut through the air.

Just as abruptly, it ceased. A hush settled over the forest. The strap at his right knee was cutting into him again. It could wait, movement would give them away.

He lay still, breathing softly. His dark crimson cloak covered him almost completely, letting him fade into the forest gloom.

His companion shifted his position slightly. Constantine moved a little forward to get a clearer view of the path below. His hand gripped the pommel of his sword.

The lead Persian scout halted, raised a gloved hand to stop the riders behind him. He scanned the forest and the incline. His helmet glinted as he turned one way then the other.

Then the Persian scout stared straight at him. Constantine stared back. There was no way the man could see him. A column of evening sunlight shone in the air between them. Midges and dust motes swirled in its beam. Perhaps the man was looking at them.

The Persian riders whispered to each other. Their lead scout threw his head back, sniffed the air.

"Find the Persian camp," Constantine had been told, before he'd led the scouting mission out that afternoon. The officer hadn't bothered repeating what almost everyone knew, that no other scouting mission had managed the task in the previous three nights, since they'd been skirting the mountains.

A blood-red ant crawled onto the back of Constantine's hand. His skin prickled. He watched as it navigated its way up his thickly haired arm. Then another appeared, on his middle finger.

He scanned the line of horsemen. One of the Persians had drawn his sword and was examining it.

The lead Persian scout shook his head as if irritated, said something which made those around him laugh, then backed his horse off the trail and waved those behind him to pass him by.

Towards the rear of their line were four prisoners, boys, pickings from a local village most likely, all naked, bound at the wrists, and trotting to keep up with the horse each was roped to. Some of their faces were purple from bruising. One whimpered as he hobbled along trying to keep up.

Anger rose through his chest. Even the most debauched Senators in Rome sickened at the practices of the Persian King. If the stories he'd heard were true, blinding would be the next thing in store for that boy. His terrified screams as they did it would put fear deep and far into the hearts of the others who'd been taken with him.

When the last of the riders and prisoners had gone past, the Persian officer followed.

Constantine waited, listening to the birds, until the sound of the horsemen died. Then he stood, turned to the Armenian guide rising to his feet beside him.

"Let's follow them," he whispered.

"Are you sure? This is why your previous scouts went missing. They got too close to the enemy."

Constantine jabbed a finger into the man's chest, hard. "We're not going back empty handed. But we're not following this track either."

"Where are we going?"

"That way." Constantine pointed at the ridge, visible through the trees, in the direction the Persian had taken.

The Armenian sighed. "My friends tell me you Romans will lose this war. That I should change sides, before it's too late. The Persians pay well, they tell me."

Constantine stepped back, as if measuring the distance between them. A bird took noisy flight through the trees.

"Your emperor should give command of these scouting missions to men who know these lands, not to Romans." The Armenian spat, then checked his sword hung properly from his belt.

"You know, you are lucky," Constantine replied.

"Lucky?" The Armenian speedily brushed dirt and twigs from his stained leather tunic, then threw his hands in the air "I'm a scout attached to a Roman army being chased by a Persian force intent on its annihilation. Yes, Fortuna surely smiles on me."

"No, Lucius, you're lucky because I'm giving you another chance to prove how loyal you are." Constantine raised his sword a little from its scabbard.

Lucius' eyes widened.

"We will find the Persian camp, Lucius." He let his sword drop back into its scabbard.

"Isn't Roman gratitude a wonderful thing?" Lucius turned on his heel, headed for where the horses were hobbled downwind.

When Constantine reached the horses, Lucius had already mounted. He didn't look at Constantine, just kicked his horse and

LP O'Bryan

headed away in the direction Constantine had pointed, sitting high in his saddle, scanning all around as he went.

III

Lower Armenia, 297 A.D.

Through the flap of the tent they were waiting outside, Juliana saw the ash-stained face of one of the Magi, the Persian priests, observing her. He looked inhuman, like a ghost, or one of the incubi her village elders kept warning her about.

The pain across her back, where the eunuch's whip had cut into her flesh, still burned at her skin.

The Magi had never been interested in the captives before. This was the first time she'd seen any of them even look at her since the early days of her capture.

She sniffed. She could smell myrrh, the curing incense. Her mother often used it. Its smell lingered, unmistakable. She bit her lip. They must not see her crying.

The sound of the Gathas, the Persian mysteries, being chanted, echoed over the camp from the Magi tents each sunset, but tonight the chanting from tents dotted around the camp sounded different, more insistent, as if building towards something. She glanced through the tent flap again, pulling at the rope behind her, linking her to the others. They both muttered curses at her, low enough that only she could hear.

The priest at the back of the tent stared at her, unblinking. As the light faded around them, one of the eunuchs came through the opening. She knew him. It was the one who'd whipped her earlier. The one she hated.

"You'll all get food when you tell us which of you'll be the volunteer for the morning, my little ones," said the eunuch, ushering them forward. "The one who volunteers will help bring forth the

13

Daeva, for our Queen of Queens. Her wrath must not be provoked, so decide quickly. We must tell the priests the volunteer's name soon. They do not like waiting." He beckoned them forward and into the tent, then left, closing the flap as he did, saying something to the guard stationed outside.

A yellow beeswax candle on a brass tray near the center pole now provided the only illumination inside the tent. Its low roof reminded Juliana of a red-carpeted cave whose encircling walls seemed to breathe in and out as the candle fluttered, and whose arched roof bulged inwardly, as if supporting something unseen, though she knew only the drifting smoke from the cooking fires separated the tent from the earliest and brightest of the evening stars.

The tent creaked, as if straining against something.

The girl to Juliana's left broke the silence. "It cannot be me." She had a pinched face, as if she'd never eaten well, or much at all, and her accent, from Al-Arabia, was difficult to understand.

"We should sit," Juliana replied. They sat in a semi-circle around the brass tray, almost touching each other's knees. The carpet they were sitting on was thin, its red pattern faded almost to the weave. Beneath it she could feel the uneven ground.

"Mine . . . both parents dead. You know this. The Magi magic not work if a girl has her blood line on the other side. You know this too," said the girl from Al-Arabia. Juliana shook her head. She didn't know this.

"Picking threads will be fairest," she said. "We will make one shorter than the others. We always did this in my village." The girls looked at her blankly. She continued, her tone more certain now. "Each of us will have an equal chance for freedom."

The girl from Al-Arabia's voice rose to a high pitch as she replied. "We cannot pick threads, Roman. The magic will not work if I'm chosen. I told you this. The Queen will be angry, very angry." She stared at Juliana, a determined look on her face. Juliana looked at the other girl, the eldest of the three, the one who hadn't spoken so far.

She looked directly at Juliana, then wriggled forward to stroke Juliana's knee. Her hand brushed Juliana's thigh, her expression enticing, knowing.

"Which of us will it be," she said in a sing-song tone. Then she lowered her voice, stroked Juliana's thigh again. "Maybe we will all get lucky. Think about it Juliana, we could be sold in Ctesiphon together when this campaign is over. Men will pay their daughter's dowry for a pair of birds like us. You're too young to be a dancer, but we'll make a good pair of song birds. Do you think you'd have been happy as the third wife of some half-broken hill farmer? Partner with me, you'll enjoy it, I'm sure." She stuck her tongue out, wiggled it up and down.

"The eunuchs listen to me, Roman. I'll tell them the magic will work better when the volunteer is an orphan, and reluctant." She sounded confident, the way older girls always sounded in the village. The girl from Al-Arabia let out a whimper.

The older girl gripped Juliana's thigh. "Agree, Juliana. I'll make you tremble with delight." A bead of sweat on the girl's forehead flashed in the candlelight as she leaned towards Juliana. A small bare breast brushed against Juliana's knee.

The sounds from outside the tent, the chanting, distant shouts, and the neighing of horses sounded different, as if something had changed, a veil had been lifted. Laughter echoed. Her breath came fast. She wanted more than anything to go home.

Like rumors of the sea, the thought of girls being with each other was something far off, that she would find out about later, much later. Her mother had deflected all questions about such things until the time her blood would come. Even what that meant she could only guess at, though some of the other girls in the village had warned her that the time would not be far off and that it would be painful. They also said many other things she didn't believe.

She blinked.

The volunteer would be freed. The guard had said it.

The girl from Al-Arabia stared at her, her eyelids tear rimmed, like a bowl about to overflow. Juliana looked at the older girl again. The girl she'd once thought could be her friend. Her eyebrows were raised. A prickling ran across Juliana's thigh, under her thin cotton trousers.

"I'll be the stupid volunteer," she said.

She pushed the older girl's hand away. The rope, still binding them together, tangled as she did so. She shook it free.

The girl from Al-Arabia sighed.

The older girl called for the guard. She spoke to him, pointed at Juliana.

He laughed. A long, curved knife bulged from his belt. It looked odd, too big. The eunuchs usually went about with smaller weapons.

She remembered a story she'd heard in her village years before. A boy from Persepolis, the son of a passing trader, had frightened all the children with tales of secret Persian ceremonies during times of war, ceremonies where special knives were used, where human entrails were read to foretell the future. A cold sweat broke out across her chest.

It couldn't be true, could it?

Practices like that had stopped long ago. Hadn't they?

IV

The City of Alexandria, 297 A.D.

Helena reached for the letter in her scribe's hand, pulled the scroll of papyrus from him, and took it to the marble table.

"Light that candle." She pointed at the large yellow beeswax candle in the center of the table.

The scribe hurried away.

As she waited for him she read the letter one more time, to commit it to memory.

Helena,

It is the wish of our Emperor Diocletian, the most glorious and esteemed, that our son, Constantine, be protected, as he has always been, and come to no harm serving at the emperor's will.

I am unable to request he come to Alexandria to attend you. You are provided for, as would be expected of an ex-wife of a Caesar. Your request to travel to Rome is also denied. Do not test the bounds of our agreement.

Constantine Chlorus

Caesar of the Western Provinces, Treveris, Gaul.

She pressed her balled fist hard into her breastbone. In front of her lay the shortest letter she'd received from Constantine's father since they'd parted six years before. It had none of the flowery language his earlier letters had been filled with. The war against the Alemanni had clearly taken its toll. Or were there other reasons for him distancing himself from her?

The scribe returned with a taper. A small flame glowed inside his cupped hand. He lit the beeswax candle.

Helena put the edge of the papyrus to the flame and watched as fire engulfed it. She let the ash drop into a silver bowl, then took a silver pestle from the table and crushed the ashes into a fine dust.

"Find me that priest who has been seeking another audience with me," she said. She pressed her lips tight and closed her eyes.

"The one who speaks of eternal life?"

"Yes, him."

The scribe bowed. He was the last of the slaves she had with her from her time with her ex-husband. "You mean the one you complained of who looked at you too plainly, when he first came here?" He kept his eyes on the ground. "I hear he sleeps with all his converts, the men and the women and the children too."

"I don't care if he rides daemons. He claims he can grant miracles. Let's see if it's true."

With a trembling hand, she smeared the first finger of her right hand in the ashes of her ex-husband's letter, then rubbed the ash on her cheeks. He would find her in mourning when he arrived. It would be better that way.

V

Lower Armenia, 297 A.D.

They were riding slower now, ducking to avoid the lower limbs of the trees, their horses jumping over the occasional fallen tree trunk and tangles of branches, while dirt flew into the air behind them.

Constantine was filled with hope. This could be the way to win the respect of his father. Lurid tales about the last two Roman emperors who'd led armies into Persia had been told and retold in the Roman camp. Anyone who brought Roman vengeance to the armies of Persia would be worthy of command.

"It's almost forty years," a centurion had told Constantine, his face contorted in anger, "since that Persian King of Kings, Shapur, put to death our great emperor, Valerian. First the Magi cut his skin off, then they stuffed it with straw. They had him in one of their fire temples for years. Perhaps they still do."

Defeating Persia had never been easy. The Emperor Galerius, who led them, would need good fortune. He would need Constantine's good fortune. This was the moment he'd been waiting for.

"Prosper through the ranks," had been Constantine's father's last piece of advice, when they'd parted four years before. Ever since, he'd devoted himself to that goal without reaping much success, or the promotions that had been expected of him. The fates had treated him with contempt, denying him things that fell easily at other officers' feet.

He had to find a way to change things.

Eventually Lucius slowed to a halt near the lip of a gorge.

When Constantine stopped beside him a wolf howled, far away. He tightened his grip on his mount's reins and patted her neck to reassure her as he listened for answering calls from the rest of the pack. None came. Below them lay a dried-up stream bed.

They slid their horses slowly down the steep embankment. The gorge was as deep as a city temple was high, with only enough room along the bottom for their two horses to move forward side by side. A sheen of sweat prickled over Constantine's body. He held the reins tight, resisting the urge to scratch at the flea bites on his calves. There was no breeze in the river bed as they moved along it with the sun lowering fast.

Whitened granite boulders were strewn around, as if they'd been discarded from some giant's building works. As they made their way down the channel its decaying walls steepened, widened, and the trees above each edge disappeared, leaving only the deep blue of the late afternoon sky above. They were well beyond the forest now, back on the plain across which the Persian army had been pursuing them. Clumps of grass and pale blue and yellow flowers grew along the lip of the gully. The only sound the crunching under their horses' feet.

Lucius led the way until they came to a rocky corner where the gully walls closed in. He gestured to Constantine to be quiet, then dismounted. They tied the horses' reins to a rock. Lucius pointed forward.

They stopped at the corner, peered up and along the gully. A line of heads on wooden spikes stood out like a stark warning along the right-hand lip of the gully. Flies, like a black funeral gauze, swarmed about them. Even from where they were, he could smell the sickly whiff of rotting flesh.

"This is an opportunity. The Persians don't place guards near their dead. Let's get closer."

Constantine was used to the sight of death and the smell of it. Flesh rotted fast in this part of the empire.

They climbed the wall of the gully in silence, hand over hand. At the lip, loose earth crumbled as he felt about for a handhold.

Lucius gasped. Constantine reached out, steadied him before he slipped and stones clattering beneath them alerted anyone nearby to their existence. He held Lucius tight.

Lucius grinned like an idiot. Constantine reached for the lip of the gulley, pulled himself up. The sight that greeted him was not what he'd expected.

VI

Lower Armenia, 297 A.D.

The four eunuchs who held her spread-eagled adjusted their holds, triumphantly. She looked down, saw her nakedness glistening in the honeyed light from the oil lamps.

She stared again at the shadows dancing languidly on the roof of the tent and thought about going home, walking the track back to her village, seeing it again from the river as it nestled in its fold among forested hills. Her mother would be waiting at their door, her grandmother too. They'd hug, all questions forgotten.

Someone lit a lamp. The shadows on the roof of the tent fled. A smug older face loomed over her. Something cold touched her inner thigh, moved upwards, patted at her, rubbing between her legs, feeling but not penetrating. She went rigid, then shuddered like a snake casting off its skin. The eunuchs held her tight.

Shame throbbed through her. Her eyes opened wide.

Embroidered on the roof of the tent were stars. They sparkled in the lamplight. Perhaps they were diamonds.

It had all started so well the day the Persians came. She had raced excitedly into the narrow street to see what all the noises meant. She'd wanted to be the first to see what the traders were selling and take the news to her mother. Then she'd heard screaming. "Persians, raiders, Juliana, come back, come back."

Halfway down the street armored horsemen with red cloaks and fearsome gray swords appeared, as if they'd been magicked up. Smoke drifted behind them. The sky itself wore a shroud.

She'd tried to run back to her house, but she'd been hoisted roughly by the neck of her tunic. She'd struggled, gasping, felt a thud to her head. Then she'd heard her mother screaming.

His sword sang, slicing through the air. He held her clamped tight under his other arm, her blows, scratches, no more than a source of amusement to him. It was the first time she'd felt true terror, true powerlessness. Now she felt the same.

If only she'd listened to her mother. She shook again. A long, deep convulsion. Then her body arched, as her thighs were pulled further apart.

VII

Lower Armenia, 297 A.D.

It is said each person sees seven sights of wonder in their lives. No more. This had to be one of them.

The largest camp Constantine had ever seen lay like a stain across the grasslands with an azure haze hanging above it. The banners, tents, picket lines and smoking fires of the Persian camp melded together in the distance like a giant creature sprawled out.

In the glow of the setting sun he took note of every detail, calm now, his breathing steady. The boredom of marching every day in the heat and the knowledge that the Roman army was being pursued had left him agitated for weeks, wanting action. Seeing the enemy, their pursuers, felt good, even if, spread out like this, they looked far more numerous than their own army.

What surprised him, though, was the absence of any proper defenses to the camp. No palisade had been raised, no ditch appeared to have been dug.

White pennants flapped on top of a group of grand circular tents at the near edge of the camp. Persian nobles' tents, he guessed.

Then a shout rang out. Instinctively he lowered his head. Lucius copied him a moment later. He reached for his sword handle. Had they been seen?

An answering shout echoed in the distance. Then another further along. He raised a finger in front of his face as he leant back close to the gully wall. They hadn't seen him or Lucius, not yet, anyway.

His mind raced. An attack could be launched from here. A dawn raid perhaps. Honors could be won, promotions. This could be his chance.

But if they were to mount an attack it would have to be done quickly. By morning any slim advantage the gully gave them would be lost. Tomorrow the Persian army would move on. He looked back towards the forest. They had to go.

VIII

Lower Armenia, 297 A.D.

The bulk of the Roman army rested in hide tents in neatly laid out rows within the rectangle of low palisade walls the forward Legionaries had constructed towards the end of that day's march in the wooded foothills of the great Palendoken Mountain.

The cart track through the foothills the army had been following had not been used, except for hunting purposes, since a nearby gold mine had been worked out during the time of the Emperor Marcus Aurelius.

The tent of the emperor who'd led the army into Persian Armenia had been positioned, as usual, at the center of the Roman camp. Inside it he waved an ivory-handled knife in the face of an optio, one of his junior officers, his voice gruff with menace.

"Tell me everything."

"My lord, all they did was ask when we're going to engage the Persians. They're not dishonoring you, my lord. They made no other comment." The optio trembled, despite him being a seasoned soldier.

The emperor traced the tip of his knife up the man's cheek to the corner of one of his odd-shaped eyes. The man blinked spasmodically. Galerius gripped the handle of his knife as if he would plunge it in, skewering the eye. Then, with a disappointed sigh, he pulled it away.

"Come back when you have something I can use. I want to know who the cowards are. I will spare you, if you find out for me."

The optio bowed low, retreating rapidly.

Galerius had vowed that morning to flog anyone complaining of the slow progress of the Roman campaign. He'd been hoping someone might have been found by now for the punishment he'd devised. He'd been looking forward to forcing his Egyptian concubine to watch as well. It would do wonders for her manners.

He sat down slowly onto the ivory and rosewood campaign chair. It had been specially reinforced for him. His flattened nose and the pale scars on his wide face were the marks of his journey from defiant centurion to feared emperor.

He pressed the ball of his fist into his forehead. He hated running from the enemy. They would have to fight soon or face the prospect of defections from the mercenary troops and scouts he'd promised rich pickings to.

He could be confident of one thing, though: the quality of the Roman legions he'd assembled. They were the best in the empire, hand-picked veterans from the Danubian border provinces, who thought only of fighting and dreamt only of victory. These were his men, chosen so there'd be no mistake.

But to have any hope of victory he needed to know where the Persians were and what they were up to. He slammed his hand against the arm of his chair, rattling its joints. He stood and began pacing. Deception and surprise, the handmaidens of the god of war, could only aid him if their blindfolds were removed.

Where were the scouts? What were they doing?

He should never have trusted that spoiled ingrate with such an important mission.

IX

Lower Armenia, 297 A.D.

Constantine leaned forward. The horse's sweat-slicked mane flicked like a loose rope against his face. He had to concentrate. He rode fast. Maybe too fast. Thankfully, the fates had been kind so far. The moon had risen as darkness had engulfed the woods. Its light filtered through the thin ranks of trees. He always enjoyed the pleasure of a night ride, the sway and rhythm, the exhilaration in his chest as his mount found the track to take and their pace quickened.

He raced out of the wood. His thighs and shoulder muscles were stiff from the ride. His mount's stride lengthened. He tightened his grip on the reins, leaning forward again, whispering, enticing the animal to race faster.

A sentry hidden near a solitary tree shouted for the password, ordering them to halt. Constantine shouted the password, swayed as his mount raced on. The palisade wall could be seen like a pale scar in the distance.

He could see guards at the gate, their spears out in front of them. Their breastplates and greaves glinted in the moonlight as they came closer. Lucius pulled up beside him in a spray of dust. Constantine slowed his horse to walk ahead and heard an order ring out. Someone had recognized him. He saluted. The gate of sharpened stakes was pulled aside. Lucius rode behind him as they cantered through the quiet of the sleeping camp.

The first person he'd report to was the Legate of the Jovians, the emperor's personal guard. Standing orders said scouts must report to the Legate, but too much of the night had gone already. If he could persuade the Legate to rouse the emperor, there might just be time for the army to be readied. If he had to wait for dawn it would be too late. The nights were too short at this time of year. He had to rouse the emperor.

Two stone-faced guardsmen crossed their spears in front of the Legate's tent as they rode up.

"The Legate is not to be interrupted, unless we are under attack," one of the guards said, before Constantine even had a chance to speak. He knew from the man's officious expression that it would do no good to argue. He looked around. The camp lay still. The only sound, the heavy breathing of their horses.

Opportunity slips away fast. Soon it would be gone.

He took a deep breath.

"To arms!"

He wheeled his horse, bellowed again, louder this time, as if he'd been unleashed from sense. "Jovians! To arms! To arms!" He sounded different, as if someone else's voice echoed over the camp in the darkness. Lucius' mouth hung wide in amazement. Wild dogs barked in the distance.

Men stumbled from their tents, some clearly half asleep, but ready to fight, their swords drawn. Two centurions clutching spears appeared beside him before the echo of his words had passed, looking around eagerly. Constantine grinned as more men rushed forward. They roared questions at him.

He shook his head in reply. They gripped his legs, as if at any moment they might pull him from his horse. He raised his hands. The men around him went quiet. The quiet spread outwards like a baton being passed from man to man. He licked his wind-cracked lips, both scared at what he'd done, and exhilarated at how free he felt.

"Centurions," he shouted. "Assemble the men. The time for fighting has arrived. We'll teach the Persian chickens not to rest while Roman wolves are about. The daughters of Ctesiphon are waiting." A lusty cheer rang out. Fists punched the air.

A babble of questions launched towards him. He ignored them all. More legionaries appeared out of the dark. Two centurions stood at the back of the crowd, staring at him. They were smirking condescendingly. He wanted to say something to them, to slap their smiles away, but he had other things to worry about.

An orderly threw the flap of the Legate's tent back and a roar bellowed out.

"Constantine get in here!"

If he couldn't get the old cynic on his side he'd be on punishment duty, or worse, before the moon set.

The Legate, Marcus Julius Sextus, was a lean, sturdy veteran with spiky gray hair. Unusually for a Legion commander, he favored decency towards his men, not brutality. He'd earned his men's respect because of it.

"I see no need for your stupid theatricalities out there," Sextus said when the questioning was done.

Constantine and Lucius stood to attention in front of him. His angry expression was gone. He gripped Constantine's shoulder.

"Your father lives the same way, always looking to parade himself."

Constantine was about to reply when Sextus raised his hand. "Say no more. Galerius, no doubt, is already raining bruises on his orderlies because his precious sleep's been disturbed. Take your news to him with my blessing. And bring the Armenian." He pointed at Lucius.

"But I warn you, you've picked a bad time. He's a wounded lion these days. It would have been better if you'd stayed out of his reach." He paused, bit his lip, looked at Constantine. "In fact, I should go with you."

Constantine held himself still. This would be the easy part.

Sextus gave a thumbs up and a growl-like cheer ran through the lines of men still forming outside the tent as he and Constantine hurried past, with Lucius trailing behind.

At each corner of Emperor Galerius' council tent torches sent ribbons of smoke and flame up to the stars. A guard stood to attention by each torch. For a moment Constantine wondered what he was doing.

No. He wouldn't falter. Opportunity lay ahead.

"The honorable commander of the Jovians," a guard shouted as they passed through the entrance flap.

"I hope to all the gods he's got a bloody good reason for keeping me from Morpheus," Galerius roared.

He stood at the other end of the tent behind a long map table. Constantine stopped one step behind and to the side of Sextus, just a little inside the tent. Lucius followed behind, so close Constantine could hear his breathing. He wondered if Lucius had ever been inside an emperor's tent before.

Galerius' thin pearl diadem sparkled in the lamplight. Around him, in a deferential half circle, stood the protector of the imperial intelligence agents and three senior officers of his personal guard.

All were bare headed, except for Galerius and a giant, who wore a black hood pulled down to cover his face. Galerius stood taller than the officers around him. Expectation filled their expressions, as if each man faced either his execution or his triumph. This would not be how Constantine would command, when he came to power. He moved his feet, trying to settle into a more comfortable position.

The dragon pattern rug felt odd under his sandals, too thick, its acanthus leaf edges reminiscent of the distant palaces he'd stayed too long in before joining the Jovians. A scent of pinecone incense tickled his nose. A marble bust of the Emperor Diocletian, Galerius' father-in-law and mentor, sat nearby on a thin pedestal. Behind it, a tiger skin rested on a rack made of jeweled spears.

"Who roused my legions?"

Sextus walked two paces towards the irate emperor, then bowed low.

"My lord, good news." Sextus sounded hesitant. "This will turn our campaign."

The air in the tent sucked at Constantine's breath, as if he stood by the door of an oven.

"Just one piece of good fortune can change the course of a war, as you know, my lord." Sextus motioned Constantine forward.

Every eye turned to him.

Constantine held his expression still. He stepped up beside Sextus and bowed as low as the legate had done.

"My lord, I roused the legions," he said, as he stood up straight. "I have news from my scouting patrol."

Galerius looked at him as if he'd crawled into the tent, not walked.

"You know my orders. All scouts must come direct to the Protector or his officer when they return," roared Galerius, his fists in the air. "You do know this, don't you?" This was not what Constantine had expected. But he knew not to reply.

"I pity you." Galerius' tone oozed contempt. "Having a father like yours only shows up your many weaknesses."

Constantine felt his cheeks burn. It had been months since he'd been berated so publicly by Galerius. Constantine felt like drawing his sword and lunging at the bastard.

"I seek only victory, my lord. The glory will soon be yours," he said.

"How will I get this victory?" Galerius said.

"The Persians have camped near a gully only a few hours' march from here. It's the nearest I've ever seen them." He looked at Galerius. The man had to see his opportunity in this.

"Their nobles' tents are an arrow flight from the edge of the camp. I saw the pennants myself, my lord. Only one row of perimeter guards have been posted. Their camp is defenseless right now." Enthusiasm got the better of his training, but he didn't care.

"If we attack before dawn we'll take them unawares. I'll volunteer, my lord. I wish to be a part of the raid and to lead it." He stopped. Galerius snorted. The other officers were sneering. Blood pounded in his neck. Could they not see the opportunity? He gripped the handle of his sword.

"This is the truth," he continued, addressing the room now. "A great victory awaits you all, my lords, like the one that gave Persia to Trajan."

Galerius raised a hand for silence, then walked towards Constantine. His knee-length cotton tunic tightened like a skin around his massive frame as he moved. When he came close his finger stabbed into Constantine's chest, the only man in the tent who matched his height and build.

"Maybe, but the last time you were part of a raid, you had to be rescued," he said.

He brought his face up close to Constantine's. Their noses were almost touching. Galerius' breath stank of stale wine. "You see, I decide when we attack, not you." Veins stood out on his forehead as he pulled his lips back in a show of rage. His gums were black with garum.

Constantine pressed his lips tight, looked towards the back of the tent. Two young orderlies, their faces pink as if they'd just bathed, stood there like statues, carefully avoiding his gaze. They both looked terrified.

Galerius glared at him a little longer, then turned away, as if he'd remembered something.

"This is a good time to tell you about a letter from your father." His tone was friendly. Constantine stiffened. He hadn't had a letter from his father in over a year. Why had he written to Galerius? Distant shouts could be heard as Galerius drank a long draught from a gold goblet on the map table.

He turned to the men around them. A smile beamed from his face. His officers grinned back almost as one. They reminded Constantine of the chorus from a theatre show he'd seen in Nicomedia.

"Your father had some sound advice for us all, as usual." He turned back to Constantine. "He said I should give you all the dangerous duties, leading the first cohort, for example. He said you're to receive no more special treatments and . . ." he paused.

His shadow swayed across the tent wall as he gestured irritably to the nearest orderly, mouthing something at him. The boy rushed to a wooden chest at the back of the room. Within moments he'd returned with a small papyrus scroll held out in front of him.

Constantine hissed air in through his teeth, imagining what Galerius might have planned for him. He would love to impale the bastard.

As the scroll was unrolled, its gold imperial seal swayed beneath it from a strip of purple silk. The orderly bowed, held it up for Galerius to read.

"Yes, I'd almost forgotten the best part," he said. "Your father has celebrated the birth of a son. Wonderful isn't it? Best thing he ever did, discarding that tavern girl mother of yours. Though I hear she was a favorite of many men years ago." He smirked.

Constantine's hands turned to fists at his side.

Galerius continued. "This new son will be appointed his successor, he tells me. No doubt that'll be the new empress' wish. New wives always want the old brood out of the way quick. They are most demanding, aristocratic women, I think you will find. If you are lucky ever to find one after this."

He pressed his palms against the side of his leather tunic. He'd expected his stepmother to be against him, since his father had told him he would remarry, but he'd not expected her to scheme to exclude him from the succession so soon.

"We are all you have, Constantine." Galerius looked around, grinning. "You do not even qualify as a member of the imperial family any more, now you've been removed from the succession." He shook his head in a mockery of sympathy.

"Well, don't worry, boy, we'll not strip you of all honors, yet." Galerius let the scroll drop on the map table.

"We had your future divined after we received this letter. Our most reliable soothsayer predicted you'll never inherit your father's titles. No one should try for what's beyond their grasp." Galerius' beady eyes reminded Constantine of a boar's, greedy and pitiless.

"He also foresaw our victory over the Persians, and that you'd be part of it, so your good news does not surprise me. The dawn raid will be mounted. And you'll lead the cohort into the Persian camp. Your father's will must be respected. It's the end of skulking around in the rear for you." He looked at his officers. They nodded energetically.

Constantine willed himself to stay quiet, to hold the curses at the edge of his tongue. He'd never skulked in the rear. He'd been following orders. Galerius's orders. Bathhouse whores spoke more truth than this bastard.

"We will win this war," Galerius continued. "And it's time you played your part."

And then it came to him. The officer who led the first cohort into battle could make a request of the emperor. It was a tradition going back to before Aurelian's time. If the officer survived, the emperor would almost certainly grant his request.

"My lord, may I ask for the lead officer's reward, when the battle is won?"

"Yes," replied Galerius. He sounded irritated. "But understand this, boy, if the raid fails, and you lose me too many Jovians, you'll regret it for the rest of what will be a truly short life." He pulled an ivory-handled dagger from a scabbard attached to his belt, walked up to Constantine and placed its tip to his cheek. Constantine felt something wet on his chin. He didn't flinch.

"Ambition has its price, Constantine. Let's see if you'll pay it."

Constantine stared straight ahead. One eyebrow twitched.

Galerius glared at him, as if he knew Constantine's thoughts and how much he was hated. He wiped the blade slowly on the shoulder of Constantine's tunic.

"Know this, a single cohort of your Jovians is all you need to carry out this raid. And don't come back empty handed. Your stupid face will not be welcome here if your raid is a failure."

The temptation to strike out at the emperor filled Constantine like water near to boiling. Galerius waved his hand dismissively.

Constantine struck his right wrist to his left breast in salute and with Lucius and Sextus behind, headed out of the tent. He had got what he'd wanted.

He remembered the other officers laughing when a coward had been given the task of leading the first cohort. It would stiffen the man's courage, they said. It had also killed the man. He touched his cheek, saw blood on his finger when he pulled it away. He looked at the slick redness. How many wounds would he have in the morning?

"I see Galerius still likes you," Sextus said, as they walked back through the camp. He nudged Constantine. "Let's show him how a raid should be done. Remember what we did that last morning outside Alexandria?" He gripped Constantine's shoulder. "Tomorrow will be your day for honors. If what you say about the Persian guards is still true when we get there, this'll be as easy as finding a cunt in a Roman whorehouse."

Lucius put his hand on Constantine's arm. "What reward will you ask, my lord?"

"He cannot name it until the time comes to ask for it. It's bad luck if he does," Sextus replied.

"But..."

Sextus held up his hand for silence.

As they walked fast through the moonlit camp, Sextus questioned Constantine about the route the Jovians should take and asked him to describe again the layout of the Persian camp. Constantine kept his answers short. He needed to think.

Why had his father agreed to disinherit him? Why had his first real chance to prove himself come so late? His only hope was the request he'd make of the emperor, if he survived the raid.

He spotted a slave carrying a water jug and called to him. The man poured cool water over his cupped hands. The smell of Galerius faded as he washed his face. Then he drank some. Nothing could be done about his stepmother, not yet, not from this far away. First, he had to survive, and survive with honor.

A little way ahead, Lucius bent and drew something on a patch of bare earth. When Constantine joined him, Lucius pointed at what he'd drawn, then rubbed it away. Then he saluted them both, turned, and walked off.

As he watched him go, Constantine imagined Lucius drifting off to sleep in the arms of one of the thin, charcoal-eyed beauties he'd seen in the Armenian baggage train. He felt a pang of envy. It had been a long time since he'd laid a woman. The Jovians didn't allow whores in their baggage train.

He considered eating, he hadn't had anything since that afternoon, but decided against it.

He looked up at the dust of sparkling stars spread out overhead, as bright tonight as ever he had seen them. The prospect of imminent death heightened every sense. Clinking echoed from the camp around him. The faint, but cool breeze prickled at his skin and in his mouth a sweetness clung from the water he had just drunk.

Soon it would all begin.

The command for silence barked out as the Jovians assembled in the parade area. Six hundred men were lined up in long rows. They were his Jovians, a single cohort from a legion he loved. Many of these men would not live to see another night.

He looked out for men he knew, nodded to them as he passed, noting the polished breastplates and the correct positioning of weapons. He'd made the right decision to wake them.

Sextus called the officers together. Excitement buzzed like a swarm of bees through the ranks. Men winked conspiratorially at him. A warm pride settled inside him. Who could doubt him now?

No trumpet call or speech marked the departure of the three thousand, eight hundred and six men of the 2nd Jovian Legion from the camp. Night marches make men quiet. Only the scuff of hob-nailed boots and the soft clink of shifting armor broke the silence as they made their way across the grass towards the shadow of the forest.

His mount was one of his favorites, an older black stallion with a white blaze on its forehead and long graying socks. He was a reliable horse, a quality likely to be in demand before the following day ended.

Settling in the saddle, he pulled his cloak tight around his shoulders against a midnight chill. He opened two of the side clasps on his wire mail coat. Behind him the Jovians marched at time and a half, not as fast as they could go, but quick enough. They would have to keep up that pace for hours, and then fight.

When a far-off dog, probably one of those following the army, began a plaintiff howl, he glanced back. The rows of spearheads and helmets behind him glinted, as if they'd been dipped in the rock oil that seeped from the earth in these parts. His head craned as he followed the snaking column back along its arc.

Behind the four hundred and eight men of the first cohort he could make out the Legate's mounted bodyguard on grays, four abreast, red tassels dangling like bloody garlands from their bridles. He could not see Sextus but knew he'd be riding somewhere towards the rear of the grays. Looking further back, a gold Legion eagle and dragon standard stood out at the head of six cohorts, the main body of the Jovian infantry. Two mounted half centuries, the rearguard, could just about be made out far back towards the darkened Roman camp.

An older optio rode quietly beside him. The man had yellowing skin and three-cornered eyes. Constantine knew him. He came from one of the nomad tribes, a Scythian who he'd had to order once to stop beating one of the pack horses. The man wore his slick black hair long, past his shoulders, and had a clump of amulets and charms jingling around his neck clicking against an old, crudely-mended wire mail coat.

"Have you prayed to your gods, my lord?" said the optio. They were the first words he'd spoken since they'd left the camp. But he still didn't look at Constantine.

"Why should I do that?"

The optio turned suddenly and leaned towards him, almost unseating himself from his saddle. "You could seek the help of your family gods, that's all, to help prepare your next journey." He pushed his face close to Constantine's. His eyes bulged as if they might pop.

Constantine stared back at the man, refusing to be intimidated.

"Don't expect any help from this lot." The optio motioned his head towards the men marching behind. "They wouldn't have coins to close the eyes of their own mothers. But a man like you, my lord." The optio sighed, as if he knew something he shouldn't.

"I won't be needing coins."

The optio turned and shouted to the men marching behind.

"Heh, Illyrian bastards, I told you the new officer would have the balls for a fight."

A muted cheer went up. The men began chanting a marching song concerning what parts of the enemy's anatomy they would take as souvenirs. The low chant spread down the ranks until the optio turned and barked, "Silence!" A hush spread back along the line as if a blanket had fallen.

"You have some qualities to bring to the fight too, optio, don't you?"

The optio grunted. "Yes, my lord. We Scythians fly above the grass like black kites and wake men from their beds with a point at their throat."

38

Constantine punched the air in reply.

They were close to the darkness of the tree line now. It looked as if some shadowed metropolis lay ahead, one whose battlements had been worn by time and uncounted campaigns into a jagged line from horizon to horizon. He licked his lips. They were dry. His tongue too. The shadows could be hiding Persian scouts. If they fled back fast to their camp, any chance of a surprise attack succeeding would be gone. So much hung by the thinnest of fate's threads.

This would be only the fourth time he'd engaged an enemy, and the second he'd led men, and the first surprise attack he'd ever been on. He knew how it should be done, his training had made sure of that, but he also knew how much could go wrong. And he needed nothing to go wrong.

X

Lower Armenia, 297 A.D.

Juliana groaned, pressed her hand over her mouth, and rocked. Her mother would be angry. She'd never have allowed Juliana back in their house after what had happened. To be touched down there, even by a half-man, would bring shame on their house, even if the insult had been brief, as if he was checking for something.

She was alone in the tent, sitting on a plump cloud of cushions, a cream silk ribbon tied tight around her forehead. Tiny silver disks jangled from it as she moved. The muslin tunic she wore reached down to her ankles. It reminded her of something a priestess might wear.

Sticky yellow dust had been smeared over her face, her arms, and her legs. It reeked of ox fat. Swirly symbols had been painted on the backs of her hands. All the time the drone of a priest's chant could be heard nearby. The sweet taste of the drink lingered in her mouth. She'd slept for a while after she'd drunk it, feeling as if a weight sat on her head, despite every instinct telling her to stay awake.

She rubbed her hands when she woke. The symbols on them smudged. She sighed.

A haughty voice rang out. The chanting stopped. The priest still watched her. Or was he a different one? The chanting restarted.

An image came to her, floating in front of her; a knife held high, streaked with blood, her mother's ash-blackened hands reaching towards it as it came down. Her mother had died too easily. She would not be like that. She touched her lips and swallowed hard. Please, when would the dawn come?

XI

Germania, 297 A.D.

Blood flowed onto the forest floor around Crocus, turning the mulch red. To his right, two of his axe men were butting helmets. They had won. In the distance, Roman victory horns blew.

As a chieftain's son of the tribe of the Alemanni, he was expected to remain loyal, even if his elder brother wanted to steal his wife and kill his children. But he couldn't. When the Roman Caesar had launched his campaign to drive the Alemanni away from Germania Superior, Crocus had seen his chance. Twenty axe men had come with him.

After this victory, he would have a thousand axe men by the feast of the dead. If this Caesar kept his word.

Whimpering made him turn his head. He passed his battle axe from his right to his left hand. When finishing off an easy enemy, it was wise to use your weaker hand.

He stumbled over a dead body, the man's head spliced in two. Gray brain mush had been splattered all around, causing his sandals to slip under him. The whimpering stopped. But he knew where it had come from. A large oak tree stood out against the whitened hulks of the spruce trees, which filled this part of the great forest. At least ten dead bodies lay in the space around it. One of his own men lay there, his face calm, but his body split in two with blood in a pool all around it.

He rounded the tree and gasped. A Pomeranian boy, from the land close to the winter sea, was huddled at its foot. Blond hair hung around his thin, pretty face.

The boy stared up at him, his mouth open.

Crocus looked around, checking for any enemies that might still dare attack him. But there were none.

He glared at the boy, bent down. "Hide under the bodies," he said. He pointed at a pile of blood-soaked bodies nearby.

XII

Lower Armenia, 297 A.D.

"We're approaching the land of the Cimerii," the optio said, turning to look at the men behind. "I hope none of you runts is afraid of the dark."

A few of the men marching behind sniggered. Most stayed silent. The shadowed tree line came closer with each step. They'd have heard the same stories Constantine had about the daemons that roam these forests.

He looked up. The moon lit the valley like a giant torch. A breeze ruffled his hair. He shivered. The coolest breeze he'd felt in a long time tickled at his face. Was the weather changing?

A silver gilded cloud sailed towards the moon, as if it might snuff it out. When he'd been assigned to his first campaign across the Danube four years before, he'd imagined his father riding into camp on moonlit nights such as this, and them laughing together. It had never happened, but the hope had been enough, when things had looked bleak.

They passed under the trees, their path no more than a hunting track now, the column of men tightening as a snake would as they went in.

"Them Persians will pull out their beards when they see us, my lord." The optio lowered his voice, looked around to see who might be listening. "Let's hope they get no time to form up ranks. If they do, this raid will be a stupid waste of good men."

"The Legate knows what he's doing," said Constantine.

"Yes, my lord, I'm sure whoever set this party going knows exactly what he's doing." He looked Constantine up and down. "I

43

suppose if you have half your father's luck we'll be finished soon enough."

Constantine shook his head, held his reins tighter. It was the same every time he'd been appointed over men older and more experienced than him, who turned out to know less than he did.

"Keep your voice low, optio, or none of us will be heading back at all."

"I know when to keep quiet, my lord." The optio spat out his words. "All the men want is a chance to win back the honor of the Jovians."

"And if you keep prattling I'll put a gag on you." Constantine leaned towards the optio and wiped a fist across his mouth.

The optio stared at him, his eyes narrowed.

The track ran down into the boulder-strewn bed of a dried-out stream. It was a while before the stream widened.

"The Persian nobles' tents are visible from where we attack, optio. I expect we'll find their King's family there. That's where I will be heading."

The optio turned to him. "I expect there'll be boxes of jewels in their tents too. Persian women like jewels too, I am sure."

"That's not what we're looking for," said Constantine. He peered into the gloom.

Thin oaks ran away in all directions. They looked like the columns of a ghostly moonlit palace. Intertwining branches arched like a roof overhead. Stars sparkled here and there like distant jewels. The faint clinking of the men behind rippled in the air, as if some animal was awakening. He looked back and felt a tingle of excitement. The time to prove his courage, to face down every doubt, had arrived.

Most of the legionaries would, he knew, be praying about now for the delights of victory or, if the fates were not to be so fortunate, a speedy death. A swell of whispering passed through the ranks. He knew what that meant. Men would be renewing their Mithraic death pacts, about who would finish off who to avoid being captured alive.

Or they'd be passing on last messages for loved ones, should they fall. Such things were not for him. All his promises had been made to people very far away. He gripped the pommel of his sword, checked it moved freely in its scabbard. Most of the other officers used the regular cavalry sword, the spatha. His was similar but wider, lighter, better balanced, its handle covered in a gold mesh, its scabbard strips of amber and sky-blue lacquer.

He valued the present from his father above almost everything else he owned. It had been given to him to mark his acceptance into the Jovians. The best armorers in Rome had fashioned it from tongues of Hispanic iron twisted and forged flat. The blade, which could cleave a man in two, had a snakeskin pattern of wavy silver and black charcoal embedded in it. Only the tiniest of bumps on its blade marked the few times it had been used in anger.

"That's a fancy sword, my lord." The optio grimaced, displaying his broken teeth and a flash of resentment in his eyes.

"Are the men still in formation, optio?" He'd learned to ignore fishing expeditions. Every time he'd given anything away in the past, he'd heard it repeated back to him later, garbled and mostly wildly distorted. He'd been warned to expect jealousy, as he was the son of a serving emperor, but the way some men twisted his words never failed to surprise him.

The man nodded, turned his horse. "I'll check, my lord," he said, before disappearing back along the line.

Constantine glanced after him. The man had probably heard who Constantine was and presumed that meant he lived a life full of compliant slaves and soft concubines. Even his sleeping in the tent of the centurions every night didn't change what some men wanted to believe.

The next watercourse they entered almost fooled him into thinking they'd reached their destination. Then he saw it had water at the bottom. As they climbed out the other side the moon fell below the tree tops and their progress slowed.

He had to be thankful that the Jovians had been instructed by the optio, on his orders, to carry their shields strapped to their backs with a chalk line marked on it, and all scabbards wrapped in rags, and all cloaks worn tight. The chalk made it easier to see the man in front in the darkness.

When they came to the edge of what appeared to be the right dry gully he was almost sure they'd lost their way and contemplated riding ahead himself. All doubt vanished when he saw the outline of the decomposing human heads in the distance. An owl hooted. It was a good omen.

He dismounted and passed the word back that all horses were to be held in a picket line under the trees. The men behind him crowded round. There was no time to wait. More were coming up each moment. With his skin prickling at the thought of what was to come, he led the way down into the gully. Everything could happen quickly now.

He scrambled down into the blackness, thinking at any moment they would be shouted at by Persian guards. At the bottom, he stationed a Jovian to wait and point out which way the men should follow. Then he waited until the next few men were down before continuing. All he could see now were the stars overhead and the black edge of the gully high up on each side. They moved quietly forward, like rats in a drain pipe.

When they reached the place just below the skulls, he sent a hand signal back for everyone to spread out and await orders. A wave of faint muttering welled briefly behind him, then subsided. As it did, he felt the tightness slip from his shoulders. They'd made it. They'd arrived before dawn. And if any Persian guards stationed above this part of the gully had heard them, they'd surely have called out by now, and raised the alarm. The fates were smiling on him. The raid would succeed.

He peered around in the gloom. On the horizon behind them he could make out the purplish bulk of the Palandoken Mountain and a starlit sheen of snow at its peak. Local villagers had warned them not to disturb the djinn that lived up there.

His stomach tightened. He understood why the men respected those who'd been on night time raids. Waiting quietly in the dark, knowing how close your death might be, was not for the nervous or weak willed.

And he had more to think about than the next few hours. Galerius could have exaggerated what Constantine's father had written or the letter could even be a forgery. It was certainly not beyond the slimy bastard to do that. He might even do such a thing for the pleasure of watching Constantine's face as he read it.

But if he died on this raid, everyone would testify how he'd volunteered for the duty. His father would be proud. He rubbed his fingers against his eyelids, forcing away the tiredness dragging at him.

But what if his father had agreed to discard him, based on some bitch's mothering instincts? *Please, god, don't let my sword arm waver.*

A muffled noise came from some way back, then the crunch of sandals hauled Constantine from his thoughts. A shadow loomed. He gripped the handle of his dagger. A voice whispered.

"Constantine?"

"Sssh. Be quiet, fool."

The shadow dropped down.

"That's no way to speak to your commander." Sextus sounded amused.

"I didn't know . . ." He stopped. He'd made enough of a fool of himself.

"This raid is too important to be left entirely to the likes of you," whispered Sextus. "What's your report?"

"Nothing to report, my lord. We're ready, waiting for first light."

"A Persian patrol has been overpowered in the forest. We're fortunate they were out of earshot of their camp, but their late return might be noticed, so stay vigilant."

"Courage and fidelity, sir."

"Courage and fidelity, and . . ." Sextus hesitated.

"My lord?"

Sextus sighed. "Galerius ordered that no Roman officer be captured alive, Constantine. You understand, don't you?" That sigh was the nearest he'd ever come to criticizing the emperor. He touched Constantine's arm, then gripped it for a moment as if saying goodbye.

"Don't you?" he repeated, more firmly.

"He won't be doling out any ransoms for us, is that it?"

"The belongings of any officer who fails to return will be auctioned off at noon. It's always the same with Galerius, you know that, Constantine. Take no more risks than you have to." He paused, as if thinking of something. "I've told all the centurions to await your move. As soon as the light threatens, get the men started. Go as far into their bloody camp as you can, and . . ." He gripped Constantine's arm again. "I'm sure they'll auction my belongings well before your pitiful cloaks."

"They wouldn't dare," Constantine whispered, but Sextus was gone.

He stared at the ground underneath him. Could he see more clearly? No, it was still dark. Iron-gray dark. It seemed as if dawn would never come.

A sparrow let out a cheerful chirruping somewhere in the distance. It sang a few excited notes then relapsed into silence. It had realized its mistake.

A Persian watch cry echoed far away. His fists balled. Sweat sprung onto his forehead. Cold sweat. Another watch cry echoed nearer, much nearer.

Constantine waited. A Persian guard could be peering at that very moment into the gully, wondering what each shadow meant, dismissing his fears as childish paranoia. When Constantine had been up there at the edge, he'd seen only indistinct gray shapes below; the floor of the gully had been inky black. They would not be seen.

Another answering cry rang out. Directly above them. This time it sounded like a boy. Then he heard whistling. Had a Jovian gone mad? No, the tune wasn't Roman. The Persian boy whistled away his fears, pacing the edge of the gully, probably waiting, like them, for the dawn. He would be nearby when the Romans swarmed out of their hiding place. He would, most likely, be among the first to die.

It's truly better that we don't know what the fates have in store for us.

The whistling moved slowly away. It was a spirited tune, ideal for keeping the boy's spirits up before his duty ended.

A faint radiance appeared at the horizon. The stars in that direction had faded. He waited. Gaunt faces appeared one after the other around him, as if surfacing from a gloomy pool. Along the near side of the gully he could make out the bundled shapes of men lying down. They looked as if they were lining the hold of a giant galley.

Dawn came fast in these parts, he knew, but still he waited. He had to be sure he could clearly see the ground ahead for at least five paces. They had to be able to run. He had to wait. His skin prickled on his back. He rubbed his eyes, looked at the ground. Wait. Wait . . .

Now!

"Form up," said Constantine, to the two centurions who'd taken up positions on either side of him. He pushed himself to his feet, eyeing the edge of the gully overhead. The men around him stood.

For a moment nothing happened. A legionary grinned at him, tight-lipped. Constantine grinned back, lifted his hand, waved a forward motion and began to climb the gully wall.

Up they went. A crimson wave. Creaking filled the air. The pre-dawn quiet only a memory. He pulled his sword, dug its pommel into the gully wall as he went up.

The edge of the gully was close. At its lip they would be most vulnerable. If Persians were massed beyond, waiting for them, the attack would be doomed. His fingers plunged into pebbly dirt. The skulls on stakes were gazing malignly down at them. His nose wrinkled from the stench of decomposing flesh.

His hands reached the lip of the gully. He pulled himself up, peered over.

Serried ranks of round leather tents, colors softened by the pre-dawn gloom, spread away across the plateau as if they'd always been there. The camp was even bigger than he'd remembered. His nostrils flared as he breathed in fast.

Pennants fluttered from the tops of most tents and in the quickly brightening light he saw a long picket line of horses and thin black-haired Persians in their long, pale tunics moving among the horses ferrying water skins. The Persians were up!

But no alarm horn rang out. And a dozen other Jovians were peering over the edge like him. No one had seen them, yet. He scrambled up, stood. Jovians appeared one after the other all along the edge that ran toward a wooded ridge.

"Line up," he said, as if addressing just the men beside him. It felt odd speaking after worrying about making noise for so long. A centurion shouted at legionaries nearby to form into a skirmish line. Another gestured in frustration about a hundred paces beyond, as he formed his men up. Constantine looked ahead, raised his sword, leaned forward and ran. His heavy sandals thudded into the ground. A wave of thuds followed all around him.

His arm went higher, the sword light in his hand, the exhilaration of the charge filling him up, making him light headed.

A shriek rang out. A woman's cry. They'd covered no more than twenty paces. A horn echoed over the camp. Others answered, booming far off into the distance, like angry elephants calling out to one another.

XIII

Lower Armenia, 297 A.D.

"It is time." The priest said the words as if they were a gentle prayer. Two young girls walked slowly into the tent. They were naked except for golden necklaces with ivory carvings of feet and hands, and blue evil eye amulets around their necks. Their bodies shone a golden brown, their breasts small but firm, all hair shaved between their legs.

They were staring at Juliana. Then she remembered. They were the girls who she'd seen running in the camp earlier.

Juliana stood, her fists trembling by her sides. She wanted to be strong. She wanted to be brave. She wanted to be sick.

The girls took her by the arms, led her out of the tent and across the cool flattened grass towards a group of larger tents. A wisp of dawn extinguished the stars. A hint of incense came to her from the priest as he walked close behind. He had a knife in his belt. She hadn't seen that before. She thought about running, but two other young priests were walking with them, observing her every move. She could hear the swish-swish of their robes and, far away, a horse neighing.

The priest in front pulled open a flap in one of the tents. Inside, in the center of the tent, stood a thin ebony column. On top of it rested a golden human skull. A chain curled down the column. She knew who it was for. She stopped at the entrance. The priest turned, took her hand, and pulled her gently forwards. She did not resist.

XIV

Lower Armenia, 297 A.D.

"Courage and fidelity," Constantine roared. The call echoed along the Roman line, spread back along the line of the gully towards the forest.

"Wipe the Persian scum away," a legionary roared directly behind him. They were the nearest Romans to the enemy camp.

And then they were halfway to the Persian tents. His gut tightened. He told himself to count things, how many paces to go, how many men he could see, how many tents, how peaceful the camp looked, who he would strike first, who he would strike next, who after that.

The Persian camp awoke. Men were staggering from tents clutching weapons. A small troop of archers in blood red tunics appeared in an open area straight ahead, as if the Romans had been expected. But there were too few of them for that to be true.

The archers' tunics were emblazoned with a golden lion. They fitted arrows to their bows with gloved hands and loosed a hissing flock straight towards the Jovians.

As one, the Jovians raised their shields and ran on, crouching just a little. Arrows whistled by, clanged into shields, like angry bees. An arrow thudded into Constantine's shield.

"Kill them all!" someone shouted.

The thrill of the charge coursed through him. The arrows had ceased. He looked around the edge of his shield. The Persian archers were unsheathing short, curved swords. Ten paces to go.

He roared an order. A shower of short spears flew. Archers fell, impaled. He picked a target, braced his shield, held his sword forward.

Chunk!

He'd pierced the archer in the chest. The man swung his sword at him. Constantine swayed, stabbed again, stumbled. No! He righted himself, glanced back. The archer had fallen, blood spewing from his mouth.

Screams curdled the air. Some were cut off abruptly. Others were roars of defiance.

He ran on towards the tents, heard himself bellowing. He hated Persian arrogance, their defiance of Rome. He loathed them for killing so many of his comrades. Roman war horns sounded, their high-pitched call something every legionary knew. The call to battle. Courage spread through him like hot wine.

He passed a shabby looking tent. No one stirred from within. He ran on. A Persian emerged head first through the flap of another. He raised his sword. Constantine took it on his shield and stabbed quickly into the man's soft unprotected belly, angling up, turning against the slight resistance, slicing hidden organs, hitting finally against bone as watery blood flooded down his arm. A sound like escaping wind came from the man's belly.

He could see every line on the man's face, the deep creases, the sleep dirt in his long eyelashes, a puckering on his lips, an old healed scar across the man's forehead, his Adam's apple puffing out as if it might burst, but most of all, a look of amazement in the man's eyes.

His face bulged. His eyes turned up. Only the whites could be seen now.

Another Persian, a boy, the first man's slave or catamite most probably, crouched further back in the tent. He too held a sword, but it shook pitiably, like a live fish.

Constantine jerked his sword back. The belly of the Persian pumped out blood. He pushed the mess into the tent towards the boy, then looked around. In every direction fighting raged in a whirl of swords and blood. But the tightness that had curled around his stomach like a rope had eased.

"Watch out." A shout and an approaching shadow made him jerk his head, just in time to miss a wildly swinging blade. The curved

Persian short sword, the Akinakes, which the boy had clearly never been trained to use, continued its arc past him. Too late, he realized his mistake. Constantine swung at him. The expression of hope on the handsome slick-skinned amber face turned to terror.

The boy looked down at his blood pouring freely.

He slumped away.

The iron reek of blood-filled Constantine's nostrils. He should have become hardened long ago to quick, bloody death, but still he felt pity, especially for the poorly trained, those with innocence still filling their faces.

He looked around. Legionaries nearby were trading blows with half-dressed Persians. Others were looking round, slicing open tent flaps. Most men, he knew, busied themselves with useless tasks in raids, not killing, not moving forward, if they were not kept in order. He had to maintain discipline. They were Jovians, not rabble.

"With me," he roared, standing with his sword raised. Legionaries raced towards him. With his sword swinging through the air they set off into the interior of the Persian camp, a line of legionaries with him. They had to move fast. The Persians would be forming up somewhere for a counter attack.

Soon the din of battle faded. They'd passed into a part of the camp with empty tents, their flaps hanging open. It amazed him how haphazard it all appeared, as if they'd placed their tents wherever they stopped.

The sun, well above the horizon now, cast long shadows over the flattened grass. He could feel already how hot the day would be, smell the dryness in the air. A tremor ran down his arm as he held his sword up. He swung it to exercise his muscles as he ran.

Then he glanced back. The troop of legionaries behind him had grown to at least twenty. The optio brought up the rear. Had the man been set to dog his tail?

Constantine jogged on past blue bowls and silver jugs set out on a carpet between two tents. Brightly striped awnings shaded the area. He slashed at the awnings as they passed.

Drums started up somewhere up ahead. Dum, dum, da-da-da, dum. Persian war drums were unmistakable. They resonated like a distant earthquake.

At last, Constantine saw what he was looking for, white pennants dangling from tent poles. He let out a shout of anticipation and headed towards them.

He rounded a large tent and came to an abrupt halt. The men fanned out beside him.

A troop of Persian guards waited ahead in parade ground order, as if they were about to be reviewed. He counted ten. Each wore a knee-length, gray chain tunic, yellow cloak and pointed red turban. Each had crow-black beards cut into a long point below their chins. Invincibles. The Persian King's bodyguard. He stared. It was the first time he'd seen Invincibles up close. They appeared to spend more time caring for their appearance than fighting.

Posturing would not be enough to force his men to run away. The odds were good. Two to one at least. He grinned.

The Invincibles threw their javelins.

His shield went up. One slower Roman fell groaning, but most of the javelins clattered harmlessly away. If this was the only guard for the nobles' tents, they were in luck.

He gave the order, "Small tortoise." His troop joined shields, four abreast around him. The optio appeared by his side, breathless.

"My lord, you must go back." The optio raised his hand. Constantine looked at him. Defiant shouts came from the line of Invincibles.

"Be quiet, optio," he roared. He elbowed him away. What was the man thinking? Could he not sense the opportunity here? The optio's face blanched as if he'd been doused for days in a cask full of piss.

"This is what we're here for, boys. Let's go," roared Constantine.

Excitement, pride and a gulp of fear mixed inside him like an ancient alchemist's brew. As one they stepped forward.

A Persian officer, his beard indigo blue, his bald head heavily tattooed with swirling blue markings, screamed at his men while brandishing a long, curved sword above his head. Constantine wondered what hopes for glory the Persian officer entertained.

His arm throbbed as they went forward. His breath came in heaving blasts. The Invincibles ahead took on the grim look of men well used to fighting. Each carried a mace or an axe.

He held his breath, kept his sword still. The two troops crashed shields. Constantine, on the far right of the line of Jovians, jabbed up, testing an Invincible's mail. A mace slammed over his shield, just missing his head.

Bastard! Constantine jabbed quickly up and under the Persian's mail. The man screamed. His shield shook but held. Constantine thrust again, harder, then turned to support the Jovian to his left.

Not one Invincible ran away.

The last one took twenty blows before he went down. As the man was being finished, Constantine checked the wounded Romans. Three legionaries were dead or dying. Their wounds were bad, a dangling, lopped off hand, a dripping, open skull, blueish pulsing entrails, enough to sicken anyone who thought war a glamorous business.

He looked away. The whimpers, shouts and grunts of dying men always affected him. Not everyone dies as stoically as they'd hoped. He nodded to a centurion glaring up at him, trying to speak. He bent low, saw the wide gash in the man's side, and finished the man off with a sword cut across his throat.

"Go home now to your family," he whispered in the man's ear, as blood poured down his neck.

Words of comfort, a quick death, it had to be done. If he himself was dying he would have prayed for the mercy of a Jovian, before the enemy could take him or torture him to death, plucking eyes and splitting noses.

The drums of the Persians were louder now.

He had to be quick.

Some of the Jovians were already moving among the white tents with their flapping pennants. Constantine roared at them to halt. They turned back to him.

"Look for letters, maps, hostages. Search all the tents nearby and bring everything to me."

Most of the Persian nobles would have escaped as soon as the alarm had been raised, probably taking anything important, but maybe they would find something.

He stooped to examine the sword the dead Persian officer had been wielding, raised it, cleaned the blood away on the man's trousers. The blade was thin, clearly of the highest quality. He felt its edge. Blood seeped from his thumb. He whistled softly. It had been rumored Persian swordsmiths had discovered a lighter, more flexible form of iron. He sheathed the sword, then slung the scabbard over his shoulder.

Somebody screamed. Other voices joined in the clamor. From the noise, he would have imagined a harem was being slowly strangled. He jogged towards the sound, the Persian sword banging against his back. A fat eunuch lay coughing, feebly dribbling out his last at the entrance to one of the larger tents. Constantine stepped around him, sword in hand, and peered inside.

A row of oil lamps on high tripods illuminated the tent's interior. A throat-tickling fragrance of sandalwood hung in the air, turning it blue. Sumptuous red carpets covered the floor. Scenes of tiger hunts picked out in gold thread decorated the walls.

In the center of the tent he saw the source of the dreadful noise. Two young women were on their knees, wringing their hands and screaming louder than he'd ever heard women scream before. Two Jovians were holding swords above their heads as if they were trying to stop the racket, although they were only making matters worse. A smile parted his lips. He saw why the Jovians were gawping.

The young women wore baggy black trousers with yellow waistbands. Their feet were bare, as were their plump upper bodies. Their naked breasts swayed as they cried, and their black hair, plaited into hennaed tails, swung like a pack of snakes about their heads.

"Down your weapons," Constantine said. The legionaries turned towards him. His gilded, purple-edged breastplate was enough to warn ordinary Jovians who he was. Most of them would know him without it. He sheathed his sword. The girls turned to him but instead of stopping, their wailing rose to an ear-splitting pitch.

An older woman kneeling a little way back didn't join in the screeching. She was maybe twenty-five, the same age he was, though it certainly didn't look like she had wasted half her life on pointless duties and out of the way frontier postings as he had done.

Then it came to him. The other girls were protecting the older one, keeping the legionaries at a distance, distracting them. She wore a silver mail shirt that ended at her midriff. Her breasts were not exposed. A mane of braided black hair flowed over most of her back.

Persian noble women never cut their hair, he'd heard. Could she be one? Perhaps a distant relative of the King? She certainly looked the part. A finger thin band of pearls ran across her forehead. White, silk ribbons hung down on either side of her face. Whoever she was, she knew the grip that beauty holds on men.

She stared back insolently at Constantine.

It was the stare of a pure bred, who expected to be treated differently, better. She didn't appear at all daunted by the intrusion of the Jovians or by Constantine's gaze. That was interesting in itself. But who was she?

The woman raised a hand and pointed disdainfully at his face with a crooked finger, as if he were her slave. Her cat eyes, highlighted all around with kohl, stared hard at him, daring him to resist her, insisting he look away, look down, now, acknowledge her superiority.

"I am the Queen of Queens, the Divine Incantress of Zoroaster. I order you to defend my person, and that of my King's sisters, from these brutes. You will be rewarded. Well rewarded."

Time slowed as she spoke. Had she said she was a Queen? She spoke an accented lilting Greek, the official language of the eastern Roman provinces and most diplomacy, which meant she was educated. His mind raced. He'd not expected this. She fingered a flame-colored and tear-shaped stone hanging around her neck. She stroked it, as if it might protect her.

He walked up to her and peered at the pendant, a red garnet, the largest he'd ever seen, an object a queen might indeed possess.

She maintained her haughty expression as he came near. He sensed her distaste as he moved even closer. He leaned forward, caught a whiff of her perfume.

In a flash, with the speed of a leaping cat, she slapped his cheek. Hard. The wailing stopped. Good. Everyone looked at him. His cheek stung as if it had been burnt. He raised his hand, pointed a finger in her face.

"Touch me again and you will be sorry."

The Jovians made ribald comments about what she might want or, better still, what she might get if she struck him again. He stared at her. He knew her type.

"Leave," he shouted to the Jovians. They were reluctant, but after a few moments they went to stand outside the tent doorway. They knew better than to ignore direct orders. He turned to her. His cheek still stung. He raised his hand again, as if he might strike her this time, and held it high, a determined look on his face. She didn't flinch.

"Where did you get this?" he asked slowly. The musk of her perfume almost overpowered him, like unwatered wine.

"It is mine," she replied stiffly. "Given to me by the King after his defeat of the Shah of Bactria. It is an ancient jewel. The last of Queen Pandoraxa's. It purifies the blood of nobles and curses all others who dare hold it. Do you plan to steal it?" Her eyes were wide and, unblinking, like a snake's. Her gaze flicked to his purple breastplate, then back to his face.

"I'm not here for baubles."

She lifted her hands high as if in thanks. The front of her mail shirt arced open. He caught a glimpse of silky brown skin where her breasts started.

"I will help you now, Roman. Get out of here, quickly. My King of Kings will be here soon, and your heart will be food for his dogs after you eat your own eyes if he finds you here."

He looked around. She was right. They would have to go soon. But she would go with them. He would not lose the prize that could make this raid worthwhile. One of the legionaries at the door peered inside.

He heard a crying sound.

"What's that?"

The Queen shook her head as if she'd no idea what he meant and had no desire to answer him.

"Who's back there?" he pressed.

She said nothing, her expression as disdainful as if he was a slave who'd dropped a tray and would soon be made to pay for his stupidity. He took a step around her. He'd no time for this. At any moment troops of Persians would be on top of them.

"It is just a girl. A slave. She is nothing."

"Show me," he said. "Show me at once." She was trying to hide something.

She sent him a glare of contempt and shook her head, slowly. She would not obey him.

He sighed. It was always going to come to this. Ask first, then demand, then force, his father had taught him. Some of his fellow officers left out the first part, asking, but he included it.

He unsheathed his sword.

The effect was immediate. The girls began wailing again. You'd have thought he'd run them through already.

She pushed her chest forward, daring him. It was his turn to smile. He moved his hand, as if to take her pendant.

She stepped back, spoke sharply to the younger girls. They stopped their wailing. Then she turned, strode to the back of the tent, and pulled aside a flap in a wall hanging. Beyond lay another linked tent.

It too had a domed ceiling and similar carpets. At its center stood an ebony column on which a skull had been mounted. A golden skull. The hairs on the back of his neck rose. Sitting by the column, leaning dazedly against it, shivering, was a naked girl of no more than ten or eleven summers. A green fish tattoo stood out on the girl's right shoulder.

One of her hands pressed between her thighs to cover herself up. She was whimpering. The Queen glided through the flap. Constantine, after glancing at the legionaries by the door, followed her. Two were looking at him with wide-eyed incredulity. He raised his hand to them as he went, indicating he knew what he was doing.

60

But when he passed through into the other tent his confidence faded. It wasn't the syrupy sweet incense, which he'd never smelt before, there was something cold and unnerving about the room, which made him uneasy.

"We make sacrifices here to the great daemon, Aesma Daeva, that he will reveal the end of this war." The Queen stopped near the whimpering girl.

As she turned he saw a slim silver dagger in the hand she held close by her side. He should have searched her. He stopped out of her reach.

The other girls had followed them and after a curt word from the Queen they began dancing around the girl at the column. She took to whimpering louder, like a dog waiting for a beating.

A Jovian called to him. "My lord, do you need us?" They were out of sight.

He answered. "Stay there. Keep a lookout. Shout if you see Persians."

The two dancing girls' breasts swayed again, as they swirled their plaited hair from side to side and ululated as if intoxicated.

"Prostrate, Roman. This is the skull of your beloved Emperor Valerian. The divine Valerian. One of your many gods, was he not?" said the Queen. She nodded toward the skull.

"Do you like my King's sisters? They are his Ministraie." She gestured at the girls. For a moment, he imagined she was offering them to him. His gaze flicked towards them and then back to her. She wouldn't fool him that easily.

"I'm sure your emperor wouldn't mind," she continued. "I hear he enjoys such things. I can watch." Her tone had turned soft, honey sweet.

The girls' movements were wilder, more abandoned now, as if some unheard tune was speeding up. A jingling of bracelets and the stomping of feet filled his ears. As they passed behind the skull he stared at it.

"See how the fixing holes in the back were bored." The Queen had seen where he was looking. "Those holes were drilled while Valerian still lived. You can tell from the re-growth. Do you see?"

61

An amused note, a note of triumph, filled her voice. Her rescuers would be here soon. Perhaps they were outside. What was that noise? He couldn't hear anything with those stupid dancers.

He had to move. He should drag them all away at once, but like a dread compulsion, the strangeness of the scene had him spellbound.

"Stay here, Roman. Unless you're afraid of what a virgin's entrails will show you."

The Queen held the knife up. She wasn't offering it. She wanted to use it.

Lives were sacrificed every day in the arena and slaves, he knew, were liable to have their throats cut for any insubstantial offence. But the idea of an innocent's life, slave or not, being wasted to foretell the future angered him. He remembered his father remonstrating with an official about the subject years before, when he was nine or ten. He'd always admired his father for that.

He walked towards the Queen. When he was close enough he raised his left hand high in the air and opened it abruptly. As soon as her gaze jumped to it he seized her knife hand. It was a trick only the untrained fell for. He bent the knife from her grip and smiled. Then he pushed her away so forcefully she took a step back and stumbled, crying out in horror at his impudence. He went to the whimpering girl.

While the Queen got to her feet he examined the girl. She looked healthy. Perhaps a recent captive. The Queen spat like a wounded vixen, but she stayed away from him. Her pinched expression and the hate in her eyes made it clear she would love to see him suffer.

He helped the captive to her feet. She clutched at his arm like a baby, her body trembling, her mouth opening and closing like a tiny bird's. He wondered had she known what they had planned for her. He sniffed. The crisp tang of urine clung to the girl's body.

"You're safe," he said, not knowing if she'd understand. He turned to the Queen. Her composure had returned.

"Your bloodthirsty daemons will have to wait. You'll all come to the Roman camp with us, either freely or tied up like dogs. I promise you that will not be pleasant. It's your choice. Make it."

He pulled away the captive's hands, walked to the flap separating the two tents, and called for the Jovians to help him, and quick. Then he walked over to the skull and, with one blow from the pommel of his sword, smashed it. No one would believe it was Valerian's skull, and what good would it do to remember him anyway? He'd lost to the Persians.

The sisters let out a high-pitched squeal. The Queen made no sound. He ground the larger pieces to dust beneath his hobnailed sandals as two legionaries peered into the tent. Two more were behind them, bobbing up and down with curiosity.

"Come on in. This lot will be coming back to camp with us. It'll be your unfortunate duty to get 'em back alive." There were stifled gasps, and a snigger. He glared. The sniggering stopped and the familiar grim expression of legionaries under the eye of an officer, returned.

The whimpering captive had dropped to her knees beside him. Now she stared, wild-eyed, at the legionaries. She had unusual blue eyes. Clearly, she wasn't pure Persian. He wondered about her story. He imagined her staying here alone, waiting for the Persians to retake this part of their camp.

He'd saved her and had changed her fate. Was that not enough? He looked at her. Yes, he would leave her. He had enough problems with the other three.

The girl saw him looking at her and started saying something. She spoke in a local dialect, then glared at him.

Suddenly there was something appealing about her, as if he knew her, or someone like her in an earlier, happier time. Constantine felt an urge to protect her. He sighed. He was just being stupid.

His heart had been hardened by years of fighting for his life in blood-filled battles and skirmishes and was now firmly locked. His one ambition now was to make his father proud of him by his actions in every campaign he fought in.

He turned and gave orders for the prisoners to be taken outside. He motioned the captive to follow him into the other tent where, after a quick look around, he found a chest filled with carefully folded clothes. She stood two steps behind him.

At first, she wouldn't touch anything he proffered. She simply stood dumb-faced, staring at the fine fabrics, her hands held up, as if even being close to those embroidered silks and linens was a sacrilege. He threw a long blue shirt-like garment at her. She picked it up gingerly, then placed it carefully back in the chest. He shook his head, and firmly pushed it towards her again, angry this time. He didn't want blood-crazed men to see women being paraded through a battle half naked. And he had no time for arguments.

She looked around, as if someone might stop her, and then hesitantly took the shirt and put it on. He picked up some similar garments and motioned at the other girls being hustled outside. She understood.

The Queen turned to him as she was being led through the tent. A Jovian was pushing her.

"Curse you, and your kin," she said. She spat at him and laughed like a crone twice her age.

"Put her over your shoulder and run for your horse," he said, pointing at the larger of the two legionaries pushing the Queen. The man nodded.

"Tell the men to take the others the same way and this one as well." He gestured towards the captives.

The Queen looked at Constantine with hate in her eyes and then screamed when one of the legionaries grabbed her arm. The man ignored her.

"You'll make it if you move fast. Go." He turned away. Behind him came shouts, the noises of a struggle, then yelling, but he didn't bother looking round.

He went around the tent, looking for papyri or maps. Finding nothing, he went outside into the early morning sunlight.

War horns bellowed not far away.

A huge horseman appeared around the side of a tent fifty paces away. Another rider followed behind the first in a spray of dust. Both had long, curved swords. Both swords glinted. If he didn't move fast he'd be cut down like corn at harvest time. He turned and ran fast, leaping wildly over bodies and tent ropes, his scabbard clattering and banging as if it might break against his thigh. The trophy sword he'd taken banged hard against his back.

Catcalls and whoops came after him. He glanced back. He was sorry he did. Four heavy Persian cavalrymen, the most feared sort, were cantering after him. Their thigh-length wire mail coats, pointed iron helmets, and leather boots made them look like oversized vultures swooping onto their prey. He swerved around a tent and raced towards another, his head tucked down.

They would be on him any moment, their swords high in the air. A single blow could cut his head off. He knew such cavalrymen would practice that killing blow until they could do it with their eyes closed. He leapt over an injured Persian curled on the ground. His legs felt heavy.

He heard the whup-whup of a spinning mace. His skin crawled across his chest as if he'd already been hit by it. He gulped air and ran on, his legs pumping, not bothering to look back. Faster, come on, come on. He dodged a tent rope, went left.

The pounding of horses' hooves seemed almost on top of him. He half stumbled but kept on his feet. It had been too easy so far. Capturing the Queen had been a gift from fortune, the kind of thing he'd never believed could happen if he'd not seen it himself. And now he might have to pay. He gripped his sword. He could turn and make the best. He ran around the side of a large tent.

"Armenia!" A spirited shout rang out ahead. Armenian cavalry auxiliaries rode towards him, their cloaks flapping, filling the gap between the tents ahead as if he'd been dropped into the path of a horse race. They clattered by him in a moment, dividing like water around him. He stood still. He could feel the air move around him. A horse pulled up with a neighing shudder.

"My lord, I see you've been seeking victory alone. I know Romans are brave, but I doubt even you can vanquish the whole Persian army."

He recognized the voice, though croaky from shouting. The horseman pulled his helmet up. It was Lucius. Constantine grinned wide and patted Lucius' horse, as if he needed to check it was real.

His attention turned to Lucius' fellow cavalrymen, who were engaged in a noisy clash with the Persian cavalry. A Persian mace swished through the air, swords clanged, a spear thudded into the ground nearby. Yells rang out, and roars of pain, oaths, and on top of it all the neighing and whinnying of angry horses and the beat of drums filled his ears.

"Can we help them?" he roared, as Lucius dragged him up behind him.

Lucius shook his head.

"We're only assisting your retreat, not helping your raid, my friend." Lucius wheeled his horse around. "That way we are following Galerius' orders."

"You've stirred up a nest of hornets."

The thump of the Persian war drums grew louder by the moment. The early morning air reverberated with the noise.

With a shout to his men, Lucius turned his horse and they galloped away.

"Stop at the edge of the camp," he shouted in Lucius' ear. He needed to oversee the end of the raid.

"Yes, my lord, a thank you is most welcome. I am Lucius and you'll repay me, I'm sure." Lucius grinned avariciously.

A swarm of Persian arrows followed them as they raced between the burning tents to the edge of the camp. One struck the back of his breastplate with a clang.

He dismounted, then heard the three-blast signal for retreat blaring out from Jovian war horns. In the distance, Jovians were running in disarray from the interior. Further along, a troop of Jovian cavalry raced, firing burning arrows into areas of the camp not on fire. A billowing curtain of smoke hung over the Persian camp. A spiral of wheeling vultures whirled nearby. They would feed well today.

He sniffed the acrid stench of burning tents. Surprise had allowed the Jovians to ravage a significant part of the Persian camp, but the price would be heavy.

He looked around for the Queen. She had to be somewhere nearby. He turned his head, trying to see between the tents, as they cantered along the edge of the camp. Then he saw them and, pointing, he urged Lucius to ride towards the tents. The Armenian cavalry followed. When they reached the captives, they were squirming on the shoulders of their Jovian guards. They were probably hoping if they delayed things, their countrymen would free them soon.

"Lucius, get your men to take a prisoner each over the front of his horse. Then ride these prisoners back to camp as if the hounds of hell were at your back," he said, as they reined in next to the captives. Then he slid off the horse.

"You do like pretty faces, my friend." Lucius grinned. Then he turned and roared orders at his men.

The Persian Queen gave Constantine a look of venom before she was bundled onto a horse. The girl he'd rescued was the last to be lifted up.

"Lucius, this one is to be treated separate from the others. She was their prisoner." Lucius gave a thumbs up.

The girl had a look of wonder on her face.

"This one is not to be ransomed or sold back to those Persians, Lucius. Put my name against her record. Now go. I have to rally the men."

He looked around. He could see lots of Jovians making their way out of the interior of the Persian camp. He had to form them up. An orderly retreat would save lives.

"Don't worry, you'll get your cut when she's sold," said Lucius. "Have you been injured?"

Constantine looked down. Blood dripped onto the grass from his right hand. He lifted it. A long cut across his forearm just below the elbow, on the outside, bled slowly into his arm guard. He was lucky. The blow hadn't severed his arm. And now the cut throbbed, and he couldn't even remember when he'd taken it. It would have to be tended to soon.

He had no time to bind it. He held his sword arm up to stop the blood flowing onto his hand.

"Stay away from your emperor's surgeons, Constantine. I hear they remove good limbs for any minor injury at all. You'll end up with a burnt stump if they get their hands on you." Lucius saluted, turned his horse and headed away after the prisoners.

"Form up!" Constantine roared, his sword in the air. Some men nearby ran to him. They stood to his left and right. Others followed. Soon ten of them were standing abreast.

In the end, he rallied almost two centuries of Jovians. They stood their ground as a rear guard for other Jovians, who he urged to hurry past them. After beating off a counter attack from a Persian cavalry unit, they finally slid down into the gully and headed back into the woods to join a stream of other Jovians making their way back to the Roman camp. He could hear shouts behind them at first, but they died away.

When they arrived at the Roman camp he had to wait three hours for the Jovian's own physician to examine his wound. He didn't seek the emperor's physician. An overworked assistant bound it up, after the cut was painfully probed by the physician. The assistant applied a cold herb and honey compress before binding the wound. He muttered prayers to Asclepios, the god of healing, as the binding was finished. It was well after noon before Constantine presented himself at the tent of the emperor.

The sun beat brutally down overhead, like every afternoon in the summer between the headwaters of the Tigris and Euphrates. He was used to heat, but this valley was exceptional, even by the standards of the east. He waited in the shade of a wide awning attached to the emperor's tent with two other officers. Neither man looked happy. They didn't converse, in case the emperor might be disturbed by their chatter. But they did stare at the sword he was carrying. It was clearly not Roman.

Wild cheering erupted at one point from inside the tent. When he asked the next orderly who came out what was going on, the man replied in surprise.

"Have you not heard?"

Constantine shook his head.

"Emissaries from the Persian King are demanding the return of his Queen and his sisters. Imagine! He's offered an immediate truce and good terms. The emperor ordered a search. The Persian queen has been discovered among the captives!" The man raised a fist in victory.

"Praise the emperor, avenger of Rome. We are victorious!"

Constantine said nothing. He had made it happen. Soon enough everyone would know.

The orderly held his hands. "You are Constantine, yes?"

Constantine nodded.

"Give me your weapons." The man's expression darkened, as if he was expecting trouble.

Constantine stared at him. It was not unknown for officers to leave their weapons outside, but it usually signaled the person asked to do so was not trusted.

"Orders from the emperor." The orderly moved his hands closer to Constantine. "You can collect them when you leave."

For a moment he thought about refusing, but the many guards nearby would not make insubordination easy and he did not want to kill men he knew.

He handed over the sword he had captured, then took his short and dagger from their scabbards and passed them over too. The orderly examined them, then went to place them on a rack nearby.

"The Persian sword is a gift for the emperor." The orderly nodded and placed the sword Constantine had captured at the end of the rack.

He knew, instinctively, that Galerius would be unlikely to praise him, but he'd have to listen and grudgingly grant him what he deserved. It had been a long time coming. Too long. He kept his expression fixed when the orderly at last beckoned him into the emperor's tent.

"What are you doing here?" shouted Galerius, as soon as he was ushered in. "I thought you were dead already." A group of officers standing around the emperor looked on impassively.

"I've come for the favor promised on the Jovian raid's success."

"What?" Galerius roared. "But you've only been successful in saving your own skin. You ran off, I'm told by your own optio, when the fight became desperate."

With a sinking feeling, Constantine knew how stupid he'd been. He took the Persian scabbard from around his neck and laid it on the ground. Galerius had to listen to this evidence.

"I did not run off, my lord. I took the sword of the commander of the Invincibles guarding the Persian queen. This is proof of my actions. I gave it up at the entrance to this tent. I searched the tents of the Persian nobles. I came upon a troop of Invincibles and with the help of my men we overpowered a troop of Invincibles. We took prisoners after we defeated them, one of whom was their queen." He stepped back. Galerius had to believe him. He felt a sudden chill in the air.

"Many have already claimed a part in the Queen's capture, Constantine. You are late to the list. You ignored the integrity of your unit as you went off in search of personal glory. You should be ashamed, rescuing a slave girl, when it was other officers, officers who followed orders like your optio, who held off the Persian counterattack and made our victory possible. Know this, you disgust me." He raised his finger and pointed it at Constantine.

"Think on this. I've had two officers beheaded already this morning for cowardice. If you think your lineage will save you, you're mistaken. I will have discipline in my army. Only my friendship with your father stops my hand. Go, leave my presence. I hereby demote you to the rank of legionary recruit and assign you to digging latrines for the next twelve moons. You shall not lead a unit again under my command or even take any active part in a campaign. There's no room for cowards in my legions." Galerius had gone from angry to enraged.

The ground swayed under Constantine's feet. He'd guessed Galerius would find a chance to humiliate him, because of his father's refusal to go along with Galerius' plan to outlaw the Christians, who he blamed for every calamity, but this was worse than he'd expected and a shocking blow to his hope of leading a legion.

Blood pumped in his neck. He wanted to kill Galerius. His face felt hot. If only they hadn't taken his weapons. It might well be worth dying to enjoy seeing Galerius with his neck cut open.

He pressed his lips together. Could there be a way out of this?

Such hasty demotions rarely occurred, but that didn't make any difference. He'd sworn to obey Galerius. A field trial had taken place, and an instant verdict had been handed down. That bastard optio. He had twisted everything. He looked around. Was he here? No. But there were others who could give evidence for him.

"My lord, is Sextus here to speak for me?" It was his last hope. He felt like a bruised gladiator about to receive a final death blow.

"Don't pretend you don't know that Sextus was carried dead from the field this morning!" Galerius' voice echoed with rage. "The loss of that one man is like the loss of a Legion. He was by you when the attack began, I am told, and soon after that you ran away. All this is undeniable. How many officers do you want to give evidence against you? I've heard all about your actions on the field already, and so will your father. Now, I have given my judgment. Go. And spare me your denials. Follow my orders."

His stomach cramped, as if he had been struck and a cold sweat broke out on his brow. One of the very few men who had stood by him, and possibly the only man who could save him from the emperor's wrath, was dead.

He couldn't believe everything that had just happened. It was as if a veil had been lifted. How could he even reply without it sounding like an excuse now?

He turned to go, knowing that as soon as he exited the tent his fate would be sealed. He'd make a few simple farewells and then move his bed roll to under the awning where the shit hole diggers lived, downwind of the regular troops, as they often stank like the holes they dug.

His hands were fists now. He couldn't beg. And he'd be throwing his breath away in argument if witnesses were ready to give evidence that his actions had been cowardly. The emperor would simply say he'd failed the biggest test of his life so far.

No right of appeal existed against an emperor's judgment on the day of battle. He turned and walked out.

The sunlight outside glinted hard, bleak. Resigned to his fate, disgusted and exhausted, he took a look around.

Striding towards him was Lucius, grinning. He raised his fist when he saw Constantine. "Why so glum? We have victory, my friend."

Constantine told him what had happened.

"Wait. I've been called to see Galerius. Let me see what I can do," said Lucius. "Do not do anything hasty."

XV

Alexandria, 298 A.D. - One Year Later

Helena disentangled her limbs from the priest's. She wrapped a thin purple veil around her and went to the couch, by the balcony overlooking the city.

"Bring wine and cheese," she said.

The young male house slave, who had been standing in a corner waving a fan, walked quickly towards the door, as if his life depended on it. It gratified her to see how eager the new Nubians were.

"Hosius, wake up!" She went to the bed, slapped the priest's bare thigh hard.

He groaned, shifted his body away from her. Then he turned onto his back.

"You do not want to share the mystical marriage again, Helena?"

"We will do it again, after the letter is finished." She pointed her finger at him.

Hosius groaned louder this time, then reached for the silver wine goblet on the bedside table.

"Composing this type of letter is not an easy task, my lady." He slid from the bed, walked to the marble-topped table by the door, under the painting of Hercules tricking Atlas to take the sky back onto his shoulders.

He unrolled the papyrus scroll, placed silver weights in the shape of slippers at each corner, and peered down at it. Most of the text was done. It needed only a last line and a florid signature.

"Have you decided how we will end it?"

Helena stood beside him. "Yes, write this. The return of my son is essential. I cannot live another day without him." She stroked his bare shoulder.

Hosius leaned forward on the stiff-backed chair, picked up the silver pen, and dipped it into the matching ink pot.

He began writing on the papyrus. He looked at her when he had finished.

"How many titles shall we put with your husband's name?"

"Augustus is enough. He will be that by the time this arrives."

Hosius wrote carefully and finished with a flourish, then sprinkled pumice all over the papyrus, before lifting it and letting the pumice fall away onto the marble floor.

"It is done," he said. Just then the bell of the night watch could be heard, first nearby, then further away, echoing through the room.

Helena lay on the bed. The young Nubian slave boy had returned.

"Have you seen how big this slave gets?" She giggled.

"I do not care." Hosius slid onto the bed beside her.

"He told me he can summon daemons to do my bidding."

"Then he is a follower of Satan."

She reached for Hosius, took his chin in her hand, and held it tight.

"He is not. But maybe I should change to his god. A god that he claims gets more results than you followers of Christ."

Hosius put his hands out, as if in supplication. "This letter will work, Helena. I have prayed over it. You know any delay in your son's release has been a sign that he is needed where he is. The one god will not allow you to suffer a moment longer than is necessary. I know that."

"He better not. This had better work. I am getting tired of promises, Hosius." She pointed at him again.

"I promise you it will."

"Good. Now, do you want to go back to bed?" She laughed, stuck her tongue out at him. "And if you pick the right answer, I will let you stay for the whole day."

74

XVI

Nicomedia, 306 A.D. - Eight Years Later

"Come on, you will like it." The slave master pushed her head down towards his cock. As she took it in her mouth he felt for her breasts and groaned. Soon she could feel him nearing the end, so she pulled away and retched into the dirt, bringing up some bile. He growled in disgust. Her hand came up to finish the job and within moments his seed flew high into the air.

"Bitch! You should have swallowed it."

She forced more bile up, coughing and retching into the dirt. "My mouth is not the right place, my lord. You might catch something from me." Then she pulled herself into a womb shape. He stood back and let his tunic fall, covering him.

"That was your last chance. I've turned down every slave boy who begged for you since you first came here, and every time this is all I get. I don't know why I waste my seed with you. There's far prettier waiting for me who will do everything I want, you ugly bitch. Let's see how you feel tomorrow." He laughed, turned and stalked out of the low roofed outhouse.

Juliana had learnt, soon after her arrival on the estate seven years before, that their master had crippled a previous overseer for getting two slave girls in the household pregnant. The mistress in the house had accused the master of doing it. The current overseer had to get enjoyment from the slave girls in a way that didn't give them a child, but which still satisfied his regular needs.

She lay still on the packed earth, listening, breathing, waiting, hope and despair turning inside her.

The outhouse was cold from the cutting midwinter winds that had gusted all that evening through the tall cypress trees that sheltered their master's villa. She found the skimpy blanket he'd thrown here earlier and pulled it tight. It was as useless as a cobweb against the cold, but its presence reassured her.

She knew what he meant about her last chance. She'd never walk again through the drifts of cherry blossoms that fell along the dusty path to the villa in the spring or take slow evening walks through the sweet pine forests nearby, when the work of being a house slave was done.

She pulled at her hair, wishing it longer. It had been cropped short when she'd first arrived. Ever since, they had made her keep it that way, forcing her to cut it every week with a shearing tool. Juliana had never been told why. But she could guess. The master's wife, Hera, had probably ordered it to ensure young slave girls did not easily attract the attention of her husband. Hera deserved to lose her husband. Anyone who found fault with everything some slaves did, deserved it turned right back on her.

Then a wonderful thought came. Perhaps her father would see her in the city. Her mother had always said he'd know her by her face, it so clearly resembled her own. Juliana held on tight to that possibility.

She'd been given to a foster mother when she first came to the estate, though she'd felt a little old for that. But the woman was childless and doted on Juliana as if she were her own, saving scraps of food for her and altering her best tunic as a gift at Saturnalia a year before, when they reckoned Juliana had reached her sixteenth year.

No one else could have a foster mother as wonderful as hers. She felt an ache of emptiness. She remembered her foster mother crying when the slave master spoke to them both the day before. She'd understood his many threats were at last to be made good.

"This one is too mean to be useful and too ugly to make a wife, even for a slave. She will get her last chance soon," were the words he'd used, and he went on pointing at her. "You'll learn how fortunate you were to be on an officer's estate, with an overseer who protected you and asked little in return."

The words her foster mother had said after the overseer had gone came back to her.

"Promise me," she'd pleaded. "That you'll keep yourself pure." She'd smiled at Juliana, stroked her face, as she'd done a hundred times before every time Juliana was troubled.

She always nodded when her foster mother had talked like this, and anyway, the story she'd told her about an infant being discarded in a rubbish pit at the bathhouses by an unmarried girl had sickened her. Though sometimes she'd wondered if the story had been her foster mother's.

"I will," she always replied. Even after he'd started calling for her.

Now she had only the wind to keep her company. And the years she'd spent on the estate were like waves that rolled away into memory. She sank slowly into a troubled sleep, trembling awake many times as the never-ending fears surfaced about what was coming for her, and only regaining sleep after long periods of shaking.

The following morning, when Juliana and the slave master reached the cobbled roadway that circled the bay of Nicomedia, the sun was well above the horizon. The wooded valley they'd come from was far behind now and the snow-covered Libon Mountains were at their back. Ahead across the small bay she could see their destination, the Roman city of Nicomedia, capital of the Eastern provinces.

Its gray brick city walls and red tiled roofs were, from this distance, no more than a jumble of shapes, but she could make out galleys and fishing boats by the stone dock, and above the city, columns of smoke drifting up towards a blanket of silver-gray winter clouds.

They'd set off before daylight and already she was hungry. All she'd been given before they departed was a cup of milk and some stale bread. She shivered. The thin, faded red woolen cloak she'd been given provided little protection from the wind.

Juliana twisted her face, trying to turn from the wind. Being tied to the back of the cart by the rope around her waist meant she walked, but the fear of falling and being dragged forward never left her.

She'd been off the estate before, since she'd been brought here, but not like this. And to add to it all, it had been raining on and off, and the cobbles were slippery. As the cart rumbled on the rain began again, soaking her through.

"Look girl. The palace of Nicomedia." The slave master turned to her. The clouds had broken over the city and rays of light lit up the roofs.

"When you end up in a village whore house, girl, with your eyes on the ceiling all day long, you'll remember this sight, before you pass away from the wormy pestilence." He cupped a hand to his ear. "Oh, listen, I think I can hear the screams from the slave market." He laughed.

But all she heard was the wind blowing in from the sea that stretched away to the left, wave-filled, dark and frightening looking. It was the biggest stretch of water she had ever seen. Who knew what monsters lurked there. She turned away from it. Straight ahead, across the bay, a sparkle of gilded rooftops stood out against the horizon. She looked down. What were palaces to her?

To her right, the land was parceled into fields and orchards and crisscrossed with watercourses and small bucket-chain waterwheels. This land looked prosperous, like their valley. She felt a pang of separation. Lime washed villas, just like her master's, with gently sloping red-slated roofs, could be glimpsed through the cypress trees that surrounded them.

"The new emperor has moved into his palace." The slave master turned to look at her. "I heard they go through slaves like an olive press goes though olives. Maybe that's where you'll end up, girl, keeping some under-gardener's bed warm 'till he passes you to the kitchen boys."

"At least I will be away from you," she said, softly.

"What was that?"

"Nothing, master."

He flicked his whip at her, though he didn't hit her. "Come on, run faster. You'll soon wish you'd treated me different, when your new master breaks you in."

He winked at her. "I'd like to watch that. Perhaps I'll make it a condition of your sale." He laughed, exposing blackened teeth. Then he cracked his whip over the slowing horses.

Juliana shivered, cursed him as a dung eater, letting the words slip out slowly, then she bent forward as she ran. Everything she'd grown to rely on was disappearing behind her, as if it had never existed. Her chest heaved. She fought the feelings away. She would not weaken any further. She had been saved for something. She'd heard another slave saying it and as soon as she had, Juliana knew it applied to her, with all she'd been through, not to that house slave who'd never experienced anything worse than a passage of the moon with little to eat.

The cart rumbled on.

But who would buy her? Would she be lucky in that?

Soon, the walls of the city loomed. She'd been to Nicomedia only once before, helping out on a trip to purchase spices. They'd had no reason to go to the slave market that day, but she'd heard about the crowds, the public examinations of naked slaves, the awful waiting and the salivating men. It was always men. Many of them old and half broken. Men who went there to take their pick of whatever woman, boy or girl they saw. Every taste could be indulged at the slave market.

"Don't forget, girl, if you run and they find you, and your new owner demands his money back, your life is mine to do what I will with it." The slave master made a fist, as if he was looking forward to that.

She didn't reply. Soon it wouldn't matter. Someone else would own her.

She gazed for a while at an aqueduct that strode across the fields towards the city, a giant Roman arm reaching out across the sullen winter landscape. The might of the empire made visible for all to see.

They joined a queue of carts waiting to pay the tax at the main gate of the city. The mules pulling the cart behind nuzzled close to her. One looked straight at her with big brown eyes gazing out from a dirt-encrusted face. Its hot stinking breath warmed her, but its gaze was sorrowful. She held up her hand, but before she could pat it the mule's teeth shot towards her, snapping shut just short of her fingers.

She jerked her hand away just in time. It was hungry. She held her arms crossed close to her chest. The animal looked dolefully at her, as if she'd taken away its lunch. She moved away from it until the cart pressed up against her back.

Shouts rang out and with a jolt the cart rolled forward. The stream of people walking past grew as they neared the gate. Slaves of all races passed, legionaries off duty and on, motherly matrons, dignified old men and plump children. Many of the slaves had thick cloaks or fur-lined tunics. They made her feel even colder just looking at them. If anyone looked at her, it was with disdain, as if they were repulsed. She saw some faces that seemed kind, but they never saw her.

The wall of the city towered above them now. Helmeted guards looked down from the ramparts, watching as the line of carts edged towards the gate. Today was market day. Most of the carts would be on their way to a traders' stalls or to the shops around the Forum. A slave girl walked past with a kind looking mistress. She yearned with a painful longing to be that slave girl, to have all this over, to find a kind master or mistress.

Someone laughed. It echoed from the high gate as the press of bodies and carts eased forward. A wave of conversation swelled around her. She wanted to go home. Or to run.

But she couldn't.

Two raggedy boys slipped in and out among the carts. They screamed when a driver sent his whip cracking towards them. They didn't see her as they dodged past, their gaze firmly fixed ahead.

A hawker, selling finger-length fried silverfish, stood to the side, his tray in front of him. Her mouth watered. Next to him a man sold flat bread, round and speckled with sesame seeds. She was ravenous. Her stomach twisted as the smell of the bread reached her. She looked away, closed her eyes, forced herself to think of something else. In her mouth was the taste of dust. In the air the hum of anticipation grew, like the noise bees make around a hive.

High, iron-studded gates stood open on either side of the road. A forbidding stone arch blocked the sky. It seemed to her that at any moment they might be closed to repel attackers, and anyone unlucky to be left outside the city would be forgotten.

Polished bronze symbols of the radiant sun, "Sol Invictus", were affixed to the center of each door. Two guards in dull iron breastplates and high red-tufted helmets stood to attention on each side, restricting the flow of people through the gate. An official in a red tunic stopped every cart. His assistant poked about in each of them.

When it came to their turn, the slave master handed over something and bobbed his head. The official looked Juliana up and down and gave a quick glance at the empty cart.

Beyond the gate they were engulfed in a wave of noise. The whistling of flutes, horns being blown, and chanting added to the clamor.

Juliana got an urge to run away into the crowd.

"Does no one clear a path for priests these days?" a man called out in a high-pitched voice. "Clear a passage, clear the gate. The priests of the sun are coming."

Juliana craned her neck to see through the crowd. A group of shaven headed, ash-smeared devotees moved towards her. Two small golden statues were being held high in the air behind them. Further back, a golden and radiant symbol of the sun swayed as the procession made its way towards the gate. The road cleared in front of them, people crowding onto the high pavement on each side, carts disappearing down side alleys.

At the front of the procession, young female flute players and timbrel janglers danced in short sea-green robes, which stopped well above their knees. Their heads were adorned with laurel wreaths. Their long legs attracted glances from all the men around as they swayed by.

The slave master cracked his whip and trundled the cart down a lane to their left, beyond the stone guardhouse and before the first row of colonnaded tavernas and shops. He stopped and turned to leer at the procession still passing.

"It's the reopening of the seas," he said, his expression gleeful. "There'll be plenty of traders in the market. You'll be best bought by some oily Egyptian who'll ship you off to his Kushite brothel. They're desperate for pale skins there. I heard a well-endowed Kushite can split a little girl in two." He grinned in anticipation.

At the tail of the procession aged and dirt-encrusted beggars, emboldened by the festival, were appealing for alms. They pushed cupped and shaking palms at every onlooker. Few gave, but the beggars simply mumbled something and moved on. Dogs barked, and street children pointed and jeered, delighting in the misfortune of the beggars.

Juliana looked to the sky. Everything felt different in the city. There was too much going on. They moved down the narrow alley way until it turned out into another crowded street.

The slave master got down now and led the cart onwards with a hand on the horse's mane. At every street corner the taverns were busy. Young serving girls stationed outside the larger taverns urged people to enter with them, to taste the house delicacies, stuffed olives or the best herb cheeses in the empire, or the wine of the gods.

Some shouted invitations to men to sample the tavern's girls, who they said were all guaranteed to be fresh from the country. At one window, they passed a crowd that had gathered. When it parted briefly, she saw a bed and on it a young man lying naked on top of an older looking giant of a woman, his bare ass rising and falling. The crowd laughed.

Ahead, the high marble pillared front wall of the Forum came into view. As they neared it the crowd thickened even more and there were lots more slaves. But she saw only two others tied to a cart like her. Most simply walked obediently a few steps behind their masters. Shouts of recognition rang out further up the street, followed by laughter. Many of the slaves looked apprehensive, as their masters marched forward on some mysterious mission.

Groups of men in twos and threes were standing on each side now. They were eyeing the slaves as they passed. Most of the men were gray haired, worn looking. A few might have been traders, from god-only-knew-where. She looked around. A group of young men with excited eyes whispered and smirked together, staring at her.

Juliana's head felt as if it was being squeezed. Some of the men looked cruel. They had the wide-eyed expression she'd seen in slave boys who liked to drown kittens or pluck the wings of butterflies.

A wizened old man in a filthy tunic, his hair matted, his face a mess of scars, followed a blond-haired slave boy no more than ten years old. The boy wore a short tunic exposing spindly white legs. She wondered why he was so thin. Then she looked at her own legs. They weren't much different.

She looked behind. No one followed them.

But to her left, outside a tavern, a young man in the cleanest toga she'd ever seen was staring at her. A moment later, on the periphery of her vision, she saw him turn to one of his drinking companions. The other man jerked around, spilling his goblet of wine but, without paying any attention to the shouts of others at the table, he beamed delightedly at Juliana.

"It's that girl you whipped to death last summer, come back to haunt you," the first man shouted.

The other young men at their table turned to stare. Juliana stuck her tongue out. The slave master turned, looked at her, flicked his whip in her direction. She flinched away from it. He stopped the cart, jumped down, and walked back to the tavern.

"Did you want a price, young masters?" He gestured to Juliana. "Perhaps you boys might share her. A virgin is worth a lot these days. Follow me and we'll have the papers made out before you know it. I'd sell her to you now, only I have to follow regulations with this one." He leaned over the table, towards the boy who'd spilled his wine.

"She was won in the great Persian campaign, you see. Booty of the Divine Galerius himself. I've been waiting weeks for permission to sell her, but now you can have her. In her prime she is. I'd say she'll buck the first time, but she'll give you a bit of fun."

A man leading a cart behind shouted at them to get going.

Juliana looked at the young man who'd made the comment, then quickly dropped her gaze. He said something to his companion that had made them both laugh. A tavern girl in a short tunic appeared with a bucket of scummy looking water. She flung it on the tiled floor beneath their table. Then she leant over in front of the young men, her breasts almost popping out. She looked at Juliana and scowled. The slave master muttered something to the men and then went back to the cart. Juliana didn't look back as they moved on, but she was sure she heard laughter directed at her. She didn't care.

They arrived at the slave trader's street. A group of female slaves were on display at the first colonnaded shop and, despite the cold, some were naked. Others wore only a loin cloth. A few wore short tunics. Most had their name and origin painted in red on a small rough board around their necks. Her head felt light.

The thought of being naked in public sent waves of embarrassment burning through her. Memories of what had happened to her as a child came roaring back. Visions that lived in her dreams, making her wake in a sweat occasionally when she thought they'd been forgotten. She'd been told that only barbarian slaves were stripped when they were sold. She'd hoped and hoped that meant she'd escape the humiliation.

Almost none of the slaves on display seemed to care about who stared at them, indeed some seemed to enjoy it, smiling lustily at the men around them, but a few of the naked girls looked timid and childlike as they turned away from the gawking men. The display of nakedness made Juliana's mouth dry up as they moved up the street. *Don't let them strip me.*

Now she knew. A good master would never buy her. Why would he, when he had such a choice? Further up the street, some of the traders had only two or three young girls tied up outside, others had more. Some had young men as well. They too were nearly all naked and she couldn't stop herself staring. One brown skinned boy grinned at her and made a swaying motion with his hips, shaking his long penis. A passer-by laughed. She overheard someone ask, "Would you eat that?" Another older man made an oohing noise at the still gesturing boy.

Juliana's ears tingled.

Another shop had three svelte, black skinned girls who jostled each other and jiggled their breasts and smooth hairless bodies at any man who looked at them. They laughed uproariously at the reactions they received.

Occasionally she saw older slaves, but not many, and sometimes child slaves, wild eyed, petrified. Their apprehension appeared only to bolster the smug superiority on the faces of potential purchasers who stopped to stare.

With a jerk on the rope holding her, they halted outside a trader's shop. It was, to Juliana's consternation, one of the poorest looking of all. Stained walls and the taint of urine and disrepair were accompanied by a gaudy depiction of a naked giant hurling blue thunderbolts painted beside the doorway to a shadowy interior.

The slave trader who appeared a moment later from inside did not look at all prosperous. His tunic was dirty and his black hair long and oily. The way he moved around, he looked like a pig nuzzling for food.

"You're late." The trader spat the words out. "Someone's been looking for you."

He stood in the doorway as Juliana's slave master undid the rope tying her to the cart. Her hands shook. They were cold though, and her wrists were sore and burning.

"This frigid bloody bitch delayed me." Her slave master handed the rope to the slave trader. "I hope she ends up a whore for one of your tavern owner friends. They'll be able to sell her ten times over to the men who like the first spearing, she squeals so much. Come on, tell me. Who came in?"

"Hold yourself," said the trader. "We'll talk business inside."

He yanked her towards him, growling as he did so. She stared back at him. He roared, laughing. She closed her eyes, prayed to wake somewhere else. He pinched her side. She jumped and opened her eyes. He grabbed her chin, pulled it down and looked in her mouth, then nodded with satisfaction.

There weren't any other slaves on display in front of his shop, so he attached the rope binding her wrists to the first of four rusty iron rings high up on the wall under the wooden roofed colonnade. Her wrists were dragged high when he'd finished. The position was uncomfortable, but bearable. And she had to be grateful. He hadn't pulled her clothes off.

The wall she stood near had been painted red a long time ago. Now it was peeling. Stains marked where the paint had been rubbed away by other slaves. The slave master and the trader were about to go inside when the trader seemed to remember something.

He turned back and walked over to Juliana. She looked away. But it did no good. With one fast movement, with both his hands, he tore away her short tunic, and to her horror, he yanked off her loincloth. Naked, she trembled from a rush of vulnerability. Every instinct told her to cover up, turn away.

But before she could, he pinched one of her nipples. A hot stinging sensation passed through her breast. She tried to turn to the wall, but found she'd been tied in such a way that if she did so, the rope cut into her wrists.

She stiffened inside.

She would not cry.

She wouldn't give them the pleasure.

Instead, she lifted her chin and glared at the trader. He brought his face close to hers, as if he might kiss her. She made her face still. His breath flowed over her, hot and garlicky.

She caught a glimpse of passers-by staring at her and had to close her eyes again even tighter.

But even with her eyes closed she could sense the staring.

It could often be, she'd been told, a living nightmare for slaves who ended up at the slave market, particularly for those who'd lived free on a country estate, as she had done. The noises of the slave market seemed to drift away.

"Where are you from, girl?"

She heard the gruff voice but didn't open her eyes. Who would be talking to her?

"Answer me!"

A stinging blow fell on her arm. She let out a yelp, looked around.

The man standing beside her was short, he came up only to her armpits, and bald, with marbled yellow skin. A puckered scar ran from his lip to his ear. His clothes were a jumble of multihued layers, open at the midriff, where a blue-veined stomach lurched in folds over his dirty red trousers. He looked like the Egyptian merchant who'd come to their estate once, but more disheveled, as if he'd been bankrupted long ago and had never recovered.

The man licked his fingers one by one with great care as he waited for her to answer. Fragments of decaying foodstuff, onion and bread mainly, flecked his thick black beard.

"Nicaea," she said.

"You don't look like a Bithynian girl. Show me your teeth, sweetheart."

She bared her teeth at him. The Egyptian laughed. His fingers stroked her arm, slowly.

"A very fine house slave, clean too. And still waiting for her first man." This new voice had a supplicating tone. She looked around. The slave shop owner had appeared behind the Egyptian.

"She'll grace any bed, master, especially the bed of a great merchant like you. Two hundred aurei is all we ask for her. It's a great price, master. I sold one like her for twice that last week. Come on, let us make out the papers. You can take her away at once." He put a hand on the Egyptian's arm.

The man shrugged him off and stepped back. "You take me for a fool, eh? I've been a master of thousands far better than this one. You Illyrians must take better care in describing your goods, trader. I see lice on her, and her teeth are half-rotten, anyone can see that. She'll not look half as well if they're knocked out. You'll never get such a ridiculous price. But I'll help you. I like Illyrians. My sister married one. I'll take her carcass off you for a hundred." He poked Juliana in the side. She wanted to kick out at him, but didn't. Already she hated him.

"She's defiant too. Her type dies quickly from beatings. A hundred is a good offer. That fish tattoo on her shoulder makes her ugly."

"Master let's discuss this inside. If you've taken a liking to her I may be able to do something on the price. I have some honeyed wine, if you'd care for it." The slave trader bowed. The Egyptian nodded. He followed the trader through the doorway. He looked back at Juliana as he passed inside and winked. She looked away. Apprehension and revulsion roiled insider her. A hand-sized black spider scuttled towards the rope she hung from. Before it could crawl down to her, she shook the rope, then lifted her thin sandal, and with a pleasing crunch crushed the spider after it fell.

Her arms felt heavier now. She glanced along the colonnade. A giant brown-skinned slave with badly cut hair and a jutting jaw had been tied up two arches away. His loincloth was as gray as the rain clouds. He stared at her, his expression sour, as if saying - I would crush you, if I was free.

"What are you staring at, you ugly crab-ridden whelp?" The giant spat towards her. She felt a sudden fury. Field slaves on the estate always treated her with respect or they were punished.

"It can speak. What a surprise," she replied loudly.

"Listen whelp, if I had a free hand I'd come over and slap that pretty face of yours. All you're good for is lying on your back." He sneered. "And whining and sucking your better's cocks. I doubt your new master will need you for much else." He stuck his tongue out at her.

"And was your mother a donkey?" she shouted.

She wanted to say more, but with a skin-crawling premonition she looked around. A crimson-cloaked man in a dark leather tunic stood a few paces away, as if he'd stopped to stare at her. She stared back at him. Then a bolt of fear ran through her. The man looked like an officer. There were marks where medallions had once been sewn onto his tunic. And a strange feeling came over her. No, it was impossible.

The man came towards her.

"Your name and your tribe, slave. And don't lie, I know every trick." Her stomach jumped. He had the arrogant tone of someone who despised slaves, and he spoke in Latin.

"I am Juliana. Born in Nisibis, the daughter of a Roman legionary from Britannia and a Persian mother," she replied, in Latin.

The man stared at her. He shook his head.

"Were you rescued from the Persians?"

"Yes, by a Roman officer at the Battle of the Palandoken and given as booty to a loyal officer of the emperor," she replied, this time in Greek.

"And you speak Latin and Greek. That is different."

Her foster mother on the estate had been fluent in both. She'd said good house slaves should know these things, like in the old days.

"And you've grown well." He looked her up and down. She tried to turn away. Then something dawned on her.

"Have you been a personal slave?"

"Yes, master, I have." She turned her head to him.

"How much do they want for you?"

She looked down. "Three hundred aurei," she said, softly. She bit her lip. Would it work?

"Ridiculous, I'll pay two hundred, at most." He turned away, as if he were about to move on. Her mouth opened. She had no idea what she would say, but she had to say something.

"I am worth a lot more than that." She glared at him.

"Your father came from Britannia?"

Juliana nodded. He would walk away. She knew it. But she wasn't going to beg. To hell with him.

He walked to the doorway to the slave trader's shop and went through it. The saliva in her mouth dried up.

She waited, shivering now. Could it be a good sign meeting this man again?

"Foolish, stupid," the Egyptian shouted, as he came out through the doorway. "Bad luck, little girl," he said, as he came towards her, his tone taunting.

Her hands gripped the rope. She waited for the worst.

"Be warned." He spat in the palm of his hand, then rubbed his palm across her breasts. She twisted as far away from him as she could as the slime oozed across her skin.

He walked on down the colonnade. She watched him, relief growing fast inside her. He stopped by another slave girl.

The slave trader came out and untied the rope holding her hands. He passed her a soiled gray tunic. She rubbed the cloth against her breast to clean away any mark the Egyptian had made. Then she pulled the tunic on. Her arms were comically uncoordinated in her rush to cover herself. When she looked up the officer was standing in front of her.

"I'm Lucius. You'll come with me. The papers are done. Stay close. We heard you were to be sold. Your owner has warned me about you, but if you know your place you'll find me reasonable. Be good and you'll be rewarded." He spoke as if to a child, but she was used to it. She bowed in response.

This was better, much better, than she'd dared hope for.

"Follow me." He turned away.

She nodded. She knew better than to run.

Lucius went to the giant slave Juliana had been bantering with and after asking him a few questions, while Juliana stood nearby hoping he wouldn't, he bought this slave as well.

The giant walked behind her as they made their way through the streets, eyeing her up and down and grinning in a disconcerting manner whenever she turned to see if he had run off.

Unfortunately, he seemed as pleased as she was with their new master. Eventually they reached stables near a different city gate to the one she'd entered by, where Lucius told them to wait in an outer courtyard. Juliana asked to relieve herself. He nodded. After using a crude slaves' facility at the city gate, she returned to the courtyard.

"You have me to protect you now, whelp," said the giant in a low voice as they waited, surrounded by horses whinnying and the commotion of the busy stables.

She put a finger to her lips, shook her head and frowned. The giant made a face at her, as if he knew all about serving a new master and certainly didn't need her to tell him. They were given bread and water by a slave while they waited. With a sunny feeling of relief buoying her she ate ravenously, ignoring the giant.

Then Lucius appeared on horseback. He waved at them to follow, then forced a path through the crowds at the city gate. There she learnt their new master's full name, Lucius Aurelius Armenius, when he was hailed by a guard.

Soon after they were heading down a dusty track into the countryside. By walking fast, the two slaves were able to keep up. Eventually, nearing midday, they entered through the high gate of a villa. Apprehension returned as they were led to the basement slave quarters by a well-dressed, white-haired house slave who shook his finger at her, demanding silence, when she started asking questions.

So much had changed so quickly. She still felt relief at escaping the Egyptian but kept wondering what she would be asked to do under her new master.

The villa and its estate were an unknown world she would have to learn all about. She would have to learn the rules fast, and how to fit in with the slaves already here. New slaves would be ignored and spat upon if they didn't quickly accept the long-established slave hierarchy they'd joined.

The kitchen boy couldn't restrain himself from showing off, as he told them where they kept the slaves' food. He gave them bread, olive oil and cheese, but only enough to stop their hunger. Then he talked about their new master.

"He is the son of the richest Armenian merchant in the whole world. He has killed a thousand Persians with his bare hands." The boy stared, wide-eyed, at them. "His father raised troops against Persia and the master led them. They ravaged twenty cities and he kidnapped the harem of the Persian King. He is a friend of the emperor." He narrowed his eyes. "But new slaves must wait many moons to serve the master." The boy tilted his chin up, exuding superiority. "You will have to. . ." He stopped mid-sentence.

"Ignore this fool. It's not for boys to tell you what you must do." The old house slave had come over to the bench where they were eating. He banged his knuckles against the kitchen boy's head.

"Run away, stupid boy," he said. The boy scampered off, holding his head.

"It's an honor to serve our master," the old slave said. "But don't prattle about him, unless you're looking for trouble."

Juliana kept her eyes down.

That night she slept peacefully in the tiny cell she'd been allocated. The cell was only a handbreadth bigger than the recessed bench she slept on and had been cut into the wall of the main corridor in the slave quarters in the basement of the villa. It had only a curtain separating it from the corridor, but she was used to that. She fell asleep thinking about her father, trying to remember what her mother had said about him, though her words grew dimmer every year, like a candle being walked into the distance.

Something about her new home had revived her hopes of finding him. If things could change so much in one day, perhaps they could change again. It helped too that her fear of being raped had diminished.

Earlier that evening she'd heard that slave girls in other people's houses often threw themselves at Lucius' feet, wasting their time and his, and making fools of themselves.

She woke early the following morning, a vivid dream disturbing her. The old white-haired slave had been in it, but as a young man, his hair almost black. He'd been naked in a room with black pillars and a group of men in togas, laughing and placing gold coins down on a marble table.

"Why so glum, little Juliana?" The giant slave, who'd been purchased at the same time as her, nudged her arm. Everyone called him Tiny. He'd appeared beside her as soon as she'd sat down at the wooden bench outside the small basement kitchen.

"I am not glum." She continued tying up her sandals. The basement corridor made her feel at home. The warm dusty smell of fresh bread filled it. A column of bright sunlight lit up a square on the stone floor near her feet, and swirls of dust sparkled in its shaft.

"Worries are sent by daemons. My mother, she used to say that." Tiny tapped his shoulder as he spoke, as if to ward off the daemons he spoke about.

The sound of trilling sparrows reached them from the doorway out to the kitchen yard. She turned her head to listen to them. He tutted and went out. His comments had been friendly since they'd arrived, despite the continuing coolness of her responses. It would take more than a few kind words for her to trust him.

"You will probably never meet the master again," said the cook, as she helped in the kitchen after they'd had breakfast. Juliana had simply asked would they be serving their new master soon.

"If you by any chance meet him, remember to bow low, girl, and to never speak unless spoken to. He must be treated right, girl. Do not forget it."

The head of the kitchen slaves scowled at Juliana and folded her arms. Juliana had seen a wooden rod hanging on the kitchen wall, within easy reach. It looked new. Her old slave master had broken rods on the arms and backs of slaves many times.

They spent the next few days helping in the kitchen, becoming familiar with the chores of the household. Juliana was set to washing and scouring, Tiny to heavier tasks, carrying and fetching. He'd spent the last few years accompanying his previous master on a journey to the trading forts along the Danube. He told them in numbing detail about every extraordinary thing he'd seen there. Juliana became irritated with his tales. They mostly ended up being about girls he'd met, who'd all been beautiful and friendly.

After two days, they were told Lucius had called for them and they were to wait in the outside yard. She shivered under a thin cloak she'd been given and tried to avoid the inquisitive glances of other household slaves as they went about their business.

There seemed an unusual number of tasks that needed doing in the yard that morning. Juliana guessed that the whole household waited expectantly to find out if there were any other duties the new slaves had been purchased for. The wall at the back of the yard, under a colonnade of small recently repaired pillars, had been painted long ago with vivid scenes against a now-faded crimson background.

She kept glancing at the open doorway, wondering when the master would come. She'd always hated waiting to see a master before. On the few occasions she had to, when she was very young, she'd almost vomited. Hoping to avoid that she held her arms tight around her stomach. Then Tiny leaned towards her.

"Today you'll find out why you were purchased, little Juliana, and if the master wants you to start warming his bed." He sniggered.

She looked at him. Did he know something she didn't? The waiting, the newness of everything, the horrible old slave who seemed to do nothing but watch her all the time, and now this, it all filled her with a terrible dread. She screwed her face up and turned as far away from him as she could.

"But I'd be surprised if he did choose you for that."

"What do you mean?"

"The master's got more choices than a Numidian slave driver, not being married that is, and having different mistresses visit him every night."

She felt him pat her shoulder. She brushed quickly at where his hand had been.

They waited without talking as the sounds of the villa continued around them. Occasional shouts from the stables and the clatter of dishes from the kitchens were the noises of a busy household. These she was used to. What was to come that morning, was what concerned her.

"Can you smell the sea?" Tiny lifted his head back as he spoke. "We can't be far from the port. I'm told galleys arrive every day from Rome. Our master travels too, every year they say, and he takes slaves with him on his journeys. I heard he's planning to go again, that the villa's stores are being run down because of it."

Juliana knew little about Rome. Few freemen she'd met, never mind slaves, had ever even seen it.

"I never want to go there," she said. One of the other slave girls she'd talked to in the few days since her arrival had told her that Lucius' father used to take their white-haired slave master to Rome with him. But he'd stopped, as he got older. Juliana had told her about the dream she'd had.

"You don't decide your fate, little Juliana," said Tiny.

At that moment Lucius appeared in the doorway. They both bowed low, almost together, as he came towards them. Her hands were trembling.

94

"I hope you two haven't picked up any bad habits. Slaves in this house are as lazy as any I've ever met. We leave here in a few days, on the Ides, and I want you both dressed properly, not in those rags. You'll disgrace me at the palace like that." He looked them up and down, shook his head, and let out a resigned sigh.

"Remember this, slaves, give me one cause to regret buying you and you go back to the slave market or the nearest one I can find. Displease me greatly, and you'll have more to worry about than that. I warn you. A slave I cannot trust does not deserve their life. Is that clear enough?"

Both of them nodded.

"Your loyalty is suspect as far as I'm concerned, but I do what I'm asked, and you will too. You'll be taught how to behave at a palace, and other things your barbarian mothers could not have known about. Learn quickly."

She swallowed. He'd said something about a palace. Had she misheard or misunderstood?

"Don't let my house down," he said. Then he pointed at them. She stopped breathing. "I'll be watching you all the time. Now go on, go."

They bowed again, eyes down, and made their way to the kitchens.

"Did he really say we're to go to a palace?" Tiny asked in an excited whisper as soon as they were out of Lucius' hearing.

"Not you, just me." She poked his arm with her elbow.

"They have fountains that spew wine there, you know, and ten dancing girls for each man, and twenty slave boys to service every woman." He made a loud kissing noise. Juliana's mind raced. Why were they going to a palace? What would it be like?

"Come with me." The ancient slave looked exactly as she imagined the Oracle at Delphi must look. She led them to an empty store room at the back of the stables where she drilled them on many things, like how to bow, how to keep your eyes to the floor while taking commands, and how to reply when spoken to by a member of the imperial family, though she assured them Hades would freeze over and be shipped to Nicomedia to cool its storerooms before that was likely to happen. She also harangued them nonstop.

"You sure are so stupid. Go down lower, oaf!" was a favorite, and she often slapped Tiny on the back with a rod, but he always looked around while she did it, as if it didn't bother him.

"How can I teach you in two days what it took me years to learn? I cannot do it. If you make a mistake it will be on your heads. They can cut them both off, for all I care." She slapped Juliana for absolutely nothing at that point.

"I've not seen the inside of a palace in thirty years, and now you two come along and you're off with the master the next day. It's not right." The crone slapped them both again, to teach them what was likely to happen at the palace, she said.

They learnt what they could. Tiny looked ridiculous bowing low, and Juliana's manner when intoning "My lord" was all wrong, so the old slave said. There was so much more to learn.

Two days later she woke early. Today she'd visit the palace of Nicomedia, where the emperor of the east lived. Anything might happen. She lay awake in the dark in her cell, waiting for the sounds of the early rising slaves.

Soon she heard scuffles echoing along the bare brick walls. The slaves' day had begun, and the sun had still not risen.

The suddenness of the attack shocked her. One moment she lay in the dark, alone, the next, blows from a rod were landing all over her back.

"Stop! I've done nothing."

Arms pinned her down. The blows continued, this time on her legs, hard and sharp.

She squirmed and twisted, sharp pains burning at her skin, lashing out with her arms, waving her fists high in the air. She brushed the rod aside. The blows stopped.

"Evil one be gone," a voice hissed. Then a scuffling noise filled the room, like rats disappearing, and finally all she could hear was the sound of her own heavy breathing.

She would have to sleep on the floor for a while, to be ready for them if they came back. Clearly, they didn't intend to kill her, just to make her suffer, and possibly end up too injured to go out with the master that day.

She clenched her fists. They weren't going to succeed. She would ignore the pains from her back and legs. She would pretend they didn't exist. Like she'd done with a thousand other punishments she'd been through.

After washing and their usual breakfast of leftover bread and cheese, Juliana and Tiny were given freshly cleaned dark-gray tunics, and darker, but thankfully heavy, cloaks. They were told to wait by the stable gate. Outside, in the crisp cold air Juliana, determined not to think about the pains from her body, noticed for the first time the crumbling wall plaster and the weeds growing along the top of the flat stable roof.

Even the gravel underfoot barely covered the path to the stables and a sodden pile of firewood had fallen over nearby.

Lucius appeared with a bright red cloak swirling behind him. His only greeting to them was a nod. Then he started shouting for the stable hands to hurry. Horses were led out and slaves rushed forward to help him mount a shiny black stallion. Two smaller mottled-brown mares were clearly intended for Juliana and Tiny. Tiny's eyebrows rose when he saw how small his horse was. But they mounted, and without a word or glance Lucius turned his horse and passed through the gate to the street. Juliana's muscles ached from the beating. Her arms and legs felt stiff and she had to swallow hard and press her hands into fists all that day to stop the groans that wanted to force themselves out of her throat. And the riding made it worse. She'd only rarely been allowed to ride on her old estate, but she'd usually enjoyed the feel of a horse beneath her, though not now.

She looked back, saw pure resentment on the faces of field slaves standing by a broken wall watching their departure. The villa's slaves would be cursing bitterly the fortune of their master's new additions. Few of them would have been taken anywhere by the master, never mind accompanying him to the palace on horseback. Juliana held her reins tight. Jealous slaves always plotted revenge. It was their way of passing time. She would never again sleep on the plank in her cell. The next time they came, it could be with knives.

But that was a worry for the future. She was riding again. A gust of icy late winter wind pummeled her. But the cloudless blue sky lifted her spirits.

She and Tiny followed a respectful single horse length behind Lucius, as he guided his horse past carts and the odd chariot on the road into the city.

Near the city wall they turned off onto a wide roadway paved with torso-sized white stone cobbles. On each side stood high gray and red brick walls of villas. The traffic was mostly in one direction now and she realized after a while that the great and worthy from the whole province of Bithynia must be travelling along with them, some on horseback, others in chariots or behind dark curtains in handsomely decorated carts. A few were even being carried in sedan chairs. They passed a barrel of a man in a spotless toga who whipped his horse as it tottered under him. The man's polished head looked like a boil about to burst.

"He'll be on his fat face soon," whispered Tiny. "Why doesn't he hide in a cart like the rest of his patrician friends?"

She looked at Tiny's horse. "He's not the only one in need of a cart," she said. Tiny just stared at her, venom in his eyes.

Lucius leaned up in his saddle as if searching for something. A formidable brick wall at least two stories high had come into view up ahead. Along the top of the wall thin slits overlooked them.

Where the wall started, at the entrance to a wide laneway, a group of men waited on horseback. The road rose steeply beyond them. The walls on each side were close by now. She felt hemmed in, in a corridor of brick and stone.

A row of low, black pine-mothered hills stood to her left. She guessed this villa's walls enclosed a ridge running down to the water. She'd glimpsed a dark bay occasionally through breaks between the walls of the villas.

Lucius trotted ahead to where riders were gathered in a circle around one man on horseback, like legionaries gathering round a standard. The man at the center was not only physically larger than the men around him, his whole appearance was different. The sight of him sent a deep shiver through her.

His cloak was dark purple, and he held himself steady, unmoving as Lucius approached him. The men around him were his guards, she guessed. She slowed, and Tiny did too, as they all came nearer, and then stopped about twenty paces from the group.

She saw the man's face clearly for the first time as the horsemen parted, and he greeted Lucius. She had to look away at once. His status shone from him. But there was something else, something unsettling.

She knew his face. She knew his heavy eyebrows, his high forehead, his short wavy black hair. But from where?

And then, as if a door had swung open, it came to her. It was him. The man who'd saved her years before. It had to be. And if he wore the purple, that could only mean one thing. Would he remember her?

She looked again. A name she'd overheard years before came back to her. Constantine. Was this Constantine, the son of the emperor of the western provinces, who was living here in the east? She mouthed his name then simply stared, though she knew she shouldn't, tingling as if she'd been struck, as he greeted Lucius.

And then, to her astonishment, his gaze swung to her. He frowned. She bowed and held it low and then wondered if she'd bowed at the wrong moment. She looked up.

They had already turned their horses. He and Lucius set off up the road together, deep in conversation. The tightness in her chest eased. He hadn't noticed her. She followed Tiny, who'd already set off after them. He looked back at her, shook his head and grinned, as if he knew her every thought. She narrowed her eyes at him. He laughed as if she was a lost cause. When he turned away, she scowled at all their backs.

The road ran along the wall until the ground levelled off as they entered a dusty square. Giant wooden gates with an elaborately decorated stone arch above them dominated the center of the right-hand side of the square - the only break in the wall.

On the other side of the square, the blackened stumps of what must have been a large building stood out like a broken tooth in the center of an otherwise perfect mouth. The year before she'd heard about the razing of the great church in Nicomedia and stories about executions of Christians, followers of the one god.

On the far side of the square stood a colonnade of open fronted shops. She saw the sign of the guild of scribes marked above some of the doorways. Tall cypress trees, like green daggers, ran in a line in front of the pink and gray stone palace wall.

The magnificent gates towards which they were headed were flanked by a pair of yellow marble pillars veined with purple. In front of them a well-dressed crowd jostled. More people were joining all the time, like flies attracted to a feast. Lucius was not attending some small audience with the imperial staff, as one of the house slaves had suggested. This was something more.

As they came close to the gate people moved aside. Many stared at Constantine. They looked as if they were observing prey. Then she noticed they were staring at her as well. She stared back. Everything about her, from her thick sandals to her unbridled hair, marked her out as a slave. But she didn't care. She rode with an emperor's son.

Tiny leant towards her. "Try not to look so happy."

She winked at him.

Just then Lucius turned to look at them. He scowled at her. All around them people were stepping back, pushing and shoving others in the crowd in front of the gate. An occasional muttered complaint died away quickly as they passed.

The guards at the gate must have recognized Constantine, as the gates creaked open and they were waved forward. Juliana was the last to be let through the half-open gate and for a moment she thought she wasn't going to make it, because of the crowd pressing close behind her, but she did. A slave in a pure white tunic came up to her in the wide graveled area beyond the gate. Everyone else had dismounted, so she gave up her reins. The guards Constantine had come with seemed to be staying with the horses.

Lucius motioned for her to come with them. Then she and Tiny followed, a half dozen paces behind, as Constantine and Lucius were escorted by an official with a bulbous stomach, thin arms and a long neck who looked to her like some upright rodent. He led them down the avenue.

She could not believe how perfect everything looked. They passed by life like statues of gods on a row of plinths. She'd never seen anything like them. The gravel underfoot was whiter than any she'd ever seen. Her breathing quickened as she wondered what else she might see. Ahead, Constantine and Lucius took no notice of the surroundings.

In the distance smoke spiraled into the sky behind a tall, marble pillared building at the end of the avenue. It looked like a temple she'd seen once but was even more magnificent. It looked as if the tops of every pillar had been dipped in gold. The statues in a line above the pillars looked like gods caught by some soothsayer's alchemy, waiting for some magical command to free them. At their center a golden eagle stretched out its wings.

And she felt a strange sensation, as if they were being watched.

XVII

Nicomedia, 306 A.D.

From a grilled window above the double height doorway and directly below the giant golden eagle with outreaching wings, it was possible to watch people coming and going to the imperial palace of Nicomedia, unobserved.

Behind the grilled window stood Galerius, the emperor of the east, the senior emperor of the Roman world, looking glorious in a jeweled toga. At the very moment Juliana sensed they were being watched, Galerius scratched distractedly at his beard as he stared down the avenue. Behind him the short, grotesquely fat governor of Bithynia bobbed up onto his toes to peer out over Galerius' shoulder. They watched Constantine and his retinue as they progressed up the avenue.

"What will you do about his request, my lord?" said the governor.

"I will do what I must. Do you see who's with him?" The governor didn't answer. Galerius continued almost to himself. "I am haunted by this bloody mongrel. He is like the pox. If I'd known he'd be coming back after all these years, still whining, I'd have ignored that meddlesome Armenian when I had the chance all those years ago. When I think how his father still will not do as he is told my blood boils." He groaned and slipped an oil-softened hand under his tunic to scratch at the scabs under his belly. "Why doesn't someone kill this Constantine for me? I'm sure there are plenty who could arrange it." Galerius waited for the governor's response.

The man raised his eyebrows.

Galerius turned back to the window. "I cannot be the one to do it or to order it done. I gave a sacred vow. I must return Constantine, unless I want a war with his father." He turned to the governor. "Carry these words to Maxentius in Rome."

He put his arm around the governor's shoulder. "Come on, governor, tell me about your new Egyptian girls. I hear they squeal mightily."

XVIII

Nicomedia, 306 A.D.

The total contrast of everything here against the world beyond the palace walls was what surprised Juliana most about the imperial palace. Beyond the walls, mud reigned everywhere. Here every leaf looked polished.

"This must be what the palaces of the gods are like," she whispered to Tiny. He grunted in reply.

In front of the giant pillared building servants in yellow tunics threw flower petals over the path of the arriving guests. A small crowd had gathered at the doorway, like children waiting for their Saturnalia presents.

Juliana and Tiny walked behind Constantine and Lucius. She gawked at everything. Tiny whispered to her, "Close your mouth. Everyone will think you're a fly catcher." Juliana closed her mouth.

"Galerius certainly knows how to spend the treasury. I thought he'd give up on absurd parties," Constantine said to no one in particular, as they waited for the guards at the door to finish with the guests waiting in front of them. Juliana and Tiny were a few paces behind, eyes lowered.

"He has to prove he's truly an emperor, in case Diocletian asks for his scepter back. Having a senior and a junior emperor in the east, and the west, has not been the great solution to the empire's woes that Diocletian hoped it would be." Lucius stamped his feet as he spoke, sending dust swirling.

A scent of lemons gusted through the doorway. Juliana's mouth watered. Slaves were shaking oil onto the upturned hands of each guest as they entered the palace. She rubbed her palms against the sides of her tunic.

The massive bronze doors were covered in carvings and jewels. They shouted of wealth beyond reason and glistened on each side as she passed through them.

Tiny sniggered as his hands were oiled.

"Do even slaves get their hands anointed?" he asked the golden legged slave girl in a dangerously short tunic, as she dribbled lemon water onto his hands.

"It is the empress' order." The slave girl gave him a patient look. Then she dribbled oil on Juliana's palms. Juliana rubbed them together, as she'd seen everyone else do.

They were in a large hall with a high purple ceiling. Rows of black marble columns lined each end of the hall. She felt small looking at them.

Another slave girl, dressed in the Egyptian style, bare breasted and wearing only a white linen sheath, approached Constantine and bowed. Juliana edged closer to hear what she was saying.

"I will take you directly to the empress. Your companion can come. I will show where your slaves will wait. Follow me, my lord." With a swish of her braided hair the slave turned on her heel and, without waiting for an answer, strode away. Constantine turned to Lucius and shrugged.

They all walked after the slave. Tiny and Juliana trailed behind, as if an invisible cord connected them. They went through a door and down a wide corridor.

Four guards stood to attention by a high door at the end of the corridor. They were barring the path to a small band of nobles, who, it became clear, were trying to gain entry to the quarters beyond.

As they approached the door their guide pointed at a side door, and then to Tiny and Juliana. Lucius whispered to Tiny. Tiny motioned Juliana to follow him.

"We're to wait here," Tiny said, when she caught up with him. "I hope there'll be food."

Juliana watched Constantine and Lucius passing through the high doorway at the end of the corridor. A pang of jealousy ran through her as she saw them disappear through it.

In the waiting room, there were four other slaves. They turned away dismissively as she and Tiny entered. A marble table, against one wall, had pitchers of wine and water, and trays of stuffed olives, cheese, and honeyed cakes on it. The smells from the table made her queasy.

Tiny poured a goblet of wine and passed it to her. It was unlike anything she'd ever tasted, bursting sweet and fruity on her tongue.

"Do you remember the slave market?"

Juliana nodded.

"Why do you think we are here?" Tiny continued in a low voice, as he helped himself to some honey cakes.

Juliana shook her head. The smell in the room, the sense of being close to powerful people, had brought back a memory of her time in the Persian tent many years before. She pressed her hands together, started breathing slowly as her slave mother had taught her to do when her dreams would wake her with half-stifled screams.

"I hope it isn't all some trick," he said, looking round.

She didn't reply. She wondered where Constantine had got to. Tiny looked at her. For a moment, she thought he'd read her mind, but all he did was laugh.

She sat and thought about the terrible things that had brought her here. She remembered the way the Persian soldiers had burnt their whole, and when she'd returned to her house everyone was dead and she was plucked from the ground while she was screaming wildly outside it, and a cloth placed over her mouth while the smell of burning flesh filled her nostrils.

The door of the room opened. Six guards filed in, the clatter of their hard sandals echoing from the walls. Juliana froze, her breath stopping in her throat. The guards were accompanied by the girl who'd brought them to this room. She pointed at them. "Seize them," she said.

The guards took Juliana and Tiny roughly by the arms, ignoring all questions, and without explanation pushed them from the room. Juliana was almost carried down the long corridor. Something terrible was going to happen. Tiny had been right. It had all been a trick.

Behind her, Tiny had four guards holding him. He knew better than to struggle against them.

Or maybe he was waiting for the right moment to lash out.

XIX

Treveris, Gaul, 306 A.D.

Crocus pulled the flap on his tent up and looked outside. A watery blue sky greeted him. The gods were appeased. His daughter was on her way to see him. He dropped the flap, turned, went across to the rush mat at the back of the tent and sat, cross legged.

He recited the prayer to Woden, god of war and magic.
You are the one I believe in.
You are the doom of my enemies.
You are the stealer of victory.
You are my father, Woden.
Be here with me today.

Rustling from outside the tent brought his head up. The tent flap opened and in walked his daughter. Her red hair engulfed her head like a flame, exactly as it had done for her mother, passing all the way to her waist.

Crocus stood, and they hugged. A tear came to his eye. He grunted it away. Loki would not trap him today.

"Sit, we will talk."

They sat opposite each other on the rush mat. The air thickened with the smell of human bodies, last night's stew, and horses. Swirling patterns filled the tent walls. Only the pile of blankets at the back gave any clue that this was also where he slept.

"You have done well, Father. Mother sends her blessings." His daughter smiled. It was the smile of her mother. The smile that had made him weak for her.

"There is another reason for you coming, Daughter. What is it?"

She coughed, looked around, leaned towards him, and put a hand on his bare knee. "We have heard that the son of the emperor of the west will come here."

"That is not sure, yet. Galerius may not release him. He may die on the way here. He may not exist at all."

"He exists. He is coming. My mother saw it all in a dream. The birds spoke to her."

He shook his head. "Always the dreams. Always the birds. You know this is why I had to leave your mother. She wrecked my head with her dreams and her birds."

"My mother says you left her because you like war. You and Woden have a pact, she says."

"That is also true. But why does Constantine's arrival in Gaul concern your mother? Tell me that?"

"My mother says the age of daemons is upon us, that this Constantine will bring them with him to Gaul."

Crocus leaned back and waved his hands, like a bird unfolding its wings. "She sees far too much, your mother."

The girl shifted nearer to him, her eyes as black as pitch, like his.

"This Constantine must be killed. His body must be cut open and his heart burnt for the daemons to leave our land alone. This is what my mother says."

Crocus grunted. "Again, your mother wants a heart. I will consider what is best for us before I decide."

"We know you can do it, Father. We know whose side you are really on."

XX

Nicomedia, 306 A.D.

Constantine and Lucius had been escorted down a corridor and out into the Empress Valeria's private garden, a colonnaded courtyard with young cedars lining each wall.

At last he would know the answer. His familiarity with the palace added to his impatience.

He'd felt an urge to rush forward, not to wait to be shown where to go. He'd spent parts of each winter for the past ten years, while on leave from the Jovians, living in rooms here under the scrutiny of unbelievably nosy officials. He'd only escaped when finally permitted to rent his own villa after Diocletian had abdicated the previous year, and they'd all vacated the palace for Galerius to take up residence.

The slave girl led them to a small plain door at the far end of the courtyard, turned, and put a finger to her lips. She inserted a bronze key slowly into the lock and opened the door gently.

The sound of lyres, discernible only as a distant murmur while they were outside the door, rushed from the room as soon as the door cracked open. They slipped inside. Small knots of guests stood in respectful silence around the empress' pillared reception hall. From the ceiling rows of broadly striped canopies hung.

Couches swathed in red, green and purple silk were arranged at the center of the room around a green marble table laden with golden goblets and platters. Bluebells and snowdrops, portents of an early spring, overflowed from golden baskets beside the table, and hung in garlands along the backs of the couches. Every fold of silk, curl of hair, and intertwined flower garland reinforced the impression of heart-stopping beauty.

Sitting upright on a gold-armed backless chair was the empress, plucking at a lyre. Two fair-haired youths sat at her feet, accompanying her. Constantine moved to the edge of a circle of onlookers. Lucius waited nearby.

The empress stopped playing and waved him forward. Enthusiastic clapping filled the room. He stopped in front of her, bowed his head low, and waited.

Valeria was an old friend. They'd both been virtual prisoners in the palace years before, at the beginning of his time in the east. She was Diocletian's daughter and her every movement had been closely watched. They'd become good friends, but too often after that she'd been away when he visited. And then he was appointed to the Jovians.

"Constantine, you have interrupted us. I hope you have a good excuse." She shook her finger at him, her tone cross, but her face a picture of delight, her eyes wide, beaming like an owl's. He felt once again the old, futile longing.

He knelt, reached forward for the edge of her purple silk robe. He put it to his lips and kissed it, slowly.

"I have no excuse, my empress, except for my impatience to see you." He spoke softly, so no one else could hear him.

"I have been waiting for you too." Her tone was sweet and cool now, like a sensuous woman's skin.

"And who is this?" She looked at Lucius.

Constantine leaned towards her. "That is Lucius Aurelius Armenius, an old friend."

"This is the man who spoke up for you when Galerius wanted you demoted?"

"The same."

"Aaah, I heard you had an Armenian friend who threatened to get all his fellow scouts to abandon that campaign if your sentence wasn't overturned, and that you should be proclaimed a hero, and that your accusers were liars."

"Yes, he did all that."

"You were truly lucky that day, Constantine. Maybe it's a sign." She clapped her hands. The lyre players restarted their song. Then she stood, walked to an empty couch beside the table, sat, and patted the space to her right, indicating he should recline in the place of honor. She let the purple silk stola she wore ride up her thighs as she made a space for him. Her legs were pale, sleek and long.

She waved away a couple who were sitting together on the other couch by the table and within moments they were almost alone. The rest of her guests around the room began talking to each other in a studied way, hardly glancing at them.

He took his place beside her. Slave girls dressed in the Egyptian style rushed forward to offer him a goblet of wine and delicacies from laden serving trays. Their bare breasts bobbed in front of him as they served him. He made sure not to stare at anyone but her.

Valeria's stola had white pearls glistening down it like spray from a waterfall. It was split at the top, as if it was too small for her, and only covered the upper part of her arms. Dangling between her barely covered breasts a necklace of amber beads gleamed. The urge to take hold of her grew. He knew only too well how she had captured the heart of an emperor and had broken many other hearts and lives.

He leaned forward to breathe in her musky perfume. "You've made this Egyptian style popular, Valeria. I hear the traders have run out of silk from here to Alexandria." He growled under his breath, involuntarily. She was so alluring.

Her eyes flared.

"So, how is our new emperor?" he said.

"Oh, Galerius, he'll be along soon. These parties bore him." She waved her arm dismissively as if to banish everyone else in the palace "Now, my sweet Constantine, let us talk about more interesting things. I've been told you still refuse to get married. I do hope you're not pining for me." She reached over and touched his hand lightly. A warm sensation travelled like honey up his arm. He moved closer to her.

"You know I've never been content with imitations. True beauty comes but once in a thousand years." He let her see him gazing along her legs to her golden sandals.

She looked at him with a mock solemn expression, then threw her head back and laughed. She reached for her wine goblet, but a young expressionless slave boy lying on the floor nearby, who Constantine had hardly noticed, passed it straight into her hand.

"You've heard about the rebellion in Britannia, haven't you?" She paused to look at him. "Where is that anyway, somewhere beyond Gaul?"

Constantine nodded.

"I can never tell one restless province from another in your father's domains in the west. They say a magistrate has been murdered."

Things were moving faster than he'd expected.

"And good timing to present your request again, so my husband says. But, more importantly," her voice softened to a whisper, "did you get my message?"

Constantine nodded. "I'm grateful, empress. I..." He lowered his voice. "You see, I had a dream. I was riding out with my father to teach the Caledonian barbarians a lesson in Roman justice. I've been told by a soothsayer that it's a prophecy."

"I do hope your dream comes true." She touched his arm.

He put his hand up, gripped hers held it, his desire growing.

Her voice trembled as she spoke. Her eyes were fixed on his. "I hope you've made preparations."

He nodded.

She looked round, as if she'd sensed something. A faint bell tinkled briefly. She pulled her hand away. He glanced around as Emperor Galerius strode through the main doorway with an expectant look on his face. Behind him a cloud of officials and eunuchs swarmed. Constantine stood, knelt by the couch and bowed his head low. All around the room he could see people bowing or kneeling.

"Up, everyone up, up. There's no formality in the empress' rooms." Galerius came closer. "I hope you're not bothering our beloved on her birthday, Constantine." He sounded out of breath.

Constantine bowed, but not as much as he should have. Some slave had told Galerius where he was.

Before he had a chance to say anything, Galerius continued. "Well, my sweet, will I get rid of him for good this time?"

She nodded, almost imperceptibly.

"Come then. We will settle our business." Galerius raised his hand.

The crowd bowed as the emperor strode out of the hall. Constantine took one last breath of the sweet, alluring air around the empress and bowed low to her. He sighed. She shook her head wistfully. He saw Lucius looking perplexed nearby. He motioned for him to come too and without a single glance back, they hurried after Galerius.

The band of guards and officials that scurried after the emperor grew as they progressed down the marble-floored corridor.

They turned a corner, passed along a pillared hallway whose walls were covered in depictions of gladiatorial skill, and went up a wide marble staircase into what Constantine knew was the most beautiful room in the whole palace. The emperor's private reception hall had been built on the highest point of a spine-like ridge, just before it fell away in a sheer cliff directly above a rocky shoreline.

The room was two stories high at least. Recessed alcoves around the sides held statues of many of the divine emperors. Gold-edged mosaics gleamed on the floor and in spectacular fashion one corner of the hall was cut through by arches. Through them he could see ominous rain clouds sweeping over the bay of Nicomedia, as if they were pouring from some giant's cauldron. Single-masted fishing boats and galleys plied through lines of foam-flecked waves like toys sailing across a rippling pond. The view from this room always made him feel like a god.

In the center of the room two steps led down to a circular sunken dais inlaid with a mosaic tabula map. The map showed the names of the cities and main forts along the largest highways of the empire, radiating in elbowed spokes from Treveris on the left, Rome in the center and Nicomedia on the right. Beside the map, stiff and aloof, stood a group of four officials, pristine in their white togas and pale faces.

The emperor paced to the far side of the sunken dais. He motioned for Constantine to join him. When he was by his side, the emperor of the east, Gaius Galerius Augustus, gripped Constantine's arm, digging his nails into the skin.

"You do like to play games, don't you, Constantine. Well, your games are all over now. Our spies have reported large movements against the empire from the Danube all the way to Britannia. It has happened before, but this time things are different. Everywhere invasion looms. I am told the attacks are coordinated. For Rome to survive we must fight back. We must fight back together."

Constantine hated being lectured. He struggled to keep his expression attentive. The officials standing nearby were nodding in agreement.

"Our successes, pushing back the Persians, crushing revolts in Egypt, will all be in vain, unless we act as one." He paused. His voice rose as he continued. "With the empire's divisions behind us, we can forge a new golden age with belief in the traditional gods, Rome's gods, binding us, so we can win a great victory. If not. . ." He raised his hands in the air.

"We will lose everything." His hand gripped tighter on Constantine's arm. "But before the victory, your father must root out all treachery in his provinces in the west. He must follow our edicts, or who knows what will happen." Galerius shrugged his shoulders, as if indifferent to the fate that Constantine's father was bringing down on himself.

"Your father has requested that you be sent to join him for a campaign to deal with Caledonia." He looked Constantine in the eye. "But do you still wish to go back to his rain-sodden provinces? You could always live fruitfully here." He smiled amiably.

Constantine shook his head.

"Then we must give your father what he desires and keep our long-standing promise to you as well. But first." He released Constantine's arm, then patted it, as one might a wayward client's. "You will swear to a few small conditions."

Constantine kept his face as expressionless as he could. "Emperor, you can always be assured of my loyalty, and my family's loyalty."

Galerius looked amused. Such a promise was the very least he expected.

"Yes, yes, but you must also promise to help rid all our lands of any threat to the peace of the empire. And you will swear to never make war against me, or against those I command, and finally, but most importantly, you will make no claim to be your father's successor, unless I agree in advance. Swear these conditions in front of these witnesses and you will be free to go to your father."

Constantine felt the weight of the moment stiffen the air around them. But now, at last, as the moment of his freedom came near, he felt no joy. All his years in the east had passed so quickly. There was much he would miss. Galerius' conditions didn't bother him. They were no worse than he'd expected. And between Galerius' words there were enough openings for many things to pass. The prize he'd waited so long for, his freedom, was within his grasp, and it was ironic that after all this time the key to it lay in words alone. He felt numb. Was it going to be this easy? He raised his hand.

"I swear to never rise up against you, to make no claim to be my father's successor unless you agree, and to act as you wish to defeat our enemies." His voice was calm, loud.

"And to never raise a hand against any men I command," added Galerius.

"Yes, that too I swear."

"Good, good. You are free to go to your father. Make haste if you wish, we'll not detain you any longer." He turned to an official standing nearby and gave him a thumbs up. The man handed Constantine a palm-sized bronze sheet with the emperor's insignia impressed upon it.

"Your discharge pass will allow you passage through to your father's provinces, my lord." The official spoke in a low monotone.

Such a small thing to hold such power, Constantine thought, staring at it. He took the pass and put it in the pouch attached to his belt. He knew what he had to do next.

He knelt and kissed the edge of the emperor's toga. Galerius laid a hand on his shoulder. Constantine rose, kissed him on both cheeks.

"I will keep my word," he said, as he drew away.

Galerius had the look of a viper contemplating lunch. Constantine bowed and retreated. He could go. He felt a surge of relief at last, then an urge to run from the room. His day approached. He could sense it, like people sense the sea from far inland.

Lucius congratulated him and pummeled his back when they were finally alone. Constantine hardly heard him. Everything had changed. A shroud restricting his vision had been shaken off. He gripped Lucius' arms.

"Finding that Persian girl we rescued all those years ago was a good omen, Lucius. You were right. She will be our living testimony to what happened in the Persian war. When we present her to my father he will know we are speaking the truth."

He'd dreamed often about his arrival in Gaul. How his father would lead an entourage out to greet him and appoint him commander of his Legions in the west. And if that was too much to expect, perhaps commander of just one Legion. How could his father refuse him?

"I have a favor to ask," said Lucius, looking sheepish.

"Not another miracle-making soothsayer who wants a letter of introduction to my father, I hope," said Constantine.

Lucius shook his head.

"What then?"

"Please, come to my father's estate. He wants to talk to you before you head for Gaul. I know you want to leave here quickly. But my father can help you." Lucius' words tumbled out as if practiced. "He has a fast ship ready to sail for Rome. You could use her. "

Constantine hummed. Passage aboard a fast ship was exactly what he needed. With the favorable winds at this time of year, he could be in Rome in days, not weeks, and then sail on to his father's provinces.

"Of course, I'll come, Lucius. You'd think I wanted to steal your favorite mistress, by that worried look on your face. Shall we go now?"

117

"My father said to come as soon as we have news. The slaves will come with us. I wouldn't leave them in that nest of agents at your villa or mine. Galerius' agents are capable of seducing anyone. We can be at the estate by nightfall."

Constantine had wondered why the slaves had been brought along to the palace. That explained that. But what would Lucius' father want in return for all this help?

"You'll have to lose your guards along the road. My father hates imperial agents snooping around his estate. You'll be perfectly safe with us. You know that." Lucius grinned.

Constantine shrugged. "This new lot are certainly brick faced enough to be Galerius' agents all right." He punched Lucius' arm. "Come on then, let's get away from here."

They passed down the corridor, guards bowing away from them, and ended up at the open door of the room where Juliana and Tiny were supposed to be waiting.

"Where are our slaves?" said Constantine, when he saw they weren't there. He turned to the guards who were stationed by the door to the empress' rooms.

"I've no idea, my lord," the head guard said, a look of injured innocence on his face.

"You must have seen them. You are responsible." Constantine pointed at the man. "Personally responsible."

He considered the possibilities. The guard must have seen something. He went over and jabbed his finger in the man's face. They stood facing each other. Constantine shook his head slowly, as if regretting what was bound to happen next. The man looked up and down the corridor, licked his lips, then spoke.

"Some slaves were called to the stables earlier, my lord."

Constantine strode away. He knew where the stables where. "This place gets worse every time I come here," he muttered.

When they reached the stables, to his relief Juliana and Tiny were standing near the main doors. They turned towards Constantine and bowed as soon as they saw him.

"Where have you two been?" he said.

Juliana and Tiny looked at one another like children who'd been caught stealing.

Juliana spoke. "We were told to wait for you here."

"Don't move from where you're supposed to be in future, do you understand?" interrupted Lucius loudly.

Constantine's guards brought out the horses quickly, and when they were ready they filed out through a side gate onto a quiet, muddy laneway.

Before long they'd left the palace walls well behind. Gray clouds filled the sky and a cold wind blew in his face. A shiver ran through him. He urged his horse forward.

He'd been refused leave to go to his father so many times for so many reasons he'd sometimes felt convinced he'd never be released. That he should expect nothing but tricks. The wind whispered across his cheeks as he rode. *Soon,* it said. *Soon you'll be away. Soon you will show them what you can do when you're not shackled.*

XXI

Nicomedia, 306 A.D.

Seeing Constantine calmed Juliana, but she still wanted to be as far away from the palace as possible. Someone wanted to cause problems for them. But why?

"What do they want with us?" she whispered, more to herself than Tiny, as they rode side by side in the middle of their small column of riders.

"For us to do what we're told," replied Tiny in a matter of fact manner.

The guards had taken them down into the catacombs below the palace building. Built into the solid rock, the low roofed rooms echoed with their footsteps and distant disembodied voices. She'd felt real fear at that moment.

They'd passed patches of slimy moss on the walls and a guardroom overflowing with grunting and laughing guards, then went down more steps. It grew ever darker with each turn of the steps as the stinking oil lamps became less frequent. She'd wondered then if Constantine and Lucius had also been arrested and the clutch of an awful dread had kept her mouth tight shut as they were hustled down an arched corridor.

And then a skin-crawling wailing had surrounded them. And as abruptly it stopped. The silence, heavier now, oppressive with expectation, was broken only by the shuffling of feet.

They'd halted in front of an iron-studded door, slightly ajar. The lead guardsman banged brusquely. A gruff voice answered. The door creaked open. Juliana's mouth dried. A large vaulted room full of strange and fearsome apparatus waited for them.

A grotesquely bloated man in a stained leather tunic stood with his hands on his hips just beyond the doorway. A piercing cry echoed. Juliana looked round the room. Her knees became weak. All the implements she'd heard of were there: racks with chains, masks with spikes facing inwards, seats with spear like protrusions. A large wheel hung from a wall.

She'd been told by other slaves all about the persecutions of Christians carried out in the name of the emperor, and she knew that she should forget every prayer her mother had taught her, in case someone overheard her.

Could they have guessed? Was that why she'd been brought here?

And then she saw the source of the wailing. A thin pitiable girl, perhaps fifteen summers old, struggled in the clutch of a leather-aproned dwarf who reached only to the girl's shoulder, but whose arms and chest were massive, as big as Tiny's at least.

The dwarf held one of the girl's hands towards the embers of a glowing brazier. He grinned delightedly at his new audience and jabbed the girl's hand towards the heat again and again. Her screams cut through Juliana like a blade.

"This is what happens to slaves who disobey Galerius' orders," said the lead guardsman. He glared at Juliana, then dragged her forward into the room by the arm. Another guard pushed Tiny in after them.

She wanted to look away, but she couldn't. The girl had seen them. She cried piteously at them, as if they might save her. A sliver of smoke rose in the air as the girl's hand touched the embers again, and her cry became a howl, a wail that went on long after her blackened hand had been pulled away from the fire.

"Do not ever tell what you have seen here. If you do, or if you ever refuse a request by Galerius, this is but a taste of what will happen to you." The guardsman's voice sounded like a snake slithering.

Then they were hustled away to the sounds of cloth tearing and further gulping and wailing.

"Remember this lesson," the lead guardsman said when they were pushed unceremoniously against the wall of the stables. "When you're asked to do something in the name of our beloved Emperor Galerius, no matter where you are, no matter what it is, do it. That's not too difficult, is it?"

They'd both nodded. Juliana's mouth was as dry as dust and only her determination kept her upright. She'd seen slaves being punished, but the cruelty she'd just witnessed was more than that, it was evil in a way she'd feared ever seeing again, but it made her want to be strong, not weak.

Constantine and Lucius had appeared soon after. Well, it seemed soon after to Juliana. She was in such a daze she couldn't really tell.

So, when finally they left the palace behind, she looked over her shoulder and wished herself even further away from that awful place, and as quickly as possible. She wondered too, what had happened to that girl, what she'd done to be taken down there.

"That's not my idea of a palace." Tiny leaned towards her. "I didn't get to see any dancing girls." The color had returned to his cheeks. He looked at Juliana for a reaction.

"This is all as strange as a belly full of snakes, you know that don't you? And look at this one." He gestured towards Constantine. "He rides as if all the Harpies are on our trail."

They rode on, away from the city, along a wide graveled road. She read the milestones marked with the distance to Chalcedon, and back to Nicomedia, and wondered where they were headed. Later, her main preoccupation became finding a comfortable way to sit, to prevent the iron hard saddle from rubbing too often again and again at the same place on her inner thighs. She'd only ridden around the estate before when one of the field hands had wanted a horse exercised or as a favor. This nonstop riding had her praying they'd stop after every milestone.

They passed two cohorts of legionaries marching at a steady tramp, heading towards Nicomedia. Some of the officers recognized Constantine. They hailed him as they passed.

Juliana and Tiny's smaller horses found it difficult to keep up the pace set by Constantine, especially Tiny's. His horse's head started drooping. To her relief, they stopped to rest soon after at a small single-tavern village by a shallow rocky stream that ran for a while alongside the roadway. The surrounding forests had been pushed back here, and fields had been marked out with lines of stones as if someday walls would be built.

The tavern keeper served fresh, very thin bread and boiled chicken. Even Juliana and Tiny ate well. They sat at the side of the building under a wooden trellis more suitable for summer. When they finished eating, an argument developed inside between Constantine and the centurion leading the guards who'd accompanied them.

"It's for your protection, my lord. Robbers, blood worshippers, they all work these forests. You must keep us with you." The man's tone was loud, bullying. He expected compliance. Juliana looked at Tiny. He grinned in reply.

"Are you refusing a direct order?" Constantine's voice was raised.

Juliana couldn't understand the centurion's reply, but he stormed out of the tavern soon afterwards, and roared at his men who were sitting not far from Juliana and Tiny. They all rode away without looking back.

"There goes your protection," said Tiny. "I expect we're on our way to some debauched festival. I can only guess what your role will be. You might want to be friendly to me now." He reached over and ruffled Juliana's hair. She slapped at his arm.

"I'd rather die."

He shrugged his arm, as if he'd barely felt her slap, then shook his head slowly.

"My, you are aroused easily." He winked at her.

Juliana ignored him. She'd ignored similar suggestions too many times before to count.

When they were ready to leave the tavern, she was given Tiny's horse to ride. It immediately picked up its head and whinnied when it realized its new charge was much lighter than its previous burden.

Not long after, the road ran uphill into thick, damp-looking pine forest. The tall ivy-draped trees reeked of resin and decay. Tiny gave Juliana one of his wide-eyed looks.

"I've heard these forests are overrun with bears."

Juliana stuck her tongue out at him. "And I heard all the bears in Bithynia were killed long ago."

He grinned wide, showing her his rotten teeth. "Well, don't worry, when they're all finished with you, I'll soothe your wounds." He fingered his mouth as if wiping away drool. Then he looked to see if Constantine or Lucius, talking to each other up ahead, had heard him. They hadn't. They rarely turned around to check on them.

The dark branches were close to the road now. They seemed to be reaching towards her. The high canopy of trees enveloped the roadway in deep gloom. The four riders fell silent.

She imagined her father as one of those guards back at the palace. The sick smell of burning flesh came back to her. No, if she ever found him he'd be strong and honorable. But how could she ever find him? He was probably back in Britannia. And even if she bought her freedom after many years as a good slave, all she had to search for him was a name she'd overheard once, Arell.

And she wasn't even sure if she'd remembered that right. She had to stop her foolish daydreams. Even if they were all she had.

They rode on into the afternoon, stopping twice to water the horses at streams near the road. The trees became sparse in places, but most of the time they were surrounded by forest. After hours of this, she couldn't tell how many, they turned off the main roadway and headed down a small, rutted side track. The sun dropped quickly towards the horizon.

In the distance a hunting horn echoed, disturbing the chirping of courting wood pigeons from the trees around them.

Tiny reached over and touched her arm. "Look," he whispered, "we're being watched." He pointed at a tree.

For a moment Juliana thought someone lay hiding there, waiting to ambush them. She imagined the dwarf from the emperor's torture chamber appearing, grinning, ready for a new victim. Then she saw red squirrels standing perfectly still around its base. In a moment, they scampered away, startled.

"Pan lives in these woods, and he still wields all his powers." Tiny kicked his horse and left Juliana behind as they rode deeper into the forest.

She didn't care now. She was not going to cling to him, which was probably what he wanted. What she'd seen that morning, the girl being tortured, had left her images in her head that didn't want to go away. The awful stench returned to her at odd moments too. And now they were far from the palace, anger had emerged. She prayed hard that if her turn came, she would have the courage to fight back.

The setting sun cast long shadows as they made their way up a steep wooded hill. It grew chilly. She pulled her cloak tight to keep the cutting wind out. They rounded a bend into a level area and were confronted by a stout wooden gate barring the track. A wooden palisade, twice the height of a man, ran away on each side into the trees. On one side the ground fell away steeply. On the other it rose.

Guards called out a welcome to Lucius as they rode through the hastily opened gate. Beyond it the path dipped. A valley appeared through the trees. At its apex sat a large villa with walls made of giant rocks, surrounded by wooden outbuildings and orchards of thickly leafed olive trees stretching away into the distance.

They came out of the woods on the floor of the valley and rode towards the villa. There were people sitting, wrapped in cloaks, at a row of wooden tables that went around the side of the villa. Cooking fires burned nearby. The smell of home came to her on the wind, then fled. It was a smell of goat stew and onions and flat bread, freshly baked.

Children played chasing games near the house. They stopped and stared, shading their eyes as Lucius led the way forward from the tree line. When they were near, some of the children rushed forward to slap the sides of Lucius' horse.

"This place belongs to his kin, I'd wager," whispered Tiny.

She nodded. But why was there so many eating outside in the cold? The only time she'd seen crowds on her old estate was for a bumper harvest, or once when a watercourse needed to be dug quickly in a drought.

Dark-haired slaves led their horses through a gateway into the crudely paved area in front of the villa. She dismounted. Her muscles ached all up her legs and her back. Constantine and Lucius were greeted with bows, but the slaves didn't seem to know who Constantine was. He'd put his purple cloak into the bag attached behind his saddle the first time they'd stopped to rest, and now he wore a ragged brown one. He looked like a legionary officer on leave or retired early for some awful injury.

"Welcome to the estate of Marcus Aurelius Armenius," a slave said to Constantine. "Your father's expecting you, Lucius," he said, turning to Lucius.

They were escorted through an open doorway into a torch-lit corridor at the end of which a closed, studded door barred their path. Tiny and Juliana kept respectfully to the rear. Tiny beamed at Juliana, perhaps delighted with the aroma of hot food that filled the corridor. A slave running ahead opened the door in front of them and welcoming light spilled out. The room they entered had a high ceiling, crimson stucco walls and a long table at the far end. The people at the table were sitting on low-backed chairs, the way servants and commoners did. All faces turned in their direction as they entered.

It looked like an odd dinner group to Juliana. Four elderly Roman men, with close-cropped hair and traditional whitened togas sat at one end, two shaven-headed men in the roughest dark-blue tunics sat in the middle, and a curly haired bear of a man in multicolored garb dominated the far end. At that man's side sat two brown-skinned Nubians who wore long hooded robes made from some thickly woven textile that reminded her of plaited hair.

It seemed they'd interrupted something. Lucius walked up to the bear-like man and hugged him. Tiny and Juliana hung back by the doorway.

"Father. It's good to see you." Lucius pulled away and gestured for Constantine to come forward. "I present the honorable Constantine, son of the emperor of the wast. He has come. I told you he would, Father."

The group at the table bowed towards Constantine.

"You are welcome, Constantine, son of an emperor, most welcome. And call me Marcus. Come, you will come join us, we were about to eat." He looked briefly past Constantine then gestured to a nearby slave, who ran to Juliana and Tiny and motioned angrily for them to follow him.

She could hear the others at the table greeting Constantine as they walked out. All she wanted was to rest, or at least to sit. Trays of food passed them on their way. She saw a particularly pretty female slave. No, she wasn't that pretty. Her eyes were too close together. Juliana's mood darkened.

The slave led them to a noisy kitchen where a squad of men and women bustled around, shouting as they prepared more food.

They passed through the kitchen, down a short corridor and out onto a cold balcony with early budding jasmine tendrils intertwined through a rickety sun-whitened railing. A blackened wooden table surrounded by benches faced out over an orchard of beaten looking cherry trees. In the distance, a mirror calm sea shone like ebony. A bright moon hung like a disc in the sky. She could hear children shrieking, playing games among the trees.

"Food will be brought. Please, rest." The slave pulled a bench out for them and left them alone.

"If they feed us I'll not complain." Tiny sat down heavily.

Juliana pulled the other bench a little towards the railing.

"All I want is to sleep," she said. She had seen too much that day. Tiny nodded.

As soon as they'd eaten the small fried white fish and bread served to them, and it appeared as if Tiny had settled down to consume the flagon of wine which came with the food, Juliana slipped away to find out where they would sleep. She hated sitting with Tiny and had an urge to get away from him. He was always watching her. Always making stupid jokes.

When she returned, Tiny's gaze rolled around as if he'd drunk too much. Two wine flagons stood on the table. She approached to remove the plates and take them to the kitchen. As she bent down Tiny reached out a hand and held her arm, lightly at first but then tighter as she tried to pull away.

LP O'Bryan

"Come here, girl. It's long past time we got to know each other." He pulled her sharply towards him. Then he stood, twisted her arm quickly and painfully and pushed it up behind her back, knocking her off balance as he did so.

He wrapped his other arm around her and clamped his hand to her mouth. Then he rubbed his body hard up against her. She groaned in defiance. A rush of anger flooded through her. His eyes were shining, wide with animal lust.

How could she stop him? She reached with her free hand towards the goblet on the table.

XXII

Nicomedia, 306 A.D.

In the dining hall, the household's best green glass goblets from Carthage were being raised. "Pax Romana," was the toast.

The goblets sparkled in the torchlight, as the serving slaves stood around the table with delicacies piled on the silver platters they carried skillfully on one hand. Other slaves rushed in to top up the goblets as soon as they were lowered. Constantine didn't speak much. He spent much of the meal going over again and again in his mind what Galerius had said and thinking about all the worst and best things about the eastern provinces that he would soon be leaving behind.

Towards the end of the meal, as the attention of the diners became distracted by a troop of lyre and flute players, he got a chance to observe the men around him. He was sure he'd seen some of them at Diocletian's court, before Galerius had become emperor, and wondered what had brought them all together again.

Then Marcus struggled to his feet. As he did so, he tapped Constantine's shoulder and bent his finger at him. He wanted to show him something. They stood. Lucius followed towards a door at the back of the hall. Beyond, a large terrace overlooked trees in deep shadow below a bright and low moon.

A pale green marble table took up much of the terrace. It was surrounded on three sides by blanket-covered couches. Trails of smoke drifted away from oil lamps set into the wall. Their light was dim and golden.

Marcus urged Constantine to sit in the place of honor beside him. Then he ordered a warming brazier and cloaks to protect them from the cold night air, as well as wine and fruit.

When they were comfortable, and the wine had been served, Marcus turned to Constantine.

"I truly wish you the best for your journey home." He raised his glass. They all touched glasses. "Do you know what position you will be given when you reach Gaul?"

"No, I don't," said Constantine. "But I'm sure my father will find me something to do. Getting there, before Galerius changes his mind, is what concerns me. Lucius told me you have a ship."

"Indeed, I do, my friend, though it is only a small vessel. It waits in the harbor at Nicomedia, ready for my signal to sail for Rome. You are welcome to sail with her." He paused. "I will be very happy to help you."

There will be a price for this.

"Come, let us be open with each other, Constantine." Marcus' smile was that of a skilled merchant, a man used to forging alliances and doing deals.

"I have a proposal for you. I dearly want Lucius to take a message to your father. This is where I need your assistance." He gestured with both hands, palms up, in front of him.

"Will you encourage your father to give the matter his attention? If you feel you cannot, do not worry, my ship will take you to Rome anyway. I cannot ask you to do something you're not happy with."

Constantine sipped from his wine. It was good. It had the soft taste of sun and flowers.

The old man continued. "I've been told your father had some difficulties raising taxes last year. This is a pity. But all good emperors seem to have these problems. Too many mouths to feed. It's an old story. And the payments to the legions when a man becomes emperor these days are shocking. But you know all this. I would like to help him a little, if he'll let me. Perhaps I can show you how."

Constantine nodded. He was well used to men, and women, trying to use him to get to his father.

Marcus clapped his hands. He whispered something to the slave who came forward. The man went away and returned soon after with four burly guards who staggered onto the terrace under the weight of an iron-studded wooden chest.

They had the look of retired legionaries. Marcus took a wooden key from around his neck and handed it to one of the guards. When the chest had been opened, Marcus stood up.

Constantine leaned forward. The chest brimmed to the lid with tan leather bags. Marcus took one out. He emptied a mound of gold solidii coins onto the marble table. One coin rolled off. Lucius picked it up and returned it to the mound.

"Each of these bags has two pounds of gold. This bag has some of the first solidii Diocletian minted. Others contain older coins. There are a hundred bags in here." Marcus gestured at the chest.

"We have five such chests, if my guards haven't lost any." He looked up at the guard with the key. The man shook his head sternly.

Constantine could smell a leathery aroma from the bags. A familiar smell. He'd been invited once by Diocletian to view the treasury, row upon row of similar chests in a secret room deep below the palace. Diocletian had informed him curtly that emperors rose and fell, lived and died, depending on the availability of such chests when they were needed.

"What is this message that Lucius will carry?"

Lucius answered him. "I will offer all this to your father. It is practical support for his reign, in exchange for a few small favors. Nothing unreasonable. I have sworn only to negotiate with your father. But better than all that my friend, I will come with you. I will see the western provinces I keep hearing about. And all I need is for you to get me an audience and perhaps . . . "His voice trailed off. "Perhaps your father might look even more favorably on us Christians."

Constantine picked a coin up and looked at it. It had Diocletian's head on it. It had probably been extracted in taxes by Marcus from Roman traders passing along the caravan trail through his lands in lower Armenia. He'd heard that recently over one third of the product of the empire's gold mines went each year to purchase spices and silks from far off lands, accessible most reliably via caravan trails through Armenia. The tax extracted by the protectors of those trade routes, many of them followers of the one god, was probably one of the most reliable sources of income in the eastern empire.

"I heard you Christians believe we will all be judged at the end of the world, emperors and all the rest judged in the same way."

"It is true," said Lucius.

"I can understand why Galerius hasn't taken to you. His lust for blood started early and never left him," said Constantine.

"If you agree to the plan," said Marcus. "I will send riders along the post road tonight towards Rome. They will use your name at every change of horses. And then they will disappear. Galerius will not be able to stop you if he changes his mind. He will be looking in the wrong direction."

"I like that," said Constantine.

A scream shattered the silence. Constantine looked around. Were they being attacked? He stood and looked over the balcony. The scream died.

"Wait," said Marcus, anger on his face. "My guards will tell us what's happening in a moment."

No one spoke. Constantine sat back down. Then a boy came running onto the balcony.

"My lord, one of Lucius' slaves had an accident."

"Take me there," said Lucius. He stood, moved away from the table. Constantine and Marcus followed.

When they arrived at the kitchen balcony they found Tiny cradling his hand. His face glowed pale in the moonlight. One of the household slaves, a young boy, was tying a wet cloth around Tiny's hand.

"What happened to you?" Lucius roared.

Constantine looked at Juliana. She was by the door to the kitchen, holding herself stiffly, her arms crossed.

"He hurt his hand, my lord," she said. There were shards of broken glass on top of and underneath the table.

"Is that your story?" Lucius stood over Tiny. The slave boy who'd been binding him cringed back. Tiny looked up with a pleading expression.

"Yes, master. I had an accident. I beg forgiveness. I didn't mean to scream." Lucius slapped him across the head. Tiny groaned, put his head down.

"The cost of that glass will be added to the price of your freedom." He looked at Juliana. "Nothing else occurred here? Tell me if it did. It will only be worse for you if I discover something later."

Tiny cringed.

"It's a small matter between slaves, nothing important at all," said Juliana, calmly.

Constantine put a hand on Lucius' arm.

"Come, leave them. You'll need plenty of sleep if you're coming with me."

As they left the balcony, Constantine glanced over his shoulder and caught Tiny glaring hatred towards Juliana. He would have to keep his eye on them both. There was nothing worse than traveling with bickering slaves. Lucius would have to punish them if it continued.

The following morning a biting wind had sprung up. Constantine paced his room alone before the villa woke. He'd planned endlessly in anticipation of this freedom. He'd imagined he'd be ecstatic after it came, but now it had, he wasn't. Old anxieties had reappeared, and some new ones had arrived, conjured from who knew where. What was happening in his father's provinces? How would he treat him when he got there? How would his stepmother react to his return? He had no way of knowing.

And he had no idea how his father would react to Lucius' offer, but about that he didn't care. There were too many other things to worry about.

Most importantly, was it too late for him to secure his inheritance, his rightful place in the succession? So much had happened. He'd been away so long.

He went out into the colonnaded courtyard that dominated one end of the villa. There was a clear blue sky above. The wind blew towards the sea. Good weather for sailing.

XXIII

Alexandria, 306 A.D.

"Hosius, I should never have doubted you." Helena sat with Hosius, the leader of Alexandria's Christians, in the inner courtyard of her villa in the best part of the city. The view from the upper floors extended over red tiled roofs to the port and on towards the giant lighthouse, which dominated the skyline even in daylight.

Hosius looked pleased. He adjusted his new tunic. A row of pearls stood out at the neckline. She wondered if he'd dare wear it at the meetings he held for his followers, or had he put it on just for meeting her, his patron.

"I am happy you have had confirmation your son is to be released by Galerius. Prayer, under the correct guidance, has always been effective for me, though sometimes, as you can see, it takes time."

"You also sent messengers to your friends at Galerius' court, didn't you?" Helena had a few people who would tell her what was really going on. She had to make it clear to this priest that she was not one of his imbecilic followers, who believed every crazy story he told them.

Hosius raised his hand, waved it dismissively. "If we cannot influence someone like Galerius to reduce the persecutions here, I cannot think any words of our followers in Nicomedia could make him throw anything our way."

"You are too modest. I hear you've prevented a dozen executions in this city for failing to sacrifice at the temples." She picked a date from the bowl in front of her and stripped it with her teeth.

"Again, these things are all done with the power of prayer alone." His eyes were bright now, wide.

Helena nodded. *He believes everything he claims, or he's a very good actor.*

"Do you think these two things are connected, the persecutions and my son being released?"

Hosius came forward in his chair. "I do. I absolutely do. The spirit is moving though us. Your son comes at the right time. The age of daemons is almost upon us and only by the power of prayer can we hope to stop the daemons taking over the whole world."

Helena made a humming noise. She'd heard this daemon stuff before, but it seemed like a rallying cry for the lower classes to her.

"It seems you do not believe that daemons are loose, Domina."

Helena stared at him. He rarely used that word for her, usually he reserved it for when he was most angry with her.

"I need proof. I told you this. I do not believe every scare story I am told."

"And I told you that I will provide proof if you come out of the city with me. I will show you the daemons." His arms were wide, shaking with the force of his words.

She stood. "Yes, I will go with you this time. But there is one more thing you will do for me before we go."

"You know I will do whatever you ask, Domina."

She bent down and spoke in his ear.

XXIV

Nicomedia, 306 A.D.

After Juliana picked up the goblet, she'd smashed it on the edge of the table, turned it in mid-air and rammed the base into Tiny's hand. He'd screamed as he'd assumed she had rammed the broken edge and might lose his hand. But she wasn't that stupid. If she'd slammed the jagged edge into his hand with the same force, she'd have cut his hand deeply. And for that she might lose her own too, for damaging someone else's property.

She'd dropped the broken lower half of the goblet on the floor near him. As she did he'd cursed her and punched her in the side with his other hand.

Juliana had winced but had learned long ago to disregard pain. She dodged backwards from his next blow, aimed at her head. Maybe she should have used the jagged edge after all. But he'd stopped as the household slaves had appeared. For a moment she was sure he'd kill her for striking him. But he calmed down quickly when the others appeared. He clearly wasn't as fearless as he seemed.

She had barely enough time to hiss a warning before Lucius and Constantine appeared on the balcony.

"Say nothing, or it'll be worse for you. They'll cut your little thing off and make you eat it."

He'd looked dumbfoundedly at her. Juliana thought he might reveal what had happened, out of spite, but he wasn't that stupid. Some of the household slaves looked unconvinced at his story. They kept shaking their heads and looking at Juliana. But after Lucius had accepted the explanation, that was the end of the matter.

Juliana was allocated a sleeping cell. Before she went to it, she told Tiny that if he approached her in the night she'd scream the whole house awake. She still slept only lightly though, opening her eyes at the slightest sound. At the coldest hour, when only spirits are about, she heard a banging, a loose shutter probably, and sat bolt upright in alarm. It took her a long time to get back to sleep. When she did she saw Tiny in a dream. He was younger, his face covered in blood and out of his mouth came an odd high-pitched scream.

When morning came, it felt as if she'd woken from a nightmare, only to find it had all been real. The good news was, Tiny knew she could defend herself. The next question was, should she tell Tiny what she had seen in her dream?

No, she would not. There could be a better moment to use what she'd seen about his past. Her birth mother had warned her about how the sight could be used as a reason to kill any women who knew what dreams meant.

She went to find the wash room before the rest of the household woke. Tiny was waiting in the kitchen in the dim, early morning light. Juliana stopped, about to back away, but he held his hand up. It had a purple bruise on its back. He moved it, to show it still worked, wincing as he did.

Then he stared at her, nodded. He knew she could have disfigured him for life. As Juliana wondered if he would seek revenge, he apologized instead in a long stumbling sentence. He blamed it all on the wine, and his unquenched needs.

Tiny even managed to look sheepish. She nodded, shrugged her shoulders in acceptance. Better to have him sheepish than wolf like. She asked about his hand. He shook his head as if he'd suffered no injury.

They ate breakfast in silence. An older woman served them a thin gruel with leftover bread and cheese from the night before. Another slave told them Constantine and Lucius were up and planning to leave soon. They hurried the rest of their meal and headed to the stables, where they found Lucius, pacing.

"Come on, you two, a ship awaits us. I don't suppose either of you've ever been to Gaul, or Rome, have you?" he asked, in a matter

137

of fact way that left Juliana wide-eyed. He was making a joke, surely. She shook her head.

"Look at you two, like a pair of virgins before your wedding night. Most slaves would become eunuchs for a chance to see the world." He pointed at Tiny.

"Don't panic, Tiny, I won't do that to you, yet. But if you give us any more problems, either of you, you'll both be sold as soon as we can find a slave market, that is if Constantine doesn't decide to use parts of you as fish bait on the way. Is your hand working, Tiny?"

Tiny grunted, held it up and made a fist.

Juliana could see he was suppressing some pain from it, but she said nothing.

"No more screaming if someone taps you. Now get yourselves ready, we'll be away soon." Lucius left them.

"I never thought I'd see Rome." Juliana said the words softly. She stared at Lucius' back. Few slaves she'd ever known had been beyond Nicomedia or the village they'd come from. Rome loomed, an unimagined possibility.

She could think of almost nothing else all that day as they made their way back along the road to Nicomedia. Rumors she'd heard had given her the idea Rome had been built in the clouds, and that many of its buildings were made of gold. It seemed unreal to be going there. And she knew almost nothing about Gaul except that it was near Britannia, and that thought excited her.

"I heard all about Rome," Tiny whispered, as they rode behind Constantine and Lucius. "From an old soldier who'd been there. He said it's a city of blood-painted temples and all the girls have to dance naked in the streets every week. Will we see you doing that?"

Juliana pretended not to hear him. The riding was clearly making his cock rise again. Maybe it would be better if Lucius had it cut off.

But could he be right? Then she remembered other stories.

"Is Britannia far from Gaul?"

"No," he replied.

A rush of anticipation rose through her. "My father is from Britannia."

Almost as soon as the words were out of her mouth, she regretted them. She'd been ridiculed about her parentage before. She should not have spoken about it. But her excitement had forced it out of her.

"Well, I hope we never go there," Tiny said. "It's full of blue-smeared barbarians who burn foreigners alive. Did your father tell you about the sea serpents there?" He looked at Juliana inquisitively.

She shook her head.

He reached toward her as if he trying to pull her from her horse. She leaned away from him, stuck out her tongue. After that she refused to speak to him again until they arrived in Nicomedia.

Constantine disappeared down a side road when they came near to the city. She overheard him promising to meet up with them at the port. She'd been hoping they would all travel together.

They went to Lucius' villa, where Juliana and Tiny were put to work helping pack for the journey.

"Eat quickly, the master is waiting at the dock," said the old slave the following morning.

"You're the luckiest pair of slaves ever passed through this house." His fists were balled when he spoke, as if he might strike one or both of them. "Taken to Rome, by the gods!" He pointed a bony finger at them. "I just pray you've both made enough offerings to Neptune in your lives. His sea monsters like to drag slaves from the decks of ships. They rip the bones clean of flesh and fling the sucked-out skulls onto the shore."

When they arrived at the quayside, Juliana was disappointed to see how small Lucius' father's ship was. She'd imagined something much bigger. It did have a high prow but only one mast. A dirty canvas awning covered the open deck and a wooden hut-like structure sat at the back. A single line of oar holes ran almost the length of the ship on each side. Tiny laughed when he saw her expression.

"The Middle Sea will swallow us like an elephant swallows flies," he said. Then he leaned closer. She could smell his rancid breath.

"They say if you meet a merman," he whispered, "you should tell him Alexander lives and reigns, otherwise he'll drag you to his hall in the deep." He blew her a kiss.

She looked away. He would not frighten her that easily.

The sea appeared calm, with only a slight swell, when they rowed out from the port, the crew straining at their oars, their grotesque-looking arm muscles swelling from the strain. Soon after, Juliana noticed the color of the water deepened to an inky black, and the swell became even more choppy. She sniffed. The air had a salty, invigorating tang and an odor of fish rose from the sun-dried boards of the deck. The babble of shouts that had surrounded them as they left the port had died away and only a steady drumbeat and the hiss of the oars broke the silence around them.

She felt exhilarated. An unexpected sense of freedom had risen inside her as the city grew smaller behind them. Nicomedia, the slave market, the stupid, ugly overseer, they were all in the past. Her life had been bound by endless repetitive tasks and by fear and beatings. Now everything would be different.

Out to sea low clouds loomed over spray-flecked swells. A pair of dolphins came alongside, jumping high into the air, again and again. Juliana watched them and couldn't help smiling. They were so totally free. It felt good to even be near them.

"Thank the gods, we have good luck with us for our journey," a crewman shouted, as the sail went up and the oars put away. The dolphins turned back to shore as the swell deepened.

Then she felt her stomach turn.

A brisk wind, the Euxine wind, one of the crew said, pushed them rapidly away from the land. And suddenly her head felt heavy and her brow hot, as if she'd been spinning wool all day.

All around them water heaved.

Tiny laughed as she emptied her stomach over the side. The city of Nicomedia had disappeared beyond the swells. Water surrounded them now, and a firm wind stretched their sail, flapping its edges. The ship creaked too, as if it was lumbering, trying to pick up speed. She vomited again. Then again. Every morsel from her breakfast went down into the deep. Then there was nothing left to come up. But she retched some more anyway.

The captain's mate, a Syrian with a weather-scorched face and a sly look, had come to watch her at the ship's edge. He held her ankle as she leaned overboard, and Juliana was grateful when he told her to rest in a stowage area at the rear of the wooden cabin, and that she could sleep there for the rest of the journey.

"Don't come out 'till you're right. The Captain don't want women groaning all over our deck. It'll bring us bad luck." His tone had become sympathetic, even if his words weren't. She held her stomach and tried to stop groaning.

The stowage area was crammed with ropes and spare canvas. It felt warm and safe out of the wind. The Syrian brought her two rough blankets. He patted her arm. He was a little too friendly. Juliana brushed his hand away. Then he was gone. She pushed some curls of rope against the small wooden door and after she'd moved things round, she found she had a comfortable place to hug herself to sleep.

It took a day for her to recover. In the meantime, Juliana was left mostly in peace. A wash of emotions held her in their grip as she waited for the seasickness to pass. Her reverie on leaving port was only a memory now. Every lurch of the ship left her wondering how much worse it might all get.

The Syrian brought her water and small bowls of gruel. "The ship is a trader," he told her, late on the first day, as if in answer to an unspoken question. "We won't go down. We're well used to these seas. It will calm soon. The rowers will work when the wind dies. You'll know that by the drumming." His eyes moved over her body.

"I'm saving my share of the ship's profits. I plan to buy a farm and I want to buy a slave just like you. I heard you were bought in Nicomedia. What price did they ask for you?" He leaned forward, expectantly, as if her answer was very important to him.

She turned her head away and groaned, loudly, as if she might vomit. The seasickness had mostly passed by then, but a few groans might mean he'd leave her alone.

He waited a while and when her only response was to continue to groan, he snorted in disgust and went away. She listened to the slap of the waves for a long time after that. She would have to use every trick she'd learnt to protect herself. She whispered the prayer her birth mother had taught her.

Life is fire, I am fire. Life is a sword, I am a sword. Life is blood, I am blood. Holy mother stand with me. She repeated it over and over, remembering every way she had been taught to make the words real.

The following nights were bitterly cold, but once the first day passed the spring days passed quickly and the seas were calmer. She was given duties, along with her food.

Juliana was tasked with removing military patches from Lucius' tunics and reinforcing the stitching on all his shoulder and elbow pads. When her daily duties were done, she left the stowage area and watched the men play dice. One afternoon, the Armenian, Syrian and Egyptian crewmen sang together as they rowed. She could only understand part of the song. It was about a lost love.

Constantine and Lucius spent much of their time sitting with the captain, talking, laughing or watching the sea.

She stared at the passing coastline when they came within sight of the land and wondered what each fishing village was really like. As the sun went down each night, she gazed over the darkening, wine-tinted sea, feeling the ship's movement under her.

She'd also been ordered to prepare the food for her masters, gruel in the morning, and later flat polenta bread with olive oil and sausage or dried or fresh fish. They also ate figs, cheese and jams, but these items weren't given to her or Tiny. But she tasted the crumbs and then devoured their leftovers. And at night she slept in her nest of rugs.

At first, she felt detached from the crew, but after a few days she got to know them. In the evenings now, she joked with them and listened to their stories. Every man she told her tale to, agreed she'd been favored by the gods when Lucius had purchased her.

They were lucky with the weather too, which, after the storm the first day, stayed clear with only mild winds until they reached the straits of the Hellespont, the neck-like opening from the Propontis Sea out to the great Middle Sea. That was where the luck from the dolphins stopped, so the seamen said.

It took four days at sea to reach the Hellespont, which they arrived at in the late afternoon. The rugged heavily forested coastline had hills rising high and away on each side. Villages of lime washed houses huddled together around short rocky jetties, running out like crooked thumbs into the dark choppy waters.

The rolling wooded hills of Thrace stretched away beyond the northern shoreline, hazed in a blue mist as the light faded. When the straits narrowed further, they crossed to the other shore and passed within an arrow's flight of the densely wooded Thracian side. Rocky promontories loomed.

"Look," said the Syrian, sitting near her, cross-legged as she was, beside the low wooden rail. He pointed at a wooded promontory on the far shore.

He'd hovered around her that day, no matter whether she'd replied to him or not, and as he smiled so sweetly and because he kept Tiny away and discouraged the other leering crewmen, she listened to him.

"There are the old lands of Ilium and Troy," he said. Then he told her a story about how Helen had escaped the sack of the city, and how she'd been whisked away by a trading ship from somewhere near here.

"She came to Egypt after that, I promise you. It is as true as I am here in front of you." He smiled wistfully at her.

A little later he pointed out a mound rising high, surrounded with swathes of red and white flowers. "Athena's gifts," he said, pointing over and over.

They undulated in a breeze, or maybe it was a trick of the light. A massive statue stood on top of the mound.

"That is the tomb of Ajax, hero of the Trojan wars. His statue was returned here by Augustus, after he defeated Cleopatra and her stupid lover. We Syrians pray every time we pass here." The man bowed his head.

Juliana looked out to sea. She could see beyond the Hellespont now, to where the straits opened out. The ship hummed as the current rushed them forward. On the last tip of land on the Thracian side a beacon light shone like a bright star brought down to earth.

The previous night they'd swung round on the end of their anchor in a deserted rocky bay in the lee of a headland. This night they had to row hard to reach a small island, the refuge port of Tenedos, not far beyond the opening of the straits. There they roped their craft to other traders' ships inside a small, high-walled port. She slept well that night. In the morning they took water and fresh bread on board. The Syrian told her this had been the island the Achaeans hid on while their fabled horse was being discussed at Troy.

The next day, they were out of sight of land for a long period, before anchoring the following evening at a smaller rocky island with a fine sandy beach. A white village perched high in the distance on a hill above olive groves. Darting columns of swifts swooped along the shore. The water here was clearer than any they'd passed over and when she looked overboard she could see multicolored fishes fleeing this way and that, and way below, gleaming sand, speckled with silver.

Two days later they sailed close to a village of low white houses, clustered near the headland of a wide bay. The paths between the houses were like rocky streambeds. Chickens could be seen and heard. The flat roofs of the houses were piled with brushwood and on one stood a domed bread oven. From darkened doorways brown-faced children ran waving as they sailed past. She caught a sweet scent of baking. The island was named Lesbos, one of the oarsmen told her. Then he grinned at her.

The next island they passed had stunted trees carpeting rocky claws of headlands and sheer cliffs that looked like the battlements of an abandoned stronghold. After that the sea became darker and the swells deeper, suggesting fearsome depths.

A rain squall lashed them later that day, throwing them off course, and everyone on board except the captain, who sat bound to the steering paddle, found shelter where they could until it passed. That evening purpling towers of clouds came racing towards them and that night vivid lightning illuminated the desolate headland they'd taken refuge by.

144

Juliana couldn't sleep while the lightning cracked. She hugged herself and listened to the rain splatter on the wooden planks as she rearranged the ropes and canvas again and again to keep herself away from the soaking floorboards. The storm had disappeared the following morning as if it had never happened. They sailed by a line of low hulled fishing boats searching for the shoals of juicy silverfish that were, she was told, their livelihood.

She saw beehives arranged near the next island's shore and that night heard scraps of sound drifting on the wind, children singing, flutes and laughter, far away.

"Only a few years ago pirates, operating from caves like that one, used to pillage ships that came this way." The Syrian pointed at golden hued limestone cliffs with stunted bushes clinging tenaciously to its soaring walls. "Harvesting slaves, they called it. There were whispers that the Emperor Diocletian permitted and profited from it."

He pointed out a dark and mysterious looking cave, large enough for a ship to enter, where the spray-flecked waves crashed up against seaweed-covered rocks.

Juliana slept fitfully that night. She listened to the watches being called and when she drifted off, images of blood-craved pirates and burning ships lurked in her dreams.

A strange unease had crept up on her during the past few days. That night it grew stronger, and she knew what it meant. She wanted to go home. She wanted to go back to Bithynia. No matter how cruel her old master had been, she'd known and understood everything around there.

She had to shake her head to stop the thoughts spiraling on top of each other. Her new life would be better, she told herself. No matter how uncertain, no matter what happened, she had to face it. Then she thought about Constantine.

She had a pain in her stomach then, as if she'd eaten something rotten. And later, she dreamt he spoke to her, though he had ashes in his hair.

The following evening, they sheltered by a massive headland that the Syrian said was part of the island of Delos, sanctuary and birthplace of Apollo.

"This island was chained to the seabed by Zeus himself," he said. "It is a quiet place these days, but 10,000 slaves were sold a day here at one time, before Rome moved the trade away. Did you notice how dark the sea is around here?"

She shook her head.

He moved closer to her. "The captain said you're to take an early turn on watch tonight. One of the crew is ill. It's either you or someone else will have to do a double. The captain said to ask you. He said you act like a boy, anyway."

"Tell the captain I'll do it." She turned away from him.

The sky turned cloudless that night. The stars shone like the lamps of a vast and distant city. The glistening band of the spheres glistened from horizon to horizon. Perhaps this is what Rome looks like at night, she thought as she nestled by the steer board, listening to the sigh of the waves.

Juliana hugged herself, remembering how Constantine had looked at her that day, as if noticing her for the first time. She knew what happened to slave girls who caught the master's eye. She'd seen it again and again over the last few years.

Usually there were a few days where they went around looking as if they'd found a bag of gold coins. And then a few days after that they were crying, either scared that they were pregnant or disappointed that they'd been set aside by the master.

Masters had enough women of their own level, the other slave girls always said to each other, when these things happened. And if the one who'd had a brief period between his sheets complained too much, she'd be beaten or sold off. It wouldn't do to have the mistress of the house hear her wailing.

Under her the timbers of the ship creaked, as if it too was preparing to sleep. She sat up straight, pulled her woolen blanket tight around herself. The reek of the seaweed, encrusted on some nearby rocks, was so strong now she could taste the salt in it. She breathed in deep, the scent of the fish they'd eaten that night and the hum from the unwashed bodies around the deck almost masked if she held her breath in fully.

She wondered if the smells meant the wind was changing. The strong Borean winds had served them well by taking them down quickly through the islands, but the captain hoped for a warmer Levant wind to carry them across the open sea to the Straits of Messina. They'd already been blown too far south, he'd said that evening, and he'd warned her to rouse him if any whisper of a new wind sprung up.

A scuffling noise disturbed the silence. She looked up. A huge shadow loomed. She stared open mouthed, and almost screamed.

"How is your first watch," a voice said. Constantine's voice. She gripped the edge of the rail behind her.

What did he want?

She swallowed hard. She wasn't even allowed speak to him without being spoken to first, and she'd never yet been alone with him. Yes, he spoke to her every day, but that was always when he asked her to do things, like fetch water or a knife. He'd never engaged her in conversation.

Her mind raced. Had she done something wrong? She looked up to see if she'd missed her watch call but the star Al Ghoul, the daemon eye of Perseus, still dipped slowly towards the horizon.

"Good," she said.

He put a hand on her shoulder.

"Don't worry, I'm not checking on you." He released her shoulder and sat on a low bench an arm's length away. He looked around, as if enjoying the night air. Then he leaned towards her.

"You know, the Captain expected you'd cry off from this task. He also said you'd cause problems on the journey, that you'd fall in with one of his men, but you haven't. You're tougher than you look, Juliana."

She bit her lip, wondering where this was all leading. What would happen if she said no to the son of an emperor?

His voice lowered as he went on. "Tell me about this dream reading talent Lucius says you've been gifted with." The note of diffidence in his voice grew stronger, as if he half expected her to throw herself at him and wanted to distance himself from her.

She shifted a little away from him. Lucius had only asked once about her dream reading. Why had he told Constantine?

"It's nothing master, a childish game." She should never have told Tiny about the dream reading skills her mother had taught her. She looked out to sea. He shifted closer, rocked.

Impatience radiated from him, like the feeling in an orchard as the trees waited for rain. She held the rail tight.

"Don't worry, I'll not report you to the temple priests," he said. "Lucius suggested I ask you about a dream I've been having ever since Nicomedia." He paused.

She stared at him. Was he really asking her to read his dream? She kept her face still. No way would she appear eager, like the slaves whose tongues hung out for their master's approval.

"But I need to know what you do with the dreams people tell you about."

"I keep them secret," she said. "I never reveal the dreams people tell me. This is what my birth mother taught me. I'd never betray dreams, not even if they threatened to cut my tongue out."

"But you know the meaning of dreams, the messages from the gods?"

"I say what I've been taught that a dream may mean, that is all," Juliana replied softly, matching his tone.

They sat in silence for a while until Juliana reckoned he'd decided against confiding in her. It was probably a good thing.

XXV

Treveris, 306 A.D.

The Pictish elder bowed as he entered Crocus' tent. "Brave chief of our Alemanni brothers, I come to beg your help."

Crocus shifted on the rush mat. He waved the man forward, then reached behind his back to make sure that his knives were ready, should there be any need for them.

"You are welcome, Nechtan. We are all brothers. Sit, let my slaves serve you. You must be hungry."

"I have no need of food or any other sustenance, brother Crocus. There is too much at stake for me to soften my words with such things."

The man sat opposite Crocus. His woolen cloak had a crisscross pattern. He pushed it behind him as he settled down. The man's sword or axe and any knives he'd had with him when he arrived in Treveris had been taken from him.

"What is at stake?" Crocus looked the man in his one good eye. The other held a black pit. Someone had plucked his right eye out. There were many who wouldn't survive such a punishment.

"Our world is under threat. You know what your Caesar plans for us Picts, don't you?"

"My master is a Roman emperor now, do not forget that. He has the power of the Roman gods in him."

"I do not doubt it." The Pictish elder touched his forehead, then made a gesture as if throwing something in the air. "But it is his plans for salting all our fields beyond their wall that I have come about."

"I don't expect he will succeed in salting all the fields."

"We do not want him to salt any."

Crocus sniffed. The reek of death coming from Nechtan grew stronger. He took a sip from a large cup of beer at his side. It had taken him a few years to grow used to the beer they made in these parts, but now he enjoyed it all day.

He put the beer cup in front of him. "You should have thought of this, when you were raiding along the coast of Britannia. I heard you people even raided farms outside Eboracum last summer."

Nechtan grew louder as he replied. "Not us. I swear on the name of the goddess. Are we to suffer for someone else's crimes?"

"It is a time of evil for many, my friend. These days the storms are stronger, and the snows kill. The water is poisoned in many wells. Do not tell me what I already know."

"But there must be something we can do to keep these evil things away. Perhaps the mighty Crocus would like to see the gifts we have brought." Nechtan stood, went to the tent flap and threw it open. In the dirt outside, between the lines of tents, a row of wooden crates stood. Between two crates stood a blond-haired boy in a thin tunic.

XXVI

West of Delos, 306 A.D.

Constantine spoke again, in an even lower voice, as if he thought someone was listening.

"Do you believe dreams show us the future, Juliana?"

She shivered. Talking to him reminded her of when she'd been a child, before she'd been made a slave, when she could talk to anyone freely.

"Some of them are messages about what may come, others are visions from the past. That is what I was taught, that they mean something."

He stared at her, as if he was working out if he could trust her.

"Before I tell you, Juliana, you must swear on your life never to reveal to anyone what I say tonight. Do you so swear?"

"I swear on my life," said Juliana.

After a long pause he spoke. "This is my dream. I wake looking towards the walls of a great city." He hunched closer to Juliana. They gazed out at the shimmering, oily blackness. The smell of salt and seaweed tickled her nostrils.

"An army is spread out before me, and beyond it a river flows in full flood. A terrible wailing rises from beyond the river. But I cannot move. My arms and legs are rooted to the ground. A giant, in a purple toga, is striding towards me. The wailing becomes louder. I see a horse, a cloaked figure riding it and I awake, sweating, as if I have a fever. This dream has come to me every night since we started our voyage. What does it mean?" His tone was agitated.

"I can unravel parts of this, my lord, that is all. Is there any more you have not told me?"

151

Constantine shook his head,

She knew she had to be careful. You could lose your life for predicting the wrong thing to a master. They sat side by side watching the sea and the stars. He pulled his cloak tight. Finally, she spoke.

"A river means things are changing, my lord. But you face dangers. That army. The rider means a message you are waiting for will arrive. This should give you hope. What you have been waiting for will come to pass." She paused. She had grown to hate telling people what their dreams might mean. Some, when they heard what she had to say, got angry. Others dismissed her words with a wave.

She took another deep breath and told him the final part of the reading. "I have heard it said that it is fear that roots us to the ground in our dreams, though I cannot tell for sure in your case."

"I'm not afraid." He snorted. "I can stand in the front line of any battle. I will trade blows with any man. What am I afraid of?"

She shrugged her shoulders. "The brave do not always win, so I heard."

"You are right."

The silence returned. Had she gone too far?

"Have you been told where we're going, dream reader?" he said. His tone had softened.

"To Rome, my lord. To the center of the world." She brushed her hair from her face.

"Yes, and after that to Gaul, to Treveris, the capital of my father's provinces. Perhaps he is the purple-robed giant."

She dared to look into his eyes. He didn't frown and look away as some did when a slave dared look at someone from a class above them.

"He's planning a campaign against the Picts. Lucius said your father came from Britannia. We may even go there."

The hairs down her back stood up. Not only was he telling her where they were going, as if he trusted her, his gaze had locked with hers, and he'd almost promised to take her to Britannia.

A scratching noise from further along the deck disturbed them. It was Lucius.

"Does she give a good reading?" Lucius sounded amused, half asleep.

Constantine squeezed her arm lightly, in a gesture of gratitude and stood up. The ship swayed gently.

"The usual tales," he said, dismissively.

Something bubbled up fast inside her. "Don't blame the reader if the message displeases."

She stared down at her hands for a moment, then, a moment later, she dared a look.

Constantine and Lucius were staring at her. Both of them looked surprised, not angry. She'd gotten away with it. Lucius patted her head.

She wanted to push his hand away, but she scowled at him instead. Lucius shook his head and withdrew his hand. Constantine put his hand on Lucius' shoulder, as if to restrain him, and they moved away towards the prow of the ship, leaving Juliana alone.

Juliana knew why they had gone. To them she was a slave, a servant, a person of a low and unlucky order, best not to mix with, a creature to be pitied and forgotten quickly. But she knew deep down she was more than a slave. And if she could, she would prove it to them.

The ship moved almost imperceptibly as a light breeze skimmed the sea. A rope slapped. She sniffed. Was there a new breeze?

The rough wood of the ship trembled slightly under her bare feet. She heard voices. Raised voices.

"I have to show respect. It's the way I am." Constantine's tone was loud, and angry. Did he not care who could hear him?

The first part of what he said next was lost in the breeze, but the rest carried clearly to her. "I'll be posted back within a year, two at most. That's what my father said. I remember it clearly. He said he'd send for me. And he has. He's kept his word."

Relief grew inside her. They weren't talking about her.

"You know I'll never speak ill of him, Constantine, but you must agree it took a hell of a long time for him to send for you."

"Do not say anything against him, Lucius." They fell silent.

153

Inside, she felt like a strung bow, knotted, waiting. She knew the value of eavesdropping and its dangers. The house slaves on the estate had prided themselves on their skill at it.

"Maybe he really needs you. Maybe you'll be appointed his successor once again. Why else would Galerius release you?" Every word Lucius spoke was clear now.

"It'll be twenty years or more before he is gone, Lucius. I'll have plenty of time to prove what I'm worth. I must win a lot more battle honors first. And I will." The wind rattled a loose rope, echoing his words.

She sniffed again. A new wind. Definitely. A warmer wind. She stood and padded quickly down the deck. When she got near the prow she called softly to Lucius, telling him she would wake the captain. She heard no more of what was being said between them.

The captain quickly had the ship ready for a night sailing. Several of the men, those who were new to his command, grumbled as they woke from where they slept under the rowing benches in the shadow of the sails. But when they saw the full moon, their grumbling ceased. It was a good night for sailing.

Soon after, the ship moved like a stallion released into a summer meadow.

As the island disappeared behind them, Juliana saw a twinkling light on the top of a headland. Her first watch had still not ended.

"The priests of Apollo light that fire, girl. It signals the change in wind. The coming of the Levants," said the captain, when he saw Juliana gazing back at the light.

She didn't reply. She was thinking about what Constantine had said. They might go to Britannia. Perhaps he might help her find her father. Could it be true?

She sat looking at the wake as it streamed behind them. Her life was changing in ways she'd never imagined were possible and she was changing too. Her early morning prayers were being answered.

The new wind drove them steadily all that night, and the next day. The Syrian had stories about every islet and headland they passed. They were the isles of the Cyclades, he told her.

154

They spent the following night anchored by an island called Cythera, and early the next day they were beyond it, and into the Ionian Sea. The wind still held good and the sky stayed almost cloudless for this, the most dangerous part of their journey, out of sight of land, across the sea to the Straits of Messina.

The sky seemed paler here, a more whitish blue, as if a permanent haze had descended.

"These are the Halcyon days." The Syrian stood by her while they watched fishes leaping high in the air. "Zeus' birds will keep the storms away, while their kind builds nests onshore. We should have an easy journey all the way to the Straits."

She noticed he was rubbing at his crotch with one of his hands while he spoke to her. She knew what he was doing, stood up quickly, and walked to the other end of the ship. A few of the male slaves at the estate used to take their cocks out in front of her and stroke them, if they ever caught her on her own. She knew better than to complain, but also knew their next step would be to force themselves on her. Only fear of the master finding out and turning them into eunuchs had deterred most of them.

But the Syrian had been right. They arrived at the Straits of Messina on a calm evening after two days out of sight of land. It wasn't until they'd passed through though, that Juliana understood why the crew dreaded this part of the journey.

The first taste she got of what lay ahead came when a thin column of gray smoke loomed on the horizon, spreading out high up in the air. It was some time before the island of Sicilia could be seen below it, but all laughter and chatter stopped on the ship as the column loomed nearer. Before the island itself appeared, a mountain came into view at the base of the column of smoke. It had a pale ring around its cone. When the sun set behind it, wispy trails of clouds with flickers of fire attracted all eyes to a display of the powers of the gods, which made anyone who saw it want to pray for deliverance and regret they had ever come this way.

"That is Aetna, the forge of Vulcan. The home of the Cyclops. They are awake, as you can see, but sometimes we can hear them as well," one of the other crew members told her in a whisper as they watched, mesmerized.

They made slow progress towards the island that evening and had to row at the end through very choppy seas. They would have to wait for the turning of the main current, she heard, before the captain would even consider making a run through the Straits.

The slim sea passage between Sicilia and the mainland of Italia could not be taken lightly. They anchored off a steep jagged-edged rocky shore, in the lee of a headland. The thin ash column towered eerily above them. It was the beginning of a nervous wait for their run through the Straits.

Juliana heard another crewman grumbling that they could have docked at Syracuse or Catania, ports along the coast of Sicilia, but he was rounded on with derision by an old hand, who wondered if the first man wanted to offer his own share of the profits from the trip to pay the harbor taxes.

The sun set soon after, and they swung wildly at anchor as the wind turned, and a squall dumped torrents of rain that seemed oddly gritty onto the deck. Rain soaked everything. Juliana's cubby hole door even blew open, saturating her and her rope bedding, before she managed to wedge the door closed again.

Juliana slept badly that night. The column of smoke overshadowed her dreams. Every creak of the boat made her fearful. She imagined monsters swimming up from the deep towards her. She woke with the light of an azure dawn spreading across the sky and the purple hued mountains of Italia revealing themselves across the channel in a misty gloom. The column of smoke from Aetna had changed. It grew fatter and darker now.

The captain was loudly abused by a damp Lucius when he awoke for not making a run for one of the ports along the coast of Sicilia before the squall came on, but the captain just shrugged, and pointed at the sea and shook his head as if something under the waves had prevented them docking.

"What's down there?" Juliana asked one of the crewmen a little later, after they'd hauled in the small anchor. A stench of fish rose from the man, as if he'd rolled in the food slops, and his skin appeared to be flaking. She recoiled away from him.

"Scylla and Charybdis live down there, girl. The captain is a superstitious bugger. He never stays in any port around here. He has to time the current just right, you know, and all hands have to be clear headed, he says, 'cause if we stay too long in the Straits, those two monsters'll suck us down into their steaming whirlpools or smash us onto rocks. The channel gets tighter and tighter, you'll see, until we pass through the final bit, only two leagues wide! We sacrificed to Neptune early this morning, so I expect he'll let us through, but you can never be sure with the gods, girl." He chuckled to himself.

Soon after, they passed the mole and lighthouse at the harbor of Messina. Juliana could feel the current flowing beneath them, speeding them on.

The coast on either side sat draped in the last of the morning haze, as the captain steered them towards the center of the narrowing channel. The oarsmen grunted. The sail had been stowed a little before. The drummer beat the stroke faster as the sea grew increasingly choppy. The ship shuddered expectantly as it broke through the waves.

A galley out of Messina plied swiftly across their wake on its way to the mainland, its two banks of oars swinging fast in perfect unison like a pond creature skimming the waves.

"Pull men, pull hard for the mainland. And while you're at it, pray to the Fates that Morgana stays below this stinking sea today," the captain roared.

Juliana peered ahead. She'd not taken the Syrian's shouted advice to hide and she gulped as she caught sight of a patch of swirling water directly in their path. She pointed frantically and when she looked back the captain grinned, ignoring her.

Then water sloshed over the deck. Waves broke over the side. She held tight to a rope as cold water sucked over her sandaled feet. The ship creaked as it changed course, pulling at its nails, until suddenly they reared up on a wave and hung for a moment.

25

Crash, the ship smashed down, and seawater flooded in, rushing around her ankles. Her fingers slipped a little down the wet cord.

Some of the oarsmen were calmly scooping water away with battered pots. Most were continuing to row. Then the cold seawater fell away, as the prow reared up again and they crashed over the next wave.

A sudden awful stink made her groan. Her face twisted with revulsion as she saw a massive clump of clinging seaweed swirling beside them. For a hideous moment, she thought they'd all be swallowed into it. Then it was gone, sucked away, leaving only a bubbling, swirling patch of water behind. The walls of the Strait pressed high on either side. It felt as if they were sailing a turbulent river.

"Galley! Galley!" A shout rang out.

Juliana spun round. Her mouth opened.

A giant war galley with a rearing horse-head prow bore down on them as if it hadn't seen them.

Its sides were crusted with barnacles, making the vessel look like a giant sea creature as it cleared the waves. Only the crash and swish of oars gave any indication that there were people on board her.

"Pull to Sicilia. Pull to Sicilia, pull!" the captain roared. Another voice joined in, Constantine's. She looked around. He stood by the steering paddle, while holding an oar in the air, as if he could fend off the galley by himself. Lucius swayed near him, saying something, laughing. Juliana felt a tingle of exhilaration and then the sudden warmth of desire as she watched Constantine steady himself, his short wet tunic clinging to his body. She looked away and up at the galley.

They were turning across the current far too slowly. It seemed certain that within moments that they'd be cut in two. The long twin banks of oars dropped near them with a splash, then reared up, and smashed down nearer again as the galley changed course, as if it intended to follow them.

"Oars in," the captain shouted. He pulled suddenly at the steering board.

A flood of water cascaded over them. The prow of the galley loomed over them. She could have touched it if she stood and reached up. They keeled sickeningly to one side in its bow wave. A heartbeat later the prow had gone past and the galley's oars struck them with a clatter, sending everyone ducking. One oar broke, spinning wood into the air.

Water rushed in as a swallowing wave but then they were upright, and the galley had passed, and they were bobbing low and drunkenly in her wake. Constantine had dropped the oar. Everyone bailed frantically now, swaying, and clinging desperately to whatever handhold they could find.

Juliana looked at the galley as it moved ahead. A pudgy face crowned with a shiny bald head at its stern peered down dispassionately at them. She saw superiority and malevolence chiseled into his gaze before the face disappeared.

They bailed and bailed. For a while it seemed they were getting nowhere, but then the current carried them out of the Straits and the sea became calmer and the job easier. She looked back and saw with a shudder that Mount Aetna had marked their passing with a wider, dirtier column of ash-gray smoke rolling high into the air.

"Neptune sails with us," one of the crewmen shouted. A desultory cheer went up.

The captain steered them towards the rocky coast of Italia and they anchored soon after in a small bay.

"This is the Tyrhenum Sea, the last leg of our journey," one of the crew told her. "With this Euros wind at our back, we'll be in Rome in days. The only thing we have to worry about now is blind galley captains. How that one didn't see us, I'll never guess." He shook his head.

Juliana remembered the face looking down at her from the galley. He'd almost looked disappointed.

That night she dreamt of her birth mother. Vixana reached out to her, then drifted away. Juliana wanted to follow her, but she was already gone. She woke with cold sweat chilling her and lay awake for some time thinking of her childhood and the certainties of their life and role in the village. Everything would have been so different if the Persians hadn't come.

They tacked in long sweeps all through that day. They passed tall limestone cliffs and the sea around them became an intense blue. Groves of dark cypress trees came close to the shore and in the distance, there were orchards of flowering lemon trees and grand villas. As they tacked past the great bay before the fire mountain named Vesuvius, they were pursued by a storm and had to run before the wind until they found shelter in the lee of a headland. As they did so, the mast creaked noisily as if it would snap, and they lost an oar and nearly lost the steering paddle.

Wind and rain beat down on the anchored ship for a whole day, and the heaving seas threatened, she was sure, to smash them apart. The captain laughed when he came to check on her and saw how frightened she looked.

"This isn't a real storm," he said. "This is only a squall."

She stared defiantly up at him. He laughed some more and left her in peace.

The wind had died by the following morning and the sky was cloudless. Only the feathery touch of a light breeze ruffled the glassy blue waters of the bay. It seemed as if the storm had never happened. The crew rowed the ship well out past the headland, where the wind blew stronger, and they sailed on.

It had taken twenty-one days to sail from Nicomedia. It had been a fast voyage for that time of year, she overheard an oarsman say. When they at last came within sight of the massive mole that marked the harbor at the mouth of the Tiber in the early morning, the scene of galleys and trading ships converging and departing reminded her of bees around a hive.

"Tax collectors, captain," the Syrian shouted, as he pointed at a skiff that appeared alongside. Two men were hauled on board. One loudly requested the names of the ship's officers and any passengers, before being rowed away. The other stood by the captain, directing him and enquiring about his cargo.

The dock ahead had two semi-circular moles. They stretched at least half a league out to sea. "The Portus," the Syrian whispered.

Juliana hadn't noticed him coming up beside her. She checked where his hands were. His arms were folded across his chest so she didn't move away. He pointed at the lighthouse at the end of the longer mole, then swept his arm around. "This is the greatest harbor ever built. It is the real gateway to the capital of the world. See those storehouses." He jabbed towards a long row of squat granite buildings. "They're full of oils, wine, corn and a hundred other goods, shipped here from every province round the Middle Sea and well beyond. I've carried many cargoes to those storehouses."

She stared and stared, sensing something familiar about the scene, as if she had seen it before, or in a dream.

She listened to the other crewmen talk and, as they came closer to the dock, became fascinated with all the galleys and trading vessels maneuvering, wheeling, and turning among the cawing flocks of sea gulls. Runners in short tunics stood along the mole as they passed along it, calling out for news of their cargo or events at their home port. The captain waved them all away.

Tiny, who'd been standing nearby, turned to her. He was drinking from a wineskin being passed around. He choked, spluttered, then recovered.

"Lucius' gods were with us. Let's hope the rest of our journey turns out this well." He held the wineskin out to her.

She shook her head. He turned and guzzled at it greedily. Someone shouted at him to pass it on. He kept drinking.

XXVII

Alexandria, 306 A.D.

Helena watched as her villa burned. The flames reached as high as the lighthouse. From her vantage point, down the road towards the port, she could even hear the crowd who had set it alight. The stench of burning wood and charring mud bricks filled her nostrils.

"Curse these heathens all to hell," muttered Hosius.

"How did you know they were coming for me?" She couldn't take her eyes off the flames. Her scribe had a bag of her most valuable possessions under his arm, including her very last gold coins, and the only real silver plate items, but everything else was gone now, especially the villa itself.

"I knew this morning. We have people everywhere. The Prefect of Alexandria has been scheming against you for weeks. You let too many Christians cross your threshold and he knows I spend time with you. He wants you gone from the city. His opportunity has come. My spies are quick when their own lives are in danger."

Helena looked around. Passers-by were staring at them. They had to move, but it was difficult not to keep staring. Helena sniffed. The smell of burning grew stronger with each moment. She wiped at her eyes. She couldn't let him see how much this had affected her.

"My ex-husband will support me. He will provide for me."

"But he is a long way away. The notaries say he is campaigning in Germania."

"Wherever he is, he will help me. And I will be a lot closer to him when I get to Rome." Her voice cracked in places but was still strong.

Hosius took her arm. The stola she wore was more for indoors than for the street. One of her arms lay bare.

"We must go to my house. I can seek passage for you at the port while you wait there. My wife will give you some other clothes too."

She put her hand on his and moved her face towards him.

"You will come with me to Rome, won't you?"

He hesitated, then laughed. "Why do you need me? My work is here."

What he didn't say was that his wife would not want him to travel with her.

"Because if you don't come I will have no connections to the church in Rome. I need your influence there." She dug her nails into his hand. Whatever the consequences, she had to get to Rome. "You know I will do anything for my son. That includes denouncing you to the prefect as the secret linchpin for the followers of Christ in Alexandria." She dug her nails in harder as he struggled to free his hand.

"I haven't been to one of his trials by fire, but I hear they are shocking to watch." She leaned closer. "But I am sure it is even more shocking to be one of the victims."

XXVII

Portus, outside Rome, 306 A.D.

"Would the Tribune Constantine step forward?" the centurion bellowed. "Tribune Constantine come forward at once." His tone grew strident, shrill.

The speaker stood to attention on the stone quay beside them. His commands were backed up by a troop of ten red-cloaked, rod-stiff Praetorian guards, their blackened leather breastplates trimmed with purple silk. Everyone within earshot stopped what they were doing and stared.

"Who calls for him? By what authority?" Constantine moved close to the rail, as he tried to work out what this meant. Surely Severus hadn't heard of his arrival yet? He governed Italia, but he should be busy at his headquarters in Milanium. But who else would have any interest in him? He looked along the line of legionaries to see if any carried chains or leg irons that might signal he was about to be arrested.

"We speak for Maxentius, son of Maximian." The centurion waved his men forward. They tramped up the gangplank, making it bend, and stood to attention along the deck, their hands conspicuously on the pommels of their swords. The centurion came up to Constantine and bowed. Most of the crew were helping get the ship's cargo, amphoras of olive oil, ready to be extracted from the hold and carried to the emporium trading hall across from the dock.

"You are the Tribune Constantine?"

Constantine nodded, staring at the centurion as bleakly as the man stared at him.

"You are invited to attend Maxentius at his palace on the Via Labicana at once."

An invitation was certainly better than an arrest.

"Maxentius is expecting me?" His eyebrows shot up in mock astonishment. The centurion shrugged his shoulders.

"Wait for me ashore. It'll take time for my people to get ready." He waved the centurion away. For a moment, he thought the man wouldn't go. Constantine stomped to the small cabin that had been his home for the past few weeks. He threw cloaks and tunics out of his saddlebags as he picked what to wear.

"Do you know Maxentius well?" Lucius stood at the door of the cabin, his hands on his hips, his bare arms blocking the way out.

"I've met him once, Lucius. When I came to Rome for Diocletian's triumph. He was a boy then, seventeen or eighteen. I rebuffed an invitation from him." He snorted. "He's got a long memory, if he's getting me back for that. He had a liking for young boys then and some other even sicker things if I remember. That's why I didn't meet him. I hope his tastes have changed."

"Not in three years they won't," said Lucius. "If he's the Maxentius I heard about, the one passed over for advancement the same time you were, I think you'll need me with you, and Tiny, just in case."

Constantine pulled his travel tunic on. The brown hide was soft and well creased. The faded decorative patches near its bottom edge and on its shoulders were depictions of Hercules' labors. Juliana had redone the stitching on the patches during the voyage. He wished they had time to visit the nearby baths.

"Tell Tiny to get ready. And tell that Juliana to stop moping around like a homesick foal, and to get herself ready as well." He placed a hand on Lucius' arm.

"If Maxentius thinks I'm a threat, anything could happen. I hope he doesn't want to dump us all in the Tiber. If he tries anything we will have to fight our way out of his villa. Are you ready for that?"

Lucius nodded. "It will be like old times."

Horses stood ready for them at the end of the dock. When they set off half the Praetorians rode ahead, half behind. The centurion, whose name was Rufius, rode at the front on a black charger ornamented with silvered fasteners and pendants. Juliana and Tiny rode together, directly behind Constantine and Lucius.

A line of carts at the gates to the Portus slowed them down, but before long they were cantering along the road to Rome.

"We will be in Rome by midday," said Constantine.

He held his reins tight. A strange sensation came over him, that they were still swaying, as if at sea. He felt queasy a couple of times on the ride, but the sensation subsided as they neared Rome. Mostly he wondered what Maxentius wanted with him. The man would hardly be so rash as to harm him, but there was no telling with his type.

The road, the Via Portuensis, ran by the Tiber. It was lined at each end with grand marble tombs, and in many other places by the high stone and red brick walls of unseen villas. The road kept close to the river for much of the journey until, as a low, bare ridge came into sight, it left the river and its slow-moving barges behind.

As they reached the top of the ridge, a haze of brown smoke appeared in the distance. Rome's shroud lay like a slick across the sky. Below the haze, and even from this far, he could make out the red-brown walls of Aurelian, the most recent fortifications encircling the city and still the subject of continuing controversy about how secure the walls were.

From the ridge a horizon-filling jumble of roofs and buildings could be seen. Flecks of red and gold flickered below a crowning haze diffusing into the pale blue sky. It was the Rome he knew well from two long stays in the capital, vast, glorious, a place of wonder and deadly intrigue.

The Portuensis Gate was open and swarming with people and carts as they approached. This was exactly as he remembered it. He brushed his hand against the pitted stone as they passed slowly through the outer gate. It felt cold.

Few people paid any attention to them as they entered. Rome attracted every man of merit sooner or later. The disinherited son of an emperor would barely raise an eyebrow here.

The city filled his nostrils. It wasn't the smell itself, the heavy stench of horse manure, charcoal smoke, and urine pots, but the sense of being an outsider that the smell brought back. He remembered how much had felt deliberately hidden about Rome, the workings of the guilds and colleges, the feuds of senatorial families, the clash of cults and priests, the schemes of landlords and moneylenders, and how unconcealed, like a prostitute's charms, had been the disdain of her citizens for all those born outside her shadow.

Such disdain, he knew though, did not prevent the city's inhabitants from enjoying taking a visitor's coins in many imaginative ways. In the small open square beyond the gate, hawkers and tradesmen shouted, enticed, pleaded, and extolled their incredibly low prices, available only to you, and only for a short time. You could buy every promise of health, wealth, and happiness for whatever you had in your purse, if you shopped long enough in Rome.

Yellowing four and five story apartment blocks, with colonnades of shops and tavernas at their ground level, lined three sides of the square. Ramshackle wooden buildings, stables if he remembered right, huddled along the other side, at the bottom of the city walls.

The apartment blocks continued into the distance along the wide avenues that radiated ahead like a honeycomb into the city. There were people everywhere, tavernas overflowed, slaves ran on their master's errands, and elegant women strolled arm in arm with friends. In the center of the square a fountain with leaping, life-sized marble horses spewed water, while all around children played, dogs barked, horses neighed, and from somewhere, far away, a great cheer came carried on the air and died as quickly.

They headed for the wide avenue that ran down towards the Tiber. When they reached the Aemilian bridge, Constantine turned to Lucius and pointed out a large and confident-looking pack of rats running along the marble balustrade, as if they'd just crossed from the old city.

He heard Juliana's intake of breath behind him and turned. She was biting her lip, but she hadn't screamed. Lucius had been right. They'd made a good decision bringing her. Far below, the broad, muddy river ran swiftly. To their left the Tiber Island stood in the center of the river, with lush pine and cypress trees at its tip and gray-haired veterans sitting on benches overlooking where the channels rejoined.

The city guards at the red brick gateway on the far side ordered people to stand aside to let Constantine and his retinue pass. When some of the crowd failed to move quickly enough, they used short wooden batons to beat them away.

One skinny young man, a slave most likely, was beaten until he curled into a fetal position in a gully. The crowd pressed back against the walls and people muttered curses as they rode past, discontent visible on many of their faces. It had been the same the last time he was here. Strong leadership, tempered with justice, was what these people needed, not what they were getting now. His father had said that long ago, and he'd been right.

The old part of the city they now entered reminded him of an ancient patrician duchess with her once glorious, but now discolored red brick walls and cracked marble facings the fading symbols of her half-remembered days of glory.

The road ahead curved towards the Arch of Janus. Above that, the buildings on the Palatine Hill loomed. The Temples of Apollo and Sibyl looked in perfect condition and were brightly painted, unlike some of the buildings around them, which looked in need of repair. Further along the hill, the massive archways and golden staircases of the Domus Augustana, the palace of the Emperor Domitian, also looked untarnished by time. But perhaps it too would look faded, if he went up near them.

He found himself riding next to Juliana, after they had to move aside to let a troop of city guards hurry on to their next assignment. The roadway narrowed and grew busy.

"You don't see things like that often in Bithynia," he said to her.

Four gangly ebony slave girls were loping towards them alongside an ornate flame-silk covered litter. Disregarding the chill winds, the girls wore only flapping leopard skin squares, which barely covered them. Their naked and oiled breasts bounced as they ran. The litter was being carried by eunuchs who wore black thigh-length tunics, their heads at odd angles and their limbs jerking as they ran. Two sported huge boils on their necks.

"A concubine with her guards, I'll guess," he said.

Juliana didn't reply. She was staring at the litter.

He turned to look at it. It had a painting on its side. A fish.

The curtain of the litter whipped open for a moment as it passed him. A dazzling smile beamed towards him, below huge kohled blue eyes, and beyond, lying out, the curves of an oiled body disappeared enticingly into red-cushioned shadows.

He shook his head and looked away.

They rode along the Clivus Victoriae and followed the street as it turned sharp right at the Temple of Vesta and on past the Colosseum. There were no games or entertainments that day, but around the Colosseum's vast awninged skirts, street traders did a brisk business. He saw Juliana staring again, her head thrown back as if she'd encountered the Pillars of Hercules.

They rode away from the center, now. Dilapidated apartment buildings jostled up one against the other on each side. Ragged orphans ran wild in the tiny alleys between the buildings. Shouts could be heard occasionally, as if someone, not far away, was being robbed.

"In some parts of Rome, the walls are so thin you can hear your neighbors passing wind." Constantine leaned towards Juliana. "Or when they make love. Neighbors can guess which wives pretend to enjoy sex and which entertain panting lovers, not husbands." He hesitated to see her reaction.

She looked straight ahead.

He raised his voice a little. "They even claim to know who enjoys teasing their boyfriends until they beg them to finish them, sometimes so loud the whole block hears." He blew air out, as if amazed.

"Tell me, is it like that for slaves as well, Juliana?" The stories he'd heard about the plebs of Rome were like the ones he'd heard about slaves. They were always sharing their beds, everyone said, and mating like rabbits whenever they were given the least bit of freedom.

Juliana turned towards him and shook her head. Her short black hair flicked like numerous tails. She looked flushed. She was more innocent than he'd imagined. Or a very good actress.

"No, that's not what it was like on our estate. No eastern woman would ever tease a boyfriend like that." She looked away, then back at him, stony faced.

"I wouldn't be so sure about that." Constantine laughed. He could remember a few eastern women who were as good at teasing as any he'd ever met.

"I'm not talking about prostitutes, my lord. I'm talking about good eastern women. They know the subtler arts."

He laughed again. "Tell me who these good women are, Juliana? I didn't meet anything but schemers in my whole time in the east."

She leaned towards him, looked him in the eye and said, "My mother was a priestess of the Queen of Heaven, as her mother was before her. They were good women. Anyone who follows the Queen of Heaven is." She leaned away.

"You follow her?"

Juliana nodded.

"I heard all her adepts are masters at the arts of love. I'll have to be careful with you."

"I've forgotten almost everything my mother taught me, my lord. You have nothing to worry about with me. You should know, I'd rather cut my throat than have relations with a master. That's why my last one put me up for sale. I wouldn't open my mouth for him. As I cannot for you."

He opened his own mouth, then closed it again. The time for jokes was over. After passing the next street corner he said, "Don't assume I have any plans to ask you for anything, Juliana." He kicked his horse and moved forward beside Lucius.

At last they came to the Porta Maggiore, the colossal twin arch gate on the eastern edge of the city. They rode slowly through it and out onto the wide Via Labicana. Two high aqueducts joined together up in the air a little beyond the gateway. They cast a pattern of stunted shadows over the cobbled and cypress-lined road.

They stopped at a massive gate on the right side of the roadway, just beyond the aqueducts.

The heavy wooden gate had rusting iron bands across it and was set into high red brick walls. The gate grated open only after a password had been shouted up toward a slit in the wall. Although tired now after the long ride, Constantine sat tall as they rode through. Inside, they were helped to dismount in a gravel-strewn courtyard.

"You wait with the horses," he told an immediately dejected-looking Tiny. "Make sure they're fed and watered, and ready for the journey back this evening." He noticed Juliana had a scowl on her face. He would have to tread carefully with this one. Who knew what she was thinking.

They were led through a gate into another larger courtyard. The gravel underfoot here was whiter, thicker. A column of white smoke spiraled above the red tiled roof of the three-story blank walled building ahead.

"Let's say as little as possible, Lucius," he muttered. "We'll see what he wants and then go. Eat and drink nothing offered directly to us."

Lucius nodded. He looked apprehensive.

"And you." He turned to Juliana, following close behind. "Say absolutely nothing. Nothing at all. Do you understand?"

She nodded.

They were ushered through a double height doorway and into a large rectangular atrium with a high ceiling painted a brilliant sky-blue. Its walls were decorated with colorful depictions of a pastoral Arcadia. A trio of smoldering braziers near one wall gave off a sweet odor of incense. Calm crept over him. If Maxentius had wanted him dead, the task would surely have started by now. It would have been an easy thing to arrange for assassins to jump them on the road outside and then claim no part in it.

He turned to Lucius. "No stupidity here, Lucius, understood? We all still follow his father's edicts."

Lucius nodded.

A distant chant came echoing to them. The sound made the empty atrium seem isolated, abandoned.

They sat and waited and waited and waited. The chanting stopped, and when he'd finally become convinced Maxentius was deliberately insulting him, a slave boy dressed in a sparkling white tunic came hurrying through the doorway. With a low bow, the boy politely but diffidently requested that they follow him.

"You've arrived at an auspicious time, my lord. Our beloved Maxentius is about to receive a reading from the greatest seer in Rome," said the boy, as he led them down a long pale-gray flagstone corridor.

He took them out through a doorway and into the villa's rear gardens. Trellised walkways radiated ahead towards a red brick wall, taller than two men, which shielded them from the source of a column of whitish smoke that spiraled into the air behind it. A crackling noise filled the air. Flames leapt above the wall. Then a sickly burning smell entered his nostrils, the smell of a funeral pyre. It gave the palace garden a macabre feel, reminding him of some of the stranger stories he'd heard about Maxentius.

Two purple-cloaked guards stood to attention by an ancient looking wooden door. They bowed and opened it as he approached.

Beyond stretched a red brick paved area, in the center of which flames danced from a fountain-sized brazier, with the faces of lions on its blackened sides. Around the brazier stood a circle of hooded priestesses, their hands aloft in supplication. They had white masks on their faces, and would have looked like statues, were it not for the way their robes rippled in the cool wind.

Four smaller braziers were arranged in a circle around the larger one. They too spat fire and smoke.

On one side of all this, women in pristine togas lay on two couches watching Constantine approach, while sipping from jeweled goblets.

"Maxentius?" said Lucius.

"The one with the diadem," Constantine replied, as they were led towards the marble tables.

He ignored the priestesses. The exaggerated way traditional ceremonies were carried out in Rome sickened him. It had been the same the last time he'd been here, every household he'd been invited to had held some overwrought ritual.

A veiled Nubian slave girl was refilling Maxentius' goblet, while her twin knelt with her shaven head down, holding a golden tray for him to place it on when he'd finished drinking from it.

Maxentius stood as Constantine came forward. He was short, pudgy and youthful. He exuded the conceited air that Constantine had only ever seen on wastrel patricians. The purple tunic he wore was striped with gold embroidered bands. and his thick mop of chestnut hair framed a face dominated by a red nose and blood shot eyes.

"Brother, you are most welcome. Your arrival has been timed by the gods." Maxentius had a squeaky, fake-sounding patrician accent Constantine despised. When Maxentius finished talking, he looked around to see who was listening to him and grinned. Then he looked at Lucius.

"You have your Armenian wild man with you I see." Then he turned to Juliana. "And a pretty Persian too. Does she perform well for you?"

Constantine put his hand up in greeting. There would be no point in explaining to Maxentius that he lived his life as close to the values his mother had drilled into him as he could, or that such values had already saved him from the shooting star fate, burning bright only to be snuffed fast, he'd seen less disciplined members of imperial families suffer.

Self-restraint, a disdain for orgiastic behavior, and fair treatment for slaves and freemen were concepts Maxentius and his type would probably laugh uproariously at.

"I hope you weren't delayed by riots. We had one last night near the Salarian Gate." Maxentius' tone was full of fake concern. He waved Constantine forward.

As Constantine walked around the couches, Maxentius continued in mock anger. "Did you hear we've had public buildings attacked, and the most sickening assassinations?"

Constantine shook his head, slowly.

"The enemies of Rome are the enemies of tradition." Maxentius sounded shrill. He jabbed his finger at Constantine.

"All these new eastern cults threatening us with their simplistic ideas will be destroyed, especially the followers of that crucified charlatan, Christ. I can promise you that." He slurred his last few words and leaned drunkenly forward.

The Nubian beside him grabbed his arm and steadied it. Maxentius shook her away.

Constantine had moved a little. He'd been thinking of helping but decided against it. He glanced at Lucius. Usually, Lucius would have had a lot to say about cults and about Armenians being called wild men, but thankfully he kept his opinions locked behind a fake smile this time.

"One thing is sure, you'll be ready when Rome needs you," said Constantine.

Maxentius waved him forward and hugged him like a brother, slapping his back three times. He stank of stale wine and heavy incense.

"You will join us, Constantine." He waved towards his slaves then sat down heavily.

Two guests bowed low towards Constantine and moved to a free couch around another table. Constantine and Lucius sat on the vacated couches to the right of Maxentius. Juliana stood behind them. The only sound now was the crackling from the braziers. The priestesses began a soft, vaguely familiar chant, their hooded heads bowed low, calling on the gods to favor them with signs.

One of them took something from under her cloak, walked up to the brazier and held it near the flame. Then she scraped at it with a small golden sickle. The scratchings flew glittering into the fire.

"That is the blue sapphire from the breastplate of the last high priest of the Temple of Jerusalem," said Maxentius. He sounded pleased with himself.

Another priestess approached a giant red glazed pottery jar that stood in front of their table, no more than three paces away. She squatted behind it. As she sat, the arms of her tunic pulled back. Both her arms ended in stumps. Her bony wrists looked like clubs. A disconcerting sight. Constantine had seen such injuries before, but never on a woman. And then the chanting ceased.

The lid of the jar moved, settled, then moved again. A faint buzzing noise could be heard.

Then the lid jumped and fell with a clatter to the ground. From the mouth of the jar the slim head of a black adder appeared. It stared at Maxentius. The priestess moaned, and the snake turned towards her, its black eyes peering at everyone as it moved.

In a quick movement, it slipped out of the jar. A startled intake of breath came from one of the other guests. The snake stopped.

The priestess moaned again, and the snake slithered onto her sandal, then up her leg and into her robe. It disappeared within the folds and reappeared, its head swaying, where her hand should have been. The woman moaned as she held her hand outstretched, pointing it at the sky. It sounded as if she was pleading with someone. Her eyes rolled back in her head. Only the whites were visible now.

"Attend." Her voice rang out, sharp, bleak.

The other priestesses moaned in unison. Each of them faced outwards now, looking up at the sky. Out of where the sun sets, the region of darkness, a black hooded crow came swooping low over the city. At first it was only a pinprick against the gray shroud of clouds, only visible because a priestess pointed at it. Then, as it neared, it wheeled and turned and called to its brethren, dropped down and out of sight. The priestess put the snake back in the jar.

Another bird, far up, hung poised in the air. One of the other priestesses pointed at it until it too disappeared, flying high over the city.

The priestesses conferred. After much nodding and whispering, one of their number came forward and stood in front of Maxentius with her hands raised. She had three small circular blue marks on her left forearm, similar to the marks some centurions tattooed on their cheeks. She bowed.

"The birds allow it." She spoke in a soft, emotionless patrician accent. "The river of flame will consume us all."

Constantine had to strain forward to hear her.

"A great man comes soon to power." She looked at Maxentius. "But it will take an ending to create a beginning. This is the one truth."

She bowed, turned, and walked slowly away, with the other priestesses following in a line behind.

The reading was as ambiguous as these things always were. Had there ever been a time when great men weren't coming to power?

But there was something about the way the reading had been done that made the hairs on the back of Constantine's neck stand up. No matter what he thought of all these ceremonies, such readings as he had heard from these priestesses more often turned out to be true.

Could he be the great man coming soon to power? That thought was interesting, though it might be no more than wishful thinking. But there was always the chance his father would reinstate him as his successor. Perhaps these priestesses knew about that. It was all very possible.

Maxentius clapped his hands. Slaves rushed forward and assisted him to his feet. He staggered up, then pushed them away.

"Come, Constantine, there is a feast being readied. I think we've all had enough of the augers for today."

They all followed Maxentius along a wide marble path and then through an open doorway in the main building. It led them into a large dining hall. Constantine felt tired.

He'd rested little the night before, as their ship had been preparing to dock, and his mind turning over what was to come in Rome had shortened the little sleep he did get.

Three low black-veined marble tables filled one end of the room. Each table was surrounded on three sides by long silk-shrouded couches. A statue of a bull ejecting water from its mouth stood in the center of the room. As he passed it he noticed splashes of red on the white marble near the statue's hooves. Blood.

Constantine and Lucius were taken to the same table as Maxentius. Juliana again stood behind them. She looked nervous. She'd probably never served at such a meal before. Well, there was only one way to learn. Ornate platters of figs, cheese and olives were offered first. Sweet wine was served with them. Constantine raised his glass to his lips and moved some figs around his plate but didn't eat or drink. Nobody seemed to notice.

He weighed up possible excuses for a quick departure, then became aware that everyone at his table had stopped talking. They were all staring down the room. He followed their gaze. A young woman, slender, tall, sashaying like a goddess, was coming towards them. She wore a billowing green silk robe split open to below the navel, exposing a shiny expanse of honey-colored skin. Thin gold chains kept the sides of her robe in place, but they seemed certain to slip and expose her even more at any moment.

Something flashed at her belly button as she walked, and an innocent, wide-eyed smile added to her charm. She prostrated herself in front of Maxentius and her breasts were exposed to Constantine for a moment. Firm nipples glittered from a sprinkling of gold dust. When her head came back up her eyes flickered from right to left, as if flirting with every man in the room.

"Aaah, Sybellina, my one and only angel. My beautiful. I'm so glad you decided to join us." Maxentius rose a little, then flopped down again.

"Please, come sit with us my beauty, and meet Constantine. He is also the son of an emperor, though that title seems to have less significance than it used to." Maxentius made a space at his side. Without replying she lowered herself cautiously onto Maxentius' couch. Then she lowered her gaze and draped an arm on Maxentius' thigh, like a cat protecting its food.

Her eyes were large, green and accentuated with glittering malachite in a wide arc extending beyond her upper eyelids. She seemed to be reveling in all the glances being cast her way but returned only his gaze. He wondered how many love amulets had been made in her honor. And how many protective amulets wives had given their husbands when she was around.

"I'm honored to meet you, my lord." Her bow was slight, as if she considered him less honorable than he thought he deserved. Her patrician tone had a jaded edge, as if she knew the answer to anything he might ask.

"Tell me, my lord, are you a follower of Bacchus, like my one true friend, Maxentius?" Her pencil-thin eyebrows rose in anticipation, as if no answer he gave could be any more than a curiosity. She ran a hand through her hair. Brown curls cascaded in sheets of honey over her shoulders.

"I am all for moderation," said Constantine.

She leaned forward. He felt the full force of her attention, her eyes wide, expression puzzled, but sympathetic. For a moment, he thought she'd signaled him to move closer, as if she wanted him to hear something. He shifted towards her. She responded with a movement of her lips, as if she wanted to smile at him, but had quickly stopped herself.

She turned her attention to Maxentius, as if concerned she'd been ignoring him, though the friendly sideways glance she gave Constantine as she turned made it clear it was he she'd rather be talking to.

He noticed small blue dot marks on her left forearm.

"I must be totally straight with you, Constantine. We two are stuck with similar horses, as Cicero once said." Maxentius leant towards Constantine.

"You see, I asked my beautiful Sybellina to join us for a reason." He took a gulp of his wine. As he did so, he placed a hand absent mindedly on Sybellina's bare forearm. She nudged it away, while staring coolly at Constantine. Maxentius' eyes had been following what she was doing. For a moment, he looked like a little boy deprived of a favorite plaything.

Maxentius moved closer to him. "I'm glad Galerius released you. He thinks the vine of ambition has been cut, but you and I know the world may yet need us, don't we, Constantine?" He took another draught of his wine.

"You may be right," said Constantine.

"I am, and I must now make a small request." He gestured, waving his hand in the air.

"Will you permit my friend Sybellina to accompany you to Gaul? She is my messenger to your father. It will be simpler for all of us if she travels with you. It is an easy request to grant, is it not?" His gaze drifted to Sybellina, then back to Constantine.

He shook his head. Although he felt curious about Sybellina, his instincts told him she'd be trouble. He'd spent too long waiting for this journey to need a spy with him.

"Why don't you send her on one of your ships, Maxentius. She will get there faster, I am sure, and my father will be keen to hear what she has to say. We would slow her down."

"I'm not a burden, my lord, am I?" Sybellina's reply was like sweet water falling into a golden bowl. She bowed her head to him, lower this time, and again he caught a glimpse of gold dusted nipple. She was tempting, very tempting.

A slight noise made him turn to see Juliana looking as downcast as he'd ever seen her. Had she not been taught that slaves were meant to be quiet?

"You see, the invitation is for you to come with me, my lord," Sybellina continued. "My lord Maxentius has a dozen galleys at the Portus, all of them bigger than the ship they tell me you arrived on. We are concerned for your security." She emphasized the word security.

"We will have the fastest of Rome's ships to take us, a ship with proper protection against pirates. They have infested the coast of Gaul, you know." She tossed her hair.

"I'm sure it's in your interest to take up this offer, my lord." She paused, then continued in a slightly harder tone. "Is it not dishonorable for a guest to refuse his host? Maxentius wishes only to help you. Will you refuse him?" She sounded astonished.

"How could I?" He was trapped. To refuse would be an insult that would allow Maxentius to take offence. And who knew what he might do then, what delays he might place in their path. If this was the price he would have to pay for Maxentius' cooperation, so be it.

It could have been worse. If what Sybellina said was true, Maxentius' ships would be ideal for the voyage to Gaul, and if he agreed, Maxentius would probably allow him to leave immediately. Anyway, perhaps it would be enjoyable. Who knew what might happen on a long journey with Sybellina? What should he be afraid of?

"Your decision is the right one, my lord. Now, I must ready myself. I expect you wish to leave soon." She glanced at his uneaten food, stood, bowed and left the room with the admiring glances of most of the men in the room on her.

"So, Constantine." Maxentius looked delighted. "Our little oracle priestess has persuaded you. She'd make a good man, wouldn't she?" He laughed.

Everyone looked at him. The room filled with infectious laughter. Constantine's ears tingled. Some of that laughter was directed at him. He fought a sudden urge to push Maxentius from his couch and stab something into him.

"Yes, you're right. Now I must beg permission to head back to the Portus at once," he said, as soon as the laughter died a little. He had to get away. If he stayed he'd only start a fight.

Maxentius giggled madly, as if he'd remembered some private joke.

"The evening is no time to travel through the city, Constantine. Stay, drink, we have girls for every taste, and boys too, of every age, though I can understand your need to get away. The physician who warned me against pursuing pleasure died under a priestess himself." He winked and grinned lasciviously like a man possessed by a daemon.

"We can be through the city before dark, Maxentius, but we must go now. I can assure you, your messenger will arrive safely." He stood, bowed formally, and without waiting for a response, headed for the door.

Lucius and Juliana followed him out through the palace. He heard them behind him but ignored them. Behind him a burst of music and raucous laughter rose up, then faded.

One part of him, the careful part, hoped Sybellina might miss their hurried departure. But when they reached the stables she was already there, dressed in a long woolen cloak and calling to her mare, prancing around the stable yard. She must have known Maxentius' plan. Tiny was ineffectually trying to calm the horse. Sybellina looked distraught, or she was playing at being defenseless.

"Can the daughter of an oracle not soothe a horse?" asked Constantine. He took the reins from Tiny and began murmuring softly. The horse kicked dangerously, then, eyeing him as he whispered, it went quiet.

"My freedom was the price of my mother's," said Sybellina, bowing. "I spent my childhood far from any stables. I learned to ride only recently." She turned to Juliana, who was standing near the doorway into the stables.

"What a beautiful slave you have," she said, her voice pure sweetness. "Is she yours, my lord?" Her eyebrows rose.

"She belongs to Lucius, not me," Constantine said as he mounted. He knew what she was really asking. Was Juliana in his bed every night.

The sun was sinking over red tiled roofs as they made their way back through the city. He decided to shorten their journey by cutting through the Subura, the seedy area below the Aventine Hill. It would be the quickest way to the southern outskirts. He did not want to pass through the city gates around the time they closed.

The Subura had declined even further since he'd passed through it three years before. The number of stray dogs had shot up. They barked at the passing riders from alleyways, as if they rarely saw horses. Only a few late bread shops were open here. There were no rows of fine colonnades as in the better areas of the city. Few people lingered on these streets, but noisy tavernas hummed from behind closed doors. The cold wind was icier now, making the soft glow of light from the tavernas look very welcoming.

Then they passed down a street whose appearance disturbed him. Most of the street level shops and apartment entrances had been broken into. Wooden doors lay busted open. A pitiful wreckage of furniture, pottery and emptied sacks had been thrown into the street.

A few beggars were pawing through the items as they passed. Others were dragging away anything of value. Further along, a macabre sight greeted them, a burnt-out chariot with two blackened human corpses beside it. They rode on afterwards in silence.

The sound of a mob is unmistakable.

He'd heard that sound, that torrent of stampeding rage before, but still it took a moment to register. Then he looked around.

Behind them, approaching at a run, came a gang of beggars, the blood lust clear on their faces, cudgels and long knives in their hands.

"Ride, ride for your lives," he shouted.

They were almost within the mob's grasp. It wouldn't be often this rabble got such easy pickings inside the Subura.

Almost as one, they kicked their mounts into action. Only Juliana hesitated, staring back at the crowd as her horse ambled forward. Sybellina, who was near her, kicked her horse up beside Juliana's and grabbed the reins out of her hand. She pulled the surprised animal along as she kicked her own to go faster. Juliana looked startled for a moment, then leant forward and clutched her horse's neck.

They clattered down the rapidly darkening street, Constantine and Lucius urging them on, turning constantly to check no one had fallen back.

Soon the noise of the mob grew distant behind them. Constantine turned a corner, slowed, and looked back. His breath was coming fast and thick. No one had been lost. And the mob had disappeared, as if it had never existed. They cantered past a blackened guard house and out onto a wide avenue with people coming and going. Torches were burning outside tavernas. The city gates would be closing soon.

"Never race through the city. 'Tis an unhealthy sport," shouted a watchman from a window. Then he laughed, and the sound echoed after them.

They were out of the Subura.

The mob wouldn't dare follow them. But they didn't stop until they reached the city gate.

Thankfully the gate was still open and late travelers were streaming in and out, but the traders beside the gate were packing up and scavengers could be seen lurking in small groups.

Sybellina turned to Constantine and grinned, as if she'd been enjoying her ride. Lucius was talking to Juliana. She nodded, staring down at the cobbles. Tiny patted his horse. Its head was also down.

The knowledge of how close they'd all been to death sent a shiver through him. It had been some time since he'd felt so threatened. That was not the way he wanted to die, fighting desperate, half-starved Romans. Why had nothing been done about the Subura? He shook his head. Nicomedia was a safer city than this.

He waved at Lucius to come forward.

"Change of plan," he said. "We'll stay in a tavern near here. Try one of those." He pointed down a side street with a string of well-lit tavernas on it. "You make the booking. If they guess who I am, they'll double the rate."

Lucius nodded, kicked his horse forward.

The following morning, Constantine woke with a thumping headache. A battered jug stood by his bed. He poured some water into a wooden goblet and drank. Then he filled it again and drank some more.

Despite his headache, he felt good. He'd got away from Maxentius quickly. A fast departure for Gaul was all he could have hoped for.

And now the easiest part of their journey loomed. And for the first time, their destination felt near. Yes, he'd have to be careful about Sybellina, she was more than she seemed, but that might not be too unpleasant a task, exposing her secrets.

Aside from that his only other concern, one that annoyed him more every time he thought about it, was the role he would be given when he reached Gaul. Were the long ago promises his mother had made really going to stand up, now he was about to call them in?

Her promises had always eased his childhood fears. Over time he'd felt increasingly confident that her predictions of glory for her only son would come true. He'd seen blades miss him in battle, had felt spears and arrows fly by his head, and each time they did, each time he escaped some near-death experience, he'd hoped she was right, that he was being saved for greatness.

As he dressed he hummed an old pleb tune his mother had taught him. He couldn't remember many of the words, but he knew the feeling of optimism the tune evoked.

"Their traps are sprung,
Their spells are broken,
I have come to take what is mine."

A province, maybe two, waiting for him beyond these thinly plastered walls. His time approached. He could feel it.

"You're right. Maxentius probably does takes advantage of these riots," said Lucius, after the serving girl had gone to fetch more bread.

Lucius had been waiting for him in the taverna's courtyard. The place had no other guests up yet, so they were being well looked after.

Beyond the roofed area of the taverna's inner courtyard, a bright blue sky held all the promise of an early spring. A pair of sparrows sang from a cherry tree in the center of the courtyard, and boughs gemmed with buds arched over the trellised side of the eating area.

"I bet this lady knows," said Lucius, looking over Constantine's shoulder.

Constantine turned, and saw Sybellina approaching in a red woolen tunic that extended to her wrists and knees. The wool looked soft and had gold embroidered oak leaves on the shoulders, and on its edges, thin leather strips. On her feet were riding sandals.

She had a fur hat on too, which made her look like a cavalry scout or an officer from some private militia, though the color of her tunic and the newness of her hat made it obvious that her recent experiences did not include long, dusty campaigns. Her outfit did, however, make their own washed-out rusty red tunics seem suddenly older and sadder.

"Good morning. You slept well, I hope?" Her tone was cheerful.

He looked her up and down.

She stood still, as if daring him to comment on her appearance.

"I've read the omens for the journey, my lord. The goddess smiles on all of us. I saw a sign concerning you."

He'd heard that before. He stared up at her.

When she didn't get a response from him, she continued, "Are you really ready to go to Gaul?"

It sounded as if she was hurrying wayward schoolchildren. She crossed her arms.

After a moment, she left them.

Lucius watched her go. "I expect she'll want to check the size of your purse next." He made a gesture, as if weighing a bag of gold, or something else, in each hand.

"There's nothing a seer likes better than a big purse of gold," he said.

Constantine took another bite of the bread on his plate. It was soft and still warm. Just how he liked it. Lucius was probably quoting some verse from Juvenal or Ovid, but he wasn't going to take the bait.

"You like her, Lucius," he said.

"I think she is more your type, the difficult kind."

Constantine pointed at him. "But I bet she gets you first." Then he laughed. They took their time finishing breakfast.

When eventually they rode away from the taverna (the bill having taken longer to settle than he'd thought, Lucius had even threatened the poor owner) Sybellina maneuvered her horse up beside Constantine's. A long stretch of wide road ran ahead. Above them, a blanket of dirty gray clouds filled the sky.

"Have I offended you?" Her tone was all sweetness.

"No, Sybellina. But," he looked at her and frowned. "You should know. I take little notice of omens and I never pay for readings."

"You are a man who makes his own fate, my lord. I was not about to ask you to pay for some soothsaying services." She came closer to him. "But what about your dreams? Surely everyone needs their dreams interpreted?" She shook the braids of her hair out from under her hat.

"So, you'll be disappointed. We have help in that area already, but I'm sure we'll find some way to keep you busy on the journey."

She swung around, as if she'd felt someone staring at her, and stared at Juliana riding directly behind them. Her expression was unchanged when she looked back at Constantine.

"I must have had a hundred augers trying to tell me about some danger that only they can tell me about, if I ease their mind with gold," he said.

"My readings give only hope," she replied.

"I have no shortage of that." *And I know my purpose.*

"The spirits spoke to me about your destiny, my lord. But I see these things have no interest for you. Please, forget I mentioned it." She rewarded him with a warm smile, as if hoping he'd take an interest in his destiny, particularly with her.

"Sybellina." He shook his head. "What do you think would alarm me?"

She frowned.

"The truth, my lord. Are you sure you want to hear it?"

"I do," said Constantine with a hint of mockery.

Her expression became serious. "When I heard I must go with you, a purple cloud passed over the surface of the oils, my lord, shaped like a man. Built like you, but he had a laurel on his head and he held a club, like Hercules, but two snakes were entwined about his neck. They were strangling him." She leaned towards him.

"Danger looms for you, my lord."

"It always has." His horse bumped up close to hers. "Do you travel outside Rome often?"

"No." She shook her head. "This is my first journey in two years." She squeezed his arm and only released her grip when their horses parted.

"I hardly slept last night because of the excitement. Everyone thinks a priestess feels nothing." She pushed her hair behind her ear. "But the opposite is true." She sounded wary, as if she thought someone was listening to them.

"I apologize for the way I was forced on you, my lord. I hope you'll forgive me. There are only a few of us from the temple who travel, my lord. We do so to carry private messages for the emperors. Didn't your father tell you about us?"

He shook his head.

Then she told him about her childhood in Thrace. She touched his arm often and answered every question he asked with as much detail as he could want. As they rode on, she removed her hat and her hair fell around her neck. She was as beautiful as any woman he'd ever met.

They arrived at the Portus in the afternoon. Tiny and Juliana went with Lucius to collect what they'd left behind on his father's ship. Soon after, they were all on board the galley that would take them to Gaul.

Constantine and Lucius were allocated a small cabin, which they shared with the galley captain, who had given up his own quarters for Sybellina. Juliana and Tiny slept below deck.

Constantine woke the following morning to the sound of running feet and shouted orders.

Forbidding clouds stretched from horizon to horizon. Rain had swept in from the south during the night. The captain said they would leave at once. They could make good time and could shelter further along the coast if the weather worsened. The crew rowed the galley out past the mole and once they were clear of it, the captain ordered the mainsail unfurled. They picked up speed as the sail swelled, pulling them forward like a whipped horse.

As he looked back towards Rome he felt relieved.

"Why do so many people choose to live on top of each other like that?" he said to Lucius as they stood by the ship's rail.

"We prefer to flock together, rather than risk the wolves," said Lucius.

"Doesn't that just make the wolves' job easier?" said Constantine.

"Maybe, but there's safety in numbers," said Lucius.

The galley was one that Maxentius' father had previously used to transport high officials on tax gathering missions. To his annoyance, Constantine was welcomed with a horn blowing every time he went out on deck, and the ship's officers bowed whenever they encountered him.

Maxentius' father had loved such rituals, but after this had happened a few times, Constantine insisted there was no need for any of it. After that, the horn blowing was restricted to his first appearance on deck each day. Below deck, the rowers, all free men paid a good daily rate, sat near their oars waiting for when they would be needed. They played dice, told stories, mended rowlocks or plaited ropes while they waited.

Food was served to the passengers under a wide flapping canvas in front of the rear cabin. This was where Constantine, Lucius and Sybellina spent much of the voyage. The spring weather had brought warmer days, so it was the perfect place to while away the hours, amid piles of cushions in almost every fabric you could imagine.

"We will be in Massilia in a few nights if this wind holds, and Neptune is willing," said the captain. He'd joined Constantine and his other passengers under the canvas on the morning of the second day after they'd left the Portus.

"A quick journey will be welcome," said Constantine.

The captain grinned. "Your slave, Tiny, has been telling everyone about your escapade at the Straits with the galley. Rest easy, you'll not be overshadowed by any ship while you're on my vessel."

That night it rained so hard Constantine thought the ship would fill with water.

He woke in the middle of the storm, long before dawn. Outside, the rain beat down in waves, as if daemons were trying to break the ship apart. He sat up. Lucius turned in his sleep. The snores of the captain continued. They were anchored in a small bay and could do nothing else but ride out the storm.

"Go back to sleep, Constantine. It's only the rain." Lucius groaned, and rolled over.

"This is not like the rain in Bithynia, or Persia. This is rain from Gaul. I remember this rain." A pounding gust rattled the roof of their cabin.

"Rain is rain." Lucius pulled his blanket up nearer his chin. "Maybe a private session with your favorite seer is what you need."

Sybellina had been distant the past few days, as if she'd learnt all she wanted to know about him. She'd taken to sleeping in the captain's cabin during the day, which seemed to please Lucius.

"We'll have our pick of seers soon enough, Lucius." He listened to the rain.

"And as the commander of your father's legions, you'll be able to tell the rains to stop," said Lucius. He made a muffled snort of derision.

"If he places me in command of a cohort of raw recruits, I'll be happy. I'll be free to fight our enemies, that will be enough for me, and to Hades with the rain and all the seers who'd have us jumping at their every word."

"Well, we may end up swimming to Gaul. So, let's get some sleep while we can."

XXVIII

Treveris, 306 A.D.

Crocus took the small leather bag and held it to his chest. He bowed. The priest of Brigit stared at him, his eyes wide, as blue as the sky and rimmed with red. His hair hung in oily ringlets to his chest. His leather tunic was worn away in places, but the runes on it were still visible.

"This is our last message, Chief of the Alemanni. We have seen preparations for the arrival of the emperor's son. If our vision for the future does not become real, we will take action."

Crocus stepped back. His tent was warm and the smell coming off the priest was worse for it.

"Never threaten me, priest. Or I will cut your cock off and force it down your throat. You will go home in tears to your wives."

The priest shook his head. "My life or any part of my body are not important to me. Cut me and see." He held out his arm, pulled the sleeves of his tunic up. A multitude of scars crisscrossed across every part of his arm.

Crocus raised his fist. "Be gone. I know your message. Take this back to your masters. Tell them to wait with the patience of the eagle."

He pushed at the chest of the priest. But the priest stepped back and was gone through the flap before his hands could connect.

XXIX

Off Genua, in the Ligurian Sea, 306 A.D.

Juliana woke. Everything was darkness. Rain hissed. The ship creaked. Scuttling. The rats were busy. She'd blocked their way into her cubby hole, but it wouldn't be long before she'd feel their tails swish past her face again, like in the smaller ship.

She swept her hands around her body. Her limbs ached, as if they'd been stretched. It was hard going finding comfort on a coil of rope pressed up against a row of water jugs in a storage hole, while avoiding dripping rainwater. She held her breath. Listened. Something had woken her. Not the rats or the endless dripping or the rain or the rhythmic slopping of the water, something else.

Tap tap. Her breath sucked in fast. That was it. The noise. She pulled her tunic tight over her knees and prayed, hoping whoever or whatever it was would go away. Was this the moment she'd been dreading?

"Juliana." A soft voice, Sybellina's. "Open the hatch."

Perhaps she'd go away. Juliana hardly dared to breathe. So much had changed since Sybellina had joined them. Constantine rarely spoke to her these days. Lucius was always bad tempered. Rome had been bursting with faces, but they were menacing, marble-like. And she'd barely seen any of the city. And now there was the threat of Sybellina.

How was she supposed to treat this priestess? A shiver ran through her. Some of the older priestesses who visited their village had frightened her. They could turn any man's head, or a woman's, if that was what they wanted, and not only see the future, but create it.

Tap, tap. "Open the hatch, Juliana. I know you are in there."

Juliana felt for the water jugs and pulled aside the two she'd used to block the hatchway. Then she yanked at the door.

Sybellina's face appeared, illuminated by the glow of a small green glass oil lamp. A trickle of smoke swirled from the lamp as the flame swayed crazily, twisting Sybellina's smile. Behind her, the oarsmen slept. Above, the rain pounded.

"Come out, Juliana. This is no place for a woman. You'll sleep at the end of my bed. The oarsmen will be after you if you stay here. Unwilling slave girls slip overboard too easily on nights like this."

Juliana stared at Sybellina. She'd heard a few of the oarsmen joking as she crawled into her sleeping space that evening and feared the obvious lust in their laughter. The prospect of having to fight some of them off had been a worry she'd tried not to think about. Had she been wrong about Sybellina?

She crawled out of the cubby hole.

Sybellina's cabin had a cot bed of gleaming oak with an ivory headrest, pushed up tight against the far corner. A knee-high wooden table with piles of cushions around it took up most of the rest of the free space. An animal scent of musk hung in the air.

"Before you sleep, I need your help." Sybellina handed Juliana a linen cloth to dry herself.

Sybellina put a finger to her lips, knelt in front of the table and patted the carpet beside her. She shook her head, disappointed when Juliana didn't sit immediately. Then, with elaborate care, she lit the fat candle squatting at the center of the table. Shadows swayed across the walls as draughts pressed in from the wind groaning outside. The rain beat down on the planking above their heads in violent waves.

Sybellina patted the carpet beside her again. This time Juliana knelt by her side.

She'd helped many times before with supplications to the spirits. She knew what was expected, to witness Sybellina's prayers.

"I know all about you, Juliana," said Sybellina. She sounded like an old friend imparting some long thought about insight. "Did you know I was a slave once too? I know the hundred humiliations you suffer every day. You must let me help you." She reached out a hand and stroked Juliana's bare forearm, as if her skin was silk.

Something came bubbling up, unbidden, from inside Juliana's chest. No one ever spoke to her kindly anymore. Slaves like her had to accept, not feel.

Juliana bowed her head. Sybellina wrapped an arm around her.

When she looked up, a set of small amber rings had been placed in a tight circle around the candle. Sybellina touched her finger to her lips, as if to stop her speaking. Then she placed a finger on each ring in turn. When she spoke, she sounded like a kindly teacher.

"This is the ring of earth, Juliana, and these are the rings of air, and water, and fire." She stared at Juliana, as if assessing her.

"Each of these rings has a story to tell. Tonight, they witness that I have taken a new sister." She held out her hand. "Give me your hand, Juliana."

Sybellina took Juliana's upraised hand. She guided the middle finger from ring to ring, as she uttered their names again.

"These are sacred rings. The rings of remembrance. See." She held one up. Juliana could see Greek lettering etched into it. "Each letter of each word on each ring represents something. That is how we remember the wisdom handed down. As one of our sisters, you'll be taught what each of these powerful, magical words mean. Would you like that?" She looked expectantly at Juliana.

Could she refuse?

"But first," said Sybellina. "I need your help. A simple token of our new kinship." She shrugged her shoulders, as if a refusal of something so small would be most unlikely.

Juliana shifted position. She had been initiated by her birth mother into the house of heaven when she was only seven years old. She knew it was expected that she would not tie herself to another rite. The things she had been taught, to see the past in dreams, to see spirits, and unlock what they wanted to say, and the pleasures of the divine marriage, might all be lost, if she swore allegiance to another path.

Sybellina leaned forward. For a long moment Juliana thought she was going to be kissed. She didn't move. She just stared, mesmerized. Sybellina's lips were opening wide. Her tongue licked at the air between them. She leaned forward again. The top of her tunic was open, letting Juliana see the mounds of her breasts moving as she breathed. Juliana looked away. Then back again. Sybellina was beautiful.

The moment extended, as if time no longer followed its predictable course. Shadows moved, as if they were leaning forward, eavesdropping.

"Juliana." Sybellina shook her brown tresses out. "Tell me the last recent dream reading you have done, and everything you wish for will be yours to enjoy." She gestured grandly, indicating her body and the rings on the table.

Juliana's unease churned like a pit of queasiness inside her. An image of Constantine listening attentively to her dream reading came back to her, as it had done almost every day since he'd told her his dream.

"Please, you must ask me something else, mistress." She squeezed Sybellina's hand. Her own felt clammy.

"No, you must tell me this. This is what I want to know." Sybellina's hands flew like birds fluttering in the air.

"It is easily done, surely. I know you dream readers take oaths, but you can reveal your readings to the great mother without breaking any oath, trust me. We are both from the house of heaven."

Juliana leaned back. One voice inside her head tugged at her. *Tell Sybellina. Tell her what she wants. You must. Look at all she has to offer.*

"How can we be sisters, if you'll give up nothing?" Sybellina's tone had turned quarrelsome, as if she had been injured. She pressed a hand to her forehead. Her other made a fist in the air as if she was in pain.

Juliana wanted to help. But he'd find out. And he would never trust her again.

"I've already revealed my deepest secrets to you," said Sybellina. "You must tell me what he said to you. Our pact has been sealed, witnessed by the rings. Tell me quickly. I will not tell anyone. I swear it."

Juliana's determination slipped. How could she refuse?

194

An avalanche of rain hit the roof. The walls of the cabin creaked. Outside, she would be soaked. In here she would be safe, like she used to feel in her mother's house, when the mid-year storms broke.

But what about Constantine? He could be awake, nearby, listening. Suddenly, the cabin felt small and oppressive, pressing in on her.

"I must go, mistress." She tried to stand. But her legs were someone else's. They swayed under her. Sweat slipped down her neck, between her breasts, and ran freely over her body. A compelling urge to hug Sybellina gripped her.

Sybellina's face looked pale in the candlelight, ghostly, as if some spirit inside her had revealed itself.

Juliana swayed.

A look of contempt twisted Sybellina's face. She reached under the table and retrieved a long gold needle with a hook at its end. She placed it on the table in front of her. The candle swayed, bringing life to the shadows.

"You are with child, yes. From him."

Juliana's mouth opened. Had Sybellina been reading her mind?

"No, I am not," she said. Drawing on the last of her strength she staggered back towards the door. Sybellina's face contorted.

"The wombs of all our sisters belong to the great mother. You will tell me what I seek, or your firstborn will be forfeit." She lifted the needle and pointed it at Juliana. "This is your choice, not mine."

Juliana stumbled back again. Sybellina came towards her slowly, like a cat.

"No one stands against me. It is written so in all the sacred books."

Juliana felt the door behind her, the large wooden handle in the small of her back. She turned, opened the door and darted out into the rain. She could be beaten for this. But she didn't care. Almost every memory of her real mother had faded over the years. But one thing she held onto. To trust the voices inside her when they warned her. She could not betray them.

She gulped as rain splattered her face. The warmth of Sybellina's cabin pulled at her, sucking her back, telling her she'd made the wrong choice. She pictured her tormentor waiting with open arms. Then she saw the needle in her hand.

The canvas awning that protected the rowing area trembled above her head from a thousand jumping raindrops. Gusts of rain drove in on each side. She ran down the narrow central passage to the entrance to the crew's quarters and her cubbyhole, and there she turned back. A shudder ran through her body.

The doorway to Sybellina's cabin, at the far end of the galley, was open. She was standing in the doorway totally naked, the curved outline of her body clearly visible, silhouetted by candlelight. She looked like a statue of a goddess with her hands raised. Whether she was enticing Juliana, or threatening her, she couldn't tell.

A high-pitched wail echoed through the rain, as if far out at sea a spirit had announced some ghastly premonition.

Juliana fled. When she reached her cubbyhole, she blocked the hatch behind her and lay down shivering. Friendship with someone like Sybellina had been an enticing thought. Rejecting her might be truly dangerous. Her cheeks tingled as she steadied her breathing. She should have known talking with Constantine would end up this way. She had to stay away from him. That would be what Sybellina was most concerned about. Her competition. She trembled at the thought of what Sybellina might do next. Then she pushed another water jug against the hatch door.

It took a long time for the trembling to end. She thought of jumping overboard, sinking to the bottom, embracing the cold water, and a final escape. She'd heard many times about slaves who'd killed themselves. The show of consideration Sybellina had displayed, as she'd taken her to her cabin, and the way it had been snatched away, had made her even more aware of her loneliness on the ship. But she'd been right not to tell Sybellina anything.

When she woke, the rain was only a memory and the sea, like a mirror, dazzled her, reflecting the early morning sun. The air smelled salt drenched, refreshing. Soft swells travelled across it like ripples blown across a bowl of molten silver. The sailing would be good today. She heard her name. The cook was waiting. Oarsmen milled around, staring at her. She could hardly see the far end of the galley, there were so many men about. Staying clear of the grabbing hands and the cocks a few of the oarsmen wanted to show her, kept her on deck and away from dark places where a man could grab her and smother her screams.

She ate almost nothing that day, as she waited to be summoned by Sybellina. But she wasn't, and that evening they dropped anchor by a long sandy beach, which stretched as far as you could see in each direction. The hiss of the breakers and the sway of the galley as she rocked at anchor soothed her as she helped the cook. She'd managed to avoid even speaking to Sybellina up to this moment, but now she had to serve the evening meal.

The only thing that happened though, when she brought them the main course, was that Sybellina said in a haughty manner, "Have you been hiding, girl?" as Juliana ladled out the fish stew.

She replied that she'd been working, grabbed some dirty dishes, and sped off with Sybellina's gloating eyes on her. Juliana looked back when she reached the steep stairs to the lower deck. Sybellina leaned back on her cushions, her arms outstretched, one hand close to Constantine's bare elbow, almost touching him.

She looked serene, a goddess whose life could never be touched by ordinary difficulties. Juliana thought Constantine might have said something, called her back, but he hadn't. He'd been gazing only at Sybellina. She had won him in a few days. Some people who deserved nothing were truly blessed by the gods. If only there was a way to turn such luck around.

Pleading illness, a sick stomach, she escaped soon after to her cubbyhole and listened to the sound of the sea slapping against the beards of seaweed along the side of the galley. Occasionally, peals of Sybellina's laughter came drifting down to her and as it did she started hating them all. Then she grew angry. She had been saved for a reason. She should have been dead already. This was what everybody told her. The spirits wanted her alive. They needed her for something. She would survive to see what that something was.

A memory of the needle Sybellina had shown her kept coming back to her, and a question; why had Sybellina asked about her dream reading? There could only be one answer.

Constantine must have said something to her. He must have. Juliana closed her eyes, imagined him talking about her. Perhaps he'd said she'd helped him, or that he valued her reading. Yes, it had to be something like that. Sybellina had become jealous. And she might still be. You had to expect anything from a jealous mistress. She checked the water jugs were tight against the door and then curled up tight with her back against them.

It took several days before her mind eased. In the meantime, she stayed away from Sybellina, who looked at her knowingly and contemptuously whenever she came near, as if she knew her every thought.

They arrived at Massilia in the morning, during the second hour past sunrise four days later, one day after she started eating properly again. Sleepless nights waiting for another knock on her door had not helped.

The city looked like a wall painting reflected in the blue-green sea as they rowed towards it into a light breeze. Tall apartment buildings shimmered yellow and pale pink in the air beyond the cliff of an old salt-whitened mole, as seagulls banked and dived, calling to each other. She squinted, trying to get some inkling about what Gaul might be like. But Massilia looked like every other Roman port, as far as she could see.

The talk among the oarsmen that morning had been about how different the people were in Gaul. How they'd still be hanging the heads of their enemies by their front doors if Rome hadn't civilized them, and how after all the work of a dozen well-meaning emperors, a Gaul's moustache still dripped with grease and gravy.

Relief flowed through her now the voyage was over. She could smell the city, faint at first, the occasional whiff of horse shit and dust, but soon she could smell flowers and people, though surely that was impossible.

As they waited to dock, she scanned the slaves scurrying about on the mole. Not one had a beard. Then she overheard Sybellina telling Constantine and Lucius that they must stay with a military Tribune she knew in the town. They could get the best supplies from him for the journey north, she insisted, when Lucius questioned the suggestion.

Lucius was silenced when Sybellina asked what his alternative was. Juliana had considered telling Lucius what had happened during her visit to Sybellina's cabin, but she'd quickly discarded the idea. Slaves are the master's possessions, and who wants a possession that attracts trouble, her foster mother had warned her. And every experience since had proven her foster mother right.

When everything was ready, they were saluted off the ship with great ceremony and escorted to the stables at the end of the dock. Juliana's bundle was light enough to be carried in one hand, but two oarsmen were needed to carry Sybellina's soft leather bags. She seemed to have accumulated even more since they'd ridden down from Rome. Perhaps the captain had been generous to her.

After their horses were saddled, and Lucius and Sybellina had haggled over them, the stablemaster warned them about refugees attempting to flee the city. "Do not speak to any of the foolish beggars waiting beyond the gate. Not one," he said. "It only encourages them. It's as if we're in a war posting these days with all the refugees that come crying through here." He spat on the ground and walked back into his shadowed stables.

As they passed through the dock gates they were confronted by a crowd of desperate looking people pressing forward, pleading for news and alms. The galley captain had given them an escort of four oarsmen to guard them to the Tribune's house. When the oarsmen pulled cudgels, the crowd parted, though they pressed in again as soon as the horses had passed and Juliana, who was riding with Tiny at the rear of the party, received pleading hands on both sides.

"What ship did you come on, mistress, please, will it be taking on passengers?" a voice cried out. Juliana wondered what could have made these people so frantic. The only time she'd seen similar scenes was during the Christian persecutions two years before.

Their arrival in Gaul had not passed as she'd expected.

And then she saw Sybellina and Tiny whispering together behind Constantine's back and a sudden and awful foreboding almost overcame her. They were planning something. Tiny hardly spoke to her these days and she'd stopped worrying about him. That had clearly been a mistake. He'd been so amiable recently, but the look on his face now reminded her of how he'd looked just before he'd attacked her.

She thought about riding up to Constantine and warning him. And then it came to her. She knew what she had to do. It was simply a matter of waiting for the right moment.

XXX

Massilia, Southern Gaul, 306 A.D.

"Too long I've waited," Constantine shouted, to no one in particular, as soon as they'd left the mob at the gate behind.

"Too many years I've wasted. The air is sweet here, isn't it?" Constantine slowed his horse and looked around. Sybellina put one hand on her hips, and, looking round for an audience, mimicked his little speech. Tiny, who rode right behind her, giggled.

Constantine wasn't sure how he should react. He shook his head and scowled at her. Then he saw her pout, and he laughed. There were a few nagging doubts, but there was no escaping the sensation of freedom, the feeling that his bonds had been lifted as soon as he'd arrived in Gaul. He'd escaped Galerius. Nothing could change that.

He didn't expect a proper welcome until he met his father in the far north. What mattered was that he was free. All Lucius' stupid talk about Maxentius' galley captain being treacherous was just that, talk. His concerns had vanished like the darkness vanishes when a hundred lamps are lit. He looked at the puffs of sun-tinged clouds racing across the blue spring sky and savored the moment. He'd waited years for this. Too many years.

He turned and looked back at the dock gates. No one was coming after them. His time was coming, exactly as had been predicted.

"Come, my lord, the Tribune of the 5th has a private bath, and a cellar bursting with the best wines in the whole province," said Sybellina. "He was posted here after serving on the Germania frontier. You'll like him." She held out her hand. He took it. She grinned at him, then looked away shyly. He let her fingers slip through his and wondered what it would be like with her, what tricks she would show him.

Lucius interrupted his thoughts.

"I hope his bath girls are as good as the ones in the east. You liked my father's, didn't you, Constantine?" He slapped Constantine's back.

Constantine nodded, remembering one bath girl in particular. She'd spent most of the time giggling. Her skill with the bath oils had been remarkable. Yes, he was looking forward to the comforts of land: cooked food, steady ground, pliable bath girls.

Young children playing ball in the road stopped to stare at them as they passed. He bowed slightly at a little girl with a ribbon in her hair. She stuck her tongue out at him.

Tall three and four floor apartment blocks with taverns and merchants' shops along their ground floor colonnades lined the narrow streets. Nearly every shop was closed. They passed an empty circus arena. After that the road widened and a little way beyond they came to the Via Narbo, where the Tribune lived. Soon he could relax.

The Tribune Marcus greeted them warily in the small courtyard of his villa. He was a sturdy middle-aged man with a nut-hard face and small, nervous eyes.

"Your arrival couldn't have come at a better time, my lord. It's as if the gods themselves have arranged it," said Marcus, as soon as he found out who Constantine was.

"Double bar the gates," he shouted at some slaves standing nearby. His eyes kept darting past Constantine as he fired questions at him. He even looked wistful when the galley oarsmen left to hurry back to the port.

"Did you see a mob at the port?"

Constantine nodded.

"Were the taverns closed on the road by the Circus?"

"Yes."

"It gets worse, just as I expected." Marcus turned and walked into the villa, gesturing for them to follow.

Tiny had been charged by Lucius to look after the horses, Juliana the baggage. She looks disappointed, thought Constantine as they hurried after Marcus. He shook his head. Sybellina had been warning him about the dangers of getting too close to slaves, how they couldn't be trusted.

He followed Marcus through the villa to two marble benches set in the corner of a small vine-trellised inner courtyard. There they sat and listened to Marcus' story under a tile edged square of blue sky. The smell of meat cooking wafted through the courtyard. Sybellina sat at the edge of one bench, he and Lucius on another. The mosaic under their feet was cracked and faded, bleached by the sun.

"I used my auxiliaries to suppress rioting yesterday," said Marcus. "Ten people died."

He waved away a slave serving goblets of wine. The man handed the last one to Lucius and bowed politely. Marcus walked towards him and balled both fists. He looked pale. The slave ran.

"One of the people who died was my wife's brother. And all thanks to our beloved governor. He demands too many bribes. Bribes beyond reason, my lord. And when he can't collect, he places extra taxes on all our tradespeople."

Sybellina tutted.

"Three days ago, a group of respectable merchants were arrested on their way to his palace to present a petition. They will be sold as slaves, he tells me. And what is their crime? Enquiring politely about the disappearance of their daughters and the progress of the investigation our governor promised. Ten young girls have disappeared. Stories are going around about strange practices at his palace. For the love of the gods, Constantine, we must do something."

"I don't know if I can help," said Constantine. He'd dealt with petitioners appealing against injustice before. Mostly all he'd been able to do was sound sympathetic and send them on their way. Some of them had clearly been exaggerating their woes, but there had been some, like Marcus, who had been instantly believable. If what he said was true, his father would surely want to know about it. He was in one of his father's provinces. He should be able to do something for a petitioner here.

Marcus paced up and down.

"My lord. You could go to governor Martinianus and press him to free these people. You are their last chance. The whole town will revolt if this is not settled well, like Narbonne did last year. That place has still not recovered."

Then, with a weary sigh, he went down on one knee in front of Constantine. He looked embarrassed, as if he sensed his pleading would be in vain.

"Up, Marcus, get up. I have no status here." Not officially anyway, he thought, but perhaps Marcus was right, as the emperor's son his voice should have some influence. Marcus eased himself to his feet.

"Have you sent messengers to my father?" said Constantine. "A trial to remove a governor requires evidence. Do you have such evidence? And who will pay the expense of the trial?"

"We've sent messengers, my lord. I believe your father is recruiting in Germania, so it'll be many days before he even hears of all this. And there'll be no trial, my lord. It'd be years before the case came up, and by then all this will be history." Marcus sounded defeated.

"I know your father. I'm sure he wouldn't approve of what's happening here, but we have partly independent status in Massilia, as one of the oldest protectorates of Rome. That means the governor can only be removed for acts of treason." His eyes brightened, as if he'd just thought of something.

"But if you intervened, my lord, before these people are sold, he may delay things. That will allow time for your father to reply."

It didn't seem too much to ask for. He should help these people.

"You win, Marcus. I'll petition the governor for you, but you must come with me, to give evidence."

Marcus stepped back. "My wife, my son, my baby daughter, they are all here with me, my lord." He looked around, as if he'd suddenly become concerned that someone might be listening, or that he'd been talking too loudly. Constantine remembered the sound of a baby crying he'd heard as they'd passed down the corridor from the outer courtyard.

"Without me they have nothing, my lord. I cannot be the one to give evidence." Desperation flickered over Marcus' face.

"But without evidence, a witness, I can do nothing, Marcus. He can simply deny it all, provide some explanation." Constantine shrugged. If Marcus wanted him to do something he would have to come with him.

Marcus looked from Lucius to Sybellina as if for help.

"Constantine is right," she said, softly.

Marcus licked his lips then looked down at the ground. His expression had changed, hardened. He nodded.

Lucius and Sybellina said they would both come with him. For a moment Constantine thought they were competing. He'd seen people do that around him before, but never Lucius. Or perhaps he just hadn't noticed him doing it before. Where would it all lead to? That was the question.

"You can't have all the fun, my lord," said Sybellina. "I've met this Martinianus. I'm sure you will get justice from him." She smiled seductively.

She is totally shameless.

"Perhaps this is none of our business," Lucius whispered as they mounted their horses.

Constantine shook his head as if throwing off a fly.

"Would you have me run from my responsibilities?"

Lucius didn't answer.

They were accompanied by Juliana and Tiny, even though it was only a short distance to the governor's palace. Arriving without slaves would, he knew, have been simply an announcement of powerlessness.

At the governor's palace, a troop of guards in full armor stood in line by the gate. Constantine showed the bronze pass Galerius had given him. They were allowed inside, while someone went to announce his arrival. Tiny and some of the governor's grooms took away their horses to be watered.

Then they were ushered to an iron grill gate set deep in the red brick wall that bounded the cobbled courtyard. The gate creaked loudly when it opened. Beyond it, an official in an immaculate toga shifted from one foot to the other. His eyes widened, and he stared at Constantine for a moment. Then he bowed.

"My Lord Constantine. You are most welcome, most welcome. The governor is finishing some urgent business. He asked me to escort you to his private garden. Please, if you will, my lord, follow me." He bowed again, deeper this time.

He took them down a path sentried by tall cedars, while his formal white toga flapped behind him. The scent of earth filled the air, as if the gardens were still being worked on. The path led down to a small pillared temple set in the bend of a wide and sunnily sparkling stream. A lemony odor spiced the air here.

"The governor has the garden of an emperor," said Sybellina.

The temple was dedicated to Apollo, the god of light. In place of windows there were mosaics of Apollo as an archer, a prophet, a father and a doctor, all with circlets of gold about his head.

A group of white marble benches were clustered in a semi-circle in front of the temple. Slave girls could be seen hurrying down the path towards them as they sat. When the girls arrived, they put pine kernels soaked in chrism to smolder in a nearby brazier and distributed jugs of clear Numentian wine in silvered goblets. It was mid-afternoon now, but the sun still felt warm in this idyllic spot.

The slave girls went away, but returned with figs, walnuts, olives and cheeses on silver platters. Juliana stood behind Lucius, helping to serve. Constantine ate almost nothing and drank just enough to taste the wine. As time passed, he remembered how he hated being kept waiting.

Some of the slave girls tried valiantly to distract him. They hovered, brushing up against him as they attempted to press more wine on him, or offer him some delicacy.

"Do you not like any of these beautiful spiders, Constantine?" asked Sybellina. He shook his head.

"I've had enough," he said. He hadn't come to Gaul for this.

He stood, adjusted his tunic, turned to a slave nearby who looked as if he was monitoring things, and said in a loud voice, "I must see the governor straight away. Go and tell him that."

Shock flushed across the slave's face. Guests waited until they were called.

The slave scurried away. Soon afterwards the official who'd brought them to the temple came racing down the path.

"Good news," he announced breathlessly. "The governor will see you, my lord. Your friends will wait here. I will escort you to him at once." He sounded apologetic and bowed even lower than before when he'd finished.

Constantine looked at his companions. Marcus, who had sat down beside him, looked concerned.

He followed the man through a side door in the main building and down a long corridor that echoed with waves of chatter from what must have been a large group of people somewhere ahead. They turned a corner and entered a wide high-ceilinged hall. It was crowded with people; provincial officials in smart togas, military officers in shiny breastplates, and locals in tunics of every color and style, all staring curiously at him. Then, as if on cue, everyone bowed. He grinned and shook his head, gesturing vigorously for everybody to rise. They did.

The official led him towards the far end of the room where a crowd parted like wheat before a scythe as they approached. One man stood like a rock facing him. The man was tall and fat. His flesh oozed like a roll of dough from his toga. He rubbed his shiny bald head as Constantine approached. The man's toga was edged with the wide purple brocade of a senior official.

He was also one of the last to bow, his right hand tapping at his chest only lightly.

"I am your humble governor of this your father's most loyal province. Welcome to our simple villa. You must be tired after your long journey. My household is at your disposal, for whatever you desire." He grinned. "Will you be travelling on soon, to Treveris? You must consider my stables your own, of course."

"Yes, very soon, governor. Good horses will be appreciated." Constantine looked around. "Can we discuss something in private?"

The governor led him through the crowd onto a wide, empty veranda with a view of the distant silvery sea. He looked concerned as he beckoned Constantine to a far corner. The sun dipped low, and the far-off hills had mist on them, like a purple shroud.

"How can I help you, Constantine? I'm a good friend of your beloved father. I live only to help the imperial family, if I can." He raised his eyebrows, face bulging for a moment like an overripe, slightly spoiled cherry.

Constantine looked around. No one had followed them.

"I have brought with me a Tribune. A man named Marcus," he said, gesturing towards the garden.

A look passed over the governor's face as if he'd eaten something rotten.

"He tells me you are holding a delegation from the town."

The governor jutted his chin forward so much his face looked misshapen.

"Their families are in fear, ill-founded I'm sure, that their husbands and brothers are to be sold into slavery." Constantine stepped closer to the governor.

"Marcus tells me there is every prospect of a revolt because of all this. Can we not do something for these people, governor, something to disprove these wild stories?"

"I have done nothing wrong. I informed your father of multiple threats to my person." The governor looked disdainful now, as if bored.

"Your father knows we have had many dangerous escaped slaves roaming this province for over a year. They have caused all manner of problems. Your father is aware of this. The group you speak of, they are connected with these rebels. I have evidence their daughters ran away to be with them." He threw his hands up.

"Every supporter of these rebels will be sold into slavery," he continued. "We must stand firm. Any monies raised will help recover the unpaid taxes from the estates that were ravaged last year. It will set a good example. You know all about that from your father, I'm sure. We must rule with a firm hand, Constantine. Your father always agrees with me on these things."

"Does he?" said Constantine. The governor was as slippery as any he'd met. Had he jumped into this too quickly?

208

"It is our way. Even the great Dio attacked clemency." The governor patted Constantine's shoulder.

His tone was one of patient instruction now, as if he was working hard to teach some young boy the facts of life. For Constantine, the tone infuriated. Perhaps deliberately so.

"I must enforce the tax gathering rigorously, my lord, or we'll have no empire to govern." He waved his hands higher in the air this time. Then he grinned, like a pig at the trough distracted momentarily, showing his small milky teeth.

"But there are benefits to this little rebellion, my lord. The property of the rebels is forfeit to the empire. I am holding an auction today of all the confiscated properties." He looked towards the high double doors.

"The new owners must pay all the overdue taxes, of course. So, the state will benefit, twice." His eyes bulged with glee. "I had set aside a villa near the port for your father, but now that you are here, one might be set aside for you as well." He looked enquiringly at Constantine.

"I have a witness who claims many of these people are innocent." Constantine had seen the same thing before. Officials who assumed everyone could be bought. This man's type were the bane of the empire. How could his father permit all this?

"You haven't been fooled by that traitor Marcus, have you?" The governor sounded amused, then angry. "You know he's been supporting the rebels who want to overthrow the peace of this city?"

"Why not let this man's testimony be publicly recorded, then a judgment be made?" said Constantine.

If he agreed to a public hearing, the governor would have to prove his allegations. If he was making them up, he would be reluctant. He might even bend now and compromise.

"But, of course Constantine, and as a first step let us have this witness brought before us." He raised his hand. A shaven-headed official who'd been standing by the doors ran to him. The governor whispered something to the man. He went away in a great hurry.

"Your father greatly appreciated my support in his early days, but please, let us wait for this witness to come. We will listen to what he has to say." The governor sounded unperturbed.

Both men gazed towards the sea, lost in their own thoughts. Then a commotion sounded from the garden they were overlooking, off to the side, loud exclamations, the slapping sound of someone running. A centurion in full armor ran up a side step onto the veranda.

XXXI

Off the coast of Leptis Magna, the southern shore of Mare Nostrum, 306 A.D.

A soft breeze blew from the south over a perfect sea, creating a pattern of widely spaced ripples. Soon their ship could head north across the Mare Nostrum to Sicilia. The galley had first been spotted by the look out. The Egyptian captain claimed he was well used to being boarded by Roman galleys operating out of Leptis Magna, searching for pirates, so no alarm cry went out when the galley, powered by three lines of rowers, headed towards them.

Their sail came down, and they drifted as Helena and Hosius came out of the small cabin at the rear of the ship and waited with the captain.

"Ready yourself for boarding," shouted a bearded sailor towards them as the galley neared. Helena knew there was probably nothing to fear, but there was always a chance that a galley captain would try to extract some toll from her. Then all the oars left the water and stayed upright. The galley captain timed the slowdown in his ship's pace so precisely, the galley drifted towards them at the moment they came closest together.

A thick and hairy hemp line snaked through the air. One of the Egyptian crewmen used a hook to retrieve it from the water nearby. He secured it to a rusty iron ring on that side of the Egyptian vessel.

"We have a passenger from the imperial family," the captain shouted up.

Heads appeared above them.

"I hope they don't delay us. I have business in Rome, captain." Helena looked regal in the tunic she had put on before coming out on

211

deck. It went down to below her knee, and was made of soft dark-blue wool, and the purple edging and pearls around its neckline made it clear the wearer was a patrician of the highest quality.

Hosius stood quietly at her side. She could tell he had never seen a Roman war galley of this size before at such close quarters. He stared up at the line of shields above the oar ports, and the pennants that bristled above the shields.

A cracking noise sounded from the galley above them. A part of the galley wall, up near the shields, swung open. Two men with black breastplates looked down at them.

"Hold fast," one of the men shouted. A rope ladder descended towards them. The crewman who had secured the line from the galley grabbed the ladder and, with the help of another crewman, held it lightly, letting it slip between their fingers as the men above descended and the ladder swayed in the air.

It was obvious these men were used to boarding ships. They didn't hesitate in their downward journey and a few feet from their objective they dropped with a clatter onto the deck.

The captain saluted, banging his chest and then shooting his arm out. He walked towards the men, speaking quickly as he did so.

"We are come from Alexandria. We have grain for Rome and two important passengers. Do not delay us."

The men pushed past him, ignoring the captain. Short swords dangled from the men's belts. The dark greaves on their lower legs and their shoulder plates were angled to deflect sword blows. These men were not here to simply inspect.

Helena stiffened. She took a step back, towards Hosius.

"What do you want with us?" said Hosius as the men approached. Each had a grim expression on a sun-darkened face.

Without warning, both men pulled their swords. One held the tip towards Hosius. The other swung his sword around and turned, looking for any opposition to what they were about to do.

A clattering noise sounded from further down the ship. More similarly clad men were dropping onto the deck. The captain's hands were in the air now, as were the hands of every crewman. No one would resist.

212

"What do you want from us?" Hosius' voice sounded shrill as he repeated his question.

In response, the man nearest him raised his sword, turned it, so the pommel faced Hosius, and with a practiced movement stepped closer and smashed the pommel into Hosius' eye.

His scream ripped through the air. It didn't end as the man grabbed Helena and dragged her towards the rope ladder.

Helena, almost overwhelmed by the suddenness, started struggling, slapping at the man dragging her. But then there were three men holding her and she was unable to move any more than twisting in their arms. Every muscle trembled now as the reality sunk in. But she did not scream.

The captain and the crew still had their hands up high in the air.

"Where are you taking me?" she said, her tone bitter and angry.

Behind her, Hosius screamed. Other men from the galley were standing near the rope ladder. Without a word, they grabbed Helena. Her hands were tied above her head.

As Helena was hoisted up to the deck of the galley, she looked back down. Hosius' screams had become even more high pitched. She saw why. Her chest tightened, and she screamed. Hosius was pushing his eyeball back into its broken socket, while around it a mass of bubbling blood and broken white bone glistened.

XXXII

Massilia, 306 A.D.

"Hail, governor," said the centurion, breathlessly. "It's the Tribune Marcus. He's taken his life. We could do nothing."

Stunned, Constantine addressed the man.

"Centurion, I'm the son of your emperor. Take me to the Tribune at once." He felt angry, sickeningly foolish. He should have expected something like this, should have known that his involvement could make things worse.

He felt powerless, exactly as he had when he'd first gone to the east and he'd learnt that his every movement would be restricted. But that wasn't him anymore. He was free now, not a prisoner. Anger rose inside him fast.

The governor shook his head in a mockery of grief.

Constantine wanted to strike him down, crush him. He balled his fists and wiped one across his mouth as if forcing it shut.

The centurion led them to a trellised kitchen garden beyond the far corner of the building. Ahead, beside a wooden bench, not where he'd left him, lay Marcus face up, a slick puddle of blood staining all around him, a wide gash across his throat making the puddle bigger by the moment. A dagger lay across Marcus' outstretched palm. Two slaves stood nearby, looking dumbstruck.

Constantine bent down and placed his ear by Marcus' wide-open mouth. He pulled away after a few moments. No one ever cut their own throat. He remembered how close he'd been to taking his own life. It had never occurred to him to cut his throat. Marcus hadn't killed himself. This governor had killed him. This evil son of a greedy half-mule whore.

"It does look as if he took his own life," the governor's voice trilled.

"That knife looks blood stained. This is better than continuing to tell a pack of lies. An honorable decision really, don't you think?"

Constantine turned. The governor was standing right behind him. He looked pleased.

He'd been manipulated from the moment he'd arrived. All that waiting, and for what? He would not be so naïve again.

Someday, he'd be able to dispense justice as it should be done. That day, he'd avenge Marcus. He touched Marcus' cheek. "I swear it," he whispered.

"Constantine, please, come away. We'll have this rebel's body impaled on the road out of town. He tricked you, you can be sure of that. But I don't blame you, he's of a most persuasive type. I even trusted him myself, once." He rested a hand on Constantine's shoulder.

"Suicide is ample proof of lying." He squeezed Constantine's shoulder, then released him, turned and walked away.

Constantine looked around. The governor's guards were nowhere to be seen. He'd forgotten to call them after him, in his eagerness to gloat. The two slaves were staring at Constantine, as if they knew what had really happened, and were wondering if he was going to do anything about it. Tiny flies were already flitting around the blood at his feet.

"Come, Constantine, we have a feast waiting," the governor called out, his voice becoming distant, as if he wanted to get away from the body quickly. "After you've bathed you'll feel much better. It always helps me forget things," he prattled on.

Constantine grabbed the dagger from Marcus' open hand. He raced after the governor. The two slaves, who might have stopped him, leaned away as he passed. They must have seen the grim look on his face. Inside he seethed. He could not let this go.

The governor was about to enter the house through a small side door when Constantine caught up with him. The man's hand was already stretched out to grab the iron handle.

With one expert movement, Constantine gripped the back of the governor's neck, and jerked him forward so that his head banged into the door. Then he pushed the point of the knife into the man's side, angling upwards at a pressure he knew would break the skin but not go in too far.

"Do not shout, my friend. Do what I say, or there'll be more than one suicide today." He twisted the knife in a way that was bound to be painful.

The governor yelped.

"You will bury Marcus as a hero. You will grant his widow and children their home and give them his proper pension. Do you consent to my small petition?" Constantine gripped the man's neck even tighter, looking around. The slaves had gone.

"Of course, of course, please stop. I didn't know he meant so much to you. Please." The governor's tone was nicely high-pitched, as it should be, and shaky. He clearly hadn't been physically threatened in a long time. He tried to squirm away from the knifepoint.

Constantine squeezed the governor's neck again. Silk-soft folds of flesh squished through his drill-hardened fingers. The bowel loosening stench of fear flowed.

"And if I hear you've gone back on your word, I swear to all the gods I will return to finish this job. Now." He jabbed the knife in a little more.

"We feast tonight as if nothing happened here, and I will leave tomorrow, and you will keep your word." He removed the point of the knife and slapped a hand on the governor's shoulder amiably. As the governor visibly relaxed, he grinned at him as if it had all been a big game. Then he sniffed. The governor stood in a puddle of urine. Constantine walked away and didn't look back.

He found Lucius and Sybellina sitting alone in silence in a walled courtyard at the far end of the palace compound. Lucius groaned as if wounded, stood, and paced up and down when he heard what had happened.

"When the messenger came for him he looked ashen. I should have guessed," said Lucius. He cursed the governor over and over and began laughing.

"What's so funny?" said Constantine.

"We misjudged Marcus. If he was really a rebel and Sybellina introduced him to us, doesn't that make her a rebel too?"

"I'd say you were the real traitor to the empire, Lucius, if what I've heard is true," said Sybellina.

Lucius stopped in front of her.

"There's a foul smell of the underworld about you, Sybellina. Don't try your magic tricks with us, they won't work." He raised his hand, as if to strike her.

Constantine grabbed it.

"Sybellina," he said. "Please, leave us." He had to make sure she knew who was in charge on the journey north.

She walked out of the courtyard, her green robe flicking behind her.

He dropped Lucius' arm.

"I promised Maxentius to take her to my father. Stay your tongue, Lucius. We've a long way to go yet. She's done nothing to deserve your enmity, unless you've something you want to tell me?"

Lucius looked disgruntled, but he said nothing. He simply sighed. Then he too walked away.

"Yes," he said, over his shoulder. "I need a good bath."

He found out from a slave that Tiny and Juliana had gone to arrange for all the baggage to be brought from the Tribune's villa. Darkness had arrived, and slaves had lit the lamps in the bedrooms by the time they returned. Constantine called out to them from the doorway of his room as soon as he heard Tiny's voice. They brought his bags over. Then he asked them if they'd seen Marcus that afternoon and what they'd been up to for so long. Tiny shook his head, shrugged his shoulders.

Juliana said Marcus had been taken up to the main house soon after Constantine had been escorted away and they'd then been shown to this courtyard.

"Sybellina told us she needed her bags," said Juliana. "And to get all our bags from Marcus' villa. So, we got them. We did what was asked of us. Marcus' wife was still waiting for him when we left her. She looked unwell."

A shiver ran through him at the thought of Marcus' wife and children waiting for him to come home. Anger stiffened inside him. He'd tell his father what had happened. Only he had the power to punish this governor. Constantine pressed his hands into fists. Whatever it was, he hoped the punishment would be painful. He spun around.

An old slave woman was sweeping the other side of the courtyard. At the far end, by the doorway to the main house, two guards stood with their hands on the pommels of their swords. They looked more interested in what was going on inside the courtyard than in guarding it. He told Tiny and Juliana, in as few words as possible, what had happened to Marcus.

Juliana's face paled.

"We will speak no more of this until we're all well away from here," said Constantine. He raised a finger to his lips.

"I dine with the governor tonight and in the morning, we leave for Treveris. Juliana, you will help me get ready. Tiny, you check the packhorses we're to be given. Ensure everything is ready for the morning. I will not have lame horses."

Tiny grunted and trudged away.

Juliana grinned, as if she'd been given some present. He asked her to fetch hot water. He didn't have the time or the inclination to visit the baths, which he knew would be somewhere in the palace compound. They'd undoubtedly be full of the governor's guests anyway, and many of them would have been there getting drunk and indulging themselves with any female bath attendants since early that afternoon. By now they'd be smothering drunken praises on the governor as well. He'd seen it all before, too many times. Entertaining guests had been Galerius' greatest skill. Not fighting wars.

He stripped to his loincloth and stretched his tired muscles as he waited for Juliana to return. He still missed the certainties of life in the legions, the never-ending training, the marching, the eating with comrades, the helpful slaves. The glow of the colored glass in the oil lamp sent tinted shadows across the walls and ceiling and over his brown body. His muscles were still firm. He was proud of that. He was also proud of the welter of scars that marked him. They were the

218

irrefutable proof of his courage. These Juliana should see. The scars from his decisions, from the people who plotted against him were not as visible. She would see them in the lines on his face.

He turned to the doorway. She was standing there, perfectly still, wide-eyed, looking petrified, holding a steaming bucket of water.

"Don't be afraid, girl. I'm not one of those who forces himself on their slaves. I never was. Just bring that here."

Juliana trembled as she walked towards him. Slave girls always want what's beyond their reach, so he'd been told, and he'd seen proof of it. Wide-eyed slaves used to shed their tunics in front of him as soon as they got him alone. Some of those girls had been exquisite and very persuasive.

"Avert your eyes." He undid his loincloth and took the wet washing cloth from her shaking outstretched hand. He'd got used to washing from a bucket. It was the usual way legionaries washed when in the field.

"Check my tunic for marks." He tried to sound understanding. Her mouth was wide open, as were her eyes. Perhaps she wasn't as used to being a personal slave as Lucius had said. Then an idea came to him. There was one thing she could do for him.

"Juliana, there is something you can do." He grinned as she turned to him.

"Anything, my lord," she replied, stumbling over the words expected of her.

"Go around as much of this palace as you can while we're all at this feast tonight, and report back to me anything strange you see or anything odd you hear from the house slaves. I know you lot love to gossip."

She nodded slowly, her eyes drifting over his body, then jerking back to his face.

"If you're asked, simply say you're looking for something for me."

"What, my lord?" Her eyes were staring now. He knew he was better endowed than most and her long, appreciative stare felt good.

"Make something up. Say you're looking for Bithynian wine or Thracian olives or the best cheese for our breakfast. But don't take any risks. I don't want to lose my little dream reader, do I?" She blushed and looked away.

"Now go and get some more water."

The feast began with a ceremony of welcome for Constantine. The bowing and introductions finished, he, Lucius, and Sybellina were seated at the table to the right of the governor's table, a massive lion-legged, green Spartan marble monstrosity. Thin, blood-red curtains hung from ceiling to floor in front of the windows on the far side of the room. They billowed occasionally, rewarding the diners with glimpses of a distant sea shining like a broken plate of silver illuminated by an early moon.

A scent of flowers filled the room. Skeletal thin, ash-blond Alemanni dancers from Germania, dressed in tiny animal pelts, entertained them with dances that reminded him of young wolves darting through trees in winter. A troop of grotesquely overweight jugglers followed, and then a giant African fire-eater with small skulls in a chain around his neck. Towards the end of the feast some of the more drunken revelers disappeared into the gardens with the dancers.

He was not in the mood for any of it, especially the oysters people kept pressing on him. He hated all this from a pit deep in his stomach. The luxury of his surroundings reminded him of Marcus' accusations. The fruits of the governor's corruption, the gold jugs, silver dishes and jeweled glass goblets lay all around.

If he could have his way, the room would have been cleared and the governor humiliated in rags and chains. He hated being powerless. Only the knowledge that he would soon be back with his father cheered him. Eventually his father's powers would fall to him, if Fortuna stuck with him and he got his strategy right. He looked at the governor and imagined what he would do to him then.

Sybellina had a veil of thin gold chains over her face, through which her eyes peeked at him, bewitchingly. They were highlighted in swirls of black kohl, which went all the way to her hairline. Occasionally she stretched her body. It was full and lithe, appealing to his animal instincts as she moved it, exulting in its allure.

220

Her gown was tight, seamless. Gold armlets pressed against the light amber skin of her arms. One of the male diners nearby tried to engage her in conversation but left her alone when her monosyllabic replies made it clear she was far from keen on his company. The man looked like a fat carp from a fish pool in Rome, overfed and bred for sloth. She granted him a warm kiss though, before he turned away, and that left Constantine a little envious. Other people approached Constantine during the evening as well, most of them looking for news from Nicomedia.

The Emperor Galerius had taken over from Diocletian only the previous year and people were still hungry to learn what he was likely to do, now that he'd risen to become supreme emperor. His attitude to Christians was well known, but whether he would extend or repeal the controversial edicts about maintaining prices Diocletian had introduced, was the question that all the merchants apparently wanted an answer for.

Some people were also interested in Constantine's own plans, now that he was about to rejoin his father. He was tired of answering questions about what position he would hold at his father's court. People seemed genuinely surprised he didn't know and assumed he simply wouldn't say.

A fat, heavily perspiring merchant suggested Diocletian was planning a return to power. Constantine couldn't dissuade him of this wild speculation, the man was so convinced, and he grew tired of it all. He passed his questioner to Lucius, who seemed to enjoy being the center of attention. Lucius and Sybellina, he noticed, still weren't talking.

He had only one brief conversation with the governor. Late in the evening, as he was contemplating leaving, he came to their table, sporting a barely dressed female slave on each arm.

"Young Constantine, I see you're not enjoying our girls," he bellowed. His tone suggested Constantine probably didn't like girls at all, if he didn't like the ones on offer at this party.

"How like your father. Well, there's no harm. It leaves more for the rest of us!" He pinched one of the girls' rumps. She squealed. "Why don't you stay here in Massilia and wait for the spring storms to pass? I can introduce you to some of our more interesting ways. Would a seaside villa entice you? You could stay there with your pet priestess." He laughed, winked, then stumbled drunkenly, falling on Sybellina. His hand clutched at her. She pushed him away, roughly.

Constantine shook his head in disgust.

"Well, I'll arrange for some guards to accompany you on the road. They'll be from my best legion, no less. Bandits and fugitives lurk on every side street these days. What do you say to that?"

Constantine looked up at him with disdain. The man's eyes were clouded with wine and his eyelids were drooping.

"I have dictated my testimony regarding the Tribune Marcus. It will be sent to your father, of course." The governor looked pained. Constantine's expression must have penetrated his befuddled brain. His face reddened as they stared at each other, each willing the other to look away.

"I provide the tax revenues that keep this province afloat, remember that," said the governor, proudly. "Without my gold, your father could not hold the frontier with all those barbarians in Germania. He told me so himself."

"It's not the raising of taxes I object to, it's the lack of proper justice." Constantine spoke slowly, clearly, so the governor would understand he wouldn't be cowed or forget what had happened.

"Proper justice! Why, I believe in that too. We're in good company, then, you and I, along with the poets and the dreamers. Is it not proper justice that those who oppose our rule, our word, and our authority, should be discouraged from rebelling? What is a man's life, or a hundred men's lives, against the peace of a province, or..." He gripped the air in front of him, as if gripping a heavy column and roared, "The peace and safety of the empire?"

All conversation in the room stopped. A lyre continued for a moment. Then ceased. Its last note hung in the air.

Constantine wondered if the governor had planned some surprise for him. Surely, he wouldn't dare. But the governor pulled his two slave girls to him, grinned at Constantine and stumbled away. The room filled again with chatter, like an amphora fills with water when plunged into a stream.

It's always the same, he thought. *Every man of power tests how far that power extends. His father had been right about so much.* Not long after that he looked around and noticed Sybellina had gone. He decided to leave too. Lucius was intent on getting drunk. He would leave him to it. He had other plans to think about.

He found Tiny in the stables and told him to go to the feast, wait for Lucius to finish, stand behind him all night if necessary, and then bring Lucius to his room.

When he got to his own room Juliana was waiting for him outside, sitting on a marble bench. Constantine sat beside her. She told him she'd overheard whispered talk of Marcus' death, and vague suggestions that there was more to it, but nothing more definite.

"The young slaves I talked to were more concerned about the wine they could steal, and which of them might be called on to sleep with their master, or his guests. I was invited to join in."

She looked at him, bit her lip. "I told them my master would not allow it. I told them you were not like that. They said all men are like that. I told that slave he was a dung eater. Then I came here."

"You did good."

"They seemed afraid of us," she continued. "Well, of Sybellina. Her name made some of them wide-eyed. One fool-looking one was stuttering. They told me a story about. . ." She looked up, hesitated, then clamped her mouth shut.

Sybellina was walking towards them. She was wearing the most exquisite yellow nightgown he had ever seen. It clung to her body like water, yet was cut with a slit to well below her navel. Her breasts peeked from it, enticingly. She'd taken off her veil and had loosened her hair.

"It was nothing," said Juliana. "I must go." She stood and rushed away, with Constantine hardly noticing.

He was staring at Sybellina. She came closer. He could smell musk thickening the air around her. *She is the kind of distraction I need,* he thought. She bowed, which caused her nightgown to yawn wide, revealing her breasts in their full, oiled glory. She raised her head slowly, and sat down beside him, where Juliana had been sitting.

The light from an oil lamp hanging between the doors to the bedrooms swam across her skin.

He spotted Juliana sitting on a bench at the far end of the courtyard, almost in darkness. He thought about telling her to find a bed.

"You have an eager guardian, my lord," said Sybellina.

"I value loyalty," he replied. "What can I do for you, Sybellina?" He leant towards her.

"I wanted to tell you something." She paused, as if unsure of how to say it. "You're a good man, Constantine, and you'll make a good ruler, I can see it in your eyes." She touched his cheek.

He reached up, touched her cool silky arm. She stood, pulled him up towards her by the hand. They walked to the doorway of her room. There she turned, leant towards him and kissed his mouth with a passion he'd rarely known, her tongue forcing its way inside him like a snake's.

His mind raced as it flickered like a wild thing. He wondered was he foolish to let this happen, but when she pushed her lower body towards him and her breasts rammed up against his chest, he didn't care.

A deep longing woke inside him, a beast that had long been leashed. She pushed him back against the doorway, rubbing her body against his rigid manhood. He turned her, pushed hard against her, kissing her neck, then her lips. He'd imagined this moment any number of times. Now it had come true, it was far better than he'd imagined.

"I don't want your slave to see us, unless you want her to watch," Sybellina whispered to him.

Constantine looked around. In the far corner, discernible in the gloom as only a dim shadow, Juliana sat still. She appeared to be clutching her knees. A pang of guilt rose inside him.

"You're right." He pulled her into the room. Sybellina giggled, then licked the side of his face as they passed through the doorway.

"You'll be good, Constantine, I can tell," she whispered, as they stumbled to the bed. A small brazier stood near it and a sliver of smoke spiraled lazily into the air from the glowing coals. On a carved wooden table by the brazier, glittering in the light from a lamp dangling above it on the wall, lay a heart-shaped silver box.

They kissed by the bed. He slid his hands up her shoulders and pulled the straps of her gown away, until it fell at her feet. She was naked underneath, her skin pale, her breasts large, her nipples painted blue and prominent.

He looked at her, then pulled her to him, lifting her up in his arms. He wanted to kiss those breasts, lick them.

Abruptly she pushed him away. She struggled to get free from his arms.

"Stop. I wish it were different, Constantine, but I made a vow. Don't ask me to break it. I'm not one of your giggling slave girls." Her hands held him away.

She looked unbearably gorgeous in the flickering light. The warm touch of her soft skin had been exactly what he'd needed. Her breasts were beautiful as any he'd ever seen. As she turned away from him their pendulous curves stiffened him more.

"Sybellina." His tone was throaty, full of desire. He moved towards her.

She held her hand higher. "Stop. I will give you what you want, I promise, when the time is right. I want you too, but please stay back." She looked anguished.

"Sweet Constantine." Her tone was pleading. "I have sworn my life to share my body only when the Mother Goddess permits it, and she has not so far permitted it for you and me, but she will, I'm sure."

He thought of begging her, pleading his need, but he wouldn't. Then he thought of forcing her. But he wouldn't do that either. He sighed as he fought his desire away. She stepped back, her nakedness calling to him like a siren's voice.

"Tell me when your goddess changes her mind."

He walked stiffly from her room. Perhaps there was something of the daemon about her, as Lucius had suggested, but she was a daemon he desired more than anything else. And also a test, a laurel to be won, definitely not a plaything to be discarded like so many others.

He'd known such tests before. And he'd always won them. He'd win again. Her goddess would permit whatever he wanted. His time approached. And sooner, rather than later. The words, emperor's son, whispered too strong in the female heart.

He grinned, anticipating the moment, and remembering how she'd looked. Those breasts! Their journey north together would certainly be interesting.

He turned often in his sleep that night. He couldn't find a comfortable position on the lumpy straw mattress for long, and he got up twice, seeking distraction, pacing about his room. Then he went outside into the courtyard. He could hear a woman laughing and distant splashes. He walked the courtyard for a while as the noises died away. He went back to his room, pleasured himself with an image of Sybellina filling his mind. He came quickly. Then he slept.

The following morning as he was about to start a breakfast of breads, cheeses, olives, honey and milk, served at a low table in the courtyard, Sybellina appeared. She touched his arm then kissed his cheek affectionately.

"Do you forgive me?" she whispered, as she sat.

He shrugged his shoulders. "It's nothing. Forget it." She had the same perfume on, he noticed.

Lucius appeared. "Looks like Bacchus is making you pay for plundering his fruits," said Constantine.

Lucius grunted. Then he joined them. Sybellina smiled broadly at him. Lucius returned the smiled in the theatrical manner some people use to indicate that although they find nothing to smile about, they are willing to be friendly.

The coolness between them had lifted a little. It would be good if Lucius had decided to make the best of their enforced companionship. And he was pleased Sybellina seemed willing to forget Lucius' previous behavior. She was more soft-hearted than he'd expected.

He also enjoyed the way she took every opportunity to touch him, on the hand when she passed him something, or on his thigh when she gave him the selection of soft breads that they all delighted over, and he even caught her looking wistfully in his direction once or twice. It looked like the test would prove easier to pass than he'd expected.

Soon after, one of the governor's officials, a small bald man, arrived to inform him that he would be travelling with them to Treveris, the capital city of his father's province of Gaul, and that the preparations for their departure were complete. Constantine shook his head. He was attracting an entourage.

Sybellina delayed their departure that morning. As they waited, Juliana seemed more distant than he'd remembered. She looks glum, he thought. Had Tiny been bothering her again? He decided to ask her, but in the hubbub as Sybellina finally reappeared, he forgot.

When they were all ready, the governor met them in the stable yard.

A brisk wind blew over them as the last strap was being tied on the packhorses. Dark clouds loomed overhead, like the portents of some daemon's army streaming towards them.

"Are you sure you don't want to stay? The storms can be bad this time of year," said the governor.

Constantine shook his head firmly.

"Farewell, then. I wish you good fortune." He looked pleased his meddling uninvited guests were leaving.

Once they'd started out, he didn't look back. Soon he'd be with his father and he'd be given real power. He imagined the governor scouring the appointment lists the next time they came through, and his shock when he saw the position Constantine had been elevated to.

The road north from Massilia was one of the oldest in the empire. It carried people long before Agrippa put his name to the new Roman road, and before Julius Caesar ever dreamt of conquering Gaul. It had been there since the earliest times, when Gaul had been a land of innumerable tribes and underground gods, trading slaves, amber and skins with empires all over the Middle Sea.

At first the road headed west, up through the circle of hills that surrounds Massilia, then it turned north, skirting marshes and lagoons, and headed up through a broad and fertile river valley, passing straight through small, but bustling towns and by early blossoming orchards, olive groves and vineyards, heading up, up to where the valley narrows, where the silver groves of olive trees and the green alternating stripes of vines peter out, and the knobbly limestone hills, heathlands, airy pastures and steep gorges of what the locals call the massif begin.

Their first days on that road were spent enduring fierce thunderstorms and the largest grape-sized raindrops he'd ever seen. At one point the high wind set a whole olive grove swaying like tassels. They took accommodation where they could, wherever a warm meal and clean rooms were on offer near the end of each day's riding.

He settled quickly into the rhythm of travel, listening patiently to the endless gossipy stories Lucius regaled them with and enjoying the tales of life in Rome Sybellina could be pressed to tell. The governor's official and the four guards who accompanied them kept well back behind the pack horses, and at times he forgot they were there.

Lucius made up ribald stories about the roadside sanctuaries to Pan that they passed and about the sacred groves with garlands strewn around, dedicated to some unpronounceable local god.

He took care to stay away from Sybellina at night, usually going to sleep before any of the others, leaving Lucius to engage the tavern keepers in conversation. She would come to him when she was ready. That was the way he wanted it to be.

The skies cleared the day they arrived at the old veteran colony at Arelate. The town had a faded air, as if its best days were long over. They were feasted by the local magistrate that evening, a most generous host, and early the following day rode on. Blue skies and a warm downy wind cheered their way that day.

The road ran near the swift flowing Rhone, a river that hid man-eating monsters in its fast currents, waiting for anyone who dared to swim her, so Lucius claimed. Then they were in a steep gorge, where villages were less frequent, and later they were up onto the high massif, where central Gaul begins.

The weather warmed. The winter was gone. A tapestry of flowers covered the ditches on either side of the roadway some days. A sense of hope, of rebirth, added to his growing optimism. If

Sybellina didn't come to him during the journey, she certainly would when she saw the position he'd win from his father.

He'd always enjoyed the routines of travel. He woke before anyone else and usually helped Tiny get the horses ready, checking for saddle sores, checking strap lines, bruises and hooves. Juliana would wake next. She seemed always to be cheerful in the morning too, as she helped the tavern girls prepare their breakfast.

She'd become much quieter since Massilia and never spoke more than a few words when he engaged her in conversation.

News of the imminent arrival of the son of their emperor preceded them from town to town, probably due to the occasional fast messenger who raced past them on horseback. They were welcomed by administrators or sometimes by settled ex-legionaries, or whatever other official the village or town could muster.

When, after nine days, they finally arrived at Lugdunum, the bustling capital of the central region, their small guard was replaced by a troop of twenty seasoned cavalrymen. The local magistrate told them he simply wouldn't allow him to proceed without a proper escort. It was a matter of the city's honor, he said.

Constantine's anticipation grew as the landscape changed from high barren hills to rolling countryside to flat, thickly forested plain. He was constantly pushing himself up in his saddle, wondering what lay ahead, willing the journey to be over, his future to begin.

He knew they still had a long way to go, but this was a land he'd never seen before and he longed to see it all and understand it. When they finally reached the thin forests on the broad plains of northern Gaul, after fourteen long days, the villages and towns became more prosperous.

Forests still abounded in places, but now there were huge estates cut and parts where the forest had been cut down completely from horizon to horizon. They arrived at Alesia, the town just before where the road forks for Treveris, to find that a messenger awaited them.

His father must have heard he was on his way. He'd sent word for him and his party to come directly to Gesoriacum, the main port for all sea journeys between Gaul and Britannia, where, the message said, his father prepared for a campaign. A festival and games in honor of Ceres, the mother-earth goddess, would be held in Gesoriacum before the army's departure. They should arrive in time to join the festivities, if they rode swiftly. The emperor awaited him with great joy, the message concluded.

It was the middle of March, a day before the Ides. Six more days at a fast pace and they'd arrive at the coast.

One morning, outside the small tavern they had stayed at, Lucius sought him out as he and Tiny were preparing the horses for that day's journey. Lucius looked irritated.

"I do not think Sybellina is a suitable companion for someone bound for high office, do you?" he said.

Constantine had spent a lot of time talking to Sybellina the previous evening, probably more than ever before. She had detailed knowledge about the lives of previous emperors, and how their sons had come to power, and she was entertaining too, with stories of mistresses, magic and love affairs, and although she went to bed alone soon after their meal was finished, their friendship must have been obvious to everyone.

"She helps make the journey more bearable, Lucius. That's all."

"I mean no disrespect, Constantine, but I wish you'd be more careful. If a priestess like that gets her hooks into you. . ." He looked away.

"Don't annoy me." Constantine slapped Lucius' shoulder. "She's not my type, Lucius. I like my women big and blonde, not skinny like Sybellina. I think perhaps she's more your sort. Am I right?"

Lucius nudged him. They both watched as Sybellina made her way towards them.

"She's always appearing from nowhere," he muttered.

Constantine didn't answer.

By the time they reached the coastal plain, everyone in the company had heard at least three times how Lucius had rescued Constantine from the Persians, and at least twice about every honor he'd won in his campaigns.

As they travelled towards the sea, the road crossed two wide wooden bridges set over deep mud-brown rivers. Their wooden pilings were as thick as any he'd seen. The farms were smaller in these parts and they saw many native Gauls herding or sowing around stockaded villages not far from the roadway. Constantine was amused by the tight animal-skin breeches the men wore in these parts and by their striped cloaks and long beards. No one in Bithynia would dare wear such barbarian garb. Some of the men greeted them warmly and offered them rest or provisions. They spoke in a gently lilting tongue and those that did speak Latin seemed ill at ease with the language.

The days were cooler now that they'd come so far north. At times they had to shelter from violent rain storms which swept over the plain and turned everything to sandy mud, which splattered them from cap to sandal if the wind blew strong enough. It was no soothing Zephyr.

The road ran close to the sand-duned coast then and gulls drifted in the air, calling to their mates. The sea appeared one morning as they crossed the top of a low wooded hill, like the blade of a great sword laid out on the horizon. A heavy smell of salt came carried to them on the breeze that day.

This sea was gloomier, more menacing than the Middle Sea. Waves broke far out in lines of bone-white foam and gray clouds marshaled on the horizon, like enemy forces waiting for an order to move forward.

He'd begun to lose patience with Sybellina and decided that a few days without his attentions might speed her acquiescence. The cavalry guards, who Constantine rode with for the next few days, told him stories about Britannia and how girls from that isle were friendlier and had bigger breasts than any female to be found in the rest of the empire.

The cavalry guards who'd never been to Britannia, especially swore that this was true. They also told him about the Druids who could kill you with a curse, or a look, and about the large-scale human sacrifices they practiced before the empire had arrived. One man said they still practiced human sacrifice in the places where Roman law had not taken hold.

231

The road crossed a bubbling marsh by a wide causeway. In the distance, he saw the low hill that stood, his guards said, over the town of Gesoriacum. In fields on the lower slopes of the hill he could make out lines of dirty gray army tents. He raised a clenched fist.

He'd made it. At last he'd made it. He'd been eighteen, and scared, when his father had left him with Diocletian to learn the arts of war. But that wasn't the only reason he'd been left behind. He'd been a hostage for his father's good behavior as Caesar in the western provinces and, although he'd met his father on a few occasions since, the insecurity of knowing his life might be forfeit for something he had no part in, had been with him like a nagging injury, almost forgotten, but always there for all those years.

Now, at last, at thirty-three, all that was over and the future he'd longed for, yearned for year after year, could begin. He had much to learn and a future to carve out but was determined not to be found wanting, no matter who stood in his way.

XXXIII

Portus, outside Rome, 306 A.D.

Helena looked down at the dock. A troop of legionaries had lined up where the gangplank was being lowered. She'd seen a signal passed by flag between the galley and the shore, and knew the troop was for her.

The previous three days sailing since they'd left Hosius on his knees had passed without incident. She'd spent most of the time confined to the captain's cabin. It had a golden piss pot and a window, where she could stare out at the sea, but iron bars, intended to keep boarders out, prevented her from jumping overboard to swim ashore or drown herself.

Beside the gangplank being lowered onto the dock stood three of the galley crew, ready to take hold of her. Their job was to ensure she didn't jump down into the water between the galley and the stone of the port wall. But there was no chance she was going to do that. Helena would do whatever was needed to help her son. She even looked forward to meeting whoever had arranged her capture.

It had to be someone important. There were few people who could pay for a galley to intercept someone on their way to Rome. Whoever was behind it clearly wanted to ensure Helena did not leave the ship at any of the ports they would stop at after reaching Sicilia. Setting agents to abduct her on arrival in Ostia would not guarantee that they would catch her. And there were too many small ports south of Rome to make having agents at every port impractical.

Helena walked forward to the gangplank. "No one will hold me," she said loudly.

The captain shouted an order in Greek. Two of the men waiting grabbed her arms. The third man went behind them as they carried her, a foot off the ground, down the gangplank to the dock. She didn't struggle. There was no point.

At the bottom of the gangplank, three legionaries with black breastplates waited. An officer with a red cloak and a black helmet stood to the side.

She pointed at him as soon as she was released. "Why have I been kidnapped? My husband will have you gelded if you don't answer."

The officer bowed. "You were taken into protective custody, my lady. I have orders to ensure your safe arrival in Rome, and that you do not harm yourself on the way."

He snapped his fingers. Two of his men stepped forward. One had thin iron manacles in his hands. They grabbed her hands and forced them into the manacles. The manacle had a piece of iron between each hand, which meant she couldn't put her hands together.

"Why are you doing this? I have done nothing wrong." She glared at the officer.

"We were told you are subject to violent fits when adverse news is given to you."

She stopped moving and stared at him. His eyes were dull, unblinking, as if he'd already seen too much in his life.

"What adverse news awaits me?"

"Your son passed through this port ten days ago. He was heading for his father's territories." The officer paused.

"What your son did not know was that there is an official order from Rome that he must not set foot in Britannia, or he'll be subject to the punishment of death."

XXXIV

Gesoriacum, northern Gaul, 306 A.D.

In the stone palace of the governor of Gesoriacum news of the arrival of Constantine, son of the emperor of the west, spread as quickly as if a war horn had sounded from the town gatehouse. Excited whispering spread from the flagstone palace kitchen to the wooden lookout towers. Even the rats, who outnumbered every other living thing by far, knew something was happening.

The emperor, Constantius Chlorus, Constantine's father, was busy with matters of state, meeting his Legates and other senior officers. The meeting, in the basilica, the largest hall in the palace complex by the port, had begun to bore him. The arrival of his son at the south facing town gate, notified to him by an excited messenger, gave him the opportunity he'd been waiting for to end the meeting.

"We will finish," he said. He waved dismissively at the officers around him. "We will come back to planning how to eradicate the Picts tomorrow."

"Crocus, you wait behind." Crocus was the commander of his Alemanni cavalry, auxiliaries who followed their own customs, but were sworn to fight for Rome.

The chandelier with fifty candles, hanging by a chain from the central wooden beam, swayed a little as the double height doors swung open and the salty wind from the sea swept in.

The Emperor Chlorus was in his mid-fifties. His hair was gray, but still thick, his beard well cropped. His iron-gray eyes were shadowed by heavy brows. For military briefings, such as the one he'd just been conducting, he still wore his old soot-black, chain-mail shirt with the two large medallions from his most illustrious campaigns secured in position above his heart.

From Chlorus' leather legionaries' belt hung an ordinary legionaries' dagger, the only weapon he ever wore these days. It signified his roots as an ordinary legionary. A purple cloak hung in drapes down his back. He was sturdy, fit for his years, and tall like his son, and he wore his prestige like a second invisible cloak. Almost everyone in the town knew that he had, against great odds, reunited the western empire since his elevation to the rank of Caesar fourteen years before. And the officers he commanded, who were filing out of the room, knew exactly how he had achieved his success.

Crocus waited. Braziers around the oak map table they'd been standing around kept the chill from the cloak-penetrating sea breezes at bay. The gray spume-flecked channel that separated Gaul from Britannia, from which the breezes came, could be seen from two small grilled windows at the end of the room. Crocus went to warm himself by one of the braziers. The emperor joined him.

"You hadn't much to say."

"You know my opinion about those officers, emperor. They make my blood run to ice. Did you not hear them? They think logic wins wars." He rubbed at his beard. The matted hairs would not be cut until their summer campaign had ended.

"And they all know what you think of them."

Crocus made a noise like an animal growling.

"But you're right, they are an innocent bunch, though even you must have been young once. Us two, we make the real decisions, you know that."

Silence flooded the hall.

"It's your son, isn't it?" Crocus seemed very sure of himself.

The emperor looked around, as if examining the legionary banners that hung from the walls for the first time. "Perhaps I will find him a post as a senior Tribune."

He paused and turned to Crocus. "I hear his experience is with cavalry. Do you have room for another officer?"

Crocus' expression didn't change.

He knows the art of hiding his real feelings.

"Whatever you wish, my lord. I am sure he's won many laurels. You must be proud of him. The stories in the taverns about him get more incredible every night." Crocus passed a hand over the warm coals, as if testing how hot they were.

"If half what they say is true, he's the type who'll be looking for a good post." Crocus sniffed. "But I'm not sure if our cavalry unit is big enough for his aspirations. He's the right age to lead a whole Legion, isn't he? The younger the better, I always say." He looked at the emperor, a slightly quizzical expression on his face.

He knows how I resent getting old.

"He's the right age, all right," Chlorus answered. He put a hand over the coals to test their warmth as well. "But he's been away a long time. I once thought we might never see him again. And do you know, I have no idea why Galerius released him. That toad never acts unless there's something in it for him."

"I have no idea what he wants, emperor."

"Neither do I. That's the problem."

He looked around, checking to ensure no one else had remained in the hall without them noticing. There was no one to be seen. The heavy studded doors had been closed from the outside by his imperial guards, and the long hall was quiet except for a faint crackling from the braziers. Thin lines of smoke curled up from them to disappear high among the blackened rafters.

"May I speak openly, emperor?"

"Yes, speak your mind."

Both Crocus' hands were testing the heat of the brazier now.

"Five years we've fought together, my lord. We've cut off Frankish raiding parties and we threw back two hungry tribes who wished to take the best Roman estates at the edge of our territories. I won my place at your right hand through my skill in battle, and in leading my men to victory, but I hold my place now through my wit in understanding the men around me. Is that not so?" He waited for the emperor to reply.

"It is."

"Well, I must tell you this. Every spring my daughter asks why I must go away and fight for you Romans again, and every year I tell

237

her we are accumulating booty and fighting to secure the peace of a great empire and our place in it." He stood up even straighter and pushed his chest out.

"But every year the booty gets smaller, and as for peace, it's as far away as ever. These Picts." He spat the word out. "What gold will they have? A few torcs and bracelets that when melted down won't even pay my men for a month's fighting. We need rich cities to plunder, emperor. How else can we get ready for when our axe hands grow weak and our daughters look for dowries?"

The emperor's eyebrow rose slightly. "Tell your daughter we have plans for another ten years of campaigns. After Caledonia we will take Hibernia and then . . ." He waited, weighing the effect his words were having. "The forests of the Franks. There'll be little gold, I know, in all of this, but there'll be land we can farm, and tribespeople for our slave trade. We will allocate these new lands to all who fight with us when the task is done, and I promise you, your tribe will be granted enough to easily pay the dowries of a hundred daughters."

Crocus shrugged indifferently.

"There are many risks to every plan, emperor. You know this. The greatest threats arise around our own camp fires, even from our own hearths." His hands went out, palm up, in a gesture of finality.

"You cannot think Constantine is a threat already!" The emperor laughed. He'd thought about it, but he wouldn't give Crocus the satisfaction of knowing any of his fears.

"Not a threat, emperor." Crocus replied. "But you must know if we give him a senior position in the cavalry he'll quickly earn the loyalty of his men. You know that. Even if he's half as good as they say, he'll get respect for who he is, for being your son. And then he'll want more. And he'll have some of our best as his blood brothers then. Who knows what he'll aspire to. Do you?"

"So how do you suggest I deal with him, Crocus? Remember he's not Hannibal arriving at our gates with his elephants."

How far did Crocus think he should go?

"When a son comes of age for position in our tribe, emperor, he either fights his father, submits to his father's every wish, or he is banished." His tone dropped. "And do you know which is the most

238

difficult way for a father? Winning." He pointed a finger at the emperor. "Being the victor if the fighting path is chosen. Sacrificing a son is not easy, but the price of power was always high."

The emperor didn't reply. His silence hung in the room.

"All I say is that you must consider what even the dogs know, the cubs of the strongest want themselves to be the strongest. It is only natural. Your son will pick his path, if you do not pick it for him." Crocus braced himself on the flagstone floor, his feet shifting wider. "If you need services from me, emperor, any service at all, I am your loyal servant." He bowed his head slightly.

The emperor knew at once what he was referring to. Crocus had arranged for two disaffected officers to disappear in the past twelve months and he dealt with local disaffection quickly. All that made him useful.

"I know what the dogs know, but I am no Agamemnon. No sacrifice has been demanded of me. If there's no room for him in your cavalry, I'll not force him on you. Go now, fetch him here. Fetch Constantine, I will greet him publicly."

Crocus saluted, turned and strode away.

The emperor stared into the glowing embers of the brazier. Was Crocus right? Would Constantine be a danger, not a support? No, he had to give his son a chance.

Bloody Alemanni succession rituals. They are not the Roman way. Constantine had survived the east. He deserved a place with his father. He remembered the tall adoring youth he'd sent away, against every familial feeling, to Diocletian's palace many years before. Now he should make amends.

No. That would only make his son soft. He remembered his long ago promises. You have nothing to fear. That was all lies. So, did he still feel guilty? Was that why he was so wound up by his son's arrival? Did he bring back too many memories of his mother? The dismal Helena.

He'd have to make provision for her now.

She could move back to Treveris, now that he'd vacated the city. He would notify her. But would she want to come and visit

Constantine? That would be interesting, especially if Theodora got to hear about it.

Old wives and new rarely got on well in imperial circles.

As he walked down the flagstone corridor lined with small busts of the great emperors, the aching pain in his stomach returned. Cursing the sickness that had reduced his nights to sleeplessness and dull pain, he held the palm of his hand firm against the pit of his stomach.

Prepare for everything.

That was what Diocletian always used to say, whenever he'd been asked for advice.

And he'd almost decided what to do about Constantine. He just needed answers to a few questions. Why had Galerius released Constantine at this time? Was his allegiance being tested again?

The ache in his stomach felt worse as he considered it all.

For years, he'd imagined helping his son when he returned, and now that time had arrived, the idea suddenly seemed unwise. Why was that? He'd striven hard not to spoil the boy. Had he gone too far?

He stopped, leaned a hand against the red brick wall, sniffed. He could smell salt. Salt and damp. Decay tainted every crevice in this place. It was even in the plaster. It never survived too long on this coast. He rubbed the wall. A small crimson coated piece crumbled into his hand. He examined it, looked at its perfect shiny skin and then its fragile powdery underside.

Why was everything so flimsy, so fleeting, every shiny victory so soon forgotten, every pleasure gone so soon after the moment it was felt, while all around the wolves stalked, waiting for their opportunity?

He'd fought his way up only to find his greatest task now was to thwart others who tried to follow his example. Powdery ash trickled through his fingers, drifting to the foot polished floor.

Everything would be different now that his son had arrived. He'd known that, felt it instinctively, since he'd first heard Constantine was coming. But did that mean Constantine would be the wolf? How would he know?

The last piece of the plaster crumbled through his fingers and fell to the floor.

XXXV

Gesoriacum, northern Gaul, 306 A.D.

The stone walled traveler's rest room inside the south gate was cold, despite the spring sunshine outside. The busy sounds of the town, clanging from the swordsmiths, shouts from traders and the neighing of horses came to Constantine clearly, and after the many days of near silence on the road they added to the anticipation and excitement growing inside him. They wouldn't keep him much longer, he was sure of that. They couldn't. His father could not. Almost every clatter of hooves made him start in expectation.

A rumor must have gone around that the son of the emperor had arrived. Legionaries and officers peered into the room whenever they passed. He thought about closing the flimsy wooden door but decided against it. He wanted to see everything that happened in the cobbled yard, and anyway these troops were his father's, they would want to know about him.

And all the clean-tunicked officials that passed by would follow every word of everything that happened to his family. He would be at the center of a thousand gossipy conversations that day. He breathed deep and with pleasure. This would be his world too.

He gave out new duties to Tiny and Juliana as they waited. Tiny was to check their horses' feeding and exercise routines and was to make sure any new ones they were allocated were given suitable stables.

As for Juliana, she was to find the kitchens and make sure the food served them was what he and Lucius liked. "You should know all about that by now," he said. Sybellina looked at him as if she was surprised he still trusted Juliana. He looked away.

"And tell the chefs I never eat boiled sausage. I always hated it. If they ever serve it to me, I'll stick it up their shit hole with the point of my dagger. That should convince them." He laughed.

They waited some more. Sybellina rummaged through her bags and pulled out her green cloak, the one with the gold embroidered edges. Then she pulled out an ointment and dabbed some onto her cheeks.

"You look better without all that stuff," he said. *She's about to lose her chance for me,* he thought. *She knows she'll be on her way back to Rome soon.* He felt glad he hadn't asked whether her goddess had changed her mind during their ride from Massilia. She didn't expect I'd be able to resist her. Now she'll have to come after me if she wants me. Sybellina was smoothing her cloak and picking fluff from it in the light by the doorway.

She turned towards him. "If only everyone was like you, Constantine." She paused, looked at him, then turned back to her task with a sigh. "I was thinking, now you'll have all the slaves you need, would you pass Juliana on to me, to help with stupid tasks like this." She picked at her cloak in sudden and obvious frustration. "You will name your price."

Juliana was sitting on the floor by the doorway. She looked up, wide-eyed, when her name was mentioned.

Sybellina's tone was petulant when she continued. "What will the emperor think of me if I arrive like this?" She started rubbing at a stain on her cloak, trying to remove it with spittle.

"Ask Lucius," said Constantine. "Juliana belongs to him, not me." He turned to Lucius who was sitting near him on the wooden bench that ran across the back of the room. Lucius' eyebrows were raised. He shook his head in mock disbelief.

"I would have thought Tiny would be a better pick for you, Sybellina. He seems to be your devoted body guard these days, so much so I believe he drank a love potion," said Constantine.

Tiny, who was sitting on the floor in a corner, looked intently at the red tiled floor. He blushed a little when his name was mentioned.

"Neither Tiny nor Juliana are for sale," said Lucius, flatly.

Sybellina sniffed. Juliana went to her, took the cloak and began picking at it.

"Stupid ugly pig!" Sybellina slapped Juliana hard across the cheek.

Juliana spun back and fell to her knees, clutching at her face. A trickle of blood ran down her cheek. One of Sybellina's rings had cut her. She cowered away from Sybellina, whose hand was raised again.

"Never beat a slave that doesn't belong to you," said Constantine. He had moved quickly and now held Sybellina's wrist, turning her towards him as he twisted it.

"You like your clumsy little bed warmer, do you?" said Sybellina, as she faced up to him. She stuck out her tongue and with her free hand cupped his testicles through his loose woolen tunic. No one had dared do that since he'd been in that high-class brothel in Alexandria. She squeezed, then pulled her hand away. No one else had seen what she'd done, they were standing so close together. "You're bigger than I thought," she whispered. She tried to pull her arm away. He held her tight. She leant towards him, teasing him.

"Do you know how much this cloak cost? I could buy two stupid Juliana's for the price of it. Release me or never touch me again." She was like a pampered child, the type who relishes making other people's lives unbearable.

Juliana had moved to the far corner of the room.

Constantine laughed as if Sybellina's threat amused him. He pushed her away roughly. Sybellina swirled her hair around her as she turned from him like an overconfident whore.

He had an urge to slap her ass until she begged for mercy.

Suddenly from outside, commands sounded. A troop of legionaries was being called to attention.

"Good timing," said Constantine.

The doorway darkened, and a scruffily uniformed centurion walked in. He looked around, then motioned Constantine to follow him. Outside, astride an oversize dirt-brown horse, was a red-bearded barrel of a man wearing a gray mail coat. Constantine grinned. Old friends are always the best. Crocus jumped down from his horse and bent low to kiss the hem of Constantine's cloak.

"My lord, it is so good to see you again. Rome was far duller after you left, which was why we had to leave. Your father sends regrets that he could not meet you in person. He's burdened with official business, as always. The army departs soon. You've been fortunate to catch us. You always were lucky. Do you remember that girl?" He slapped Constantine on the back and turned towards the others. Constantine introduced Lucius and Sybellina.

Crocus and his Alemanni officers had made his brief time at Diocletian's Triumph in Rome a real pleasure. It had been the only time he'd felt truly safe in many years. He wasn't allowed stay with his father while he was in Rome, because of Diocletian's paranoia, but in the confusion of the late autumn revelries nobody remembered that the Alemanni auxiliaries were the close allies of his father.

Horses were brought out as he reminisced. They mounted up. Crocus rode with Constantine beside him. As they left the courtyard he looked back. Juliana was standing looking at him, a sullen look on her face. Tiny was saying something to her, but she wasn't paying any attention. He turned away. It was true what they said about slaves being ungrateful.

Everyone in the street stared as they rode past, many speculating loudly as to who he was. "Will the army move on now, my lord?" someone shouted. He'd seen towns garrisoned like this before. Sometimes inhabitants almost abandoned the town until the Legions were gone. He'd also seen townspeople who couldn't leave scrabbling like frightened mice for food until their protectors had gone. He looked around. There were more beggars here than in similar towns in the eastern provinces, although they all held their hands out the same way.

They entered a large courtyard, the type normally used for marshaling troops. Thin pine trees stood around its edges. Salutes were shouted out as they passed through a heavy wooden door and out into a smaller colonnaded courtyard. Guards banged their swords to their shields as they entered. He noted the number of them and wondered what it was the garrison commander feared. Was this part

245

of the empire still so lawless that doubled guards were needed on every doorway? They waited to be announced into the basilica meeting hall at the far end of the courtyard.

He pictured his father waiting for him with open arms. Lucius said something. He didn't reply. He hadn't understood what Lucius had said. He took a deep breath, then followed Crocus through the doors.

At the far end of the long hall was his father. He knew him immediately, though he looked far older than he remembered him. He was sitting on a Greek style throne, the kind that had no back support and golden arms like lion's paws. The lavishly embroidered purple toga he wore looked out of place in the gloomy hall. As Constantine walked forward he saw the thin pearl band on his father's forehead. So, he too had taken to Diocletian's changes.

Behind his father, in an attendant semicircle, stood a group of officials in dazzling white togas. An expectant hush descended as he approached, like that moment in the circus when a gladiator's fate is about to be decided.

Constantine strode purposefully forward. A group of onlookers, petitioners and traders mainly, had parted down the center of the room on his arrival. He could hear them crowding behind him as he walked forward. He hadn't seen his father in over two years, and that had been only briefly, at Diocletian's Triumph in Rome, and all the time he was there he'd never felt free enough to say what he thought. Now, at last, he could. He had returned. A rush of sentiment threatened. He fought to quell the feelings welling up. The promise of returning to his father had been the rock he'd clung to whenever despair had threatened in the east. The yearning to see his father had been the mission of his life.

This was the man who'd made him. The man who'd played games with him through the rocky orchards at their home in Moesia. The man he respected more than any other. A shiver ran through him, as if an arrow had flitted past his ear. He straightened his back. He had to do this properly.

He had to be utterly sure of himself, utterly confident, utterly a real emperor's son, striding up the room, his cloak flicking behind him. Then no one would notice the too-stiff way he held his expression, his struggle to hide his emotions. He reached the far end of the room and prostrated himself on the mosaic floor directly in front of his father.

He placed his hands out wide, his forehead touching the floor. It was the fullest act of submission possible. He waited to be told to rise. It was an honor, not a humiliation as some barbarian chiefs claimed, to prostrate yourself in front of an emperor, a man chosen by the gods. He forced away all thoughts of rising.

The onlookers murmured. This was the dutiful son they'd heard about. The son who'd come all the way across the empire to be with his father. Surely now, the gods would grant their emperor an easy campaign, and the gentle winds needed to carry his army safely to Britannia. This arrival was a good omen.

"Arise, son. You are most welcome. Come. Come close." The emperor opened his arms. His unhurried tone had an imperiousness to it. He was well used to ordering things as he wanted, though his guttural accent still gave away his origin from the western provinces of the lower Danube. Some things do not change.

Constantine embraced his father and looked behind him. Thank goodness his first impressions had been right, his stepmother the empress was nowhere to be seen.

"I have come to offer my sword." His words came with difficulty, as another rush of warm feeling towards his father almost overcame him. He pulled away, pressed his lips together, and ground his teeth.

"Who have you brought with you?" The emperor looked quizzically over Constantine's shoulder. A feeling of unease rose in Constantine, then dissipated as quickly as it had come.

He waved his companions forward and presented them after they too had prostrated themselves. The emperor greeted Lucius coolly. Sybellina, he stared at a moment longer than was necessary. The empress was definitely not nearby, if his father was taking an interest in beautiful messengers. He remembered how his father paid little attention to women when they'd met up in Rome and how impressed he'd been by that.

"I'm happy to meet you, Sybellina. If you're a priestess of the cult of the Sibyl, you must have knowledge of our future. Do you?"

She nodded.

"Good. We always find it a little difficult to see the future clearly."

"I am honored to be here, Imperator. I have a private message for you, my lord." Sybellina bowed low.

"Good. Good. You must come to the feast honoring the return of my son." The emperor turned, motioned for Constantine to follow him, and walked slowly towards the rear door of the hall.

Constantine, disappointed that his father had paid so little attention to him, followed him out through it and across a courtyard, one pace behind him, and into a long dining room set out for a meal with goblets and wine jugs and large golden dishes.

Lyre players struck up jerkily as they strode together up the dining hall. In moments, a soothing tune flowed around them.

"Welcome home, Constantine." The emperor turned and hugged him again, more warmly this time, but there was still something distant about him, as if he was distracted by something. It was not the welcome Constantine had hoped for, but he consoled himself that he should not expect too much on their first meeting.

Slaves swarmed around, urging them to sit. They did so and the crowd that had followed them from the basilica sat at tables set near the walls as if each person knew instinctively where their place was.

Delicacies of the region were served first, stuffed mushrooms and other things he mostly didn't recognize, then the usual Roman fare appeared. The roast thrushes tasted good, as did the spiced boar and the braised hares. Wine and a dark local beer were served, and at the end of the feast huge cheeses and earthenware plates of small honeyed cakes were laid on the tables.

Lyre players and a troop of singers chanted traditional Roman songs as they ate, both fast and slow. But no lewd, almost naked dancers appeared to entertain them, unlike such feasts in Rome or in Nicomedia, since Galerius had taken power.

When the meal was over most of the guests departed quickly. Many visited the emperor's table before they went to express their joy at the reunification of father and son. He'd always felt hypocritical when forced to join in rejoicing with the emperor in Nicomedia, his position had always seemed so tenuous, but now for the first time in as long as he could remember he felt truly content and at home. The well-wishers seemed sincere too, perhaps that was how people were in Gaul.

But he wanted to have a private conversation with his father. There was so much he had to tell him. After a few more guests had departed, the emperor rose to his feet and indicated with a nod that Constantine should follow him.

Constantine went after him, his mind racing. Why did his father look so frail? Was he ill? He'd been like an oak the last time he'd seen him, his face all red and healthy. Now he looked gray and more aged than appropriate for his years.

A full moon lit the small private courtyard his father led him to. He'd waved away their torchbearers a moment before and now dismissed the two red-cloaked bodyguards who'd accompanied them from the feast.

"I expect you know how difficult it is for me to be alone with anyone," said the emperor. "But it is time you and I talked."

Wooden benches faced each other in the square trellis-bordered center area of the courtyard. Constantine, after being waved towards it, sat on one. The echo of ironclad wheels grinding on cobbles came to them from beyond the courtyard walls. The noise grew louder.

His father held up his hands for silence as Constantine started to speak. Then he stood, his head at an angle, listening intently, his mouth half open. Constantine started to say something again, but his father shook his head sternly. The sound of the wheels faded slowly. Then a guard called out far away and an answering call came from somewhere further along the town wall. That call was different, longer.

The emperor turned to him. "My apologies, I've begun a new watch system. The calls let us know how the whole town is after each circuit and at each watch."

Constantine raised his thumb, tried to look impressed. His father sat beside him and placed a hand on his arm.

"I am proud of you, Constantine. You bring honor to our family."

It felt good to hear those words.

"That is why." His father gripped his arm. "You must be given a proper job, a role in keeping with your position, something that will help my campaign, and our objective."

XXXVI

Rome, 306 A.D.

The legionaries with the black breastplates ran behind the chariot. They were lucky the two horses had been set to a walking pace, but Helena wouldn't have cared if they'd all fallen by the wayside clutching their hearts.

The officer with the red cloak and black helmet held the reins of the two horses tightly. He'd barely spoken to her during their journey along the road to Rome. Now, at last, they were nearing the city, which loomed ahead with the smoke from its cooking fires and temples turning the sky gray above it.

"I will scream when we get to Rome's gates, if you do not tell me where you are taking me and why." Helena had been trying since they'd joined the road to Rome to get information out of the officer. Up until this moment she had failed.

The officer turned to her.

"Now that we are within sight of the city, I am free to tell you that I was ordered to take you wherever you want to go in Rome, and then I must escort you back to Ostia, leaving the city by nightfall."

She pointed at him. "That won't allow me even enough time to visit the baths. Who gave you these orders?"

"I am further ordered to give you a gift for your son, which you are to take to him in Gaul."

"And if I don't agree to all this?"

The officer cracked the reins, so the horses sped up. They passed a farmer's cart carrying amphora to the city.

"If you do not agree I am to take you to the Tullianum to be imprisoned. Charges of supporting the outlawed Christian sect have been prepared. You will also be charged with treason in Alexandria, supporting enemies of the empire."

Helena stared at the road ahead. The gravel on the surface most of the way up to this point had given way to regular shaped pink blocks. Whether the change was due to the fact that more blood was spilled the nearer you got to Rome, or that the road's designers had simply decided to make the entrance to the city more inspiring, was hard to know.

What she did know was that she did not have much choice. Almost everyone sent to the Tullianum, the prison on the slope of the Capitoline Hill, ended up executed. They didn't have to wait long either. The courts made special arrangements to try anyone charged with treason.

She turned to the officer. "What is it I am to take to my son?"

He reached into a pouch on his belt and passed her a small brown vial. Its stopper was sealed with string and covered over in red wax.

XXXVII

Gesoriacum, 306 A.D.

"The care of my provinces weighs heavier each year. I should have learnt more than war when I was your age."

A shadow of unease fell over Constantine. He shifted in his seat.

"You are young. You can broaden your skills now. And help ease my burden."

The emperor licked his lips, slowly. His tongue was dark red. He paused.

Relieved at last he had an opening, Constantine jumped in. There was much he had to say before any decision was made about his role.

"I know you'll find a place for me in the army that suits all these concerns, Father. You must know my experience is ideal for your upcoming campaign." There were other things that needed to be discussed, though. He'd been going over them in his head during the meal.

"I hope we can also discuss other matters, father." He leaned forward. "The man I came with, Lucius, I met his father before I left Bithynia and I promised to arrange for his son to deliver a personal message to you."

His father looked angry. His lips were pressed together as if he was holding himself back. Memories of shouted reprimands came to him, thickening his tongue. He took a slow breath. Sweat prickled his brow.

"I have told you all about Lucius. He saved my life on the Persian campaign," he said.

His father shook his head.

"I wrote to you about it. If Lucius hadn't stood up for me, I'd have been demoted to the ranks and humiliated for who knows how long. You know what Galerius is like. He wanted to get to you through me." Frustrated at the coolness of his father's response, he looked down at his feet. His father's sandals were ordinary, drab, like a lowly centurion's.

He continued, as he stared at his father's sandals. "Lucius risked his life for me. He gave evidence for me and had his commander do it too. They both swore to my courage. I was fortunate they were in Galerius' tent that morning. They did not have to speak up." His voice was trembling a little. It had all come back to him how close he'd been to disaster that day. He pressed his fists against his thighs to steady himself.

"Lucius went as far as to laugh in front of Galerius, to say I deserved a laurel, not demotion. If the Commander of the Armenian auxiliaries, his Commander, hadn't been there to back him up, I know what would have happened. You must give him a hearing. He has some offer from his father. An offer you might consider."

"All of this is news to me," said his father slowly, almost indignantly. "We received no letters from you in all the time you were in the east. Your mother despaired. She has been writing to me ever since. My new empress took it upon herself to help her. She used her influence to get Galerius to confirm you were still alive and would be freed. And it has worked. Her letters are the only ones he ever responded to."

Constantine knew at once what that meant. His stepmother, the empress, had written the letter urging Galerius to place him in the front line all those years ago in Persia. When he'd met his father in Rome, they'd had so little time, there had been so many ceremonies they'd had to attend together, he hadn't any time alone with his father to ask about that letter. In any case, he had survived, and Galerius had softened a little towards him after their victory over the Persians.

The excitement in Rome had distracted him as well, and he'd been wondering whether Diocletian's abdication meant he'd be released. That had been his focus while in Rome.

"Did you see the empress' letters to Galerius?" Constantine blurted out.

His father looked at him sternly, his brow creased. "I don't ask to see my wife's correspondence. Are you suggesting I should?"

"No." Constantine shook his head, tried to look unconcerned. Theodora had been scheming. Was she still at it? She wanted him out of the way, that would be normal. Stepsons were often despised. Well, he'd be with his father on the upcoming campaign. This would be his chance to claim his rightful place beside his father, while his father was away from his stepmother's influence. He had been right. He bowed his head. He had to be cautious. Change the subject.

"There's another matter, Father. The governor of Massilia." His voice slowed as he picked each word carefully. "We disagreed. The man is corrupt and a murderer. His actions cast a shadow over his whole province." He checked himself. His tone was becoming vehement.

"Nonsense. That governor is one of my best," his father snapped back.

"He had a Tribune who was under my protection killed. The man was about to give evidence against him."

His father raised a hand.

"Stop now, Constantine. The governor of Massilia has my full support. He's the only one who ever took on corruption in the merchant classes and their blatant tax evasion in that province. If I had a man like him as a governor in each of my provinces, all my problems with coin would be solved in a year."

"He murdered a good man for speaking out." Constantine's voice was raised. His anger showed clearly in his tone. He had to suppress it. He couldn't risk a confrontation with his father.

The emperor stood, slowly, as if his bones ached. He pointed at Constantine. "I need loyalty and obedience in a son. I have no time for barrack room sentimentality. My decision is final. A governor has the power of life and death over everyone in his province. You know this, but you question his decisions." His finger jabbed towards Constantine.

"He decides who lives and who dies." The emperor stepped back. His hand became a fist. Then it opened, and a smile came to his lips, as if he'd just thought of something.

"The festival of the Goddess Ceres begins in these parts. You may wish to drive our team in the main chariot race, if you want to display your prowess, that is." His expression was magnanimous now, as if he'd presented Constantine with a costly toy, hoping it might placate him.

Constantine closed his eyes and thought about it.

"How long do I have to learn the team's habits, a week, two?"

"Two days. It's enough."

Constantine sighed. "And if I win, will you have the governor replaced then?" He licked his lips.

His father exploded. "You're starting the wrong way with me, Constantine. I didn't plan to tell you this now, but I perhaps I should." He stood over Constantine, daring him to rise up against him. His finger poked Constantine's shoulder. "After the festival is over you will go to Treveris. There you will be appointed a Prefect of the city and you'll learn the art of administration. Then perhaps you'll understand why we appreciate our governor at Massilia." His tone had turned dismissive.

"What!" Constantine spat out the word.

His father stepped back and was examining him coolly, his hand by his dagger. Constantine tried to calm himself. He could die here if he pushed things too far. He'd heard stories of fathers who'd killed their sons during minor disagreements.

"I know nothing of civil administration, Father. Those jobs are for lovers of smooth-skinned young boys. Do you really want me to waste myself minding dusty scrolls?" A pained silence fell between them.

Constantine turned away in disgust. He couldn't believe it. He'd been so confident he'd be placed at the head of a cohort at the very least, if not a Legion, or even the whole army. In the distance, the sound of crashing plates came to him, then a reprimanding shout. The air had grown warmer, but it was lifeless. He thought of things he might say, arguments he might make, but nothing came out of his mouth.

"I didn't know you valued the dangers of war so highly." His father sat down on the bench opposite him. "But if I ask you to do this for me, will you please me?"

There were few better ways to test the depth of a man's loyalty than to ask him to do something he hated. Perhaps that's what this was, a test.

Constantine stared straight ahead, his lips pressed together, filled to the neck with disappointment. "If you order me, I will do it, but I came to Gaul to help you in your campaign this summer. I have led Legions. You must know that. And I've won laurels in three campaigns. I could be very useful in your campaign. Do not waste me on administration."

The emperor held up his hands as if he'd relented. "Stop." He took a long breath, hissed it out, then pursed his lips. "You may come with me to Britannia. You may be one of my military advisors and help me ready the men. But you will not fight. I will not risk it. Once the campaign begins, you go to Treveris." He spoke the final words slowly. He was used to offering such compromises.

"I make war only so that the empire can be at peace. Peace and prosperity, they make the Pax Romana. That peace brings safety to millions. There is nothing so sweet as to live in a well-protected city, a well-administered city, a city where you can listen to tales of people striving to win peace or honor, using their wits to win what you already have won. Now, I have spoken too much already, and I am in no mood for arguments."

Constantine had to accept the offer. He had no choice. At least he could go to Britannia. He would not be dismissed at once. There'd be time to change his father's mind.

He bowed his head. "I am grateful. I do want to serve you, Father."

The emperor called out for a servant.

"Show my son to his rooms," he said, when the man arrived.

Constantine bowed towards his father, then followed the harried looking servant. The man kept his gaze down whenever he spoke, indicating which way they would go. Constantine barely noticed, and hardly saw the corridor or the people they passed. He was wondering how he could change his father's mind.

They'd been allocated the best guest bedrooms, but they were still small. Gesoriacum was no imperial capital. Constantine and Lucius' bedrooms were beside each other. Sybellina's was on the far side of the small courtyard their rooms opened onto. For some reason, he'd thought she'd be sleeping elsewhere. He found Lucius in his room and told him the news.

Constantine tried to give the impression he was happy with the role he'd been offered, and Lucius thankfully made no derogatory comment about it, but he sensed shock and was sorely tempted to criticize his father. But Constantine had learnt over the years to keep his thoughts to himself, especially any critical thoughts about his father.

They stayed up talking for a while, but Constantine soon felt tired. Someone had lit the oil light in his room. His bags had been unpacked too. He hadn't seen Sybellina nearly all evening and it came to him, in a final depressing afterthought, that his hopes of winning her were slimmer now. She'd learn soon enough what had happened between him and his father, and she'd understand what an administrative position in Treveris really meant.

His elation while waiting to see his father earlier that day, Sybellina's vindictiveness to Juliana, and the way she'd teased him, all seemed so long ago now. Sybellina had been almost ready to come to him, he was sure of that. If only his father could be persuaded to change his mind. Otherwise he'd have to forget about Sybellina, and a lot of other things.

It had all turned out differently to what he'd expected. He looked across the floor. Even the mosaics here were only crude imitations of what he'd left in Nicomedia. He made a fist, pressed it to his lips. His defense of Juliana wouldn't have helped him with Sybellina either. He sat on his bed, undid his sandals. Why did he feel so protective towards a slave girl? Her beaming face came to mind. She was more attractive now, that was true. She was blooming like a dirty rose does when plucked from the dust and placed in sweet water.

258

So why not have Juliana tonight, if I want her? Why wait for Sybellina?

No. I will not force her. Especially not here. His father, and especially his mother, had forbidden such pleasures with the slaves when he was young, and despite being teased for this in the east he'd never taken part in the orgies of slave rapes that had accompanied some of their victories.

He remembered an old dream. One he'd cherished for as many years as he could remember. In it, he took his place at his father's side, learning to command multiple Legions, take war councils.

They ruled together.

A cold and bitter feeling seeped into him. Why was his father set on this path? Why did he want to give him so little?

XXXVIII

Gesoriacum, Northern Gaul, 306 A.D.

At dawn, as the first stirrings of the town could be heard echoing distantly, a lone figure in a purple toga sat on a stone bench in a private courtyard. Two opposing walls of the courtyard provided views through low arched openings braced by green Spartan-marble pillars, no wider than the thickness of a wrist. The man was staring off through one set of openings at the sun rising through the thin blue mist that cloaked the smudge of the distant forest.

The emperor had woken early. He had a headache. That boy was so ungrateful. Did he not know that everything he enjoyed, his father had risked his life to win? Why did he argue so? It was humiliating, and frustrating. He would have to be taught gratitude and respect again. The qualities of an honorable son. The qualities Theodora was always prattling on about. If I'm not careful, that boy will bring shame on us all. Perhaps that's why Galerius loosed him on me.

He called for a slave.

Not long after, a woman draped in a thick cloak was ushered into the courtyard. The slave who accompanied her bowed low as he waved her forward.

"Welcome, Sybellina. Come in." He raised a hand in welcome.

Sybellina walked forward confidently and prostrated herself fully on the tiled floor in front of his bench. Then she rose and bowed.

"To be in your presence is an honor, my lord."

Her lilting voice was a net to draw men in, he knew. She'd certainly been well trained.

"Come. No need for formalities at this hour. Sit beside me. You're a beautiful young creature. But you know that. Tell me, are you really as quick as a salmon, and as wily as a vixen, as my agents in Rome tell me all you priestesses are?"

Sybellina sat beside him, undid her cloak. It dropped from her shoulders. Her gown was held in front by thin taut leather straps.

"Who would say such untruths?"

"Indeed," he said. "So, tell me your message, Sybellina."

"Maxentius sends greetings, emperor," she said in a rush, as she bowed her head. "He wishes you the success of Hercules in your campaign and desires to bind his house tighter to yours." She paused, bit her lip.

"Say it girl." He waved his hand, as if coaxing something up from inside her.

"Maxentius has a sister, Fausta, my lord. You met her, he tells me. She is young, but ready for the marriage bed, and eager to marry into your great family."

The emperor let out an amused tut.

"Aaah, but I am already married, girl, and into his illustrious family. I won't put aside his half-sister for his sister, no matter how young she is." He rocked back and forth, shook his head, raised his eyebrows and looked at her.

"My lord, it's not you Maxentius is thinking about. It is your son, Constantine." She lowered her eyes.

"I see," he said, slowly. "And you've told him about this?" Was this Galerius' plan? Elevate Constantine and sow division within his family?

"No, my lord. The message was for you alone. Fausta is a most suitable wife. Her offspring carry the seed of the great Emperor Marcus Aurelius. And she will bring a large dowry."

The emperor ran his hand along the smooth, lovingly-crafted wood on the arm of his chair. He sniffed. A whiff of bread from the bakeries in the town came to him, carried on the early morning breeze from the sea.

"I'll consider our reply. I assume you're to take a reply to Maxentius."

"Yes, my lord, as soon as you give it."

"Well, you'll have to wait, girl, and join our retinue. Now, tell me about your training. Do they still treat some priestesses like prisoners in Rome?"

"We would never consider ourselves prisoners, my lord. I trained in the arts of divination and healing, though recently many in Rome no longer wish to learn about their future, so our coffers are low." Her head bowed. "I shouldn't be burdening you this way. Should I leave you?"

"No, not yet, Sybellina." She was very good, he had to give her that. "My treasurer will make a donation, of course. But tell me about you and Constantine, have you, you know, become close?"

"My lord." She shook her head vigorously. "We have strict vows."

"Yes, I know." He placed a hand on the wood in the middle of the foot-wide gap between them and splayed out his fingers. "There is another matter, Sybellina. It's the reason I brought you here." She looked at him directly. He sensed eagerness. That was always gratifying.

"It is a personal matter." He paused, studied her face. "My soothsayer suffers a sickness, brought on no doubt by fear of my wrath, due entirely to his many ridiculous divinations. I would like you to read the augers for me this morning, Sybellina. Will you?"

"I am your servant in all things, my lord."

Was that disappointment in her tone? It could be.

"Very good." He reached across, stroked towards her bare arm, not touching the skin, but feeling the ends of the downy hairs on her forearm and the heat from the skin below. She kept her arm still. Was her training in divination, or something else?

"The Temple is through here." The emperor stood abruptly and led her towards a small wooden doorway carved with spirals.

They passed down a corridor, met only slaves, and then they were outside, in front of a temple to Hercules, set in the center of an enclosed, deserted, colonnaded courtyard, the pillars of which were thin and covered in plain red plaster. The temple, he told her, had been built soon after Julius Caesar's men had first captured the town, more than three hundred years before. It looked that old and was big enough to house a large elephant, or maybe two.

In front of the red columned temple stood a wide platform, approached by three broad granite steps. He gestured to Sybellina. She bowed, walked ahead up the steps, and then paced out an equal-armed cross, the division of the world, at the middle of the empty platform at the top, inside the colonnade of pillars. In a low voice, she intoned supplications to the gods as she worked.

On finishing her chanting, she stood at the center of the platform, her face up, awaiting the augers. The emperor stayed at the bottom of the steps observing, then followed her gaze into the pale blue morning sky. Puffy white clouds edged with red drifted towards the recent sunrise. They waited, standing patiently, until a cawing flock of gulls appeared from the west, swooping down over the town.

She flung her arms up.

"The augers agree, Nuntatio, my emperor. Your campaign will be favored. It pleases the gods." She came down towards him, frowning and hurrying as she came close.

"You are suffering! What is it?" She touched his arm.

He was about to reprimand her but didn't. He'd tried to hide the pain but holding the side of his stomach brought much relief. He'd had similar attacks before in the early morning. She was very observant.

"It is nothing, nothing at all. I've had stomach cramps for a few days, that's all. It will go away."

"And does it get worse after you feast, or after you exert yourself, my lord?"

"Umm, sometimes," he replied.

"My lord, I know a remedy that may help you. We treat many members of the imperial families in Rome. Will you try one of our potions? I'll bring it to you later. I assure you, you'll not be poisoned." She said that part with conviction, her eyes fixed on his. "We are sworn to protect the imperial families. You know that."

"Thank you, Sybellina. My physicians are bumbling fools." *She knows I can have her potion tested and her life would be forfeit should the mixture kill.*

He led her back into the low roofed palace, her hand resting lightly on his arm.

They passed through the dining hall. Constantine and Lucius were there. Constantine was clearly taken aback to see Sybellina with his father, so early in the morning. He half stood, then sat, then he stood again.

"Sybellina, Father."

"Constantine, good morning," said the emperor brightly. "Your friend Sybellina has read the augers for the campaign for us all. The signs are good, she assures me, which is better than what my normal soothsayer tells me. He keeps seeing evil portents." He shook his head, then sat at the table opposite Constantine and patted the place beside him for Sybellina to sit.

She gave a brief triumphant smile, and sat beside the emperor, linking his arm. Constantine looked as if someone has taken away his favorite toy. The emperor suppressed a grin.

"You can practice all day with the chariot team if you wish, Constantine," he said. "I've already sent word you'll be there after breakfast. Practice is the key to many things."

"I shall take my leave," said Sybellina. "But I'll be back." Her eyes flicked down to where the emperor's hand still pressed against his side. He moved it. His pain was too obvious.

He kissed her hand, called for one of the slaves and whispered to him. The slave followed Sybellina from the hall.

"You will keep Sybellina with us?" Constantine sounded surprised.

"She's to wait until I have her answer," said the emperor. He turned to Lucius. "I understand you're a cavalry officer. Constantine tells me you train new recruits."

"I was assigned to help start Galerius' new Jovian cavalry division," said Lucius.

"Excellent, I have need for good cavalry officers."

"I am expected back in the east," said Lucius, in a worried rush.

The emperor raised his hand. "You also carry a message for me, don't you?" They could hear the stamp of legionaries drilling
264

beyond the high brick walls. Shouts roared out. He drummed his fingers on the table.

"I do, my lord." Lucius's eyes darted one way, then another. He reached for his goblet. His hand was trembling. Good. A slave replenished the goblet with honeyed milk.

"It is a delicate matter," said Lucius.

The emperor looked around at the slaves. There were too many around them. All with their ears open. He waved his hand. They disappeared.

"So, come on. I never punish messengers."

"It's about the persecutions, my lord," said Lucius. "My father wishes to make a proposal."

The emperor leaned forward.

"I must go to the arena," said Constantine, abruptly. He stood, and with the briefest of bows left his breakfast mostly uneaten behind him.

XXXIX

Gesoriacum, Northern Gaul, 306 A.D.

Constantine spent the whole day getting to know the horses he was expected to drive at the chariot races. He'd been a regular winner some years before, in the races his Legion had held from time to time on the orders of Diocletian, and he knew well the importance of understanding your horses and getting to know them. Chariot races were one way for middle ranking officers to impress the men under their command, before leading them into battle. It took courage to race chariots.

The Circus arena for the chariot races had been constructed outside the town walls. It was a small circuit, compared to some he'd raced, even the temporary arenas his legion had built outside their forts, but it had the familiar wooden spine down its center, wooden tiers of seats along each side, and gates at the top end from which the chariots would hurtle at the start of each race.

Two days later the festivities began with the slaughtering of a bull in front of the Temple of Ceres near the forum in the town. A procession, headed up by a statue of the bountiful Ceres, held aloft by scantily clad maidens, was followed by trumpeters and chanting, shaven-headed priests. It wound its way to the Circus, where the charioteers were blessed and the matae, the turning posts, were anointed with the pouring of oil.

It was customary for the emperor to wait for the seats around the track to be filled before entering his box under the flapping purple awning. At the Circus Maximus in Rome statues of the gods were arrayed below the imperial box, but here carved local sea gods sufficed.

266

Constantine went to help with last-minute grooming in the marshalling area. He was there when he heard the trumpeters announce the arrival of the emperor. Like the sound of a great animal stirring, everyone in the arena stood and with one voice cheered and whooped. A bitter sea breeze made the hairs on his arms bristle as he and a groom pushed their way through the commotion of horses and handlers to the gates.

"Hail, Caesar Augustus, our beloved Emperor Flavius Chlorus," the heralds roared.

They were answered with a great cheer. The center gate from the marshalling yard was opened and to a tumult of roars and cheers the charioteers marched around the arena in three rows, their sandals kicking up the sand.

They were all blessed with oil flowing, this time in front of the emperor's box by a wiry priest. Each charioteer basked in the cheers of the crowd, as if each roar was for him alone. Young women blew kisses, pulled open their tunics to expose their breasts and waved invitingly at the charioteers as the priest chanted. It took an effort for Constantine to keep his expression stern as the blessing finished to laughter and roars.

The day's events began with a young recruits' race. That was followed by a race for the local tribes. He could tell from the expectant faces in the tiers of seats that many of the legionaries had gambled every denarii on these races.

As he observed the crowd through a gap in the wooden gates he saw Sybellina arriving in the imperial box like a goddess, her hair swathed in a golden veil, which sparkled as it fell over the thick folds of her green cloak. There was an 'ooh' from the crowd. His eyes narrowed. Sybellina acknowledged it all with a bow to the emperor, then another to the spectators, which revealed most of her breasts. They roared. They loved it.

He'd been wondering when she'd arrive. A priestess from Rome would give the proceedings glamour. She'd probably acknowledge him in front of the crowd too. He'd barely seen her in the last few days, but almost against his will he'd been looking out for her. But what he saw that day stunned him. She sat at his father's feet and looked around, as if she was his favorite concubine.

She looked ridiculous.

He went to finish his preparations in the marshalling area. Everything had to be checked, then checked again. But his mind was wandering. His father couldn't be with her. He couldn't. It was all just a show. He tightened a strap too tight, then had to loosen it again.

He had to win, or at least do well. Everything was in the balance now. If he showed courage he'd be respected. He licked his lips. There was sand on them.

Unable to resist, he went back to the gates. She was still there by his father, but she was leaning away from him, talking with an officer. The excitement around the stadium was infectious. The cheering lifted his spirits. He looked through a gap in the wall, raised his fist and roared the lead chariot on in the race that had just started.

The crowd groaned as a local son tumbled, smashing head first into a wall near him, marking it with blood. Slaves rushed out to retrieve the body. Pale bone poked out from the charioteer's neck. Blood dripped. A roar went up. The race had been won by the greens, to hoots of derision from the crowd. The bubble of excitement expanded around him as he fought his way back to his chariot. Charioteers were shouting at grooms, grooms were roaring at slaves, slaves ran about as if the ground was a fire under their feet.

Then the trumpeters blew to announce the main race. He stepped onto the springy wooden platform of his chariot. In his mind, he saw himself winning, receiving the laurel from his father to the acclaim of the crowds. Sybellina was blowing him a kiss. His father would know he shouldn't send him to Treveris. He would know his worth. He would keep him by his side.

Constantine gripped the soft leather rim of his chariot and waited for his horses to be led forward. Sand churned around them as the chariots and horses were positioned in the starting gates.

They were ready. He licked his lips. Sweat trickled down his nose. He wiped it away quickly. He could smell sweat and blood and shit and fear.

The horses shuddered, responding to the baying crowd. Get out of the gate fast. That was what the stablemaster had said. It was what every stablemaster said.

The spectators came to their feet. Only one thing held the chariots back now; an arm-thick chalked rope.

This would be the first time most of the crowd would see their emperor's son.

A winner's name was never easy to earn.

He pulled at the strap holding his leather helmet tight under his chin, then leaned back, balancing his weight over the single axle, pulling the reins of his two shivering horses, ready to release them.

A trumpet blew. A high note.

The race was about to begin. The crowd hushed. The cries of seagulls echoed in the sudden silence.

The reins were wrapped around his fists now, so he could use his bodyweight. He pulled lightly at them. His horses neighed, straining to move. He looked along the line. His opponents stared straight ahead. They would give nothing.

The horses pawed the ground, each set feeding off the excitement of the next. A tremble passed through the reins.

Focus on the rope.

As soon as the cloth fell from his father's hand, the rope would be lifted.

It twitched. It twitched again. The crowd roared.

"Purple!"

The gate opened. He flicked the reins. The chariot jumped under him, almost throwing him. He gripped the reins tighter, spread his legs, remembering what his first chariot master had told him. He leaned sideways as the dust from the chariot in front flew into his face and the boards under him rattled like angry snakes as the chariot flew forward.

The race was a blur from that moment on. At every turn it seemed as if he would fall and his chariot be upended, as he fought, cracking his whip on and on to drive his horses forward. He felt the flick of a whip across his shoulders as a man behind tried to unseat him. Then the whip hit his shoulder. He shrugged it away. He wouldn't be unseated so easily.

There was only one chariot ahead. The crowd were roaring. The last lap loomed, the dolphin lap counter at the turn showing clearly that he had to make his move now. The chariot ahead was close enough that he could hear the urgings of the driver, see him look back, his face drawn, muscles in his neck tight like ropes.

And he saw his chance. He could go inside. He jerked the reins, pulling them hard to the left. A huge spurt of sand rose in the air as the chariot wheels creaked, then bounced high unsettling his feet and sending him crashing into the wicker side of the chariot.

One hand instinctively went to the rim. The chariot bounced again, this time onto the other wheel, which creaked loudly. Ahead there was only the winning post. A roar filled his ears, "Purple, purple," as his horses put their ears back. One of them turned its head. Its eyes were wide, rolling. He cracked his whip over it.

XL

Gesoriacum, Northern Gaul, 306 A.D.

"You are my slave, not his, Juliana," said Lucius.

"But if he wants you, I'll not refuse him, and when he grows tired of you, you can always run back to me. Maybe then you'll be more willing." He winked at her. She looked down at his feet. How big they looked in his military sandals.

"I'll be with Crocus' cavalry from tomorrow. I have a riding tunic that'll need cleaning every day, but when that's done, and properly mind, you can serve Constantine. I'm sure you'll have no problem with that." He made a pleased face at her.

Juliana nodded, keeping her expression as blank as possible as Lucius walked away. What concerned her most was that she'd heard they would sail to Britannia soon. The thought of travelling to the land of her father filled her with anticipation, which made her wish each day and every duty would pass quickly.

Constantine was recovering from his injuries, sustained after his chariot tipped over just beyond the winning post, and she was sure Sybellina was using the opportunity to employ charms and spells to enchant him. Juliana attended his room as often as she could and fortunately Sybellina said nothing about her conscientious cleaning routine, though she did not see her spreading salt on the floor to disturb any spells set in Constantine's room.

The cleaning regime was necessary, as far as Juliana was concerned, because Sybellina's scent hung sickeningly in the air for an unnaturally long period after she'd departed from her visits to Constantine. Juliana had not yet found any charms hidden in his room though, but she knew she needed her own powerful charm to protect him properly from Sybellina's spells.

Back in Bithynia Juliana was well used to creating charms, talismans of hope, for other slaves on the estate. They had worked too, usually in matters of love that were not about Juliana herself. Self-directed charms were always the hardest to get right.

In this case, with Constantine, she needed a charm that would have a high probability of working. He could not become Sybellina's plaything. She was a dark witch who could only harm him. Adding other spells to Juliana's own would give him a chance to fend off Sybellina's magic. And those extra spells would have to be bought.

But she had no money, and she didn't dare steal. So, she would be patient. Her chance would come. Constantine was not finished in his dealings with her. And Sybellina's guard would fall, her watchfulness dim. It was only a matter of time.

Some nights Juliana dreamt she was administering to Constantine's wounds, as she'd spied Sybellina doing. He was lying naked before her, as he did for Sybellina. She was rubbing soothing oils into his body. All over.

She woke after those dreams in a sweat, her nipples erect, a tingling heat flowing between her legs. And when she was finished touching herself, she prayed no one had heard her, and wondered what effect Constantine was having on her, that even she didn't fully understand.

She felt an echo of the same heat whenever she was near him now, and she enjoyed it, enjoyed circling him, cleaning his room, helping him in any way he wished. She had tried taking on Sybellina's airs too, the way she held herself, upright, like a stiff flower, and the way she spoke, clear, but with a glow of enthusiasm, but he never noticed, or at least he didn't say anything about it if he did.

During each day, aside from looking after Constantine and her other duties, she also helped check supplies for the imperial household, which were being counted before their departure. Tiny was helping move these supplies to the galleys tied up at the dock. Most of the fleet however, the legionaries transport galleys, were pulled up along nearby beaches. Some were anchored a little offshore.

To her it was an incredible sight every time she went to the dock. All those ships. All that activity. Each person intent on their task. It felt strange to be a part of it.

A portent of change to add to all the others came to her one afternoon when she visited the docks to give Tiny a message. Flocks of seagulls were moving constantly about the sky. She looked at the gulls, closed her eyes, reached towards them with her mind, warning them that their easy pickings would be gone soon.

When she opened her eyes again the gulls were descending on the dock as one, sweeping down, scavenging between the legs of the men carrying sacks of grain. Among the men they were targeting was Tiny. They had found him for her.

Most evenings that week Juliana and Tiny met in the basement of the main hall in the palace, further along the corridor from the narrow individual cells set into the walls where the slaves slept. She was still wary of him and had no intention of being drawn in by his stupid attempts at friendship.

As they ate the leftovers that served as their final meal each day she usually simply nodded or gave a quick answer if he asked her anything. He told her often he'd forgiven her and asked her repeatedly why she hadn't forgiven him.

Sybellina addressed her in a reasonable manner now too, as if nothing had ever happened between them. This made Juliana more nervous than anything else. Could her refusal to give Sybellina what she wanted have been so easily forgotten?

On the morning of the day before their departure, as Juliana was crossing the kitchen courtyard, Tiny beckoned her to him from the corner by the slops bucket. She wondered at once if she should scream, but he looked distraught, with his hands held out, so she walked hesitantly towards him.

"Please, Juliana."

She looked behind her. There were slaves in the kitchen who would come running if she screamed.

"What?"

"It's Sybellina," he whispered. Then he looked around, as if he thought someone might be listening. A cloud passed in front of the sun and the courtyard fell into shadow. Juliana's mood darkened. She raised her eyebrows.

"Please help me, Juliana. Tell me what to do. I swore to. . . She is. . ." He stopped, looked down, composed himself, then more words rushed out of him. "I can only serve her if I keep my promise. She says I will be cleansed, fit to help her. I don't know what to do." He looked distraught, his face scrunched up, as if he was struggling with some awful burden.

"You can refuse her," she replied.

"But she itches at me, like a worm inside. I cannot sleep. Is this a spell? Please, Juliana."

"Has she given you potions to drink?"

"Yes, vile liquids."

"Refuse them from this moment, if you wish to be free of her."

"But she tells me she will purchase me from Lucius." He looked at her, his eyes pleading. He wanted reassurance, and more, which she wouldn't give. His mouth was working, as if he wanted to say something else, but couldn't get it out.

"Tiny, listen to me. Sybellina is dangerous. Do not go near her again. Do not trust her. Now I must go."

His mouth was open, as if there was more he wanted to say, but it was too awful to speak about.

"What are you not saying?" She leaned towards him.

"She…" He stopped.

"Tell me."

He was shaking. She put her hand on his. He relaxed, slumped a little.

"She cut me. She collected the blood in a bowl." He shuddered. "She made a sign over it. Then drank it."

"Show me."

He held his arms out. There was a bloody scab half way between his elbow and wrist.

"She said not to tell anyone."

She held his hands tight. Then she stepped back from him. This was the lot of slaves. They had to accept everything and anything. She'd heard of things like this before, involving male and female slaves doing things to secure a position with an adored mistress or master. Some slave girls painted their bodies, others had to submit to whips and the cutting out of tongues or even being blinded if they'd broken some rule.

Often cruelties happened just for the sake of it, because their owners could do whatever they wanted with no consequences, even unto the death of the slave.

Juliana gripped his shoulder, then went away. She felt sad for him, but also relief and then guilt. Sybellina had moved on. She was focusing on Tiny. Perhaps now she would get her chance with Constantine.

That night she was woken by shouts and running. Slaves peered from their cells to see what was happening. Screaming pierced the air. Agonized screaming. The voice seemed familiar. Juliana followed as a rush of slaves poured through the kitchen.

In the courtyard, under the light of a full moon, surrounded by slaves, lay Tiny. Juliana's eyes went wide, then wider again, as she took in the scene. Dark blood flowed over the rough ochre tiles, spreading out beneath him. An icy cold hand gripped her heart.

She'd seen two slaves who'd hung themselves, still dangling from a tree, and others brought back dead after fighting with villa guards, but she'd not seen a slave who'd castrated himself, and her vision from tales of such events, about slaves who'd been induced to do it in a ritual to some goddess, had been nothing like this.

Blood was oozing, gleaming. Tiny looked like a half-butchered animal. And still the blood flowed. And he was bellowing again, like a speared pig, and panting, as if he'd been chased by dogs. Moments later, guards with shiny breastplates shoved past, ordering everyone away.

Juliana tried to step forward to help but was elbowed viciously by another slave. Her last glimpse, before the guards surrounded him, was of Tiny's hands curled in the air grotesquely, his face as ashen as the moon, contorted in a pained rictus.

Juliana pushed through the crowd. She had to tell Lucius.

Someone she passed said, "The stupid ox will be dead soon, he's done it all wrong."

A woman laughed. Then abruptly the bellowing stopped, and all the crowd's mutterings died away. Even the guards became silent. There was a cough. Then a long gurgle.

Her stomach heaved. Her hands shook. Her legs wanted to buckle. Blame might fall on her.

He had warned her. She'd failed to tell their master. She was sweating cold drops. More slaves and officials and more guards pressed by her as she made her way into the kitchen.

The head of the imperial household's slaves came towards her. A bald headed, powerful looking ex gladiator. He glared at Juliana. She side-stepped out of his way. A slave dying was not uncommon but dying in such a way could be a bad omen on the household.

"You knew him, didn't you, Juliana?" an older slave woman said. Juliana turned. The woman motioned her forward.

"You are lucky, my girl. Our new emperor has forbidden torturing slaves who know things," the woman whispered, looking round. "You must say nothing, nothing, remember my words. Some want the old days back, you see, and to have us on racks with our limbs broken for daring to say something they don't like." She looked around, clearly scared, then shook her head firmly, a finger tight to her lips, her eyes wide.

The next thing Juliana heard was Lucius shouting for her. She straightened her tunic and with the woman shaking her head behind her, she shoved her way back to where Tiny's body lay. People were drifting away, except for some guards and officials. A puddle of blood seeped all around the body. She could smell it, sweet, earthy, cloying.

"Do you know anything about this?" Lucius shouted, as she came closer. He gripped her arm, shook her. Veins bulged across his brow.

She hesitated. She should tell him everything, shouldn't she? But she couldn't.

"No, master, no. I ran from where I was sleeping. It is terrible, master. I don't believe it. This is impossible." She hoped she sounded innocent.

Lucius spun around. "Who found this slave?" A hand rose in the air. "Was he alone then?" Lucius strode purposefully over to the slave. He gripped the man's bare arm so tight the skin turned white around his fingers.

"Yes, master. There was no one else here. He was wailing," said the slave.

"Who carries out burials here?" shouted Lucius. A hunched man came forward and bowed low. "Arrange for this stupid dog to be buried, tonight, in the outcasts' pit. The dogs can have him." Lucius turned and was gone.

A wave of relief, then briefly anger at Tiny, at how stupid he was, then deep remorse flooded her like a weight as Juliana watched them take the body away. She sat in the courtyard alone after everyone had gone, listening to the wind and the occasional barking of dogs in the distance. She quivered every time she heard some more excited barking starting up. She gazed at the stars as the barking quietened. The pinpricks of light were like distant candles being held by some celestial audience. Who would ever know what those lights really were? She prayed. She prayed to the goddess of her mother, the Heavenly Mother, the same goddess as the priestesses who came by the estate every year preached about, the goddess of light, of love, and of fire. She prayed for Tiny. She prayed for herself, held her arms up. They shook as she prayed

Winged Goddess come,
Lady of the Moon,
Lady of the Sun,
She who holds all hearts.
Who listens to our prayers,
Mother of the Gods,
Full of Grace,
Save us this day,
And at the hour of our death,
Forgive our sins, amen.

She put her hands over her eyes. When would it be over? The pain. The not knowing what was to come. Her tears flowed. They were for Tiny, and they were for her too. Everything was so different here. At every turn, there was a threat. No one rested in the middle of the day, the rain was miserable, and the food was different, greasy. It made the latrines stink and the smell of them stung her eyes far worse than it had in the east.

Her life there had been hard, but she'd felt close to her real home, her real family, far away on the border with Persia. Her childhood, her life before being captured, didn't even seem real anymore, as if she was remembering a dream.

And what would her future hold? More fear?

She'd thought she'd become used to being scared, but she hadn't. And there was one thing sure now. Sybellina was capable of anything. An image of Tiny's body being taken away like a bundle of rags came to her and she shivered. Would that be her future too?

XLI

Gesoriacum, Northern Gaul, 306 A.D.

The camp of the Alemanni outside Gesoriacum stood on the supposedly poor ground close to the marsh south of the city. Crocus didn't care. Soon the Alemanni would get the respect they deserved. And anyway, it was a good place for summoning the spirits of the underworld.

"Get the prisoner. Bring him to my tent," he shouted at one of his bondsmen, as he strode through the group sitting cross-legged in the open area around which the officers' tents had been set up. There were at least thirty bondsmen there, each one sporting the twisted ribbons in their hair representing the part of the great forest their families came from in Germania.

He sat on the red mat at the center of the tent and ordered the cauldron to be brought. It was time to feast.

It was set up in front of him.

When the prisoner arrived, Crocus ordered him stripped naked. The man was a member of the Brigantes tribe, which was appropriate for what was to happen. His hands were bound behind him and he was forced to his knees in front of Crocus.

"Will you give willingly so that another of your tribe may be granted luck by Wooanaz and their journey gifted with the spells of good fortune?"

The man shook his head. His eyes were wide.

"Do you accept you were caught stealing from our camp a few days ago?"

The man nodded, slowly. His expression hardened, as if he knew what was coming.

"You will accept the penalty, then."

The man sniffed, as if holding back tears.

"Drink this," said Crocus. The man had been left without water since his capture. He would drink anything now, even a concoction that would wake him up and ensure he experienced everything that was to come.

"Put him up," said Crocus, softly.

The man struggled as he was taken, but his hands were bound tight, so he couldn't do much more than wriggle and bend. He was laid out and then his feet were bound, and his knees, and a gag with a speaking stone in it was placed in his mouth.

He struggled violently as he was hoisted onto the ring set at the meeting point of the tent's staves. But after a few more breaths he quieted and hung above the cauldron. His eyes were closed now, his expression calm, as if he was praying to the God he'd preferred as a child.

His eyes opened again when the iron wire was placed around his neck. They stayed open as it was tightened with the torc set at the back, twisting round and round, the wire cutting slowly into the Adam's apple. He tried to scream. But already his windpipe was too restricted to get out more than a whistle.

Now his eyes were as wide as they could go, blood shot and bulging, but still he lived, and his blood ran from all around his neck and dripped down into the cauldron from his blood soaked hair.

Crocus stood after a while, took his gold goblet and went to the cauldron. It was already a hand's breadth full of blood. He dipped the goblet in and put it to his lips. He sipped. Yes, the blood tasted good. The sacrifice would be successful. The blood cake would be made and shared with the men. They would know then that they were bound to a new purpose.

He made the sign. The wire was brought tighter and the skin ruptured all around the prisoner's neck as his flesh opened wide like the mouths of the gods seeking blood.

A violent shudder passed through the prisoner's body.

Crocus stiffened, turned, as a breeze opened the flap of the tent to let the man's spirit out.

XLII

Gesoriacum, Northern Gaul, 306 A.D.

When she reached the sleeping cells, she took a small, nearly finished candle and went to where Tiny had been sleeping. Already there was almost no trace of him. His spare blanket and extra tunic had been seized by some opportunist slave, probably before he was even dead.

And there was a strange odor there too. It made her more afraid. A dirty and empty cotton bag and a soiled spare under-garment lay discarded on the floor. The only other thing she found was a thin bronze bracelet, which gleamed at her from under his cot when she looked there, holding the candle in front of her. It had been missed by whoever had been here first.

She picked up the bracelet and went back to her cell.

Early the following morning, after a night of waking to every noise, she was summoned by Lucius.

"Take your things today to the galley we've been assigned. The master of the imperial household will tell you where to go." He came up close to her. "Are you sure you know nothing about what happened to Tiny? You must have talked to him." He glared at her.

"We rarely spoke, master. I didn't care for his company." She looked down.

"Why?"

"He was close to…" She paused, then she said it. "Sybellina." She wanted to say more but didn't dare. And another part of her wanted to take back the little she had said. Who believed a slave?

Lucius' tone softened. "Well, you must forget all this. Tiny was overcome by a daemon. I've seen it. You shouldn't be exposed to such things." He squeezed her arm. "You must keep away from Sybellina, do you understand?"

She nodded. He released her.

"Smile, girl. The wind has changed. Everything is right for our departure. Your father was from Britannia, wasn't he? Do you know what part?"

"The land of the Brigantes, master. He . . ." She hesitated.

"Yes."

"He had a family name, master. Arell, from the family of some queen."

"How do you know all this?"

"My mother, my real mother, she told me stories about him over and over. He was supposed to come back for us." A wave of emotion rose from somewhere deep inside. She bit her lip to control it. Memories flooded back. She coughed. Then again.

"You want to say something?"

She put a hand towards him, as if she would clutch him, but she didn't. "I never thought much of this, master, but my mother told me once that I had the secret power of my father's blood in me."

"What power is that?" He leaned towards her.

"My mother called it the power of the raven. The ability to see the guilty secrets in people's hearts. Their past misdeeds and evil acts."

Lucius took a step back. His eyebrows went up.

"Have you seen mine?"

"No." She shook her head. "I don't think the power is strong in me. Only once or twice in my life have I felt people to have evil secrets they are carrying around." She looked into his eyes.

He stared back at her. "And you have that feeling now."

"Yes, I do."

"About who?"

"The Lady Sybellina." She blurted it out. "She carries evil inside her. I am afraid, master. Afraid how all this will end." She waved in the air, including everything around her.

"We must be on our guard then, Juliana." He leaned closer to her. "And I hope you will find out more about this power of yours in the land of your father. We will travel through the territory of the Brigantes." He turned and walked away.

She bowed at his back. This was the news she needed. She still felt sick at the thought of Tiny's bloody death and what it meant about Sybellina's powers, but maybe there was hope for her. Maybe, if she asked in the towns they passed through, she might find her father, or his people. Her father might be powerful. He might buy her freedom. Hope soared inside her.

She collected her few belongings and went down to the dock. At first, she was refused permission to board the galley they'd had been assigned to, but then the head of the imperial household spotted her and waved her forward. She was told to wait below deck with some other slaves in a cramped and damp smelling area past the rowers.

Constantine, Lucius and Sybellina came on board soon after. Juliana was called to help settle Constantine and Lucius' baggage, which had been brought on board piece by piece. They had been given space in a low wooden structure on the rear of the upper deck. As Juliana was setting up hammocks for her masters, she saw Sybellina behind a thin curtain in a dimly lit corner. She was sleeping there.

At first, Sybellina seemed not to have noticed Juliana. Then Sybellina woke and lit an oil lamp, which silhouetted her against the thin curtain as she changed her gown. Juliana couldn't help staring as Sybellina moved around, naked behind the screen, applying oils to her body.

Juliana could see why men wanted her so much. She was slender, had large breasts, but more importantly she seemed sure, confident of herself, and her body. The sight reminded Juliana of a young tigress she'd seen at the games a long time ago. She watched Sybellina, noticing the way she moved, then copied her movements, mostly in her mind.

Then Sybellina blew out the oil lamp and walked past her with her nose in the air. Juliana finished what she was doing and went to explore the ship.

Below decks, slaves, legionaries and rowers mixed together. Half the rowing positions were taken up by legionaries. They all slept where they sat, and rowed when called upon. Other legionaries lay in the gullies between the benches, their packs and weapons beneath them. There was much excitement, as for some of the legionaries this was their first sea voyage. Many were sick later.

Juliana discovered that she was one of only two female slaves on the ship. The place they had been given to rest was in a corner behind the water stores, where, on this vessel, a guard was permanently stationed.

The departure of the war fleet that day was a heart stopping experience. War horns blared from the ships and were answered from the shore. Along the beach, galleys and wide bottomed merchant vessels pulled away from the shore. Towards the horizon, ships sailed away. In the port, late passengers dashed along the quay and almost-forgotten pieces of baggage were hurriedly loaded. Then, after the last ropes were cast away, they were moving, lumbering out to sea, as the rowers pulled, and the rowing masters beat their drums, echoing one another into the distance.

"This wind should take us across the channel in half a day," the other girl assured her, as they watched from the middle of the deck.

The sky that morning was a just-washed bright blue. Small puffs of clouds, like pieces of cotton she'd seen once at a market, scudded across it. The tide had turned.

"All the signs are right for a good crossing," said the girl. She squeezed Juliana's arm.

Then a noise, a keening, came to them. As one, they both scanned the shoreline to see the source. Juliana's mouth opened wide when she saw the crowd of women standing, pressed together, on the gray pebble beach beyond the dock, wailing as if every last one expected to be slaughtered. She'd never seen or heard anything like it.

"Those Alemanni," said the other slave girl with a sniff. "They bring shame on all Germania. You wouldn't see the Chaucii crying like that, just because their men are off to war." She pushed her dark curls back and secured them with a heavy red hairclip. It seemed too valuable an object for a slave.

Juliana looked back towards the port, saw people crowding onto the dock. Others were streaming onto the beach behind the

285

Alemanni women, where rows of fishnets were drying. It seemed that everybody from the town, from the simplest in their rough woolen tunics to the rich in their fine togas, had come out to watch the fleet set sail.

It looked as if the town's permanent inhabitants, who'd cowered in their houses, felt free to appear again. Slowly the wailing was drowned out by shouts from the ships, and the creaking, sliding noises of the oars. And then, above their heads, there came a whoosh as the sail was raised.

"My master says that I am part of a great campaign," said the girl, as they pressed together at the side planking near where the stairs led down to the rowers.

"Few women are so fortunate, he tells me." She linked arms with Juliana.

Juliana didn't reply, but she didn't push the girl away. They watched together as ships around them dipped in and out of the rolling swells. Juliana felt pride and a tingle of excitement at being part of it all, and the prospect of actually setting foot in Britannia, a place that had always seemed impossibly far away.

"Masters are full of shit," said the girl. Then she giggled.

"He tells me we'll clean Caledonia of every runt who stands against the peace that Rome bestows and that we'll bring prosperity to all Britannia, a finally unified colony." The girl sighed as if remembering something painful. "Who can resist the might of Rome now?" she said wistfully. Then she pulled herself closer to Juliana and whispered in her ear. "How often does your master fuck you?"

Juliana looked her in the eye. "He doesn't. Not yet, anyway."

She breathed in deep. She was about to visit the land of her father. The thought sent a shiver through her. Then she raised a fist to her chest. Here she could be the person her birth mother had foretold. It had seemed impossible that she would find her destiny in the land of her father, the eager words of a seer who'd wanted her to see hope ahead, but the words had come back to her on the voyage and it all seemed possible now.

XLIII

Londinium, Southern Britannia, 306 A.D.

It took them two days to reach Londinium. The crossing was quick, less than half a day. Juliana saw white cliffs in the distance, unlike any she'd seen before. Then they turned away from the shore and the wind died, and for the rest of that day they battled currents as the galley was rowed slowly northwards. At times it seemed they were going backwards and the curses from the officers striding the deck not far from where Juliana huddled confirmed her fears. The sea was darker here than any she'd seen. The stories she'd heard of great sea monsters lurking in these parts seemed totally plausible.

The hidden monsters, the Cetos, could be pulling at the underside of the boat. Perhaps they would pull it down under the waves next.

Then the wind changed again and just before dark, with her fears quietening, they reached a place she was told was near the mouth of a great river, though she saw no signs of it. They anchored by an island with a stone temple on a low headland. A lighthouse on the nearby mainland marked the entrance to a large port. Most of the galleys would dock there. Rutupiae, she heard the place called, and from comments overheard she found out that almost all the legionaries would make their way to Londinium by road from there.

There was much talk about marshalling camps for the push north, and which officers would stay on board and who would go ashore here.

"Pretty slave girls are always welcome in Londinium, girl. You know it's among the most prosperous cities in the empire. Even runaways do well there. Do you fancy that?" said one of the crew to

Juliana in a thick accent, as a haze of smoke filled the horizon as they sailed on the following morning. When she turned to him he winked at her. She looked away quickly.

"And why not?" His voice was almost a whisper. "With friends you can do what you want in Londinium, not what your master tells you."

A cold sharp breeze made her pull her woolen cloak tight. Despite his unwelcome presence by her shoulder, an unusual and unexpected sense of possibility, of freedom, teased at her. Running away had never seemed an option before. Did slaves really do such things here in Britannia?

But she didn't reply, she'd been warned often enough about encouraging men, especially when your master might see you, and within moments the crewman was called away with a shout. As she watched him go she felt an urge to call to him. But there were too many people about. Too many people watching her. And the fear of what happened to runaways who were caught, who were often flayed alive or crucified, kept her lips sealed.

Whenever she got a chance that morning she stared out across the water, measuring their progress, anticipation growing inside her. On both sides there was land now. They had entered the mouth of a great river. Marshlands spread away into the distance on the far side. Flocks of seagulls and mallards wheeled and as they passed some seagulls came to fly around the galley calling out, as if replying to the oar drum and the shouted curses that drove the rowers on.

Great mud banks stood desolate out of the water in places, like the crowns of submerged giants. Birds she'd never seen before with long beaks and a pattern of black and white on their backs were standing on the mud banks in groups poking their beaks into the mud.

Beyond the marshes dark forests loomed. Lonely looking fishermen could be seen on the nearest river bank, oyster and eel gatherers, someone told her, and there were occasional watch towers beside impoverished looking villages on areas of slightly higher ground.

As the banks on each side closed in, plumes of smoke could be seen rising up from walled villas set back from the shore, before drifting lazily into the gray clouds that closed over the landscape like the lid of some giant cauldron. Juliana stared in wonder, spending more time than she should have at the side planking, as the city came closer. A sense of anticipation filled the air. None of the officers seemed to care, as they usually would, that she wasn't doing something, sewing a garment or fetching something for her master.

There was something different about this land. Rome had been all marble and temples, with statues lining its approach. The approach to this city was dirtier, excrement floated by, and as the bank of the river closed in billows of smoke could be seen streaming from long timber and brick walled enclosures.

Then something bumped against the galley and many men looked over the side. She did too. A bloated body, double its normal size, without a head and with ruptures on its back, went past just below her. The smell filled her nostrils and her mouth, making her gag. She turned away and walked to the other side of the galley.

Everything looked wrong. They were passing a long building with a strange galley pulled up on the bank beside it. Even the bricks of the building were wrong, thicker and bigger and more oddly shaped than bricks in the east. Her skin prickled. Was this really where she came from?

They were being watched too, from the shoreline, but there was no joyous waving. Did people here see only invaders when Roman galleys came?

They were relying solely on oar power now to move forward. The thump of doubled oar drums and the watery swish of oars rising out of the river filled the air.

She looked ahead. The emperor's galley, which had been a little in front of them all the way up the river, was near now. It was the largest ship she'd ever seen. It had two long rows of flashing oars, was lined along the water line with shields, and had at its prow a massive ram carved in the shape of a sea serpent. A purple and gold banner fluttered from a crossbeam high up on its single mast. Who would not know that the Emperor Chlorus had come to Britannia?

It took most of that morning for the galleys to navigate the mud banks. The tide rose and as the rush of the river abated they turned a wide bend in the river. Ahead, a stone bridge, with wide arches, crossed the narrowing channel. It was the first crossing point she'd seen. Along each bank sat wooden quays. The ones on the northern shore looked sturdier, newer. The ones on the south looked little used. Legionaries lined a quay on the north side, awaiting the arrival of the emperor. Their curved red shields gleamed, their central bronze studs standing proud in a row, like statues.

On the south bank people in dirty tunics lined up along the quayside. Only a few of them wore proper togas. Desultory cheering rang out, then died.

The emperor's galley was having difficulty in the narrow channel, but eventually, and with the help of pilot skiffs and ropes cast ashore, it pulled up to the quayside.

A smaller galley, with a part of the emperor's personal guard on board, visible on deck for all to see, docked next. The galley Juliana was watching it all from was then hauled tight to the quay. Juliana, who was standing with the other female slave in a quiet corner of the deck, whispered her excitement to her companion. The emperor's guards went quickly ashore and formed a phalanx in front of his galley.

"The emperor must wait until his own men are ashore," said the girl, with a note of satisfaction in her voice. All around, people were getting ready to disembark.

"My master says some high official was murdered in Eboracum. The emperor's security will have to be tight." Juliana looked blankly at her. "You must know Eboracum," said the girl smugly. "It's the biggest city up north." She waved her to the horizon, then tutted.

Juliana replied in Greek. They'd been speaking Latin, everyone here seemed only to speak Latin, and she knew the girl would have no idea what she was saying.

"I'd very much enjoy seeing your ass whipped, before you're sent to work on the fattest and oldest men at the baths here." She laughed at her own joke.

The girl sniffed, ignoring her.

"My master says the raids out of Caledonia are causing panic all over Britannia, and even further. No emperor will be lost on his watch, he says. I hope not. He's promised to free me." She smiled triumphantly.

Juliana looked away. It wasn't hard to guess what favors she'd granted for that upcoming privilege.

They watched as a troop of dignitaries lined up to welcome the emperor. Trumpets sounded, and the eagle insignias of the Legions under the emperor's command were marched ashore. A knot of high officials in pristine togas followed. Finally, and to the thin wailing of wind dampened trumpets, the emperor appeared, wearing a heavy purple cloak trimmed with fur. A thin gold laurel wreath sat firmly on his head.

The welcoming ceremony was watched in silence by a large crowd, held back behind a row of legionaries at each end of the quay. When they saw their governor prostrate himself in front of the emperor however, they let out a huge cheer.

"The emperor is come. The barbarians are routed," were two of the cries that could be heard over and over.

Juliana felt the first spit of rain on her forehead. She touched it, closed her eyes. Could her father be feeling the same rain? Was he here in Londinium?

She wanted the ceremony to be over now, so they could disembark. She was not supposed to revel in her master's position, but secretly she hoped everyone ashore would notice she was part of the imperial household. When she'd first understood that she would live in the company of, and help serve, the son of an emperor it had seemed odd, totally bizarre, but increasingly she enjoyed the status her position gave her. Other slaves, the lowest kitchen ones admittedly, bowed to her occasionally now, and she'd gone from telling them to stop, they wouldn't have anyway, to liking the attention.

She'd wanted, but hadn't dared, to tell the other slave girl how close she really was to Constantine, the emperor's son, but she knew the danger in that. She had to be wary of jealous spite, she'd been told by one unfortunate who'd ended in the fields many years before. But she found it hard to restrain herself from telling someone how she'd

291

read his dreams, and that she'd nursed him back to health after his accident on that last bend of the chariot race, and how she still went to him every day, to see if he needed anything.

She'd made honeyed wine for him, and he'd even told her how he liked it now more than any other drink. She closed her eyes and remembered again how he'd said it. Then she recalled how Sybellina had grabbed his arm and dragged his attention away. Her hands clenched tight to the rail. *How could he like someone as ugly as Sybellina, with her pointy ears and heartless eyes?*

At last, the emperor was conveyed away on what looked like a golden chariot, surrounded by two rows of jangling mail clad guards, who ran to keep up with the horses. Constantine was escorted down the gangplank, and as he and Lucius reached the quayside he turned, caught her eye, and called out for her to join him. She was supposed to wait before following them, but she'd been afraid she might lose her master, so this was perfect. She walked as gracefully as she could down to where they stood. Her heart was thumping. He was waiting for her.

"Our baggage will be brought later, Juliana. Did you leave yours with ours?" She nodded.

"We don't want you to get lost," he said. He turned away and grabbed Lucius' arm. Chariots were rumbling forward around them, and in the distance the crowds cheered on.

Before Juliana could reply, Constantine was hailed by a young man striding along the quay as if looking for someone. When Constantine acknowledged the greeting the man bowed and introduced himself as Valerius, the son of the governor of Londinium.

Valerius was tall, at least as tall as Constantine, and he wore a dark-blue half-toga of unmistakable quality. His blond hair was worn a little longer than the usual cropped Roman style, but what Juliana noticed most was his expression of bemused wonder, and the way he held his head at a slight angle.

Constantine was treated with theatrical reverence by Valerius, who kissed the hem of his cloak, then his hand.

"You will all be lodging at our humble home during your stay," said Valerius. He bowed again.

"I've stocked up with all the best foods and the strongest beers and wines between here and Rome herself." He pushed a mop of hair away from his brow with a flourish. "I thought I'd be entertaining Alemanni officers." His eyebrows rose, and he looked around conspiratorially.

"But when news reached me that the emperor's son had rejoined his father, I insisted we host you. Have you any idea what stuffy old Alemanni officers are like? Well, I've entertained enough of them." He looked through Juliana as if she wasn't there, then touched Constantine's arm in a friendly manner.

"Come, you must greet our plebs, and after you've settled in we'll tour the best pleasure houses in Londinium. They're the wickedest from here to Rome, and I should know." He coughed, looked round again. "Or I could introduce you to the priestesses of Isis." Juliana gawped. Did he ever stop talking?

"My father prefers me to follow Mithras of course, but I find the priestesses of Isis much more entertaining. Even ladies find them accommodating." He winked at Juliana, laughed and called for a chariot.

The streets beyond the docks were lined with people from almost every tribe in the empire. Constantine and Valerius, Lucius and Juliana, and Sybellina, all went in separate chariots. Sybellina rode with an older man, an official from Valerius' household. The crowds cheered loudly when they saw the purple cloak on Constantine's back.

Juliana had never been cheered through the streets of a city, had never even dreamt of such a thing, and the sight of young men blowing her kisses, people smiling and waving, made her forget all her cares. She waved back with increasing confidence and laughed as boys ran up and tried to kiss her hand where it lay on the rim of the chariot. It was her first experience of the public pleasure of being associated with the imperial family, and she loved it.

"Women gladiators entertain the crowds in the Colosseum here, Juliana," said Lucius. They'd just passed two blond girls cheering wildly. They had, very obviously, been trying to attract his attention with gestures and winks. "They're one of the attractions of this city, I hear. The descendants of Queen Boudicca showing off their

293

fighting spirit. I'm sure there'll be games in honor of the emperor, so we can see if these women can fight." He growled at her like a wild cat.

She leaned away from him, then laughed. The idea of women fighting in the arena intrigued her, especially if they fought men. She wanted to see it.

The streets were lined with colonnades of shops of every type, from armorer to weaver. Almost all looked prosperous, freshly painted, with new wooden signs gleaming outside. A few of the stalls had tables in front, obstructing pedestrians so much people had to walk in the street, adding to the crowds gawping close to them as they passed. Some cheered at the sight of the purple. Other people just stared. But the shouts from the street hawkers and some shop owners didn't stop, either enticing people to try the wares or greeting customers, and all in a Latin dialect mixed with strange new words, some rhymed together.

When they arrived at Valerius' villa Juliana was ordered to help his household slaves prepare for their guests, and to supervise the unpacking of the baggage when it arrived.

It all turned up as she was eating a hurried early evening meal in a large stone floored kitchen. She had to stuff her mouth and rush after the slave who came with the news, to ask him if he would help her carry everything. She'd never be able to do it on her own, and again she thought about Tiny and wondered would he ever be avenged.

Constantine's baggage had grown since they'd met with his father too. He had three large wooden chests now. Two were filled with ceremonial togas he'd been given by the master of the imperial household. His other belongings, what he'd brought from the east, didn't even fill the third chest.

"How could the son of an emperor live without at least twenty togas?" Juliana said to a friendly slave girl who was helping her unpack. The girl's Latin was good, despite her being from a tribe in the far west of Britannia. Everyone in the household she'd met spoke Latin fluently, to her surprise. The girl grinned as she folded a toga.

"Is it true he's not married?" she said, wide-eyed. "And he wins chariot races?"

Juliana nodded. Suddenly she felt an old urge. The urge to tell her whole story. She hadn't felt it in a long time. Disinterest and derision had quietened her. Tales of ill luck were as numerous as the leaves that fall after the harvest is brought in. But now she was associated with Constantine everything was changing, including how other slaves looked up to her.

The girl giggled. "You do know he'll be chased by every vixen in this town. Some of them are right tarts, flashing everything at the masters." She put her hands over her eyes as if she was embarrassed. Then she giggled again. "Some of them have been preparing since the first day they heard about him!" She lowered her voice. "Even us slave girls have been washing our hair in flower scented water." The girl shook her head until her hair spun around like a flail.

Juliana could smell flowers. She had to say something.

"You should know that he never chases women. So, don't get your hopes up. And tell the others the same." The girl looked crestfallen.

"He prefers boys?"

Juliana shook her head. "No, it's not that." She closed the lid of the chest with a bang. She wasn't going to say any more.

Lucius' room was beside Constantine's. His baggage consisted of the two saddlebags he'd brought from Bithynia. Unpacking those was easy. Disappointingly, Sybellina's bags arrived separately and she wasn't asked to help with them.

Juliana adored Valerius' villa from the moment she was shown her own room. She was amazed when she saw it. It had a heated mosaic floor, gaily painted walls, woodland scenes in blues and golds, and was by far the finest room she'd ever slept in, unlike the burrow-like cells she was normally allocated. She'd no idea why she hadn't been given such a cell in the basement with the other house slaves, but she was afraid to say anything in case the mistake was uncovered and rectified.

The house was reassuringly laid out in the traditional style of a city villa, around an elegant courtyard with a marble fountain and a statue of a blue nymph. At the front of the villa there were two progressively more impressive reception halls. The bedrooms were at

295

the back of the main courtyard. A baths complex had been constructed on a corridor at the rear of the villa, and boilers there kept the water and the underfloor heating at just the right temperature. Without such heating her room would have been cold. She'd noticed how cool it was here for the time of year. The summer would be starting already in the east.

A kitchen courtyard led into the street at the very back. A separate covered corridor for the slaves of the household ran down the back and on one side of the house. It connected the kitchen area with the reception halls at the front.

Constantine, Valerius and Lucius went to enjoy the baths complex after their arrival. As she finished tidying their rooms she heard the faint sound of Lucius laughing. The sound reminded her of a distant time, before she'd become a slave. She closed her eyes as memories flooded back. At once she opened them and rubbed her face. They would know if tears stained her cheeks. They wouldn't like it. Slaves were not supposed to display their problems in front of their masters. She looked down, saw a spot on the floor, bent and scrubbed hard at the dirt engrained into the mosaic. She had hope now. She had come a long way. If anyone had told her a few years before that she would end up like this, in the entourage of an emperor's son, with a room as if she was a master's daughter, she would have shouted at them and called them a stupid liar. She stood. There was work to do.

She'd been warned there'd be a feast of welcome in the governor's palace that evening and laid out Constantine's best embroidered togas in readiness. Lucius would have to borrow one, as his own was too patched for such an occasion.

When she'd finished the preparations, she waited at a bench in a corner of the courtyard, sewing closed a rip in a toga. Only Constantine looked at her as they passed. But that lifted her heart and sent it soaring. None of them motioned her to follow them. After they'd moved into their rooms, Sybellina appeared from hers and without a word or glance at Juliana, who felt, for a sickening moment, as if she'd been caught doing something terrible even glancing at her, Sybellina headed towards the baths. A slave boy from the household padded behind her carrying a red lacquered box. Juliana watched, relieved, as the boy followed Sybellina through the iron-grill gate to the baths at the rear of the courtyard. It hadn't taken her long to find herself a new acolyte.

Soon after, Lucius appeared again. He called to Constantine, then sat on the stone bench near the center of the courtyard. He looked around, constantly. Constantine came out from his room. He still walked with a slight limp from his recent injuries, but his bandages had been removed to allow air to the wounds. He had healed quickly. Lucius waved at Juliana to come forward.

"Valerius is with that slave girl who was rubbing him down," she heard Lucius replying to something Constantine had said. Then he turned to Juliana. "Did you find some good wine?"

"Yes, master."

"Well, let's see if it is as good as Valerian claims. Fetch a jug."

"You'll get your chance with the bath girl." Constantine sounded amused. "I saw her giving you the eye when she was rubbing him down." He looked up and winked at Juliana. She half smiled back at him, then suppressed the rest and turned away.

When she returned their mood had changed. "You must . . ." Lucius stopped talking as she came forward. He scowled, then looked around as if he was checking if others might be listening.

"Wait there, Juliana. Tell us if anyone's lurking about beyond the gate." Juliana bowed and went to stand by the gate to the baths. It was not far from where they were sitting. Beyond it she could hear Sybellina ordering the slave boy. Then everything went quiet from the baths. One of the few benefits of being a slave was that you heard conversations, some very interesting conversations. She stepped towards her masters, so she could hear them better. Constantine's voice was raised.

"What are you worrying about? I'm safer now than I have been for years. What do I have to fear?"

"Think about it, Constantine." Lucius was angry. "Our arrival spiced the pot. Most people hate new things. You know that. Look to his advisors if you want to change his mind. I bet they're the ones telling him not to grant you the position you deserve. You must be careful. Every step you take is being judged."

Juliana held her breath, afraid she might not hear Constantine's response. Then, far off, there was shouting and horses neighing. And something rustled in the rose bush that twisted through the trellis behind her. She looked around, alarmed, but saw nothing.

"And you're wrong, Lucius, trust me on that. Why would his advisors stand against me?"

Lucius stood up. Juliana turned her back to them, as if she had no interest in their conversation.

"They see you as a threat, Constantine. To themselves and to your father. They'll want you far below them. In the underworld, I expect."

Her mouth went dry. Was Lucius right? Was Constantine in danger? Her skin felt clammy down her back.

"I'll show them they have nothing to fear." Constantine sounded confident.

"You're a dutiful son, truly, but you must be on your guard, that's all I'm saying." Lucius' tone changed. He sounded angry now. "Have you seen the way Crocus, that Alemanni cavalry commander, looks at you before he whispers in your father's ear? Something's going on there. I swear it."

Juliana turned her head. Lucius had his hand on Constantine's shoulder.

"So, we make an alliance with Crocus. But I want no intrigues. And tell me, did my father agree to see you again?"

Lucius tutted loudly.

"No, he hasn't. I must wait, they say. I'm useful in Crocus' cavalry. I'll be called when your father's ready."

Constantine laughed, a small bitter laugh. "And so we are all waiting." He sighed, loudly. "You'd think my father was doing this deliberately."

"It's his advisors. It must be."

"Don't start down that road again, Lucius. You have a position in the army. That's more than I have. Come, let's get ready. It's getting late, and it's cold out here. This is not Bithynia." He stood up, and with a sideways glance at Juliana, and a nod, he disappeared off to his room.

Lucius motioned Juliana to him.

"You'll help me get ready." He looked and sounded angry. Juliana bowed quickly and followed him.

As she fussed around him, adjusting the folds of his borrowed toga, he enquired about how she was. His tone was friendly now, and it came to her that he wanted something. Ever since Tiny had died he'd been endlessly hard with her, ordering her about on endless errands, fetching and carrying things he sometimes never used. Now, there was something else he wanted.

"I see the way you look at him." His words were accompanied by a grin.

"Master?" She had dropped the edge of his toga. She picked it up quickly. How could she have been so stupid? She imagined all the ways he would punish her.

"Don't fret. Your secret's safe with me." He tapped at her hand playfully, then looked at her openly in a way that dispelled most of her fear, like water washing away dirt. The relief made her grin too. He motioned her to move away and finished adjusting his toga. "You heard our conversation outside, I suppose?"

"Yes, master.".

"You will know, then, that I fear for Constantine's life." She moved further away from him. The ochre stained wall was right behind her and half-lit shadows were playing on it from the cluster of oil lamps suspended in their bronze floor-standing holder in the far corner of the room. It felt odd to hear Lucius talk like this, confiding in her. For a moment she thought he'd confused her with someone else. Then a strange sensation warmed her stomach. He was discussing these things with her because he trusted her.

"Juliana, you know you must not speak of any of these things, not to anyone." He frowned at her. His mood was changing again.

"I won't, master. You have my word."

"And will you help me protect Constantine?"

"Yes, master." Her blood was thumping in her neck, as if it expected some further shock to come.

"Good, I have a task for you. Tonight, you will accompany me to this feast for us, and I'll point out Crocus, the cavalry commander, to you."

Juliana glanced at him quickly, then down at the floor, where a good slave kept her gaze. What was he up to?

"You will find him tomorrow morning, early, and seek a private audience. Say you have a message from me. When he sees you, tell him I wish to make a donation to assist with his expenses and that I wish to meet him." Lucius shrugged nonchalantly, as if such a donation meant nothing to him. "When you return, come straight to me, and tell me everything he says and everything he did. Everything, do you understand? So, keep your eyes open."

A nagging worry was growing inside her. She'd known a slave who'd been pressed to be a messenger, to spy on one of the neighboring families back in Bithynia. The man was found soon after, hanging from a tree. As a warning to tricksters who copied Mercury, so she'd been told. She opened her mouth, leant a little forward, as if she might say something, then thought better of it.

Her stomach felt empty and hollow. Then it came to her. Was this why she'd been allocated a proper bedroom, so that Lucius could keep a close eye on her?

He shook his head, as if he knew what was going on in hers. "It's just a simple message, Juliana." His tone implied he was injured at her ill-concealed unease.

She looked up at him and felt a rush of guilt. She didn't ever question her instructions, not in any way, even with a look. She knew better. She shouldn't even have opened her mouth to reply. Keep your head down when asked anything was what had been drummed into her, with beatings for the most minor infraction. If you don't react in any way, your master will not get angry. She'd learnt that long ago, but he'd asked so politely and the strict rule of obedience, which every slave had to follow on pain of death, had seemed overruled, relaxed on their journey. She pursed her lips. She mustn't do that again. She'd seen awful, stomach-churning things happen to slaves who spoke out. And she'd need Lucius' help if she was ever to be free.

Lucius leaned towards her. "If you serve me well, Juliana, you'll be rewarded well. Now remember what I told you and make no mistakes. You have nothing to fear."

She knew at once that she'd been lucky. He wasn't going to make anything of her reaction. She excused herself, saying she had to ask the Master of Valerius' household for a clean tunic for herself. Soon she was running down the back corridor, relief pushing her on, and when she returned, grateful, with the tunic, she went into her room to change. When she was ready she came out again quickly into the courtyard where Constantine and Lucius were waiting for Sybellina.

When Sybellina finally appeared, her skin glowed as if she'd come straight from the warm room at the baths. Her hair had been coiled painstakingly on top of her head, and her diaphanous green gown fitted tightly around her slim body, with a necklace of small yellow pearls dangling from her pale neck. She looked like a statue of a goddess sprung to life.

Juliana felt ugly, terribly ugly, in her coarse tunic, even if it was clean. She glanced again at Sybellina, then looked down. Sybellina was bowing for Constantine, revealing her breasts entirely. They were pendulous and alluring. Juliana had managed to suppress her feelings towards Sybellina, but now, seeing her so obviously trying to tease him, her resentments came rushing back. She was standing a little way from them, her head bowed in the most respectful attitude of a slave, determined not to catch anyone's eye. None of this should matter, she kept telling herself. She would think only of finding her father. But she found it hard to distance herself.

And it became even harder when Sybellina's flirtatiousness extended to Lucius. And he also appeared remarkably eager to join in. Sybellina kissed him on both cheeks, and then she kissed Constantine on both cheeks before squeezing in between him and Lucius with a laugh and putting her arms around their shoulders. The tinkle of her laughter filled the air as they waited for litters to arrive at the front of the villa.

When a slave arrived to say that their litters were here, they were all ushered out into the street. Juliana had seen litters in Nicomedia, and in Rome, but neither city had as many as here, nor the

301

variety of styles. She didn't have to run to keep up with the stocky attendants, who carried each of the two litters, Constantine and Sybellina in one large one with six men carrying them, and Lucius in another with four men, but she had to walk fast, and it felt odd after all the days in Gaul riding beside or near to her masters to be following them again. She was reminded starkly of her place.

In the gray of what seemed a very long dusk the light from the torches burning at street corners made the breastplates of their attendants gleam. The people of the city stood back as the procession passed down their narrow brick-paved streets. Most of the other litter attendants weren't nearly as burly, or as well armored as theirs. Some looked worn down by their task. Indeed, one pair weighed down with a large red-curtained litter stumbled as they went by. Angry, panicked shouts emanated from the occupant as the attendants righted the litter at the last moment. Juliana almost stumbled too as she watched. She'd wanted to rush to help, but now all she did was give the attendants a nod as they passed in the street. They stared back, as if observing the passing of gods.

The governor's palace had a wide, double height pillared reception hall, which was packed with people by the time they arrived. A buzz of conversation ran through the room, like you might hear at a busy market. Local officials and army commanders with bejeweled concubines mingled with merchants and the emperor's high officials all dressed in their finest. Slaves, both male and female, in minuscule purple tunics, carried trays of silver goblets filled with spiced or honeyed wines. Bright frescoes on the walls glowed in the gently swaying light from clusters of oil lamps hanging from the roof.

They passed a man loudly pointing out new additions to the frescoes, the tribal God Rhiannon, the god of horses, and Esus, the god of nature, now occupied prominent positions on the walls alongside Jupiter and Apollo.

"Britannia is a rich province, it seems," said Lucius, to no one in particular.

Laugher and animated conversation floated round them as they moved through the hall. Constantine was hailed by an obese high official whose two equally ugly daughters were pushed forward and presented to him with insistent glances by their mother. Juliana scowled. They bowed low showing anyone who wanted to look the fullness of their milk white breasts. One of the girls grinned up at Constantine as her breasts and protruding nipples were exposed. Juliana hoped her presence and sour expression might deter them a little, but neither girl looked in her direction, though their mother glanced at her in a way that signaled she knew Juliana wasn't one of their class.

The mother asked Constantine in a wheedling tone, "And when will your father arrive, my lord?"

Constantine shrugged as a distracting commotion broke out on the far side of the room. All heads turned. People stood on their tiptoes or leaned on their partners to get a better look. A troop of four trumpeters had entered, each wielding a massive spiral war trumpet. An extended trumpet blast quieted the onlookers. Juliana felt a shiver of anticipation.

The tall wooden doors at the rear of the room creaked open as the last note of the fanfare died away. The emperor, Constantine's father, appeared in the doorway in an elaborately embroidered purple toga. There was a gasp, then a cheer, then everyone bowed low as the emperor moved forward.

A few began to prostrate themselves, but the emperor waved them up, insisting loudly that it wasn't necessary.

Time passed slowly all that evening for Juliana. She felt isolated, and in fear of what was to come. No one spoke to her except Lucius, and he just gave whispered commands to smile, stand straight or to refill an empty goblet. Other personal slaves could be seen around the room doing the same for their masters. They all looked better at it than she was.

The crowd thinned as those who'd not been invited to dine departed. Finally, after what seemed like an age, the whole party moved to a dining hall. Juliana took her place behind the table Constantine, Lucius and Sybellina were led to. When she smelled the food she was glad she'd eaten bread with cheese before they'd come. A large lump of it had been pressed into her hand in the kitchen by the girl who'd helped her unpack.

Trays of dried herring and stuffed kidneys were served first, then roast beef, and minced oysters (the best in the empire, claimed Valerius) stewed with celery and dates. Each dish was announced by its server. The smell of food was tantalizing. Her mouth watered as each one appeared.

The locals drank wine and beer as if they had a great thirst. It intrigued her that the emperor and his son drank and ate hardly anything. It was her first time observing them together, within a couch length of each other, and she concluded they were as similar as father and son could be, each a thick-necked bull dominating their table.

Half way through the feast a red-tunicked slave appeared by Sybellina's side, at the opposite corner of the table from where Juliana stood. He whispered in her ear. Sybellina, with most of the eyes in the room on her, went and sat close by the emperor at the main table. The buzz of conversation in the hall rose to a crescendo as she leaned close to the emperor and laughed her warm and friendly laugh for all to hear. Juliana looked away.

Constantine's expression darkened. The conversation at his table stopped for a moment. He turned and looked at the expectant faces around him.

"My father delights in the soothsayer I brought for him. Let's hope she brings him good fortune." He raised his goblet. The other diners at the table, Valerius, his father, his mother, and Lucius, raised their goblets and drank.

For the rest of the night Juliana stole occasional glances at Sybellina. All the men around her were clearly enthralled by her presence among them. She was like an old mare with a knot of graying stallions pressing round her. How could they be so taken in by her pale, badly-plastered make up and high-pitched laugh?? There was clearly a lot of half-blind men in Britannia, the type who needed a slave to find the straps of their sandals.

Even the plump, almost-naked dancing girls, who were desperately trying to entertain the emperor's guests, could not hold the gaze of anyone at the table after Sybellina had joined it.

She had to be using some powerful magic. How else could so ordinary a woman hold so many men in her spell?

304

Constantine had turned his back on his father's table, while he and Lucius entertained everyone around them with stories about their journey from Nicomedia. More wine was drunk and toasts to the emperor, Rome, and the imperial family passed, one after the other, from table to table.

"Come, my new friends, let me show you the real entertainments this city has to offer," said Valerius, after one raucous toast. Then he stood a little unsteadily, and motioned Constantine and Lucius to follow him. Lucius stood first. He motioned Juliana to his side.

"You will come with us, Juliana," he said, softly. "Perhaps we'll meet some of your relatives." He touched her cheek, stroking it. Some of the men were looking at her now and grinning, making her feel uncomfortable. She could smell stale wine from his breath as Lucius whispered in her ear. "Do you see the red-bearded man beside the emperor?"

"Yes, my lord."

"That's Crocus." He bowed low in the direction of the emperor's table, and then stumbled after Valerius. Juliana's stomach tightened. She'd been hoping Lucius, after the amount of wine he'd downed, might have forgotten about the task he'd given her.

Torchbearers with drawn swords escorted the group from the back entrance of the governor's palace across a small brick-paved square to one of the largest taverns Juliana had ever seen. Constantine and some others from their table made up the rest of their party. The tavern had a pair of green glass oil lamps hanging outside. Inside, it was laid out like a villa with an ornamental garden at its core for guests to sit in and watch entertainments.

Dwarfs dressed as legionaries ran and tumbled in the garden and around the tables, and as Constantine made his way past them they bumped into each other, as if they'd been distracted by the new guest. Then they unsheathed short wooden swords in mock anger at each other, to the amusement of the wealthy looking patrons. Valerius shouted at the dwarfs. They ran off screaming, to the cheers of the crowd.

Then he led them to a large table and demanded wine, beer and fruit from the beaming serving girls. Everywhere she looked there were girls preening. She insisted on filling Lucius' and Constantine's goblets herself from the jugs that were brought, and then stood behind them, glaring at any of the serving girls who tried to catch their eye.

"This is the best moon's milk, they tell me." Valerius raised his goblet. He shook his other fist in the air. "A toast to our illustrious fathers. May our brothels always be as stuffed with talent as theirs."

Everyone joined in the toast.

"You should know, Constantine, that I'm to be appointed a tax farmer in the north as soon as your father finishes up there. I do hope his Legions do a better job than the Emperor Severus'. Squeezing provincials is not my idea of happiness, but if they're in fear of the Legions the job will be a lot easier. And so, to the Legions!" Another toast was drunk.

"I may end up a coin counter too, before my father finishes here," said Constantine, wistfully. "Unfortunately, no Legion could make that job easier for me."

"No, surely not!" Valerius shouted. He pushed at Constantine, causing Juliana to spill a little of the beer she was refilling his goblet with. Constantine simply looked up at her and smiled. She looked away. She'd met enough drunk slave boys to know they'd rape a hole in a wall if the sun had warmed it up.

"You are an experienced military commander. That's what I heard. You should lead a Legion. What a waste." Valerius shook his head and drank deeply from his goblet. A serving girl with a low cleavage, exposing most of her breasts, and shifting, lizard eyes refilled it.

Soon a group of Valerius' acquaintances had gathered around them. They vied to entertain Constantine and Lucius with tales of their life in Londinium.

Then Valerius, who Juliana thought looked bored at not being the center of attention, suggested they all move to a different place not far away.

The tavern he led them all to was no more than a large circular hut with battered bronze war shields oozing their history hanging from its walls, and a thick bed of rushes strewn on its lime-packed floor. A thatched roof stood above their heads supported by blackened timber beams. In the center of the room a round pit piled up high with firewood crackled. A column of smoke drifted to a hole in the center of the roof. Long tables circled the room, and from what she could see - it was dark in parts of the room - groups of bearded native Britons crowded most tables.

The place smelt of stale beer, sweat, wood smoke and spiced wine. A wild beating of hand drums filled the air as they entered. Then the drumming stopped, as if the drummers had belatedly seen intruders. Everyone in the roundhouse turned to glower at them. They were halfway across the room, heading for an empty table near the fire. Dice players at a nearby table, distracted from their gambling, looked up at them in disgust as they passed, clearly irritated at the intrusion.

Valerius waved to the drummers, shook his fist at the dice players, and greeted nearby tables with shouts of recognition. The drumming recommenced. Most people looked away. One old man stared quizzically at Juliana as she passed. It amazed her how different everybody looked here from the previous tavern.

The stubby tallow lamps on the tables were not nearly as bright as oil lamps too. Each table here was a yellow island amid shadows swirling.

Some of the tavern's patrons wore belted, dark woolen tunics. Many wore unusual vertically striped breeches. Cloaks were pinned at the shoulder with intricate gold or bone brooches. Hair, mostly brown or raven black, was worn long. It curled over shoulders or was plaited and held back with bronze pins. Faces were shaved, but many of the men had thick moustaches. Serving women carried jugs or plates of food and wore short wool tunics, their complexions ruddy and unadorned with the heavy pale creams Roman matrons favored.

A strange language filled the air, with only the occasional Latin word thrown in. One of the men at a nearby table was wearing a thick twisted torq of what looked like gold around his neck. The men around him looked like his body guards. When Valerius saw the man, he invited him to share their hospitality.

Juliana kept looking from one table to the next, trying not to stare for too long and attract unwanted attention. The atmosphere in the round house was raucous, aggressive, as if the men here wanted everyone to know they were different, not cowed by the Roman presence all around them.

Juliana was sent to fetch wine and beer with one of Valerius' slaves who'd accompanied them. When they returned the man with the torq was sitting opposite Constantine, at the end of their long darkly stained table. He was swaying from side to side. His thick black hair fell straight and loose over his shoulders. His long moustache would have earned him only ridicule in Bithynia, but in this place it looked normal. His face was scarred too, as if it had been clawed by a bear on one side. The only thing she found attractive about him was his ice-blue eyes. There was something familiar about them. Then it came to her. They were a similar shade of blue to hers.

She stood behind Constantine holding the wine jug, so she could hear what the man was saying.

"I am Morbod," the man's Latin lilted up and down. "My father is Aengus, King of the Ordovices, from the land by the Hibernian sea. His father was Nemed, also King, as was his father before, and his before that, all the way back to the time of the first people. You ask why I'm in Londinium. Well, I will tell you. I am looking for a beauty. An Olwen, who I will marry." He grinned, displaying black teeth. "Now, before we go further with this chatter, who are you, and what brings you here to the land of the Brigantes?" He gave Constantine a granite stare.

Juliana waited, holding the jug of wine low.

"I am Constantine, the first son of the Emperor Chlorus. I am here with my father to bring the peace of Rome to all the peoples of this island. Will you drink with me, Morbod?"

Morbod took a moment longer than was polite to answer. "This your first time in Britannia?"

Constantine nodded.

"Well, we'll have no bloody feud with you yet then, so ladle out the wine."

Constantine motioned to Juliana.

She poured spiced wine for them both.

"So, who's this Olwen you seek?" asked Constantine.

Morbod sneered.

"How should I know, I have not met her yet. If I had met her, I would not be sitting here. I would be splitting her with my cock."

"I wish you good hunting." Constantine raised his goblet.

Morbod stayed at the table.

"I hear your father comes to break the old treaty," he said. Then he pushed his face towards Constantine's, while crashing his fist onto the tabletop. Valerius, who sat next to Constantine, reached for his dagger on his belt, but Constantine held his hand up and shook his head.

Morbod leaned forward some more. "Your father has been tricked. Why break with a hundred-year-old treaty and claim the rest of this island now? Why?" His tone was contemptuous. "Because your father wants to feed his land hungry Alemanni warmongers, and that's the truth. A truth the dogs in your Roman Forum know, even if you don't. The Emperor Severus paid with his life for the last attempt to conquer Caledonia. I hope your father doesn't make the same mistake, or you."

"It's the Picts who break the treaty, with their raids and their murders," replied Constantine.

"Raids to retake cattle stolen by Romans, and the death of the magistrate responsible seems a petty excuse to bring war on the heads of all those beyond the Wall," said Morbod. He leaned towards Constantine. "I hope your spies have informed you of the druid's spell that lies over Caledonia. A spell that no Roman can ever break. Hadrian knew all about it. Carausius recently lost his pride learning about it. Your father may have to learn about it the hard way too." He raised his goblet, downed his drink in one swallow. Then he slammed it on the table. Some drinkers nearby put their own goblets down and stared.

"Your father could hunt there instead," he continued, in a friendlier manner. "Pursue the Caledonian boar. Maybe he'll be luckier than Severus or my friend Carausius." A growling laugh bubbled up from deep inside the man's chest.

He looked at Juliana, who was refilling his goblet. She was standing with her head lowered in the correct way, but she felt his gaze on her. Their eyes met for a moment.

"You have a slave from Britannia, Constantine?" He looked puzzled. Then, leaning forward, he addressed Juliana. "There is the look of a Briton in those eyes. Are you from here?" He added something in his own language that she didn't understand. She frowned at him. He knew she wasn't allowed speak to her master's guests. She felt angry. Constantine would think she'd encouraged the man by looking at him. Then Lucius intervened. He was sitting next to Morbod.

"You are only half right, friend. Her mother was a Persian, but her father was a Brigantes, called Arell, she claims, though this is her first time anywhere near his island. She's a passable dream reader, so Constantine tells us. Perhaps even as good as the priestess, Sybellina." He looked up at Juliana.

She stared back, her expression hardening. Everyone around them was looking at her. Her cheeks burned from the unwanted attention. She wanted to run.

"I hear dream reading is a skill many possess here," continued Lucius.

Morbod bowed in her direction. His brow was furrowed. "Few possess the gift of the sight. It is a special gift." He put his hand up, his palm facing Juliana. "I feel it around you. You are a daughter of the great Queen all right." He turned to Constantine. "You pick your slaves well, Roman." He looked back at her.

Her mouth opened, as if she might ask him something. Then she closed it again. This was not the time.

He stared at her, then answered her as if he knew the question she was thinking. "Yes, I have seen your face before. Your kin live in Eboracum. They make the iron swords that cannot be broken. All their secrets came from the top of the world and were learnt from daemons." He spat on the floor near her feet. She took a step back, looked around.

Directly behind her, sitting on a low stool, was an old beggar with a puckered scar where one of his eyes should have been. The

310

beggar's tunic was fashioned from untanned animal hide. Shapes traced in faded purple and yellow dyes swirled all over it. He had a mat of twisted slate-gray hair hanging down like a tail over his shoulder.

The drumming was louder now, the air stuffy, the room spinning, everything in shadow, getting darker, black.

As Juliana slumped, the beggar reached out with both hands and caught her deftly. His movements belied his age. Constantine leant forward to help, but he was too far away. Lucius moved off the bench and assisted the old man.

"Give her a kick," shouted Valerius. "I find that works wonders with slaves."

"I'll bring her outside," said the beggar, softly. "She'll come around in the air." Lucius rolled his eyes. He was drunk. The beggar grunted, picked Juliana up as if she were a baby and carried her towards the door. Some of the locals cheered as they passed and winked at him. Juliana was only groggy but came around completely in his arms. "Ow!" Someone had pinched her bottom. She moved, wiggling out of his grasp. The beggar set her down.

"I'm thirsty." Her legs were weak under her. She crinkled her nose. What was that smell? Lucius, who had followed with a displeased look on his face, put his arm around her middle and guided her out through the doorway.

"That'll teach you," he said. Beyond the doorway, lying on its side, a long block of granite rested, a vestige of some old tribal monument. She sat on it. Under her sandals tufts of grass alternated with bare earth. She felt a lot better in the cooler air.

"Slaves and taverns never mix. We'll be leaving soon. Wait here." Lucius bent down and looked in her eyes, examining them.

"I'll be better soon. I just need some air for a few moments." She wanted to add that he'd be drinking piss from the tavern owner by the end of the night if he kept drinking, but instead she clamped her mouth tight.

"Don't forget your duty. You cost too much to end up being a waste. The price of a pretty slave girl is an extortion in this town. I do not want to replace you. And if you run away now I will see you cut open when we catch you."

She nodded. He shook her shoulder roughly and stood up. Then he gave the beggar who'd lifted her a coin and ushered the man back into the tavern.

She took a deep breath. She didn't care about Lucius or what he thought of her. Everything had changed. She would find her father. She could feel it in her bones. She'd met someone who knew about his people. It was a sign. It had to be. Coincidences didn't simply happen.

It was the spirits intervening. Her head felt light, as if a summer wind was blowing through it. But her mind was clear, all her fears carried away on the wind. Her father would buy her freedom. She'd seen a sign in her dreams, a bird high up only the night before, circling, flying away, then coming back to circle her again. It was a sign. Birds lived free. She would too. Now it would come true.

She looked up at the sky. Stars shone bright, like pearls strewn across the sky. He might even let her live in his villa. Constantine would visit. She laughed. Better not to think of such things, slaves existed only to be used and thrown away by men of his class. She would not be stupid enough to hope for anything with Constantine.

A woman was singing in the tavern. A hush descended until all she could hear was the voice and distant dogs barking. She couldn't understand the words, but the song was beautiful, haunting. It reminded her of something from long ago. She looked towards the doorway. She should go back in.

"They sing the lay of Myrddin too slow this far south," said a voice in guttural Latin. She looked around. The beggar was standing in the shadows.

The singer slowed, as the song turned sad. "It's the fate of all Brigantes to be drawn to the lady of the lake," he said.

She looked away.

"Is that my repayment for saving your pretty head?"

She brushed at her tunic, sat up straighter, moved her feet and got ready to run. "Does my rescuer have a name?"

"I am called Tiresias by the mighty Romans. It is the name of a blind wanderer. They like to joke. I was gifted with only part of
312

Tiresias' haul, you see, as such is the way of fickle luck." He walked towards her. The whiff of unwashed flesh came to her. The breeze caught wisps of her hair that had come loose and sent them flying across her face. She brushed them away. It felt cooler now, almost cold, as he approached.

"Your master says you are a Brigantes, from the clan of Arelldua." His voice had a mesmerizing lilt to it.

She nodded.

His face darted forward like a bird about to pounce. "Be warned then, slave. The Great Mother is all powerful. She knows the way to the one god. But it is blood that makes her spells work. Her priestess travels with you, I hear. Is that true? And her name is Sybellina?"

Juliana nodded. Tiresias' Latin was accented, difficult to understand.

"Then you must be careful, Brigantes. The powers that raised up the Brigantes are in you. I can sense it. She may too. They are the powers of Myrddin, and the son of Aedd, and of the great lady too. They help us to read dreams, see death approaching, to sow fear, and overthrow all men. They are the powers that took the Emperor Severus to the other side. You have them too." He took a deep breath, leaned towards her. "You are more than you seem. If you need help, seek me out. It is well known that ones such as Sybellina do not abide competition. Leave word for me in any place like this. Be wary though, I sense she is powerful. They train them well in Rome."

Juliana's blood was pumping fast. She could feel it in her neck. He was speaking to her as if he knew her. She had the strange sensation she'd been expected here. That he'd been waiting for her.

The verses of the song came louder now. More people had joined in the singing. It sounded as if everyone in the tavern was banging their goblets on the table together. The double beat echoed in her head. She looked towards the doorway. A golden glow emanated from it. She turned back. She wanted to ask Tiresias about Sybellina's powers.

But he was gone.

Through the doorway she saw Constantine and the others coming towards her. Morbod was behind them, his goblet in the air, toasting their departure. She stood as the group poured out. A blonde, overly buxom serving girl was clinging to Constantine's arm. Valerius was calling loudly for them all to follow him to another drinking house, but Constantine shook his head and pushed himself free from the girl. After a few irate words were traded, soothing coins placated her, and she ambled back inside.

Back at Valerius' villa, after all the cloaks had been hung up, Juliana bowed good night, and went to her room. It was not a good idea to stay around after your master had been drinking. Every slave knew that. Though there were some who didn't care, of course, they slept with their masters to save themselves from the whip, or simply to eat better. But that was not her way. She'd seen too many tearful slaves handing babies over for exposure, some more than once, pitifully trying to hide a coin in the baby's clothes so someone might take it in, or worse still, slaves suffering the terrors of the pox if they'd been shared around on nights such as this.

Her foster mother had warned her about what happened many, many times. "If you don't have to be a whore, don't, please god, don't."

She was looking forward to being alone. She had a lot to think about. She opened the door of her room. Someone had lit the oil lamp and left a covered jug of water and an extra patterned woolen blanket on her bed. It should have felt good, how the masters must feel every night, with people looking after them, but it didn't.

The beggar's words were going around in her head. She lay down. The Great Mother needed blood for her spells to work. Could it be true?

She remembered what she'd heard at Massilia, how dangerous Sybellina could be. What had happened to Tiny proved that Sybellina was capable of anything. And she'd snared Constantine's heart with a spell. That would have taken powerful magic. Magic born from blood.

She closed her eyes. If Sybellina hadn't travelled with them things would be so different. She remembered Constantine's disappointed face after Sybellina had left their table to join his father. Anger tightened inside her. Why would he care so quickly about
314

Sybellina? She was a bony fingered witch and ugly too, in her pale face creams and tied up hair. Why did he not see it?

It had to be because of a spell.

Soon it would be too late. Juliana had to face that. A voice inside said no, she couldn't interfere, she was only a slave, she had to accept it all, not gamble with her life. That she could do nothing against her masters. That way led to the tortures laid down for unruly slaves, and certain death. She had to accept it. She was a slave.

But what Tiresias had said meant she could be more than a slave, and that meant she had to do something she'd feared she might have to do since Massilia. For as long as she could remember she'd pretended not to care about being a slave, but the thought of Constantine with Sybellina made her fate so totally unjust. She was better than a slave, that was what Tiresias had said, wasn't it?

Juliana had nothing physical to remind her of her mother, but she remembered how she'd been so proud that their family had never been slaves. They had never been tallied among those whose offspring, being blinded from a young age, ground millstones endlessly, or worked inside villas and were not even allowed to speak.

Round and round her thoughts went. Would she ever be free again? What would it be like? For a while she tried to sleep, but she couldn't. It felt as if she was in a cave, her room was so big. Her cheeks ached, as if she'd been crying. She remembered things she'd heard about the power of evil, and how spirits fought inside you.

When all sounds in the villa had died away and only the distant howling of hungry dogs could be heard, she got up. Wrapping her cloak around her, she made her way out into the courtyard. The faces of the statues around its edges seemed to be frowning, disapproving of her mission.

The waning moon lit Sybellina's door brightly. A finger-sized curse tablet lay against its bottom edge. She bent down. On it there was a depiction of Erinye, the snake-headed spirit who pursued unpunished criminals. It was a warning, a marker to warn spirits to stay out, but it also confirmed that whoever slept here had not yet returned.

She put it to one side and creaked open the wooden door. A fluttering night lamp lit the room, flickering as if it might go out from the breeze Juliana had created by opening the door. She held her breath. She hadn't brought a lamp. She didn't want to be seen. Shadows jumped across the walls. A sweet odor of musk made her want to sneeze. Laughter tinkled distantly. She tensed. Every instinct begged her to run, not to take such risks, to remember how she would be punished if caught. She looked over her shoulder. The courtyard was empty, waiting.

She quietened her breath. Waited some more. The only sound she could hear was a distant shout from somewhere else in the city. This was her chance. She stepped forward.

Eyes seemed to be watching her from the shadows, aghast, as she crossed to the low table in the far corner of the room. The words of a Persian curse came to her - thieves never get what they expect. Her mouth fell open. On the table standing proud was a huge engorged black phallus, a bull's phallus. At its end a jeweled scarab glistened. Beside it there were two pale marble cosmetic pots and a large heart-shaped silver box.

Behind the phallus stood a green marble container carved into the shape of a grasshopper.

She'd heard that love potions could be made from grasshoppers. She reached for the lid, almost touched the phallus as she did, lifted the lid quickly, then closed it again fast with a loud and disconcerting click. Her hand shook as she pulled it away. The smell of decay, a rotting vapor, had seeped from the dark tangle inside the marble container. She rubbed her hands against her tunic and reached for the silver heart-shaped box.

A loud creaking noise sounded from the courtyard. She turned. Through the half-open doorway she glimpsed a light moving.

She ran to the door noiselessly on her toes, closed it, then stood with her back against the wall, her blood pumping in her neck. Footsteps echoed. They were coming towards the door.

It would open in a moment. She closed her eyes. If Sybellina came into the room all she could do was run past her, throw herself at once at Constantine's feet. If she told him what she'd heard at Massilia he might protect her, he might understand. He was her only hope now.

XLIV

Londinium, Southern Britannia, 306 A.D.

At the feast, most of the guests were long gone, but the emperor was still deep in conversation. It was the first time all evening he'd had Sybellina to himself.

"You ask me about blood ties," he said. He took a sip from his goblet. His wine had been diluted until it was almost water. It was the way he liked it.

"You should know they mean less to me than to most people. I fought my way up day by day. I had no father to help me. No family to help me up. I have proved that it can be done." He looked at her and grinned.

"But you are a force with the power of a god. Few have what you do, lord," replied Sybellina.

"Did you hear that funny little man offering to build a temple to me?" He shook his head, bemused.

She shook her head.

"Not until I'm dead, I told him. They soon lose heart, you know, when they realize they'll get no reward from me on this side of death. He said Londinium has started collecting for a victory arch already, before the campaign has even properly started. Were you here when he said that? His eyes were bulging. Or was that before I rescued you from Constantine?"

Sybellina looked serious. "The campaign is important to a lot of people, my lord. They will want to commemorate it after your victory."

"You are right, I suppose. This will bind Caledonia into the peace of the empire at last. My predecessor Severus had a good plan, but I will make it happen." He rubbed his chin thoughtfully.

"I will have my triumph in Rome. I will be the emperor who achieved what eluded all others. Our victory will change everything for this island. We'll be rid of those Picts, or whatever they call themselves, once and for all. We'll unify all these islands after that. We will totally eradicate any tribe that stands against us. It will be a good example to all the stupid painted barbarians on our borders in Germania."

"Will Constantine help you?" she asked sweetly.

He squinted, as if he wanted to examine her before replying. "I'll tell you a little secret." He looked around. Only a few revelers remained at each table. There was no one else at theirs. "I want to test him first."

She looked suitably shocked.

"I cannot put him with the forward troops. If he died in battle the Picts would claim a great victory, proof of their Druidic powers. I cannot allow any possibility of that happening. If he accepts the duties I've offered him he'll learn the things that will be most important in this empire when my work is done, the duties of peacetime, the duties of administration."

Sybellina looked at him for what seemed like ages. He stared back. He was right in his decision about Constantine. Every time he saw Constantine he knew his son needed to prove his loyalty more than anything else, for his own sake as much as anything. He'd avoided the whole issue while Constantine was in the east. Diocletian had been insistent before he'd retired that he was right to overlook Constantine for elevation to a senior position. He'd been right too. Constantine wasn't suitable for elevation as his successor. The campaign reports Diocletian had shown him in Rome were impossible to argue with. Theodora had been pressing him about Delmatius, the son they'd made together, who was a far more likely candidate to be his heir than Constantine, so she kept saying, even if Delmatius was still only a child. But she did have a point.

When Delmatius grew up he would not be tainted by failed campaigns in the east. Constantine would have to learn to accept his assigned role. If he didn't he would have to die. One way or another. It had to be that simple. He'd hardened his heart a long time ago to the reality that Constantine's life hung by a thread, never mind the fact that Theodora kept adding, in her inimitable nagging voice, that sons could be as dangerous as a worst enemy.

Sybellina reached over and touched his hand, then withdrew it quickly. "I see your great qualities in him, my lord, your vitality, your courage." She stretched out her hand again, touched his cheek, and rubbed a finger slowly across to his lips. "But more importantly, when will I pass my test with you?"

He stared at her. He was well used to beautiful women. But this one was different. She'd recited whole sections from a play by Euripides, one of his old favorites, when the talk at the table had turned to Agamemnon waiting for a wind, as he had before the start of his campaign. He'd even wondered if someone had told her his reading habits.

Then she'd engaged the governor, a corpulent Prefect and a sour looking Legate in a debate about what was the most effective sacrifice to placate the gods.

"Scapegoats will always be needed," she'd said. The Legate had claimed sacrifices were used simply to placate the superstitious.

"Sacrifice a scapegoat. Their suffering releases our guilt," she'd said. She'd looked at him then. Had she meant something by that comment? He still wasn't sure.

"Agamemnon sacrificed for his arrogance. A good scapegoat is a good distraction. It allows us to start anew." She'd laughed then, when she'd seen the serious faces all around her. Then she'd turned to him and raised her goblet.

"We are lucky to have such a wise emperor. A man who understands the need for scapegoats." They'd all toasted him then.

She'd enthralled everyone at the table. They all either wanted her or were afraid of her. He rarely stayed to the end of a feast anymore, but he felt a lot better in the past few days. He'd tested the medicine she'd given him on one of his hunting dogs of course, and when the dog had suffered no ill effects, he'd tried it on himself. The pain in his side had diminished. Most days now it was gone. It was time to invite her to his rooms. He'd been right not to send her back to Rome. They had enough priestesses there.

He enjoyed the scent that filled the air around her as they crossed the torch-lit courtyard. At the feast he'd felt the heat from her body beside him, like the heat of a roaring fire.

The head of his household slaves, an old man with a bald head, opened the doors to his quarters and bowed. All the other slaves were shooed away. Only this one would stay, just out of view, ready to serve him should the need arise. His private courtyard was aglow with torches. Plumply cushioned wooden seats under a flowering jasmine entwined trellis invited them to sit. The emperor touched Sybellina's arm, guiding her. A gold wine jug and tall green glasses awaited them on a veined marble table. The old slave came forward bowing low, poured two glasses and then disappeared.

"You look like a goddess tonight, Sybellina." He kissed her hand.

"Your attention is flattering, lord." She leant towards him, her gown opening, exposing the top of her breasts.

"Aaah, the uncomplicated ambitions of youth." He kissed her hand again, admired her silken skin.

She leaned forward a little more. Her robe slipped open some more. Her breasts dangled firm in front of her, gold powdered nipples sparkling in the torchlight.

His eyes widened.

She stood, let her robe slip away.

He noticed with a thrill of pleasure that all her body hair had been shaved or plucked away. That was a task he would enjoy.

She knelt, bent slowly forward until her forehead touched the tiles underfoot, long legs spread out behind her. Her naked buttocks were high in the air. She looked up at him.

"How may I serve you, my lord?"

XLV

Londinium, Southern Britannia, 306 A.D.

Constantine visited the villa's bathhouse the following morning. The hot room was as hot as Vesuvius. Valerius and Lucius were in the warm room, enjoying the pleasures of a bath house breakfast. Slave girls, barely dressed, hurried about, fretting over their every need, serving hard bread, hard cheeses, walnuts, boiled eggs and sweet unfermented grape juice, while they sat naked by the edge of a mosaic lined pool. Each had a different girl expertly kneading his shoulders, whispering in his ear. Constantine left the hot room and joined them.

"Did someone tell you there'll be games this afternoon, in honor of your father?" said Valerius. "You'll get to see our famous female gladiators." He stroked the hand of the slave girl massaging his shoulders. "The animal fights have started already. But we're not expected until this afternoon. If you don't mind, I'm off to test this new slave girl." He stepped out of the water, his erection clearly visible. He pulled the stone faced girl after him.

They stayed beyond midday in the bathhouse. Lucius enjoyed one of the bath house girls, twice. Valerius expressed amazement that Constantine didn't want to taste their pleasures.

"Are my slaves not good enough for you?" he asked, sliding back into the pool. His eyes narrowed. "Or are you're dreaming of another?" He paused, laughed.

"You are, yes. I see it in your eyes. It's not that priestess, I hope. You were staring at her half the night. Maybe if you ask your pater, he'll pass her on to you when he's finished. Isn't it so hateful when your father spoils your fun?" He splashed water towards

Constantine, who shook his head in response, though it clearly annoyed him that Valerius imagined he cared about Sybellina.

"I've had enough of easy girls, Valerius. Most simply make your manhood wither, as you should know," said Constantine. He stared pointedly at Valerius' small and flaccid member visible in the water.

Valerius scowled at Constantine, and then cajoled him to play dice by the side of the pool while they waited for Lucius, who had disappeared again with a different girl. Soon after a messenger came from Valerius' father, summoning him to the arena, to be present for some executions. Valerius scoffed disdainfully at the idea.

"The pleasure of watching condemned men fight to their death with a single bread knife between them is hardly sufficient to make me attend these games early. Pater should pay me to attend for the plebs' pleasures. Do you not agree, Constantine?"

"I do. I've seen enough executions to last me a hundred lifetimes," said Constantine.

Valerius laughed and dismissed the messenger.

"Would you like to go out again this evening," he said, turning back to Constantine.

"You've got a better head than me for drinking, Valerius," Constantine replied. "I could never keep up with you. Despite the temptation, I will decline. Perhaps Lucius will keep you company."

Lucius, who had rejoined them, shook his head.

"You're trying to kill us, Valerius. I drank more than I had in a year last night. I'll go drinking with you again before we leave, but not two nights in a row."

"And when do you leave?" said Valerius.

"At the new moon at the earliest," said Lucius. "We're waiting on reports from scouts and we'll have to get lots more augers read, you know, before the actual date can be agreed. We'll be here another week at least. There'll be plenty of time for sampling more of Londinium's entertainments."

Later, as they waited in the atrium for their litters, honeyed beer flavored with mulberries was served to them. It was not to Constantine's taste, so wine and water were brought as well.

Lucius went off to find Juliana. He found her mending a tunic in her room.

"You look pale," he announced as his greeting. "Have you visited Crocus?"

She spoke quickly, stumbling over her words. "I slept badly, master, that is all. I went to where Crocus is staying early this morning, but he'd gone to the camp outside the city. He'll be back this afternoon. That's what they said." She put her needle down.

"Go to his quarters and wait for him there." Lucius looked around, as if wondering if anyone was listening to him.

"Yes, my lord." She turned and left without another word.

Sybellina had joined the others by the time he'd returned to the atrium. Pale blue silk ribbons streamed from her coiled hair. She looked like a sculptor's model of a Roman priestess, an unhappy Roman priestess.

"Someone's been stealing from my room, Lucius," she said in a tone that could cut stone.

He tutted loudly.

She stabbed a finger towards Valerius. "This sort of thing happens only in the worst households. I demand that a guard be placed outside my room, day and night. Do you hear? And if you cannot arrange it, I'll speak to the emperor myself. He'll get something done. And..." She turned to Lucius, her expression viperous. "If I catch the thief who dared do this they'll pay and pay dearly."

"Sybellina, that's so terrible," said Valerius. "Do not worry, I'll arrange a guard. And we'll replace whatever's missing."

"What was taken?" said Lucius.

"A charm, an irreplaceable charm." Sybellina stood with her hands on her hips, a vision of injured innocence.

"What charm, Sybellina? I'll have my slaves search every room in the villa for it. But we need to know what they'll be looking for," said Valerius.

"It's too late," shouted Sybellina. She stamped her foot.

"Why would anyone steal such a charm?" said Constantine.

She glared at him. "I do not know, but when I find out..." A look of malice slid across her face. It was not a pretty sight.

324

"Sybellina, I told you, if we find out who did this, they'll have more than you to answer to," said Valerius. "We treat thieves like they deserve in this city. Come, try to forget about it. We must go at once, or we'll miss everything. And I'll buy you ten charms in the forum later."

He escorted a still raging Sybellina outside to where their litters were waiting. Constantine was glad it wasn't him who had to placate her. And in an odd way he felt pleased too. Pleased that something had been taken from her. She deserves a little ill luck, he thought, as he climbed into the last litter.

At almost every street corner people recognized Valerius' litters and greeted him as they passed. Constantine noticed that among the oversized busts of the emperors that lined the entranceway to the Forum, there was none of Galerius. That would never have occurred in a city in the east. As they came nearer the arena the streets were lined with hawkers, sausage vendors, oyster sellers and cake merchants, and crowds lined the streets. Echoing roars from the arena could be heard in the distance now.

"Lance him, lance him," was the shout. Then the shouting stopped. A rhythmic stomping of feet, like rolling thunder, indicated that the crowd's desire had been granted. He felt the old excitement he always experienced when he attended the games. He knew many of the gladiatorial contests might have been staged in the theatre for all the acting involved, but he'd always been drawn to the real bloodletting and the ritual. It was compulsive viewing, whatever you thought about the rights and wrongs of such contests.

The arena, a cliff-like brick structure, like the Colosseum in Rome, held ten thousand people, he guessed. Its size indicated how far Londinium had grown in the past century.

He climbed the wide marble outside stairs into the emperor's box. A great cheer went up when he emerged from a garland-fringed doorway. The purple awning over the box cracked in the wind, as if in response. The crowd cheered again, then again as he raised his fist high in salute. It was the most wonderful feeling, public acclaim. Suddenly, he wished he'd brought Juliana along to help serve him, to see all this and to feel all this, to know who he really was.

XLVI

Londinium, Southern Britannia, 306 A.D.

Juliana was waiting to see Crocus. She tapped the front of her right sandal nervously on the marble floor of the courtyard and twirled her hair around a finger. She'd seen her reflection in the bronze mirror hanging in her room and the sight had shocked her and pleased her. She'd never looked so womanly.

The clatter of horses broke the silence. She stood straighter, her hands pressed into her sides. Why had Lucius asked her to do this? He was one real bastard.

After a few moments Crocus came swaggering into the courtyard. He wore a greasy sheepskin coat and tight breeches strapped all the way up his legs. A Roman short sword in a heavy purple lacquered sheath hung from his belt. He came straight up to her, looked her up and down, sneered, then pinched her cheek, sniffed, and ran his hand over her hair.

His hand ran down to her breast and he squeezed it, hard. As he did so he leaned forward, stuck his tongue out and licked her cheek. His breath smelled like horse dung.

She shuddered, muscles tightening in revulsion, but moving as little as possible. This man had killed one of his wives in a knife throwing contest, if she could believe what the other slaves said. She'd overheard one joking about how they'd pass out if he asked them to hold an apple as a target.

She spoke as clearly as she could.

"Great commander of the Alemanni, I have come with a message, a message from my master, Lucius." What she wanted to say, was, "Do you always smell this bad?"

Crocus snorted as he undid his cloak. He passed it to a slave.

"What kind of message?" he grunted.

"I must say it in private, my lord."

He waved the slave away, then asked her, "Are you a gift?" He stroked her hair again, pawed his hand down her back and squeezed her arm, hard.

She had to bite her lip to stop herself striking him. Not now. Not now. She pressed her hands tight against her sides.

"No, I only have a message, my lord."

"Come on then, tell me your message." He walked around her.

She stood still, hating every moment she was near him. "My master offers to make a donation to help with your personal expenses." She said it in as clear a voice as she could muster.

He gripped her arm, squeezing it as if it was a rag.

"Ow." She flinched. His eyes were as cold as any she'd ever seen. They bulged as she stared at him.

"Did you tell anyone what you just told me, any of your slave friends?" She shook her head, tried to pull away. He tightened his grip. He clearly knew what making a donation meant, that he'd be expected to repay it in some way at a future date. He'd be a client of Lucius.

"Well, know this, pretty slave. If you do, I'll pluck your sultry little eyes out one by one, and then cut out your writhing tongue and feed the whole lot back to you boiled into a soft stew when you get hungry." He laughed, then released her.

It was raining hard as Juliana made her way back to the villa. In two moments, she was dripping wet. It felt as if a shroud had descended on the city. She looked around. No one was interested in her. Hawkers plied their trade under the shelter of the colonnades. Grinding noises could be heard from some shop doorways. A tavern beckoned. A hubbub of voices came out as she passed. An aroma of onions and sausage drifted with them.

She turned. A litter's occupant had screamed as he was tipped into the rain. One of his attendants had slipped. Rising up, dripping, he stared at Juliana sullenly as she went past, then roared at his attendants like an angry child. Sensing something, she looked around.

Three emaciated youths were staring at her wide-eyed from a dark alley.

She ran for their villa as fast as she could. Earlier, Sybellina had looked at her like those boys, accusingly, as if she knew Juliana had been in her room and had some retribution planned for her. A pair of greyhounds yapped as she passed the doorway they were guarding.

Juliana knew that her best hope was if the effects of Sybellina's love charm wore off soon. Everything would be different if Constantine saw Sybellina for what she was. She glanced behind her. Please, heavenly mother, let that be my last visit to that monster. She stumbled. Who was that in the long cloak walking after her, staring directly at her?

XLVII

Londinium, Southern Britannia, 306 A.D.

"How do people live in such weather?" said Constantine, as they waited for guards to form up to escort their litters back through the city.

The emperor didn't reply. The gladiatorial games had ended early on his order. It appeared to him as if the canvas awnings above the stands might collapse with the rainwater they'd collected. People had been streaming away in any case because of the downpour and the leaking awnings, so he'd cancelled the last bout. It had been a clearly rigged contest, between a loyal Roman gladiator and a Pictish barbarian, brought here to have his throat cut publicly after a one-sided fight.

The brick-lined high-ceilinged room below the imperial box echoed to the sound of rain on the wooden stairs and walkways above.

"They're used to it. Rain falls all year round here," said the emperor. "Treveris is warmer than this place. It would suit you better. Why don't you go and visit your mother there? I hear she arrived from Rome a few days ago. Britannia is too damp for people who've lived in the east." The emperor examined his son's expression. It was blank. He could read nothing.

"I'll go," said Constantine. "When your campaign against the Picts is over." He sounded very sure of himself. "I'd rather fight in the rain than be bored anywhere. I want to help you, Father."

"I am sure you do," said the emperor. "Did you enjoy last night?"

"Yes. What about you?"

The emperor shrugged his shoulders and looked away. One of his guards appeared at the doorway. Their escort was ready.

As soon as he arrived back at the governor's palace, the emperor sent a messenger to fetch Sybellina. The rain continued to pour outside. As usual there was lots to be done. Reports from provincial governors had to be responded to, letters from imperial agents read, decisions had to be made about appointments, building work needed funding, policies on runaway slaves needed to be reassessed.

The pile of scrolls never got smaller.

And he kept wondering about Constantine. There were good positions he could appoint him to, if he really wanted to. The Legate of the 30th should have retired some time ago.

But there were other things to consider. It was likely Crocus was motivated by something other than loyalty in warning him about Constantine. Perhaps Crocus and his Alemanni would need their wings clipped soon.

The messenger returned. Sybellina had been found. She'd been with Constantine's friend Lucius. They'd been on their way to some temple, but a rider had caught up with them and she'd been given the emperor's summons. She would arrive soon. She had gone back to her villa first.

He called for the best wine to be brought and whatever delicacies could be found in the kitchens.

He also dispatched a message to the master of the treasury for him to send one of the best pearl necklaces from the treasure chests at once. When an orderly arrived with the necklace he examined it for flaws, and on finding none, draped it on the side arm of his couch. Then he stood and paced to and fro.

The marble floor of his reception room was warm from the underfloor heating. The bellows and stompings of the guard being changed could be heard from outside in the courtyard, and distantly from somewhere else he guessed must be the main gate. More lamps would be needed soon, but not yet. The darkness certainly gathered slowly here. He sat and read some more letters.

It was dark when Sybellina finally entered through the high doors that led to the outside courtyard. The slave who opened the door took her cloak.

"Ah, Sybellina. I'll be finished shortly." He glanced up from a report. A net of raindrops shimmered in her hair. The golden light from the oil lamp suspended on a chain near the door reflected warmly on her skin. She bowed but stayed a few paces away from him. He looked back down at the scroll.

She would have to wait for him, as he had waited for her. When he reached the end of the report, he put it down, picked up another one. He listened for any movement that might betray her impatience, but there was none. When he'd finished that scroll, he glanced at another one, picked it up, then, as if he was bored with it, he placed it down and motioned her forward.

"I came as quickly as I could, my lord." She sounded apologetic. "But it takes time to prepare for an audience." She was wearing a pale blue knee-length tunic, split open at the front.

"And you did a wonderful job. Come now, sit beside me, Sybellina. I have something for you."

She sat close by him on the couch, then looked with a theatrically puzzled expression at the piles of scrolls and letters on the low marble table in front of them.

"Surely someone else could attend to all these, my lord."

"You are right. I'll have them taken away," he said. He called for his personal slave and had the scrolls removed. Then, after having wine poured, he dismissed all the slaves.

"You said you had something for me, my lord. Are you teasing me?" She laid a hand softly on his bare knee, then withdrew it.

The emperor reached behind him and picked up the pearl necklace. It had been glaringly visible against the purple and gold brocade of the sofa arm. He saw a flash of something cross her face, which she hid quickly. Was it disappointment?

Anger rose inside him.

She leaned forwards. Her smooth pink nipples peeked at him. His anger turned into desire.

Pearls, the pay of a courtesan, would not be enough for this one for very long. Had she heard the story of the cup bearer he'd been with, who he'd bestowed an estate in Gaul upon?

"Thank you so much, my lord, you are so kind. Really. What a beautiful necklace. I have one just like it back in Rome." She kissed him lightly on the cheek.

"Come here, you little vixen." He pulled her to him, kissed her lips hard. They were like ripe fruits bursting with juice. He tasted Cinnabar. His lips tingled. She pressed her breasts against him, pushed her fingers roughly through his hair. Then she got down on her knees in front of him and each hand went up inside his tunic. She stuck her tongue out at him as she worked to make him harder.

"You are in better health today, my lord." She blew a kiss at him.

"Come closer," he commanded.

She leaned forward, her eyes locked on his.

When he was finished he groaned, stood and called loudly for his scrolls to be returned.

"I must finish what I started," he said.

"Am I to be discarded so soon?" She scowled petulantly and smoothed her tunic with angry strokes as his slaves hurried about.

"I'll call for you again. This will not be forgotten." He waved at the bear skin rug where he'd been sitting. He knew it was good to keep seductresses like Sybellina waiting, nearby of course, guessing, with limited male company, like pheasants being cooed to and fed morsels before their plumped-up bodies were roasted.

It was, after all, what she deserved. It was what anyone who tried to manipulate him deserved. She would learn to wait. To pine for him. He waved his hand dismissively. It would teach her an important lesson. A familiar feeling of power coursed through him.

"Before I go, my lord, please, I must talk to you about Maxentius' offer." She was speaking quickly, a note of desperation in her voice. "I've been thinking about what you said, my lord. It is wise to marry Constantine to Fausta. Maxentius is right. If you don't, Constantine will only pick someone unsuitable for himself. If he's half the man you are, he needs a wife, my lord, a suitable one. Please, let me have your answer. Maxentius' support for you will be obvious to all if you do." She looked over her shoulder as if worried someone might be listening.

"You know you must be careful, my lord, there are rumors, rumors of plots against you, plots against your person."

"Don't bother me with talk of rumors, Sybellina. The day they stop plotting against me is the day I'll get concerned. You will get your answer. When I'm ready. Not before. Now go."

She looked crestfallen. He saw her eyes fill, as if she might cry. A surge of feeling coursed through him. The urge to pity was easy to resist though. And he enjoyed the feeling of power his self-control gave him. This surely was the right moment to tell her his terms.

"Go now. But wait for me. And be with no other. I warn you. I know the oaths you took. Break them and you'll not get another audience with me ever, never mind your answer. Keep your oaths and you keep my protection. And if you have real evidence about a plot against me come and tell me immediately." His tone was curt, aggressive, the tone he used to get people to do exactly what he wanted.

She looked shocked, then nodded, bowed, and stepped backwards, a little unsteadily, while still facing him. When she'd taken seven paces with her head bowed, her pearls clutched tight in her hand, she turned, and in a moment, she was gone. It was the procedure priestesses like her had for departing the presence of an Augustus.

He'd enjoyed that, enjoyed teasing her, getting her going, giving, then taking away, showing her who was the master, and how far he'd come. And how much he'd learned.

XLVIII

Londinium, Southern Britannia, 306 A.D.

The following morning, Constantine was summoned to go with his father to inspect the Legions massing on the heaths to the north of the city. Most of the troops had arrived, but a significant number of horses were still missing, most likely because of foul play or trickery on the road.

They met with the Legates and the Tribunes from each Legion and discussed the army's state of readiness, their marching orders and the contingency plans for the push north. All the officers agreed, the painted Pictish tribes would flee their hill forts and easily-taken raths when the Roman Legions approached, and that if cutting the tendons on Roman horses was the Picts best trick, their cavalry had nothing to fear. At the end of the meeting every officer swore not to make the mistake of leniency the Emperor Severus had made.

The last time such a large Roman army had ventured beyond Hadrian's wall, ninety-six years before, Emperor Severus, a wily African, had lost more than 50,000 legionaries to the mists and harrying Picts on his first march north. In revenge, Severus had planned the massacre of all the tribes north of Hadrian's Wall, and the salting of their fields. Only his death at Eboracum, while planning that campaign, had saved the Pictish tribes. The plan was subsequently cancelled by his son, Caracalla, whose only concern of course was how to consolidate his own power back in Rome. The plans for the march north had been handed down however, and now, at last, Severus' scheme would be carried out. Rome would get her revenge.

The emperor had studied the obstacles Severus had encountered. He'd decided to send three separate cavalry cohorts ahead to determine where the Picts would flee to and where they would muster.

These reconnaissance troops would maraud beyond Hadrian's Wall and by the full moon after next would pull back to Eboracum, where the main body of the army would by then be stationed. They would engage Picts they encountered, fight, then run. Such tactics should encourage the Pictish leaders into thinking the Roman campaign might be beatable and gather to counter it. If the tribes then decided to take on a Roman army in open battle, the Legions' task would be so much easier. With most of the Pictish warrior class dead - no quarter would be given - the task of clearing the highlands would be reduced.

But either way, if the Picts mustered or if they didn't, the late summer would see the end of them once and for all.

XLIX

Londinium, Southern Britannia, 306 A.D.

At Valerius' villa Lucius was questioning Juliana about her meeting with Crocus. He was sitting on the edge of his bed. She was standing a few paces away, her head respectfully down.

He shook his slowly, distractedly, when he heard Crocus had threatened her.

"We will be grateful to you, Juliana. I hold a great responsibility. Many of my people are depending on this mission."

"What else will I have to do?" she said.

"Nothing for now, Juliana, absolutely nothing."

She stared at the floor. She knew what *for now* meant. It meant that there'd be more meetings with stony-faced piss-drinkers who could split you open just for looking at them the wrong way.

"Now, tell me every word that passed between you and him."

L

Londinium, Southern Britannia, 306 A.D.

Sybellina was in the bath house. Two slave girls were working hard on her with the villa's most pungent oils. They were using long cleaning strigils to rub the oils in and the dirt out. One wall of the warm massage room was covered in a tiled wall painting depicting the Goddess Hecate, the guardian of the veil between the material and heavenly worlds. A shrine cut into the wall held a small marble statue of the goddess. Rumors of the defection of Britannia from the worship of the Roman gods to the one god were clearly lies.

Sybellina wondered would Constantine hear that she'd been with his father. She hoped he would. Everything was working out exactly as had been predicted.

And now it was time to call on Hecate. The goddess had helped the Great Mother's priestesses many times before. In the time of the Emperor Marcus Aurelius she'd brought storms down upon the enemies of Rome. She could be counted on to do something small, such as bringing ruin onto the head of the one who had stolen her charm and threatened her mission.

She ordered the slave girls to kneel, one on each side of her, then prostrated herself, naked, on the marble floor in front of Hecate. She banged her head lightly against the floor, so the goddess might hear her supplications. Finally, she turned on her back and ordered the slave girls to massage her as she recited the secret chants her mother had taught her to gain the attention of the goddess. Her breathing became labored as the massaging continued on every part of her body, as she directed, until her exhortations grew louder and finally reached a crescendo as she stuck her tongue out and her legs quivered in bliss.

LI

Londinium, Southern Britannia, 306 A.D.

When the full moon arrived, a few days later, the army broke camp and began the long journey north over the endless cobbles of Ermine Street. Members of the imperial entourage, such as the priestess Sybellina, travelled by heavy covered wagon to the rear of the main force. Juliana travelled on horseback with a group of other high-ranking slaves.

Constantine and Lucius rode with the emperor's personal guard at the center of the column. He was glad to be on the road again.

"There is no better sport than hunting men," the Emperor Diocletian used to tell him. Soon he'd be enjoying that sport again. In fact, he was looking forward to it. Every evening he had to listen to Sybellina's theories about spies being around every corner and how he had to be careful. And now he was sick of it all. She would run from him whenever he'd tried to get close to her and had even had Juliana's room searched early one morning before they left Londinium.

Nothing had been found there of course, but Juliana, her eyes wide with fear, had threatened to kill herself afterwards. Lucius had to swear she was not going to be tortured to get her to calm down. A terrible screaming, that had stopped almost at once, like the sound of someone being crucified in their nightmare, had woken him late the following evening. Juliana had denied it was her when he and Lucius had entered her room.

She'd been quieter than ever since then. He'd seen such behavior before when slaves were accused wrongly of something.

He was glad he was not travelling with Sybellina.

LII

Gesoriacum, Northern Gaul, 306 A.D.

The Empress Theodora, Constantine's stepmother, arrived at Gesoriacum looking for a ship to take her to Londinium on the very day the emperor and his army began their march north across the channel in Britannia. She was escorted by a troop of legionaries and personal slaves.

Theodora exuded the haughtiness of an elegant and attractive woman, exactly how you'd expect the eldest daughter of the retired Emperor Maximianus to behave.

Unsettling news had reached Theodora's ears. She'd decided after hearing it, that she must speak in person with her husband as soon as possible. Messengers would not do. Leaving most of her court behind she'd set off as quickly as she could in the hope of catching him before he made any decisions that he, or she, might regret.

Theodora did, however, arrive at Gesoriacum just in time to catch the post ship about to sail for Londinium.

As they neared the coast of Britannia she stood at the prow of the galley with the captain.

"My lady, you must be looking forward to having your family reunited. We heard all about Constantine. We wish you well. His return is a marvel." The captain had spoken to her on only two occasions since they'd left port. His guttural Latin marked him out as being from a tribe based around the old port at Rutupiae in Britannia, whose skills in these waters were legendary.

"Constantine is not my son, captain. He is the son of a tavern girl who my husband, the emperor, kept around out of pity, because her bastard was so sickly. If you have any good wishes for a reunion,

340

save them for me and the emperor. Constantine's mother isn't worthy of your good wishes and his connection with the imperial family will soon be over." She turned away.

The captain bowed and left her at the prow. Below her the dark sea rushed past.

When the galley eventually tied up at the wharf in Londinium, Theodora sent a messenger to the governor of the City. A detachment of legionaries and a chariot arrived for her soon after.

When she was ushered into the main reception hall where the governor was waiting for her, she let him know exactly how she felt.

"You provincials! You have no idea how to welcome an empress, do you? You are extremely lucky I don't ask my husband to have you flogged in the forum." She held out her hand to be kissed.

"I beg your forgiveness, empress." The governor prostrated himself, then stood and kissed the edge of her robe and then her ring.

"I am in need of your services for only one night, governor. I expect you've run out of all luxuries anyway, after Constantine being here. I'll be leaving tomorrow morning to follow the emperor. Have all that I might need readied at once."

"I'll make the arrangements myself, empress."

Early the following day Theodora left the city accompanied by a troop of guards and her own slaves. It was a perfect crisp morning with a clear blue sky and a light, auspicious wind.

As they rode north other travelers on the road moved out of their way as soon as they spied Theodora's purple cloak. Any who were slow to do so were brusquely ordered to clear the road by the guard leading the way for her.

Drifts of pink and white blossoms covered the gravel verges in some places, where clusters of cherry trees (Gean trees, the locals called them) huddled close by on each side of the paved roadway.

At one point, bluebells ran in a great carpet over a thin woodland to their right, which stretched to the top of a distant ridge. In some places the roadway was paved with red brick, at other times with gray or veined white slabs of stone. Occasionally it was simply rough gravel.

Yew trees, looking as old as the empire, grew beside the ivy-clad oaks that crowded at times up close to the path. Thistles and nettles flourished everywhere in a great profusion. When the road entered a valley, rushes spread away on both sides, then disappeared as they gained higher ground. In places the landscape was alive with industry. They passed woodsmen coppicing ash for spear shafts and farm tools and other workmen felling older cherry trees, for furniture most likely.

The villages they passed through bustled with people coming and going, the women in long drab garments to their ankles and the men in trousers strapped to their legs or long tunics, depending on their occupation.

The farmland was often being tended by gangs of slaves, who stopped and stared as they rode past. Theodora saw little use of the whip and shook her head at the mistakes being made by the masters here. Occasionally she saw evidence of an army or a horde of people having passed this way recently: flattened fields patterned with rutted cart tracks and signs of great encampments.

They made good time, stopping at night at the biggest taverns or at other lodgings along the way. Most of the forts they passed were located at bridges, some had whitewashed workshops open to the cobbled streets from which the sounds of hammerings and apprentices being chided could be heard.

Five days after leaving Londinium, they discovered that her husband's army was only two days ahead of them and was expected to camp for some time at the major colony of Lindum, a day's march further on. She would catch up with them there.

As they progressed further north she noticed that people wore their hair longer and that the salutes of the sentries at the forts were slower than the salutes down south and in Londinium. The local tribespeople here were clearly in need of a sharp lesson in who their masters were. How they could resent Rome, after all the benefits of expanded markets and central administration and the peace they had brought, was beyond her.

She spoke only when absolutely necessary with her guards. The senior centurion who led them was a veteran. He'd earned this prestigious duty because of his taciturn disposition, she guessed. But his manner suited her. The empress had learnt while very young that if she spoke to the slaves and guards who surrounded her, they would presume a friendship, and soon after would expect favors, or worse still, would use everything she said to start the most incredible rumors. Such were the trials of being raised in the strict confines of an imperial palace.

Even travelling by horseback, rather than by slower covered wagon, would, she knew, be enough to spark waves of gossip in her wake.

The road skirted a marsh edged with lichen and fern on the morning of the day they reached Lindum. Sodden clouds broke open and tumbled cloak-penetrating sheets of rain on them as they went on. As the rain whipped at her, anger filled her heart. He would pay for all these indignities. She'd make sure of that.

She turned her head, checked the road behind. It was empty.

But she had heard something.

She looked again. Yes, there. Out of the mist a single horseman was riding at full pelt towards them, his black cloak flapping wetly behind him, a hood pulled tight over his head.

The rider slowed to a walk as he went past but didn't stop. He simply held out a small bronze pass to the centurion who'd taken up a position beside her and was waved on. As she watched him disappear into the rain ahead, she wondered if she should have stopped the rider and asked him what mission made him ride so fast in treacherous conditions.

LIII

Lindum, Northern Britannia, 306 A.D.

Just beyond the city of Lindum, on the road north to Eboracum, lay a wide grassy sward where Roman armies camped to practice their maneuvers. The emperor, after consulting his officers and then ignoring their advice, decided that his army would rest there for three or four days, depending on when the rain stopped.

The old fortress at Lindum had been built on a limestone scarp overlooking a pool in the River Witham. A colony of veterans had been established there in the earliest days of Roman rule and the town had spread out from the fortress down towards the river. It had been enclosed soon after by a rampart, wall and ditch.

Monumental, recently-constructed stone gatehouses topped by oversized equestrian statues barred the main roadways into the town. Horses were the chief source of wealth for the local Coritanian tribespeople and the prospect of selling horses and provisions to the Roman army had brought large numbers of traders into the city the day the emperor arrived.

Accompanied by two hundred and fifty legionaries from the imperial guard, the emperor and his retinue had been welcomed at the main new gate by the governor of Lindum. Rooms had been made ready in the governor's palace where the private baths had been redecorated hastily in anticipation. Local flaxen-haired slave girls, overawed at the prospect of serving an emperor, waited there, ready to pander to his every whim.

It was late in the afternoon when the emperor finished in the bathhouse and strolled, thoroughly refreshed, into the governor's private meeting hall. A single slit, no wider than a hand, in the middle of the far wall provided an unimpeded view over the town. Smoke from cooking fires and forges rose plaiting ribbons in the air. The sounds of horses neighing, the pounding from forges, and occasional muffled shouts or peals of laughter came to him as he watched from his vantage point. Beyond the town walls a line of horses headed away towards where his army was setting up camp.

He rubbed a finger along the thin crack of mortar between the rust red bricks, testing its consistency. He'd heard that brick makers in these parts had been persuaded by druids to water down their mortar and sell bricks not left for two years to dry, though whether that was true, or simply a way for the brick makers down south to make greater profits, he did not know. Certainly, this mortar seemed a good grade with fewer pebbles mixed in than some he'd seen.

He was sure that many of the claims made about the wiles of the druids were no more than tales for frightening children. But it was not always clear which ones.

He'd received a report that the druids and their acolytes were massing on an island off the coast, beyond Hadrian's Wall, and that they were planning to flee to Hibernia, though that too could be a ruse. But what if it was true? Had the sworn enemies of every emperor who'd ever set foot on this island finally come to see they'd been irreversibly vanquished? Or was that what they wanted him to think?

He banged his fist against the brick wall. He'd give a lot to know what they were planning, whether he would face the Picts in open battle, or would they hold a fortress, like Vercingetorix had done in Gaul, and allow themselves to be wiped out as one. A flash of light bloomed on the horizon. Was it a signal?

Were their spies trailing him even now, as he'd been warned? They certainly would want to know what he was planning, and they were cunning enough to make use of any flaw in his plans. Cunning was one of their main strengths. It was a strength he should not underestimate.

Directly below his vantage point were the red tiles of a small Mithraic temple. A puff of white smoke rose from an opening in the temple roof as he gazed down at it. Some of his officers would most likely already be there, confessing their sins no doubt and appealing

345

to Mithras, their god of light and truth, for personal success in the forthcoming battles. They'd be sending messages soon, he expected, begging him to attend their sacrificial meal.

But he wouldn't go. He joined Mithraic celebrations for the rebirth of the sun every midwinter. But that was more than enough for that lot. It was all the alms-grasping priests of Mithras would ever get from him again.

A rampart of cloud, slate hued, edged in gold by the setting sun, was rolling in from the south. He felt a spit of rain on his cheek.

Soon it would be time to get ready for the feast. Every town he visited had to have one. He patted his stomach. It was bulging a little in a way he did not like. Feasts were not what he needed now, and being forced to listen to endless speeches, praising him, followed by the local magistrates exaggerating the woes of the town and the terrible problem of ever-rising prices.

If he was lucky, as he usually was, all that would be followed by testimonies about the delinquency of youth these days and the corruption of old men. All these aimed at local targets and accompanied by appeals for him to solve every problem, as everyone knew he could, with the merest flick of his little finger.

The first night in any Roman town was always the same. Every ugly prostitute and their pimps would line the main street in their finest tunics, and every criminal would show off his wife and her pearls. Sometimes the two groups were indistinguishable. This was what it was like to be emperor. And it was not what he'd imagined his life would be.

But there was one thing he was looking forward to tonight. She would liven up his table. He patted his stomach. And the sausage this far north was always good.

LIV

Lindum, Northern Britannia, 306 A.D.

Lucius had only just arrived at his lodgings in the military prefect's oversized villa when he received the summons. Leaving Juliana to sort out his things he went, in a state of high anticipation, to find out if his lure had been taken.

Cavalry officers and members of the imperial guard were milling around at his destination, the town's stables, each one intent on giving detailed instructions as to how their particular horse should be treated. Excitement filled the air. Soon these men would be enjoying the pleasures of the taverns and the she-wolf's lair.

One of the Alemanni officers told him Crocus could be found at the far end of the yard assessing a disused stable block. He found the low stone building and pressed at its rotten wooden door. It opened, creaking loudly.

A musty odor came out. Dust thickened the air in the shaft of gold evening sunlight, coming through a small round window high up on the far wall. Stacks of chariot wheels on the floor were illuminated, as if they'd been discarded by the gods. The peeling carcass of a once impressive cart had been pushed into a corner. A cloak of dust coated everything. A chariot stood near the doorway, forlornly waiting for those who'd started to rebuild her to return and finish the job.

Shouts echoed behind him from the yard, followed by the sound of a horse neighing. A creak echoed from the back of the stable.

"Is that you, Crocus?"

He was being observed. He knew it and he didn't like it.

There was no reply.

"Crocus? It's Lucius." Louder.

He paced slowly towards the gloom at the back of the storeroom. He passed a stack of wheels, turned. There was a blur of movement.

A hand clamped firmly over his mouth. The point of a blade was being pushed into his side.

"Say another word, prick, or struggle one little bloody bit and you'll not have time to even ask for your stupid god's forgiveness." The hand pressed tight across his mouth. Lucius could hear his assailant breathing. Noises from the yard reverberated through the storeroom. He consoled himself with the thought that if his assailant wanted him dead, he'd have been on the floor in a pool of blood by now. The rushing in his ears calmed.

He was pushed roughly forward.

Lucius wiped his sleeve against his mouth, then pulled his dagger from its unadorned scabbard and turned.

"Put that girly blade away," sneered Crocus, as he sheathed his own weapon. "I was only teaching you a lesson."

After a moment's hesitation, Lucius did as he was asked.

"Did I injure your pride, my friend?" Crocus grinned. "Well, I hope you're not too touchy, before we even begin this." He took a step towards Lucius. "But first, you'll swear an oath, to that stupid fish god you yellow skinned Armenians cling to and swear that you'll never speak of this meeting to anyone, any god or any man or any man god. A sacred oath on your blood and life, if you value it that is, or on anything you do value, like the cunt who shat you out. Do you so swear?" Crocus pushed his face forward to within a hand's breadth of Lucius'. The blood vessels were bulging on his forehead. Thick sinews, cables, had appeared on his neck.

"I so swear," snapped Lucius.

Crocus looked around. He went to the open doorway, peered outside, then closed the door over. The light dimmed. He padded back and stood in front of Lucius.

"I have news for you, brave bloody Lucius." He leaned in towards Lucius, his expression smug.

"Yes," said Lucius.

"Theodora, our wonderful and valiant empress, will be here soon with her grand plans for her family, thanks to your friend, the priestess of darkness, Sybellina." Crocus touched his forehead with his middle finger, looked up, raised his finger high in the air, then turned and spat in the dust, over his shoulder, as if warding off evil.

"That priestess cunt has been pressing for too many favors from our emperor," he said. "I expect the empress heard all about her and her ways. She'll have her banished as soon as she gets here. We'll fix your donation to my coffers when the empress is gone. It will be difficult to get him to listen to your cause until then. That is what you want, isn't it?"

Lucius looked at him, weighing up how far he could go with his response. Two days before he'd received a letter from his father. There'd been another edict proclaimed in Syria, Palestina and Cilicia. It was the first new edict against the followers of Christ in a year. Disaster was now being piled upon disaster for them. He had no choice. This door was unlatched. He had to push on through.

"The Fates always reward those who help their friends in some way, is that not so?" On such moments, so many hopes hung. His mission had been an abject failure so far. Only someone like Crocus could help him now. Someone on the inside.

"Well, it's not your body I'm here for," replied Crocus.

Lucius looked down. Crocus was clearly amenable, but how far would he be prepared to go? That was what he had to find out.

LV

Lindum, Northern Britannia, 306 A.D.

Constantine arrived late, as he'd planned. A blustery wind, the type that carried the smell of rain and death from far off, swirled at his back as the giant double doors of the hall were opened for him. The clusters of candles in their ornate bronze candleholders near the doorway streamed sideways, flickering like the pennants of a Pictish army, until the doors were closed behind him.

He'd put on his new black leather tunic. His gold campaign medallions had been pinned to it.

He advanced into the room. Everyone stared at him. He'd become used to such gatherings, had even come to enjoy the attention and the whispers of the people pointing him out to their companions. Two women winked at him, despite the presence of their escorts nearby. He turned away and saw Lucius at the far end of the hall.

"Where in bloody Hades have you been? I thought you'd deserted us," was how he greeted Lucius, after he'd made his way through the crowd.

"I don't desert people, you should know that. A good Roman never gives up, isn't that what they say?" Lucius had barely finished speaking when Sybellina appeared at his side in a long white skirt, slit open at the sides all the way up her thigh. Her sleek midriff was bare. A wide band made from a mesh of gold wires covered her breasts. Snake bracelets circled her olive hued arms. Her hair had been piled into curls high on top of her head, as was proper for such gatherings. A dusting of blue-gray hematite drew attention to her eyes. She was attracting some very appreciative glances.

"If you do desert us, may I go with you?" said Sybellina. She sounded almost apologetic.

"I'm sure you're too good a Roman for that," said Constantine.

She leaned towards him, whispered in his ear. "What's turned you against me, my lord? Once you would have jumped at any chance to be with me. You've found someone else, I think. Tell me who it is, so I can pluck her eyes out." She arched her eyebrows and hugged his arm in a friendly manner, as if she'd had too much wine already.

The gold mesh binding her breasts was a loose weave. Her nipples poked through it. They'd been smeared with gold dust. The mesh scratched against the leather of his breastplate. The smell of her perfume, the whiff of flowers at night with a faint trace of burnt animal fat, made him turn his head away.

You're too late, he thought. I'm not under your spell any more. Compared with someone innocent your snares are overdone.

She was not as attractive as he'd once imagined her to be. And especially not smelling like this. He wasn't sure why, but perhaps he'd seen too many party girls dressed like her. Perhaps the thought of his father with her had turned him off too. He thought about Juliana, her innocence, how different she was to Sybellina.

"Have you've greeted the empress yet?" purred Sybellina.

"The empress is here?" He looked around, startled. If his stepmother had arrived she had to be scheming about something. A sudden chill ran up his back, as if a window had been opened behind him.

"Yes, she has arrived. I hear she's with the emperor," said Sybellina in a low voice. She looked pleased. That puzzled him. Surely his stepmother's arrival would affect her too?

He felt a sense that something had caught up with him, then anger. He knew she'd be scheming with his father. Her every move was meant to diminish him.

"I must greet her. Thank you for the news."

He headed out of the hall and walked quickly to his father's rooms. Guards stood to attention, their spears crossed, barring his way.

"I'm the emperor's son, let me pass." He pushed at the spears.

"Sorry, my lord. No one is allowed enter the emperor's quarter unless invited." The centurion pointed to a marble bench.

"Rest, my lord. I'll inform the emperor you are here."

He clamped his lips together, controlled his rising frustration, and sat. The centurion slipped through the door. He saw a glimpse of marble floor. He took a deep breath and began examining his leather boots, repositioning the thin straps that bound them to his calves.

Muffled laughter echoed through the door. He wondered for a moment were they laughing about him. No. He had to remain calm. Accept it all. Be careful. He remembered what that had meant before, the last time he'd met the empress. In Rome that was. He'd been treated like the despised runt of the family then, someone whose very existence was a deep embarrassment. Since then he'd hated her. He shivered with the memory.

Every moment was like an age as he waited, but then finally, with a creak, the doors swung open and he was called inside. At the far end of the large, richly decorated room, was the empress. His mouth went dry. He got the strange sensation that time had speeded up, that things were moving faster than he'd expected. She was lounging on a purple, silk brocade covered couch in front of a dark massive wall hanging of a huntress, draped in a boar skin. The dark marble floor that stretched between them was strewn with bearskins. Bronze oil lamps glowed all around.

His father, the emperor, was standing in the center of the room. A slave moved around him, adjusting his purple and gold toga.

"Constantine, I'm very glad you came," said the empress. She nodded towards the emperor.

He bowed low to his father, walked past him, went down quickly on one knee, and kissed the glassy surface of the back of her hand. A perceptible shudder ran through her.

"Your father tells me you brought not one single gift from the eastern provinces. How typical." She withdrew her hand quickly, as if his kiss was poison. She looked at him disdainfully as he straightened.

"You are getting fat, Constantine. Going to too many feasts, I expect." She motioned him to step back, so she could examine him. He did as he was asked.

"I'd prefer to be in the field, empress. I am sure . . ."

She interrupted him, loudly. "I did not come all the way from Treveris at the far end of Gaul to talk to you about your duties." She shot the emperor a knowing look. "I must tell you some bad news." She paused, sighed grandly.

"Your mother waits for you. You must visit her at once in Treveris. She is ill, very ill." She raised her eyebrows, as if daring him to contradict her.

"What's wrong with her?" he said. He wondered if she was lying.

His real mother, Helena, had kept his hopes alive with tales of his glorious future all through his childhood, as they'd moved together from province to province following his father. She'd taught him about the legendary emperors of Rome, Augustus, Trajan, Hadrian and Marcus Aurelius and she'd promised him that one day people would tell stories about him too.

"She suffers a lot, but I know little of her actual condition. All I can tell you is that she is waiting for you in Treveris. It is your duty to go to her." The empress looked at her husband, as if for support.

It was very convenient timing, but there was nothing he could do. They would get what they wanted.

"Come now, Constantine, you are fortunate Helena hasn't been taken to the other side yet," said his father. "Believe me on this matter, I'll send for you if I need you." He slapped away the slave boy who was still fidgeting with his toga.

"If you stay in Treveris, Constantine, I'll also consider what position I can give you in our legions facing Germania. That's what you want, isn't it, a senior role over our legions? Come on then, it's agreed. Let's all go to this feast together. I don't want any disagreements, especially not in front of these provincials."

Constantine knew it would not be wise to press his father. Arguing with him in front of the empress would be a bad mistake.

At dawn the following morning, Constantine paced the courtyard of the villa he and Lucius had been assigned to. He was waiting for Juliana. He'd gone to her room but had found she'd left it earlier to start her daily tasks. He'd ordered a house slave to find her and send her to him.

When she appeared, he waved her forward. He felt strangely nervous as she approached but knew what he'd decided was right. She came towards him and bowed.

"I need your help, Juliana."

She looked taken aback.

"I must start out for Treveris this morning and I need someone to put my things in order."

"Of course, master."

"I have something else I want to tell you." Without waiting for her reply, he led the way to his room, beckoning her to follow. Inside, he closed the door, sat on the edge of the bed, and picked up the amber necklace he'd placed earlier on the marble table beside his low bed. He held it towards her. She approached slowly, looking at it strangely. There was something different about her these days, something compelling. This all felt so right. And he was totally aware of her femininity. He could even smell her. A soft rose smell.

"It's simply a token of our friendship, Juliana. You brightened my journey here. And now we are entwined. Please, honor me by accepting it." The skin on her bare arm shone like silk. He was spellbound by her presence. Desire surged up inside him.

Her hand flew to her face. She looked aghast, reached towards the necklace, then withdrew her hand before she'd even touched it. Her cheeks were red.

"I cannot accept such a gift. I am a slave," she stuttered. Then she lowered her eyes. He stood. Her black mane of hair, shining in the light from the doorway, said "touch me". He bent towards her, breathing in the smell of roses, which seemed to come from her. He took her hand gently, raised it up, and kissed it. She didn't resist. He wondered if the same longing he had ran through her too. He felt a little light-headed. He wanted her badly now. Needed her.

She reacted with a sigh, stepped back, and pulled her hand away, shaking her head like a dog throwing off water.

"Please, master, do not deceive me."

He stepped towards her, stroked her hair as if it were braids of silk. She wavered, looking around as if she might run. He opened the clasp of the necklace and placed it round her thin neck.

Her eyes brimmed. She stared open-mouthed at him.

"Juliana," he said. "I am not your master. You are under no obligation to me." The air between them was warm and thick. "This is not a deceit. I . . ." He took a deeper breath.

Could he say it? He licked his lips.

"I cannot stop thinking about you." It felt as if he was taking an oath. And for once, he didn't care if he was displaying his eagerness to a woman.

She looked up at him, found her voice. "But, master, any friendship between us is. . ." She looked hopeful, even if her words said something less. ". . impossible."

"You will call me Constantine, please." They were standing very close. He reached up, held her shoulders lightly. "I long for you, Juliana. You fill my dreams. Nothing is impossible when you love. That is what the poets say, isn't it?"

She shook her head slowly, disbelievingly.

"Please listen to me," he continued. "I will petition Lucius to grant you your freedom. I will pay him whatever compensation he asks for. I want nothing in exchange. I promise you, you will not be deceived by me, Juliana. You are the only woman I think about. Every time I see you now, I want you more. It is eating at my heart."

She had to understand that he had no intention of harming her.

She sighed, a sigh of submission.

"I want you too," she whispered. Her voice echoed like a bell in his heart. She turned her face up, opening it to him.

He moved closer, close enough to feel the warmth from her body and hear her breathing. Their lips hesitated, inches apart, then came together. Gently at first, then with a burning fervor, their passion awoke.

His deep ache, his physical longing for her, hardened, pressed up against her. She responded, rubbing gently against him, moaning. Then, abruptly, she pushed him away, struggling against his arms.

"Stop, please," she gasped.

It was a physical jolt to the sweetness that had engulfed him. Her kisses glowed hot in his memory.

She tilted her head as if she was listening for noises from outside. All he heard was a songbird filling the air with sweetness.

"I love you, Juliana, and I need you, I need you very much." He was almost begging. That wasn't like him.

She looked at him, clearly assessing him for what seemed like an age. She looked scared. Every possibility flashed through his mind. No, he would not force her. If she didn't want him, he had to accept it.

He bowed his head, broke their stare.

She reached out her hand.

They kissed again. This time she didn't resist.

She wants me. He kissed her. Stroked her neck. Her skin felt like water. The tension flowed out of him. She was everything he wanted.

He reached under her soft woolen tunic. She pressed against him. He ran his hand up her legs. She groaned. He pulled her tunic up over her head, threw it aside. Her breasts burst free. Their tongues met. He ran his hands all over her body, then pushed her legs apart, pushing her back onto the wall.

He moved inside her. She gasped his name, responding to his urgency with thrusts of her own.

More, more, faster, faster.

LVI

Treveris, Northern Gaul, 306 A.D.

Helena turned in her bed. She pulled the blankets up tight under her chin. These northern provinces at the edge of the empire were as cold in summer as Alexandria ever got in the middle of a normal winter.

She felt under her pillow. Yes, it was still there. Soon it would be time to pass the vial on. The question was, should she give it to Constantine, and risk it being found on him and all that might mean, or should she give it to someone else?

There was a second problem. Could any of them trust what was in the vial? Perhaps it was meant to make whoever took it sick, but not die, which would expose the person who'd delivered the poison.

No, whatever happened to the person who drank the vial was up to the one god. Whether they would die was not the point. What the vial would do would be to draw out the desire to kill, by providing the means to do it.

Whether the vial would ever be needed was another matter. She would leave that for others to decide. It was time to find a messenger. And if they were caught with it, the person could be told the vial would allow them to kill themselves, if they were captured by an enemy. Each person it passed to could say the same thing.

Her dreams came swiftly that night. First, she saw the she-wolf waiting, her teats swollen, then she saw a Roman army laid out on a plain, banners raised above with a red cross on each one, just as Hosius had predicted. The massed ranks were shouting in unison.

"Augustus, Augustus, Augustus."

On a podium in the distance someone was being crowned.

She awoke with a start. Who had she seen being crowned as Augustus, the highest position possible in the empire?

Had it been her ex-husband?

LVII

Lindum, Northern Britannia, 306 A.D.

"Please don't cry, Juliana," whispered Constantine as they lay sated on the bed afterwards. "If I'm not allowed to return to Britannia soon, I'll ask Lucius to send you to Treveris. I swear it. We will not be parted for long."

"If . . ." Her voice trailed away.

"I love you." He wrapped her in his arms. She snuggled up against him.

"I will spend all my time dreaming of you." He smoothed her hair.

Suddenly, a knock on the door resounded through the room. They both jumped in their skin, as if a bucket of cold water had been thrown over them.

The knock came again, loud, insistent. He shouted he was coming. They hurriedly fixed their clothes.

"Who is it?" he shouted, as he dressed.

"It is your Empress Theodora. Open this door at once!"

He waved frantically at Juliana.

"Coming," he shouted, his thoughts tumbling. He looked at Juliana. She was fixing her belt, her face ashen. He jammed his feet into his sandals, stumbled to the door.

He pulled it open. Juliana stopped smoothing her tunic.

The empress had her back to him.

Her long blue gown had a thin purple edge. Her yellow tinted hair was curled high on her head, held up by a heavy looking gold headband. She turned and scowled at him as the door creaked open further.

359

"You two have been busy," she snapped. She looked past him at Juliana, who was standing with her head bowed well behind him.

"Come here, slave."

Juliana moved cautiously towards her. Theodora waved her forward faster, until Juliana was right in front of her. She put her forefinger under Juliana's chin, pushed her head up.

"I've never understood why you like scrawny jaundiced-looking slave girls." She shook her head, her distaste evident. "I hope this one isn't going to wail, like those others, when you leave her." She moved past Juliana into the room.

"Be gone, girl, I can't stand maudlin slaves. Ask my boys to come here. They'll finish this packing."

Constantine nodded to Juliana. He hoped she'd understand. It would be better for her if she disappeared at this moment. The empress was too powerful. She was only a few years older than him, but she always spoke with the utter conviction of someone who always got exactly what she wanted.

After Juliana had departed, she began to quiz him.

"I was informed Sybellina was your lover."

"Sybellina plays only with men her goddess approves of," he said.

Her eyes narrowed. Her face looked pinched, pale.

"Did Sybellina tell you about the stupid request she carried here from Maxentius?" The empress was looking at the toga laid out on his bed. She bent down, fingered it disdainfully. It was a crude garment compared to the fine silk she wore.

"No."

"I so believe you," she purred. She lifted the toga, sniffed it. "I suppose you expect me to tell you all about her message. Well, I suppose I might, seeing as it doesn't matter anymore." She looked at him a little crookedly.

He didn't take the bait.

"Maxentius has offered little Fausta as a bride for you." Her tone was surprised, as if she didn't know her own half-sister was being proposed as his wife.

So, that was Sybellina's secret. No wonder she'd acted strangely with him. If she was conveying a marriage offer for him, she would have been warned not to let him get close to her. It would have been forbidden for her to interfere with the subject of her message.

"As you well know, your father would never allow such a match, Constantine. It would lead to civil war. Maxentius is trying to use Fausta's dowry, which you would receive, to bribe us to fight his enemies, and then put him in the position he believes he deserves. That's what he wants from this arrangement. He's always been an ambitious one."

"Why wasn't I told?" said Constantine.

The whole thing was stupid and irritating. Then he wondered what Fausta's dowry would have consisted of. Lands, no doubt, and estates, perhaps more than that. Theodora's dowry had consisted of so many estates his father had raised almost a legion from the slaves and farms that came with the land.

"Your father has decided it. There was no point in telling you about this before now. Sybellina will go back empty handed to Maxentius. Fausta can look elsewhere for a husband."

She called to her slave boys who had appeared at the door. They trooped inside. "Pack all these things quickly. Take them, and Constantine, to where the horsemen are waiting outside."

She turned to him as they began working. "I've arranged for the guard troop who accompanied me from Londinium to escort you back there. They've been ready and waiting since dawn. You were expected at the stables earlier." She looked him up and down. "But I can see now that you were busy satisfying your desires." She frowned.

"Do not forget, after you leave here, Constantine, that you are not your father's successor. And never will be." Her tone was firm.

Why did she feel she had to remind him of this? She held her hand towards him in a conciliatory manner.

"You do know that that was decided a long time ago. I'm only saying this because I care for you. My sons will be grown men in a few years. None of us want to see you all fighting or worse, killing each other when the time comes. Accept what has been decided, as they will have to, and I will see to it personally that you and your mother live the rest of your lives in peace. I give you my word." She touched her curls, smoothing them on her head.

"And there may be other rewards too." Her right hand played with the top of her gown, pulling it slightly open.

He glimpsed the curve of her breasts. He looked away. They'd been right about her. Well, he wouldn't fall for such an obvious ploy, and in front of the slave boys. Did she have no shame? Or perhaps they joined in, as one rumor had implied. He picked up the leather bag with his campaign medallions inside. They would not lose that on him. The slave boys had finished. There hadn't been much left to pack.

"I appreciate all that, empress, but I should go now. Perhaps…" He let the thought drift, then bowed and walked out. She was lucky he didn't tell his father about her. That would put lightning in the old man's veins. He shook his head.

But was she right about Maxentius? Did he want to start a war to recover his own place in the imperial succession? He thought about what answer he might have given to Maxentius' offer, if the choice had been his.

He couldn't deny it would be a good marriage, if he had ambitions. Was he not supposed to have ambitions? He balled his fists. Did he have to accept everything they told him?

No, and his father was simply avoiding trouble. It did not mean the succession was totally decided either. There was still hope. It would be many years before his father died. Many things could happen. Theodora's sons might not prove worthy or they might fall from a horse or sicken and die.

He left the room. Poor Juliana. She really had no idea.

He looked around for her, called her name twice down the corridor to the slave's quarters, but it was as if she'd disappeared. Theodora's slave boys were with him too, carrying his bags. He couldn't make too much of wanting to find her. He spotted Lucius peering out of his room. He signaled, strode over to him, waved the slave boys away. They waited at the far end of the colonnade.

"Lucius, thank goodness. Theodora brought news. My mother's sick, so I must go to Treveris today. But there's something I need you to do." He looked around. This would be embarrassing. He took a deep breath. "I want to have Juliana with me, Lucius. I feel I can trust her. What slaves will I be able to trust in Treveris?" Lucius' eyebrows shot up. He seemed about to say something, but Constantine gripped his arm, then spoke in a rush.

"As a personal favor, arrange her papers for me. I'll purchase her at whatever price you want. Send the documents to Treveris. I'll send for her." His mind was racing. No, he couldn't bring Juliana with him. The empress would enjoy that too much, especially after she'd found them together. She'd claim he was weak. But he could send for Juliana. Perhaps when he'd made up his mind about staying in Treveris.

"I might be back. If my father can be made to see sense, I'll be back before the end of the summer. Say nothing to anyone about this."

Lucius had an annoying grin on his face.

That night, at a tavern on the road to Londinium, Constantine woke in a cold sweat. An old nightmare had returned. A crowd of pleading people, their heads covered with black hoods, had been pursuing him. Their shouted words reverberated in the dark around him. "How long, master, how long before you avenge us?" He thought of calling for Juliana to help him understand his dream, then remembered where he was.

LVIII

That same evening, back in Lindum, Lucius called Juliana to his room. It had been a difficult day for her. When she'd left Constantine that morning, she'd walked away with such intensity of purpose, she'd found herself in the kitchen courtyard before she'd looked around. Then, while working at her tasks, she'd repeated his words over and over in her mind, as if by doing so, it would increase the likelihood of them being true. It was his tone, though, that had convinced her. But tone was a difficult thing to remember. It was frustrating. If only it all hadn't happened just before he went away. Why, after all their time together, did he have to wait until this day?

She'd given Constantine what he'd wanted, without any struggle, and in doing so she'd surprised, even shocked herself.

Most males on her estate had been in such fear of their overseer, they hadn't pursued her. She'd not been allowed to encourage them either. Between her foster mother's rock-solid convictions about immorality in slaves and her overseer's attempts to break her will by keeping away other men, she'd enjoyed no more than rushed kisses with a few of the most courageous slave boys. Now, when she thought about the possible consequences of what had happened, she felt ill. She'd broken her most sacred vow. She'd given in to temptation. Risked everything. And for what?

She could tell no one about her fears or ask any other slave any questions. They'd work out what was going on in the blink of an eye. But she had heard that if you held your breath afterwards you'd not become pregnant. So, she'd held her breath off and on all day, and if it did work, she was sure she must have stopped any child taking root.

364

But she knew too, that if it was that easy to stop yourself getting pregnant, every one of the slave girls who'd she seen get pregnant would have done it. Their lives wouldn't have been ruined. And they wouldn't have been sold to any bidder at the next opportunity and ended up in the mines or a whorehouse.

Pine kernel incense was smoldering in a small brazier on a low marble table in Lucius' room when she arrived there. Two glass-encased oil lamps cast a warm glow on the red frescoed walls. Lucius was sitting bolt upright on a long couch, staring at the painting of a peacock on the wall. She closed the door behind her.

"Juliana, my dear. It's been a long day, hasn't it?" He patted the couch beside him. She shook her head. It wasn't right for a slave to sit with her master.

He patted the couch again, his expression harder.

She sat as far from him as she could. He moved a little towards her.

"Did you see Constantine before he left?" He placed a hand on her shoulder.

"Yes," she replied. She wanted to say more, that she'd enjoyed every part of his body. But who knew how he'd react to that news.

"I've been given a new role at Crocus' side. I ride tomorrow for Caledonia with his Alemanni cavalry. We're off to slaughter Picts." He looked pleased. His hand tightened on her shoulder.

"You will take orders from the emperor's slave master while I am gone." He paused, looked at her. "Constantine tells me he wants to buy you." He squeezed her shoulder even tighter.

She breathed in quickly. Her mouth dried. Her skin prickled on her throat.

Would Lucius say no?

"We'll be finished killing Picts by midsummer. By then you should be with him. Not before."

Her mouth opened. She wanted to ask why he needed to kill Picts at all.

He shook his head vigorously. "No, don't thank me and don't tell anyone anything about what happened between you and him. Keep your mouth sealed, Juliana, if you want to go to him, that is. I've

365

made out the papers for your sale already. They'll be sent to Constantine. Be patient until a message returns from him."

She let out her breath. She would be with Constantine. Nothing else mattered.

Constantine had told her he'd petition Lucius for her freedom. Was he planning to buy her now, not buy her freedom? She stuck her chin out. Would she always be his slave, nothing more?

She gripped the edge of the couch. Lucius patted her shoulder. "You know, you are fortunate. Many slaves would go through torture for a chance to be owned by a member of the imperial family. I hope you appreciate your good luck and remember who stood aside to let it happen."

She nodded.

"And remember this, keep away from Sybellina. That priestess is dangerous." He reached up, brushed Juliana's hair away from the side of her face.

She pulled back a little.

He slammed his fist down on the edge of the couch. It rattled under her.

"You are still my slave, Juliana. I could have had your body anytime, if I wanted you." He stood abruptly, his fists balled at his side. "I do not force myself upon slave girls. I do not have to. You might appreciate that in the future. Now be gone."

"I am sure I will," she said. She walked away, a deep shudder of revulsion passing through her.

The pale light of an almost full moon lit her departure. She went to her cot in a small ante-chamber in the basement of the villa and fell onto her blanket. She took the necklace Constantine had given her from her tunic pocket and touched each piece of amber in turn, hoping, praying that he'd send for her sooner than Lucius expected.

She pressed the necklace to her lips as a wave of emotion swept through her. She'd given away her virginity and now she was alone.

Would he let her down?

LIX

Londinium, Southern Britannia, 306 A.D.

When he reached Londinium, Constantine had to wait three days for a post ship to take him to Gaul. During the rough sea crossing he vomited almost the entire journey. The swirling waters echoed the swirl of feelings inside him. He was hopeful that Juliana would join him, but fearful too that Theodora or his father would find a way to stop her and that they would ruin his prospects in the army. When he arrived in Gaul, the governor of Gesoriacum gave him one of his best horses for the journey east.

Sheltering in taverns at night and riding hard during the days along the wide roads of Gaul, he made good progress. He'd been given eight guards as an escort but only their Decurion spoke good Latin. The others were uneducated Belgae. He didn't mind, he needed to think.

As they moved east the flat landscape changed slowly into low, densely wooded hills, with fewer farms and villages. Ancient forests of pale birch and beech crowded up to the road in endless thickets, like rows of giant spears. The spirit, the genii of this forest, seemed watchful and angry to Constantine.

Tangles of undergrowth clustered around tree trunks. In some places the earth stretched away, leaf carpeted, as far as he could see, littered here and there with random patterns of fallen branches. Occasionally, banks of small white star-flowers enlivened the wood.

The weather held good and the sun shone warm through most of his journey, but it was a sickly warmth lacking the invigorating heat from it in the eastern provinces. Butterflies swirled, and birds swooped. At one point a daring raven stood guard as they passed near the carcass of a wolf.

The city of Treveris sat on the far bank of the River Moselle a little downstream and northwards from where it joined the River Saar. He knew Treveris had been a Roman city since the time of Augustus, occupying the level terrain between the river and the steep wooded escarpment to its east.

The day they reached the Moselle they'd been riding hard, trotting fast with new horses for most of the morning. He'd been searching for the river every time the road crested a thickly wooded ridge, and when at last it appeared he had to call a halt to take it in.

The Moselle lay before them, a giant blue-green ribbon that had fallen into a lightly wooded valley, creating a vision of arcadia. Vineyards ran in stripes up the sides of the escarpments on each side of the river. Fields, laneways, and cypress-shaded villas filled the valley, and on his side, the west side of the river, a wide brick-paved roadway ran down slowly towards the water.

As he descended into the valley along the edge of the escarpment to his left and right, gaily painted temples, most likely sanctuaries for Bacchus, guarded vineyards below. Some of the long fields of vines extended all the way down and right up to the wide, sun-dappled Moselle. It felt as if summer had at last arrived after their many days in rolling misty forests. The valley reminded him of places from his childhood in Moesia.

They crossed the river by a sturdy looking triple-cart-wide wooden bridge, after showing their passes at a busy guard post. The Moselle was wider than an arrow's flight here. It sparkled in the sunlight as eddies swirled about the bridge's monumental pilings. A long line of barges floated downstream below them as they rode across.

A racket of clattering hooves and squeaking carts filled the air. Constantine looked up. A pair of hawks flew high, patrolling. He thought about Juliana, wondered how she was, and when he might hear from Lucius.

On the far side of the bridge stood the massive Porta Moselle, a huge gate tower made of dark-gray basalt blocks. A long sullen-gray stone city wall stretched away on either side, interrupted in places by high towers with banners flapping in the breeze.

It was late afternoon by the time he arrived at his mother's villa in the busy commercial part of the city, behind the forum. When he announced who he was, there was at first suspicion, then, after the old stable master recognized him, great excitement.

All the slaves rushed about, bowing and offering him refreshments, and it was only after he'd calmed them that he was shown to her bedchamber. The villa had a dusty look, he thought, as if no one was bothering to keep the place tidy, as guests never came there anymore. The line of painted marble busts of women outside his mother's room were all off their pedestals, lying on their sides on the floor. He strode past them as the door ahead was thrown open by a slave who'd hurried in front.

At the threshold to his mother's bedroom a sickly, sweet odor of heavy rose perfume assaulted him. Helena hadn't changed.

And then he saw her.

She was sitting in a high-backed wicker chair in front of an iron-grilled window. She was attempting to get up. She looked much older than he'd ever remembered her.

Her hair was still raven black, though, and still tied up in a severe bun, the way she always wore it, but her pallor was sickly, and streaks of gray ran through her hair. He hugged her awkwardly as she struggled to stand upright. She sat back down quickly as soon as he let her go.

"Mother, what happened to you?"

"My son, my son, it is so good to see you. I was lucky to get out of Rome with my life. Maxentius made me swear allegiance to him."

"He's scheming to become an emperor," said Constantine.

"Maybe we can use him."

"That day is a long way off."

"It's good to see you. Your presence cures me quicker than a hundred temple offerings can."

He relaxed a little. She sounded like her old self.

"Theodora told me you were gravely ill." He went down on one knee in front of her. "I was planning to visit at the end of the campaign, but she said your life was in danger, so I came at once."

His mother motioned him to her, grabbed his shoulders, pulled him closer. Her eyes shone. "That evil witch will have you declared illegitimate too, if she has her way." She let him go, sank back, looked up at him, then looked away, shaking her head.

"What happened between you and her? Tell me." Constantine's voice resounded in the room.

"After Theodora visited me, I had a fever. I am sure she put something in my wine. I begged her to send the court physician, but I had to pay a passing charlatan myself instead. I had a crisis many nights ago, but it's long passed and now all I can think about is how evil she is." She waved her hand for the slave who'd brought him to disappear.

Constantine felt relieved the danger was over, but angry he'd been manipulated to leave Britannia so hurriedly by the empress and what she may have done.

"Are you sure she did this?"

She stared into his eyes.

"You cannot make anything of my suspicions now, Constantine. You must wait for a moment when she is vulnerable."

"And father still pays for everything for you?" he said.

"Yes, the witch hasn't won that battle yet, but everything will change for the better now that you're with me. We can decide what we'll do with her when you become emperor. You are staying here, aren't you?" She looked at him, wide-eyed.

He leaned forward and kissed her again on both cheeks. Her dreams of him becoming emperor were undimmed. It felt good to hear her certainty of purpose. That alone was worth the effort of coming here.

"Yes. I have been told to stay here, but I plan to write to the emperor and ask for a position with the Alemanni. As for who becomes emperor after him, he hasn't said anything about changing the official succession. But I expect I'm being kept well away from this year's campaign in case I win glory long before his new empress' precious sons." He sighed, and made a fist with both hands, his frustration clear. "He even refused for me to marry Fausta, an offer Maxentius sent."

"If you survived all those years of intrigue at Diocletian's court, my son, I'm sure you can survive the wiles of Theodora for a while." Helena's bony finger trembled as she pointed at him.

"It's better anyway that you'll not be away fighting while that woman is around your father's camp. Bide your time. What we've all prayed for will come. I've told you often enough, you will be emperor. It's been foretold. There are many people working for it. That stupid witch will not steal it all from us. You are his firstborn son. How dare she even think of stopping you!"

She shook her fist, echoing his gesture, coughed, sat back and smoothed her pale blue gown over her knees. It reminded him of cobwebs.

"Now tell me, have you decided on a wife? If Fausta considers you worthy I'm sure there are other suitable candidates too. A man of your age and position should be married and married well."

"I have no need for a wife. It'll be years before I need an alliance with any great family. And I'll not be tied to some spoon-fed patrician." He hesitated for a moment, took a deep breath, and pressed on. He had to tell her.

"I have found the woman I want to be with, Mother. A woman more elegant than a princess. Her name is Juliana."

"How did you meet her."

Constantine hesitated. It would come out if he lied.

"She is Lucius' slave."

His mother let out a cry. "No! Not a slave girl." She broke into a sob, let out another pained cry.

"I thought you of all people would understand, Mother."

"You cannot take a slave girl as a wife. You know that. We're not like other families now." She shook her head with a firmness that made it clear she would not change her mind. "It's impossible. Theodora is marrying her cousins' daughters into the richest families in the provinces, horse traders and tin merchants and those land hoarders, and all expecting to be rewarded with estates in Caledonia.

371

How could you spoil your chances by taking a slave as a wife? I will not allow it. Use her, yes, let her warm your bed by all means, Constantine, if you must, but you will marry well and soon, not least because you need the dowry."

She leaned forward, reached towards him. "If you do this you'll expose us to nothing but ridicule. What girl of quality would take you if you even talk about this?" She coughed, raised her hands to her face. A violent spasm passed through her. She coughed again, bent over as the coughing went on. He grabbed a water goblet and held it out to her.

She took it, drank from it, then coughed again.

"You have no idea what I went through to come here, Constantine. Some days I thought I would not make it. Do not disappoint me. Everything depends on you doing the right thing at every step."

"Shall I call for a doctor?"

"No, it will pass. It is something I picked up in Rome. It will ease with your support now that you are here." She coughed again.

He shook his head, his lips pressed tight. He had little choice now. If his mother was ill he could not go against her. She would say he wanted to kill her. He knew his mother. She had done it before when she wanted her way. He would wait and bide his time. For now, at least Juliana would be with him, under his protection.

He stared at the ochre tiled floor. So much was changing. He remembered his mother, Helena, as a tall attractive woman, always vivacious, and warm hearted to slaves. She'd given up all hope of another husband by staying on at his father's court for his sake, even though she knew the new Empress Theodora, hated her. He could not throw aside the person who had kept his fate tied to an emperor's and had cast aside her own to do it.

He put a hand on her shoulder, steadying her as the coughing subsided. In the Moesian village she came from, people were as tough as granite and private, hardened by tough lives, hot summers and deep snow in winter. Marrying your children well, that was what mothers there worried about. He felt a tug of exhaustion. He had to sleep. If she didn't want a doctor, there was nothing more he could do.

"I have a room set aside for you," said Helena. She clapped her hands.

The following night, at a feast in his name his mother insisted on holding, he met the governor of Treveris and was introduced to many of the senior administrators of the city, a class of men he'd always despised. Petty, pompous, rule-making men with quivering bellies and bulging eyes. If, as some of them claimed, they were military men, they were fit only for parade ground duties.

Most of these bloated blood-suckers took great pleasure in describing their virtues to Constantine in mind-numbing detail. He kept his thoughts to himself, but inside he seethed. Administrators were not real men. This was not what he wanted to be.

The only thing that lifted his spirits were daydreams of Juliana and what they would do when she got here. Every moment since his arrival, to his amazement, his gaze had leapt to the door every time it opened. She had burrowed deeper into his heart than he'd expected. Lucius' letter, the confirmation of sale, could be with him soon. He would persuade his mother to take Juliana into their household. She would be won around when she met Juliana. He would not give way on this. Everything would work out if he planned it right.

He'd done everything he was supposed to so far. But one thing felt strange, the longer he was separated from Juliana, the more he wanted her. No woman in Treveris, or the ones he'd been with in the east, was anything like her. She was different, smart, beautiful, and she was a connection to all he'd been through. And she knew his dreams and what he hoped for.

How strange it was to come so far in search of something, only to find it among those you were with on your travels.

It felt as if Juliana was haunting him.

He excused himself and went out into the town. As he walked the empty cobbled streets the buildings around him seemed to be holding their breath. Near the city gate three fresh heads dripped blood onto tall stakes. He stopped. Presumably they had been put there to deter visitors to the city from causing trouble.

It was not how they did things in the east, but there the enemy tribes were hundreds of leagues away. Here there were tribes in the great forest a day's ride away, under the loose control of the Alemanni, who needed to be taught how to behave in a Roman city.

The dripping heads made him think of all the blood that had soaked into his own skin and the dead faces he had seen. Faces that always took days to disappear from his mind.

He went close to the heads. Graffiti had been written about their tribes in Latin on the stakes they were impaled on. Some here hated Saxons the way they hated Sassanians and Scythians in the east. One of the pieces of graffiti claimed that the men ate children. The claim made him smile, but not for the reasons intended. He had heard similar claims made about the Persians in the east.

He heard a dog barking and looked around. The street was empty. He felt out of place, disconnected. He knew that while he lived here he would always be different, an outsider, both by his position in society and his family origins. Few people in Treveris, at the edge of the empire, had ever lived in the east, or even travelled there, and many had strange ideas about how lives were lived in other provinces or beyond the borders of the empire. They thought themselves superior, not only to the people from beyond the limits of their empire, but from every other province in it. They saw themselves as different.

But he saw so many similarities. He'd seen hardship etched in many faces here, just as he'd seen it in many other cities. And sickness among the poor killed here just as quickly as it did everywhere in the empire. What was needed was a more unified empire, but that was unlikely to happen in his lifetime.

He sniffed. The steaming middens, that was another thing that was the same all over the empire. The air was filled in certain streets with the stench of bowel. He looked up. The thickly thatched roofs looked just as ready to burn as they did in Britannia.

He clenched his fists. The talk among men at the feast had been about which were the best brothels in town, and how soon they could go on leave to their villas, and the upcoming games. He needed something more.

He needed something to make everything he'd lived through worth it.

That night, after he fell asleep, he saw a great army, masses of cavalry walking slowly, moving forward in seething shifting columns, an army greater than any he'd ever seen. An army that would make people rub their eyes and look again and talk about the sight to their grandchildren. An army that could change things. He woke with a start and sat up, sweating.

The sights he'd seen in the east had never left his dreams. The sights and sounds and smells of shit, and guts and blood from battlefields, they were too strong to forget. Something an Eastern sage in a town they had retaken from the Persians had said to him, which had stuck in his mind, came back to him.

"You can do anything you think you can do, if you believe in it."

But could he do anything? He considered his treatment since his arrival in the West. It had not gone as he'd expected.

But would he live to see that army? Would he even live the year out with Theodora plotting against him?

He had never feared assassination, though he knew that Theodora might have planned such an end for him. He knew how to bear such thoughts from his many sleepless nights in the East after he was first taken there as a hostage for his father's compliance to the Emperor Diocletian's will. The emperor who had plucked his father from obscurity and made him a Caesar.

And, in any case, he always kept his weapons about him. He turned to the window, pulled his knife from under his pillow. The blade shone in the moonlight. He touched the tip to the palm of his hand, as he'd been taught. Blood trickled onto the flag-stone floor.

LX

Lindum, Northern Britannia, 306 A.D.

Before he departed Lindum, the emperor ordered the main body of Alemanni cavalry to proceed as the army's vanguard. The Alemanni under Crocus were well used to this task. The route north took them along the new westerly route to the city of Eboracum, past the great fort at the new bridge over the River Don. Here they'd move from the territory of the Coritanii to that of the Brigantes. The Alemanni cavalry would then proceed beyond Eboracum to set up camp at the supply fort of Corstopitum, a few leagues south of Hadrian's Wall. From there they could raid north into Caledonia proper.

The rest of the army would remain at Eboracum, a city built on river flats at the center of a great vale, a position which allowed it command of all the main trade routes in north eastern Britannia. The outer streets of the city were filled with new and rambling villas. Roman colonists had been busy rebuilding and expanding, aided by the newly affluent natives. Many of them had grown rich on the trade in wool, slaves and fish, much of it from beyond Hadrian's Wall. The city usually had a relaxed air too, with a calm weekly market, unlike the frenzied ones, which were the hallmarks of commerce of its southern counterpart, Londinium, where they were held every day.

The afternoon the army arrived, though, the city was anything but relaxed. A welcoming festival had been arranged which was, as far as Juliana was concerned, the best they'd been treated to in all the time she'd been in Britannia. She was getting used to travelling in an imperial entourage, even if she always rode half a league behind the emperor himself.

As they rode through the main street leading from the main river gate, little girls on either side, dressed in off-white tunics, showered the visitor's path with shimmering handfuls of pink and white petals, while fife and flute players played lively tunes and bobbed and bowed at the passing visitors. At the forum a tumultuous clashing of swords against bucklers greeted them. Troops of guardsmen and members of the city watch saluted every part of the passing parade while onlookers cheered rapturously. Even the sun had come out to greet them and many slaves cheered that day as if they'd all been freed, such was the excitement. Juliana felt like an orphan who'd found a gold coin.

At one point, her every muscle stiffened as she leaned forward on her horse. "Constantine!" she shouted, excitedly, at a tall dark-haired man whose back was turned to her. Then, abruptly, acute embarrassment rose up inside her. It wasn't him. She closed her eyes and gripped tight with her thighs to steady herself on her small gray mare, willing the noise and people around her to fade away.

She'd been relieved when the Empress Theodora had followed Constantine to Gaul. She could bear the waiting a lot easier now. It was obvious that the empress had more to concern herself with than Juliana. Nothing at all had been said about her being found with Constantine, though until Theodora departed she'd half expected to be called at any moment and questioned about what had occurred. Constantine could have any slave he wanted, but there was a possibility that Theodora would want Juliana to tell her things about her stepson.

Now the empress was gone her fears had faded. Her concern now was why she was still waiting. Had there been a delay in Lucius' message reaching Constantine? Had his reply been lost? She kept telling herself she shouldn't panic, but her nights in the tent she'd been allocated on the road north were filled with an expectation she hadn't known since she'd been a child waiting for her mother to come back from the market. And it grew stronger every day she was apart from him.

The thought that she was now in Eboracum, and that her father might be near, added another twist of sadness to it. A sadness that overcame her every time she thought about her real chances of finding him.

She blinked. Someone nearby had shouted for the beauty with the black hair to smile. As she'd been warned, she fixed her gaze ahead and didn't respond. The emperor's entourage were above the plebeian rabble, so the slave master said, though she didn't feel that way.

The feast that night went on until almost dawn, but Juliana was allowed away early after the main dishes were served and collected. It was the way she'd been treated since Constantine and Lucius had departed. She guessed one of them must have said something to someone.

She helped in the kitchens the following day and discovered that the local baths had a special time for slaves and decided to visit them. The facilities for slaves in the governor's overcrowded villa near the forum were limited to washing from a large bowl. On arriving, she remembered that the time of her blood was late. She prayed it would not mean what she feared most. Had being close to Sybellina's charm affected her womb too?

Juliana knelt in a corner of the warm room at the baths, where a niche had been set up with a statue of what looked like Diana.

Was she being punished for the thoughts of Constantine that invaded her mind constantly at night, unbidden? His many qualities filled her dreams, but most of all she remembered his body on top of her, his manhood driving into her, hard and fast, again and again, making her long for him inside her. Such thoughts made her feel guilty, and ashamed. Some mornings on the road north she hadn't eaten because of it all.

Why hadn't she resisted him? Had he fooled her? Was there a messenger coming at all?

The day after arriving in Eboracum she began looking for her father. She'd quickly established that she'd not be considered missing if she disappeared for an hour or two. No one was watching her movements that closely. She'd found out from a stable slave where the smiths worked and asked in every shop on that street, near the city wall at the Porta Sinistra, was there any smith in Eboracum who'd served in the East with the legions, and who had the name Arell.

What she got for her efforts were scowls and sneers, although once she was told that such a man did exist, but when she went to his smithy he was far too young to be her father and all he did was shake his head when she asked questions. She wasn't sure whether this was wariness of anyone he did not know, or just his lack of Latin.

Eventually, after three more days of searching, she'd visited every smithy in the civilian town outside the city walls and along the river, and finally she had to accept defeat. A new moon was coming that night, but she felt empty inside, abandoned, cursed. All that night she trembled and sickened at what her future might hold.

The next morning, early, she received a summons.

"But Sybellina's not my mistress," she said to the slave standing in the doorway.

"It matters not, girl. What Sybellina asks for, she gets." The old slave was clearly angry she'd dared question his summons.

Juliana felt queasy as she looked at the old man's stony face.

"You're lucky I don't whip you so you can't sit for a week, then drag you to her anyway."

Juliana grunted in dignified assent, then put the twig brush she'd been using to sweep the corridor in a corner. What could Sybellina want? Did she know about Constantine, and about the charm? Or was there some errand she wanted her to run?

She looked at the old slave. His expression was as fixed as that of a marble statue. He wasn't going to tell her anything. Anyway, what could Sybellina do to her in the middle of a busy palace?

Anxiety twisted inside her as they hurried to Sybellina's room in the far courtyard near the emperor's quarters.

When they entered the room, after knocking, Sybellina was on her knees moaning, banging her forehead gently against the floor in a corner of the room. A single iron-grilled window let a patterned square of sunlight onto the red tiled floor. Juliana stood still, taking in the faint but audible thuds as Sybellina's head hit the floor, her low rhythmic moaning filling the air. She wanted to shout, "Stop," but she couldn't. Thoughts of running filled her head.

"Please, Juliana, send him away. Only you can help me," said Sybellina. Then she let out a low moan.

Juliana turned. The old slave was already gone.

"What can I do to help?" She edged forward, lowering her eyes respectfully, hoping Sybellina wouldn't see how truly pleased she was to see her distressed.

"I heard your kind are sworn to help people in need."

Juliana's mouth went dry. What did she know about her kin? How did she know anything about her?

"When did the sickness start, mistress?" she asked, hoping to distract her.

"Wait." Sybellina rose, shuffled to a small round table with ivory feet. On it sat a yellow beeswax candle, calibrated for the hours, two simple silver goblets and a jug. A small flame and a curl of smoke rose from the candle. Sybellina collapsed into one of two armless high-backed wooden chairs beside the table. She leaned in and cupped her hands around the candle.

Juliana felt warm, as if it was midsummer in the Eastern provinces. A trickle of sweat ran down her back. She stared at the chair she was clearly expected to sit on. Was Sybellina playing a game with her? Was this all some ruse? It felt as if a metal band was being tightened round her head.

Sybellina pointed at the chair. Juliana moved to it, perched uncomfortably on its front edge. This felt wrong. All wrong. She couldn't help Sybellina. She should go. At once. Her hands were trembling. She looked at the door, then back at Sybellina. She was holding her head at a strange angle now, smiling as if some amusing thought had just come to her.

"Please, drink with me, Juliana. I need to know you trust me. I know you're nervous, but don't be. I am not evil." Her eyes widened. She looked innocent.

Then it came to her, the door out of the room was behind Sybellina. She was trapped. She swallowed, hard.

Sybellina filled the goblets on the table with wine from the jug. It glugged as she poured. Wine splashed onto the table. Sybellina touched the spill with a finger, licked it, nodded her approval, then passed one of the goblets to Juliana and raised the other to her lips. She saw Juliana looking at the goblet with suspicion. With a flourish, she put her own goblet down.

"I see you don't trust me, Juliana." She sounded offended. "So please, take mine. I'll drink yours. If it is poisoned, I'll be the one to suffer." She handed her goblet to Juliana, who hesitated for a moment, then passed her own back to her.

Sybellina drank. Juliana looked at her goblet. She sniffed at it. It smelt fine. If Sybellina had been about to drink from this one, surely it couldn't be poisoned. She tasted it. It tasted good, a little bitter. Sybellina raised her goblet, drained it. Juliana took a sip, waited, drank a little more. Surely such a small amount could not hurt her.

"My ailment started, Juliana, my dear," said Sybellina, her tone more assured now, "when someone stole my most secret charm. And for a long time, I wondered who had done this." She shook her head in mock bafflement.

Juliana's heart thumped so loudly she feared Sybellina would hear it.

"Lucius, perhaps, or one of the emperor's officials, or some impudent slave. But there was no proof, no proof at all, until last night." She smiled with the sure purpose of a snake.

Juliana's mouth opened. She wanted to say something but felt too tired. The goblet slipped from her hand, crashed, rolled, settled very slowly, rocking back and forth. The stink of wine filled the air. Her eyelids drooped.

"Late last night, our emperor told me his son took an interest in you before he went away. A passionate interest. And I knew at once. Only powerful magic could have turned his eye towards a scrawny mongrel like you." She snorted derisively.

Gut-twisting terror gripped Juliana as if she was being held in a vice.

"Stealing has terrible consequences. You know that, don't you?"

A wolf was about to pounce. She had to run, but she felt so terribly weary. Then pain squeezed at her stomach, and set her hands shaking.

"I must go, mistress." She tried to sound normal, but her voice came out funny, all slurred. Sybellina was getting bigger, her face filling Juliana's vision.

A hand gripped Juliana's arm.

"You're so innocent, aren't you?" Tinkling laughter echoed in her head. Juliana tried to stand. But her feet wouldn't cooperate. Her vision blurred. Someone was holding her up. Laying her down on a soft bed, forcing something into her mouth. She spluttered, swallowed. A voice came blurrily, as if through a trumpet.

"You'll pay the price now, sweet Juliana." A slow chant began. It went around and around, over and over and over.

There was a smell.

Sage.

Heat.

She wanted to sleep. A whiff, a burning, penetrated her mind, wrinkled her nose, bringing her back. Though she didn't dare open her eyes. Darkness sucked at her.

"The ritual will be done properly this time, sweet Juliana. The knife will be cleansed in fast running water before we take your blood. Sleep well."

Scornful laughter echoed in Juliana's head. A hand griped her chin, crushing at her cheekbones. She mustn't react. It was not that hard. She had no energy. Her concern was about falling asleep again.

"You do know your lover's not coming back, my sweet," said a distant voice. "Delmatius will marry Fausta. And after that there will be no future for Constantine. He'll only be in the way. And we know what happens to sons who are in the way. I might have saved him, but now it's too late. Such men were not for the likes of you. All you did was pull him down, Juliana. So, understand this, soon I'll hold your love-struck pumping little heart, my sweet. And I'll squeeze it hard until the last ruby-red honey-thick drops come out and I'll have my new love charm and all the fresh blood we need." The voice became indistinct.

382

The bang of a door closing came to her from far away.

She had to get up. She had to get away. She tried to raise her head. It didn't want to move. She tried to shout. Her mouth was stuffed with something.

Her nostrils twitched, wrinkled. Something smelled bad. She opened her eyes. The room was empty. A candle flickered, casting shadows. She balled her fists, dug her nails hard into her palms, turned her head, lifted a shoulder, a leg. The effort almost drained her.

It reminded her of how she'd felt after a heavy beating back at the estate in Bithynia. But she had to focus. Constantine was in danger. She had to move. She rolled, first one way then the other, then, after three tries, she rolled off the bed and onto her side in a crash that hurt her knee. She peered up. A water jug stood nearby. She reached for it, slowly, forced an evil tasting rag out of her mouth, pulled the jug to her, took a long drink, then poured the rest over her head. Her eyes widened with shock. She didn't have much time. She had to stand.

Dripping, she stumbled for the door, creaked it open, leaning against the wall as she did so, then took a step, then another.

She was at another door. It opened. A corridor lay ahead. At the end of it stood a doorway. Sounds of the street came from beyond it, dogs barking, a child crying. Then she was at the end of the corridor, pushing. Then sunlight and voices.

"Wake up. Wake up." A slap landed on her face, stinging her. She opened her eyes.

Her head was pounding as if a knife had been pushed through it from the back. She blinked. It was night time. She was lying on a rough blanket on what felt like straw. She looked around, every muscle tensing in fear.

A face. One eye. Leering at her. Tiresias, the half-blind wanderer from Londinium. It couldn't be. She groaned in recognition.

"Where am I?" She eased herself onto an elbow. Her head felt ridiculously heavy. A vague confusion of images came to her. She remembered waking alone because of a smell, then stumbling into the corridor.

She'd been in a nightmare.

"Three days I waited for you at that kitchen courtyard gate, Juliana. Waiting for you to go on one of your silly trips around the smithies, disturbing them all. Every smith in town has been talking about you, girl. It wasn't hard to find out where a blue-eyed, raven-haired slave girl was staying, though I began to doubt you'd ever come out of that villa again. Then you fall into the street, and I had to grab you from a bunch of do-gooders who wanted to bring you back into the villa. Needed a bit of talking to, they did. It's not like the old days, you know. Everyone's out for what they can get." He pushed himself to his feet, brushed himself off, and stretched, his blue-veined arms poking out of his gray woolen sleeves. It appeared he'd been on his knees, watching over her.

"It looks as if you've gone and made enemies, girl. Big enemies. No one wastes a sleeping draught, like the one you were given, on a friend. You've slept half a day and most of the night. A new dawn approaches. Tell me the tale of how it all happened. Who gave it to you and how did you escape?" He sat on an old saddle nearby.

She looked around. They were in the loft of a small outhouse. It felt odd not to wake up in her cell with duties beckoning. A pang of guilt rose inside her. Who would do her tasks? Could she go back to them? She licked her lips.

No. Sybellina wouldn't let her get away so easily again. She might be considered a runaway already. The pain for that was death or torture and disfigurement. It was likely too that torture was what Sybellina would prefer. She could have killed her already with whatever she'd put in that drink but had instead made it weak enough for her to survive.

She had to find Lucius.

She told Tiresias about Sybellina. As she began relating the story she glanced over her shoulder, as if afraid someone might be listening.

"She will look for me. She'll not give up easily," she said at the end. She felt the familiar ache of longing for Constantine. He would protect her. He had to.

"There is someone who can help me, if I can get to Gaul."

"Calm yourself. It's common knowledge that witch of yours will be gone back to Rome after she conducts the sacrifices for the games of Apollo after the full moon. If they find you before she goes you could end up crucified, if she claims you stole something and ran away. Now tell me, girl, who is this person who'll help you in Gaul?"

She looked away. He probably wouldn't believe her.

He leaned closer. "Tell me. I deserve to know."

She looked in his eyes. There was kindness there. She debated not telling him, then remembered what her mother had said, to *always listen to the voice inside you, they are angels talking to you.*

She opened her mouth, closed it, then spoke. "The son of the emperor. I…we. . ." Her mouth had gone dry.

"Ssshhh, girl. Say n'more. I know all about it already. The emperor's slaves know almost everything." He touched his nose.

She groaned, thought about all the giggles, the slaves who'd looked at her oddly in the past few weeks. They all knew. She felt stupid. Tiresias had been testing her.

"There's someone I want you to meet, girl. With his help we could send you to Constantine, but you must do something for us." He stared at her, daring her to offend him.

"What do I have to do?" She pulled back from him, looked down, fear rising inside her again. She glanced at the opening in the floor leading down to the ground. Would she have to run?

"Constantine must come back. He must come back to Eboracum. Aye, the pot boils best with all the right ingredients." He chuckled.

A pain tugged at her. She put her hand to her stomach. A long shudder ran through her.

Tiresias patted her arm.

"Don't you worry, girl. I examined you. You have no injuries that I could see. And I had a good look. I expect you will have stomach cramps for days, though."

She turned away. Could she trust him?

"Where's your master, Lucius, these days?"

She told him about Lucius being with the auxiliaries. Tiresias looked pleased.

"Lucius will get you a travel pass. Officers are always sending slaves on errands. You'll go to him first if you want to see Constantine again, girl."

Yes, she thought, Lucius would help.

The first cocks were crowing as Tiresias led Juliana into the courtyard of the small villa to which the outhouse was attached. A rough wooden door filled one corner. He knocked four times and after waiting what seemed ages, knocked four times again. The door was opened. Tiresias went inside. Juliana followed. They entered an earth-floored low-ceilinged kitchen with battered pots hanging on its walls. The smell of warm fresh bread filled her nostrils. She felt terribly hungry. A gray-haired man stood by a polished wooden table. He was staring at her. Tiresias gripped her elbow and spoke in a low voice.

"This is Wehwalt, the woeful one. He lost touch with his first family, a wife and daughter, twenty years ago near the border with Persia." His tone was calm and there was a hint of pleasure in his voice.

"He has another name too. Arell."

A flush of warmth ran through her. Could this be her father? The man was certainly tall, as her mother had described, but he was bent, aged, not at all like she'd imagined. She looked at Tiresias. He nodded.

"You met Wehwalt's son when you called to his smithy half a moon back. You didn't expect him to answer a Roman slave's questions, did you? Your visit set his father thinking and when I started making enquiries for you, he volunteered his tale."

"You look just like your mother," interjected Wehwalt, in halting Latin. His eyes were pale blue, not unlike hers.

"I thank the great spirit, the raven and the wolf. I know your eyes. They were different to hers. Your mother's were brown. You got mine. I could never forget you."

Juliana shook her head. Was this a trick? She took a step forward. She wanted this man to be her father, but fear rose up inside her, filling her head with a roar of doubt. Were they trying to dupe her?

Or was she dreaming? She held her arms tight across her chest. Her breathing had quickened.

"I was a lot younger then. When the Legion I was part of was moved, without warning taken from our frontier duties to go to Alexandria to suppress a rebellion, I petitioned three times for leave to meet your mother, to ask her to follow me. But each time I was refused." His voice almost broke. He put his fist to his mouth to steady himself and the gleam of tears came to his eyes. He blinked.

"I am sorry I left you. We packed up and went in two days. No one was allowed outside the camp. He did it deliberately, that Legate. Treated us worse than his slaves. It was two years before I was granted a pass to seek you both out. By then the border fort we had constructed, and the village nearby were all gone, burnt to ashes. I searched for you, looked in every town between Armenia and the Middle sea, but eventually I had to give up, go back to my legion or be considered a deserter. Where were you both, Juliana?" He sounded wary, suddenly, as if he too was doubtful.

It all sounded right. How could he know these things? A well of emotion opened inside her. Tears came. She rubbed them away. They kept coming. She let them roll down her cheeks. She'd wept often and so deeply after they'd made her a slave. But then they had dried up as she'd grown used to slavery and the memories of her life before had faded.

"We lived deep in Persia with my mother's people. I don't even remember it. But she thought I should mix more with my father's blood. She had to listen to endless jibes about half-castes in Persia. We went to Nisibis, on the border. I was captured by a Persian army in a village near to it. Then taken as a slave by Romans."

The old man's head bowed further as she spoke, as if she had struck him. "Nisibis. Yes, your mother had lived there before. I remember that." He took a step towards her.

Doubts reared again. Had she really found her father?

"What stories did you tell my mother?" Only her real father could know the right answer to that.

His eyes narrowed, and he looked up in the air, as if searching for a memory. "I told her many things, about Britannia, Gaul, Rome and about the great Chieftains of the Brigantes."

"What chieftains?" she pressed.

The old man looked perplexed.

"Yes, I told your mother many stories about Queen Arelldua. I remember it now. Your mother loved stories about strong women."

She felt as if she was falling, as if the ground had been removed. This was her father.

"I told her our daughter, you, were descended from that great queen, as I am. She was the queen of the ravens and the wolves. The blood of the Brigantes' mightiest warriors runs through you. Did your mother not tell you?"

"She did. I did not believe her."

She hugged him awkwardly then and their tears flowed. She hugged him tighter and tighter as if the pain of waiting so long to find him could only be healed by feeling the warmth of his body around her. Afterwards she wanted so much to be back again with her mother, to somehow show him to her, to tell her that she had found him, but she couldn't, and she had to accept that.

"Come now," said her father. "Meet your brothers." He motioned towards a doorway at the far end of the room. Juliana had barely noticed it. Standing in the shadows was a small woman in a dark striped gown. A solemn black-haired boy about seven years old stood beside her. He was wearing a blue tunic. An older boy, a man really, watched from over his mother's shoulder. She'd been so close to them all and hadn't known it. Her mouth opened in shock.

Time flashed past as they welcomed her. The years of agony she'd been through, alone, unable to speak her mind, unsure if she would die each day, waiting for the whip, diminished with every moment as they crowded around her.

They ate breakfast together at the table. It was the happiest meal in as long as she could remember. A spread of cheeses, honeyed bread and hot porridge was served. They all sat for a long time, listening in wonder to Juliana's tale of how she came to be here. Tiresias made a joke about her wandering further than he had.

Everyone laughed. The boys' Latin was not as good as her father's, but with some help from him and her new stepmother they all managed to understand just about everything she said.

Their mood turned serious when she told them about Sybellina, though she left out some of the details.

"Only those who have lost their freedom, know its true worth," said Tiresias. "Most treat it as a child treats a toy." He took the little boy's hand, whispered something in his ear. The boy brightened.

"You must stay with us, Juliana," said her father. "We'll buy your freedom, whatever price Lucius cares to want. You have found your real family. Aye, I'm sure when Sybellina's gone you'll fit in with us like a missing pelt on a fine cloak." His wife nodded. Her little brother jumped up and down with excitement.

She was being borne along on a current. And it felt right. Then she remembered Constantine and she felt torn. She looked down. His offspring was growing inside her. She opened her mouth. The words wouldn't come for a moment. Everyone stared at her.

"I'm sorry, I cannot stay with you. Not now. There are things I must. . . It's not that I . . ." She looked from face to disappointed face. "It's not that I'm ungrateful. It's . . ." She bowed her head. She couldn't tell them the things in her heart. They'd been locked away too tight. Fortunately, Tiresias finished what she'd begun.

"Juliana's destiny is twined already with another. Someone who might help our people beyond the wall. Aye, much might change because of this. The coming Roman campaign might still be disrupted. Their standards turned away from Caledonia's doors. Sometimes a slave can lead their master." He winked at her. "If their heart is true."

Juliana shook her head. How could she influence Constantine? She didn't even know if he wanted her.

"Aaah, and I nearly forgot, I have a gift for you, Juliana. Charms to help you on your journey." Tiresias took two thin snakeskin bracelets from a pouch attached to his belt. He handed them to her.

"If you wish to hold your lover close, girl, give him one of these. It will smooth his path and bind him to you for as long as he wears it and you wear yours."

She took the bracelets, put the smaller one on her wrist, reached up to her throat for the necklace Constantine had given her. Then she remembered. Sybellina must have taken it. A tiny shudder passed through her as memories of her ordeal came flooding back.

"Something bothers you," said Tiresias.

She didn't want to say it, but she needed to tell someone. "I used Sybellina's love charm to gain Constantine's affection. But she took the necklace he gave me, so she'll be able to pull his affections back to her." There was desperation in her tone. As she spoke the words it came to her clearly how she might lose Constantine.

"You know how to use love charms?" said Tiresias.

She looked from face to face. Would they be angry that she was using powers from beyond the veil? But what she saw in the expressions around her was expectation, not fear.

"Sybellina taught me a little. My mother did too."

"What did your mother teach you?" said Wehwalt. He was leaning forward across the table, his eyes wide.

"Only a little. She was going to teach me more, but I was captured. All she really taught me was how to see the future in dreams."

Tiresias reached towards her hands, motioned her to hold them out. His eyes had half shuttered now, as if he was almost asleep. "That is no small thing. I felt some power in you before. This must be what kept you awake even after taking Sybellina's sleeping draught."

She held her hands out.

"Close your eyes."

She did so.

He pulled her hands forward, then pushed them together, palm up, as if she was holding water before drinking.

"Do not open your eyes, Juliana. Keep your hands steady and tell me what you feel." Tiresias removed his hands from around hers.

She waited and waited. She felt nothing, just the hard-wooden seat under her and the tension in her arms as she held out her hands. All she could hear was the soft breathing around her and in the distance the cawing of birds. She hadn't noticed that before, but it seemed now as if there were birds nesting in the roof.

Cold crept up slowly from her feet. Her open sandals didn't give them much protection, but she usually didn't notice the cold.

She was floating now, thoughts chasing each other through her mind. She said the prayer her mother had taught her for dream reading, repeating it over and over in her mind to suppress her own thoughts and allow the reading power to come forth.

"Queen of Heaven, help me. Queen of Heaven, help me." Her lips moved, but she did not say the words out loud.

She held herself as still as she could, her hands up, still waiting for whatever he was going to put in them.

And then she felt it. Warm, round, like the bottom of a glass jug. She tightened her grip around it. No, it wasn't a jug. It was a glass ball. And it was getting warm. She opened her eyes. Her hands were empty. She drew them back, quickly.

Tiresias's mouth jerked open, as if he'd been slapped. He stepped back, his eyes wide.

"What did you feel?"

"A glassy ball." Her tone was high pitched. "I was sure it was there." She looked at her palms, then pressed them flat onto the table, to rid the warm sensation from them. She stared at Tiresias.

"Do not be afraid. I sent a simple message from my mind to yours, that is all. This cannot harm you." He touched his hands to his mouth, as if feeling for blood.

There was none.

"You have great powers."

"No." He shook his head. "The one with the power is you. Only one in ten thousand of the daughters of the raven and the wolf have the power to feel what is in another's mind." He turned to Wehwalt, pointed at him, and then at the rest of her new family in turn. "You will speak nothing of what happened this day to anyone. If you do you will surely bring every trouble maker this side of the Middle Sea down on us all. This must be kept blood secret. Do you so swear?"

Nods came from every head, though it came slowest from her stepmother's.

391

Tiresias turned to Juliana. "Do not be afraid. Tell no one and practice your gift only when you are alone. Listen for the thoughts of others and their intentions. You will have the power of the raven to see ahead into the future. Be careful though. You may find that others want you to use your power for themselves, if they discover you have this skill. But you have the power of the wolf too, the power to survive any calamity the world can throw at you."

Juliana pressed her hands into her thighs. Questions raced through her mind. Her mother had said she was a good dream reader, but she'd assumed many had such powers. She kept her voice low as she spoke.

"Does this mean it will be hard for Sybellina to sway Constantine's heart?" She knew by asking this she had betrayed her greatest fear, but she didn't care.

Tiresias raised his hands, palms towards her. "Sybellina is a witch of Rome. They boil the bones of babies to heal their patrons and use their nakedness to bewitch any man they choose. I do not know how strong your lover's affection is for you, but it will need rekindling if you are to defend it from Sybellina's wiles."

"I must ask you also to help our cause," said her father, leaning forward.

"What cause?" she said.

"Our cause is the fate of the tribes beyond the wall, and the fate of all our kin who are free from Rome's grip." He paused, coughed. He looked older than ever.

Tiresias continued for him. "The Roman emperor plans a final solution for everyone beyond the wall this summer. The emperor speaks of slaughtering every man, woman and child and burning every village and salting every field as a warning to the tribes in the south and across the seas not to raid and not to plunder, or Rome will reach their homes and kill every kin they have." He shook his head. "The emperor wishes for a triumph, to seal his glory in Rome."

Her father put a hand on hers. "The legions must be stopped."

She gripped her father's hand. "I do not have the power to stop them, but if a chance comes for me to help in any way, I will, I swear."

He opened his arms. They hugged. Everyone in the room hugged her in turn. Wehwalt was last. He whispered in her ear as he did so. "You were foreseen. You are more powerful than you know."

LXI

Eboracum, Northern Britannia, 306 A.D.

While Juliana slept, Tiresias was busy. He headed by a wide circuit, checking at every turn that he wasn't followed, to a tavern by the east gate. It was the area of the city where traders from beyond the empire gathered to tell tall tales and find whores who didn't mind what type of payment they got, Roman silver or Pictish spirit-imbued gem stones.

"I thought you weren't coming," said the tall, raven-haired girl with the feather tattoos on her bare left shoulder. Her dark eyes were wide in the light from the oil lamps.

Tiresias knew that her wide pupils meant she'd been drinking more than the common ale the tavern served. She'd been drinking She-wolf blood, a potent mix which could transport the drinker beyond the veil to the spirit world.

"The time is drawing near," said Tiresias. "Join the whores who service the Roman garrison. But set your price far above what the ordinary legionary can pay. We will arrange for you to be seen by the master of the palace."

The girl scowled. "I will fuck anyone, you know that, if it will bring death to our enemy." She leaned closer to Tiresias. Sparkles of blue shone in her hair from the lamp light. "Will this?"

He put a hand out and cupped her breast through her deerskin tunic.

"You have been blessed by the mother with the power to stop an empire. Your chance is coming to use this power, Inion. Make no mistakes." He squeezed hard.

She reached across fast, took his neck in her hand, and squeezed it.

"You had better be speaking the truth, old man. If you are not, and I whore myself for nothing, I will find you and cut your head off and eat your brains after roasting your skull for a whole night. That should kill the taste of the old man I could smell from the moment you came in this room."

Tiresias looked her in the eye. "A new age is dawning. You will help its birth. An age of love will be born from death. I accept your challenge, bitch."

She released her grip. His neck was red from where she'd held him, but he didn't flinch or rub at it.

But his voice was even more of a growl when he spoke. "Tell your brothers and their friends to find a place inside the walls of Eboracum. We will need a diversion and at least ten swords at the new moon."

"Only ten," she replied, laughing. "No problem." She lifted her hand and waved at someone behind him.

Tiresias turned. The table behind them was packed with young men. Many had the blue dot tattoos of Pictish outcasts on their foreheads. They all, to a man, had their goblets up to salute the daughter of the wolf, Inion MacTire. Each had a smile on their face, as if they were smitten.

LXII

Eboracum, Northern Britannia, 306 A.D.

Juliana and Tiresias left Eboracum the next morning. There was no time for waiting, he said. Her father provided the horses and a pass from his smithy showing they were on an errand. Parting from her new-found family was difficult, but her father made it easier by promising she'd always have a place to return to, and if she ever needed the gold to buy her freedom, she'd have it.

She was thrilled at that, but nervous about where fate was now leading her. Her life had been given back to her by her escape from Sybellina and she was sure her father was right, something hidden inside her had helped, but she also knew that the powers of the raven and the wolf were such that anyone gifted with these powers not only had the power of foresight, but also had the taint of death around them.

"Be careful, Juliana, you are one of us now," her father said as she mounted her horse.

"I know," she replied. After a wave goodbye she rode out into the street with Tiresias ahead.

She wondered if they'd made the right decision as they approached the city gate. Running to Lucius didn't seem such a good idea now she was doing it. Perhaps she should have stayed hidden with her new family. With them she'd felt safer than she had in years.

As they came near the gate she was sure at any moment Sybellina would appear and call for her to be arrested. Tiresias smiled when he turned to her. She reluctantly returned it.

And what would Lucius' reaction be to her unannounced arrival? Would he believe her story? She'd wanted to ride directly to

Gaul when she'd seen the bronze pass her father had given them, but Tiresias had insisted that Lucius had to be found first.

"You'll need more than a smithy's pass to get onto a Roman galley and cross to Gaul," he'd said. "Your father's pass will be of no use further than Lindum. I know these things." He'd tapped his nose.

She felt a surge of hope, though, as she thought about the confirmation of her bloodline from the great Queen that her father had told her all about. Constantine could make her his wife, if he wanted, now. There was so much she had to tell him.

As they passed under the stone arch of the city gate, to her great relief, no one took any notice of them at all. They didn't even have to show their pass.

They rode hard all that morning. Moorland turned to forest and the cobbled road with its neat curbstones turned into a raised causeway made of heavy gravel. Long sweeping vistas of wooded glades opened up around them. Sometimes the trees and banks of brambles or bracken grew in an impenetrable wall right up to the road.

They rode further and further, thrusting on towards Caledonia. She noticed a gradual change in the landscape, an occasional and sudden glimpse of a bleaker wilderness. The cloud-swept sky drove squalls of rain onto them as it got slowly darker, but Tiresias pressed on until eventually he found shelter for them in an abandoned farmhouse.

A jug of watered wine had been left there by someone and some hard week-old bread wrapped tightly in a deerskin. They ate it all with chunks of dry sausage they'd been given by her stepmother. That night, as she waited to sleep, she thought about her new family. She prayed her journey would not end in disappointment and that she'd see them again.

Early the next morning they rode into a mist-shrouded valley accompanied by the echoing cries of wolves, far off. At the head of the valley they turned off the main Roman road onto a barely visible side track.

"This is the old hunters' way," said Tiresias, as they walked their horses while the sun cleared the mist away. When it had done its job, Juliana marveled at the bare, purple hills which appeared around them.

After staying at a farmhouse again that night, this time occupied and very friendly, they set off early, while the dawning sun reflected through dark clouds a little above the horizon, like the lit ramparts of some great gold-edged city.

Late the following afternoon, before they'd found shelter, fires reflected in red on the low clouds ahead, as if a great feast was being held beyond the hills. They spoke little that evening. Tiresias was no longer the affable character from the town. Out here, there was little Roman politeness about him.

His face looked ashen, weary, and sometimes he looked around abruptly as if checking whether they were being followed. Survival in these wilds was reserved for the fit, he said, and those who knew the old ways. "Pity provides no refuge in the hills," he repeated, a trace of regret in his voice, whenever they passed an animal carcass.

The rain, which battered them at times, dissolved everything into a gray wet dimness that made her wonder what had happened to the summer, and if they were really headed towards the fabled lands of ice, the ultimate end of the world, and not simply Caledonia. The rain also made her reins slippery, which eventually brought stinging blisters to her hands. She was used to sheltering regularly in taverns and drying out properly from rain storms, not pressing on and on.

She looked around regularly. Her instincts said she was being hunted and, in her dreams, she felt a dark presence hidden, but lurking. Every traveler they met stared at her. At one point she became convinced that Tiresias was leading them in the wrong direction. She had to recite a prayer in her mind to distract that thought from coming back to her.

Then, early one morning, the track led downhill and she felt better. They skirted a dark wood alongside a river and joined a wide gravel-bedded Roman way. She saw the stone towers of a large fort guarding a low wooden bridge ahead. Rain drenched them suddenly, but they moved on, and the clouds were whisked past them by a blustering wind.

As they neared the fort they met a unit of bearded, long-haired Alemanni cavalry, who quickly confirmed that Lucius could be found ahead. A rush of delight tingled through her. If she'd got this far, she could find Constantine too.

Her baby would have a father.

The road forked before the next bridge with a small Roman camp on the far side. "I believe your master is there," said Tiresias. Then he bade her farewell. "I have other matters to attend to."

She thanked him profusely for all he'd done. He moved his horse beside hers and hugged her briefly. "Be not too trusting, Juliana. Remember this, the courage of the wolf and the cleansing power of the raven will protect you against all evil forces." His expression was serious, almost a scowl. He patted her arm lightly, turned, and headed away without once looking back.

She stared after him, wondering if she would survive long enough to see him again. As she approached the bridge waves of cold fear rose up inside her, each one stronger than the last. She'd felt protected riding with him. She whispered to herself, "I can do it. If I came this far, I can do this too." She smiled at an astonished looking guard on the near side of the bridge as she approached.

"Where do you come from?"

"Eboracum. I am here to report to my master. He is a senior Roman officer who will cut slices from you if you interfere with me." She stared down at him, her expression hard as stone.

"Which officer?" He did not look impressed.

"Lucius the Armenian."

He glanced over the bridge, as if expecting someone to appear. She held out the thin metal pass.

After examining it briefly he waved her on and across the bridge. When she arrived at an arched wooden gateway on the far side she was politely but firmly asked to dismount and then taken to a small room nearby. The waves of fear were coming faster now. What if he'd heard she'd run away and decided to punish her the way run-aways were supposed to be punished? Her connection with Constantine might not be enough to save her, if her actions enraged him.

The guards were cautious here. The atmosphere in the air was different, as if they expected to be attacked at any moment. Guardsmen cast cold glances at her whenever they passed the doorway, and their hobnailed sandals crunched closer, then away, then closer, like how the practice snaps of a torturer's whip intensify his victim's fears. If Lucius was in the fort beyond, why was it taking them so long to let her through?

"Juliana?" She looked up. Lucius was standing in the doorway, wearing a shiny black leather tunic. He'd let his beard grow. Black curls ran wild over his face, which now had the red hued weather-beaten look of someone who spent most of their life outside. He called to the gate guards.

"She is my slave girl. Don't get too jealous, you lot." He turned to her. "Come, Juliana. You have news?"

"Yes, master." She bowed, but not as low as she would have done before. She felt relieved at seeing him, but the next step was not going to be easy.

As they left the gatehouse she heard muttered comments. "That Caledonian girl's not enough for him?" and "Do his slaves ever need training?" And "I'd like to show her mine." Finally, Lucius turned and shouted.

"If you lot weren't so pox ridden from coupling with Baal, I might have considered your requests for leave." The muttering stopped. He turned to Juliana.

"Don't mind them. The camp followers up here are no match for a pretty slave from Persia." He nudged her and winked.

"So, what brings you here? Constantine not enough for you?" She shook her head, nervous again.

He tutted. "Don't be so serious, Juliana. "

"It's not that, master. I've heard nothing from Constantine since you left." She looked down, blurted the rest out. "I think his life's in danger. We must . . . did you . . .?" She hesitated.

"Ssshhh, wait." He gestured a quick cutting motion.

They walked past circular stone granaries, heading towards a tightly packed area of dark-brown leather tents by the parade ground. Two picket lines of horses were being groomed nearby. Many of the cavalrymen tending the horses grinned at Juliana as they passed, as if Lucius wasn't there.

Four bedrolls took up the back of Lucius' large officer's tent. Inside the entrance, just under the awning, two folding stools and a storage chest, which served as a low table, had been set up. It had started to rain. The plopping noise on the leather roof was loud but it brought a welcome sense of privacy. They pulled closed the awning and the light dimmed.

On the chest sat a small bronze oil lamp. It gave off a dim light. Lucius used it to light another larger gray long-wicked lamp which seemed crafted from the mud of these parts. He sat on one stool and motioned for her to sit on the other. It didn't feel right, she was still a slave, but she was tired and did as she was told.

The sound of watch trumpets could be heard in the distance. The trumpet calls died away until all they could hear was the patter of the rain.

"How do you know Constantine's life is in danger?"

"Sybellina said so, master."

He rubbed his hands against his tunic, cleaning them.

"I can smell evil from that one." He took a deep breath, closed his eyes. "What happened?"

She told him how Sybellina had tricked her, how close she'd been to death. She said nothing about Tiresias. He shook his head in disbelief as the story unfolded. Then she told him what she'd overheard about Constantine. His eyebrows shot up as he took in the news.

"I'll get word to Constantine." He patted her hand. "I'll send a messenger at once."

Juliana shook her head. "We can't rely on a messenger. Please, master, I must go to him. Let me do it. I cannot go back to Eboracum." Her hands were fists by her side. She felt awkward at having made such an appeal. It wasn't expected for slaves to be demanding.

Lucius looked at her for a long time, then abruptly sucked in his breath, as if he'd made a decision. "You can go to him. I'll be in Eboracum for the games of Apollo. If he decides to come back and confront his enemies, that could be the excuse he needs. Tell him I'll

401

be waiting. There are many ways I can help him." He stepped closer to her, lowered his voice.

"I sent the papers to him about him purchasing your freedom. He's probably arranged it already. You'll be free soon." He put a hand on her shoulder.

Relief rose inside her. She put a hand to her teeth to steady herself. She was going to see him. She was going to be free.

"But you'll have to look the part of a messenger."

As soon as the rain eased he went to find her a new sleeping roll, brown woolen breeches, a green auxiliary's cloak and, most importantly, an official auxiliary Legion messenger pass. He also came back with a hard leather helmet with a raised ridge around its edge, which with everything else, made her look like a boy when she tied her hair up beneath it.

The small bronze pass had an official eagle insignia etched into it, along with a request etched in thin lines of script to grant the bearer free passage. Lucius had made enquiries to see if anyone was about to travel to Gaul. He discovered that two injured decurions were about to go home on sick leave in two days.

She would have to wait at the fort until they were ready, but after he talked to them in the infirmary, they agreed to let Juliana accompany them, as long as she was issued with a good horse and didn't hold them up. One of the men had almost lost his hand. The other was on a less than speedy recovery from a deep thigh wound.

On the morning of her departure, Lucius pulled her to the side of the wooden stable block where she was to collect her horse.

"Constantine must demand his rights. He is his father's eldest son. But make sure he seeks me out before he does anything reckless." He leaned closer. "If anyone can persuade him to stand firm, it'll be a woman." He raised his fist and grinned.

"When you return, if you get back in time for the games, ask for me at the main gate house at Eboracum. Say your name is Lucia." He pressed a bag of coins into her hand. "Spend this wisely, and don't talk about Sybellina with anyone else but Constantine. Slaves disappear very easily, you know that. I don't want you thrown to the dogs or to a troop to bicker over who goes first at you."

She bowed and thanked him, and as soon as he'd turned his back, unable to restrain herself, she peeked in the soft leather bag. She'd never had so many coins. They were all the new silver ones too, the ones people had been talking about, that she'd never seen.

As they approached the stables where the decurions were waiting he warned her brusquely not to show the bag to anyone. Then, after she'd mounted, he smoothed out the bottom of her cloak as it lay over the back of the horse.

"I will bring him back," she said, looking down at him.

"I know. I see a spirit of determination in you, Juliana. Now show us where your fate will take you."

It was a great morning for riding, perfectly crisp with a light breeze, but still she felt nervous. She kept asking herself - how will Constantine react when he hears my news? She'd seen pregnant slave girls being thrown out of their houses in the middle of winter. Some had ended up scavenging the city dumps or working as whores. She couldn't bear that life. Whatever it took, that fate had to be avoided.

They made good progress, passing long lines of packhorses heading north, carts heading south and only a few native tribespeople on horseback. Twice she spied teams of hunters on foot up in the hills accompanied by wolf hounds. Summer was coming and although most days were dry and warm, a damp mist, brewed by Typhon, encircled them some mornings, forcing them to wait at the rest house they'd stayed at until it departed.

When they reached Eboracum, they stayed outside the city at a tavern on the road south. That night, horrors filled her dreams. Wolves could be heard sometimes in the forests, howling at their fate, but that night it was not wolves that woke her. It was fear of Sybellina and a knowledge that she was close.

They were challenged early the next morning when they passed a large encampment of legionaries, but her pass, and her companions' passes, saw them on their way quickly and soon after, to her relief, Eboracum was far behind.

Strangely her horse was startled by a grass snake that afternoon and she was thrown to the ground. Her companions laughed when they saw her dazed expression as she sat at the edge of the ditch.

They offered to assist her search for injuries. She refused, loudly, got straight back up on the horse, and ordered them all to keep going.

They passed through Londinium in a day, stopping only to eat. Once they were on the far side of the river, by way of the great bridge, they headed along the southern estuary of the river past the villas of what she was told were the original, and now wealthy, early Roman colonists, and then headed onwards towards the port of Rutupiae.

They set out across the channel between Britannia and Gaul the day after they arrived at the port on a post ship manned with banks of oars and fitted with a wide sail. The crossing was choppy, making Juliana vomit again, but the wind blew in the right direction and later that same day they arrived in Gaul. The following morning, they were back in the saddle.

The days fell away after that in a rhythm she was now well used to, a good breakfast of warm porridge and bread if they were lucky, followed by long periods in the saddle, watching everything around her. They ate a light meal in the middle of the day, then dinner at a small post house, usually a dark stew with meat she never asked the source of. She imagined, at the tiny rate they were paying for accommodation and food, that all she would get would be the name of some animal she'd never heard of.

Her companions rode with her as far as the road junction, with the turn for the valley of the River Mosella. They were heading south towards the frontier lands of Germania Superior. They had become friends during the journey and had, contrary to Lucius' warning, wasted little time with tavern girls or trying to bed her, which she put down to the fact that they were both longing for their wives and still aching from their injuries. Both bade her a warm farewell when they parted. She'd told them she was going to see her lover in Treveris, but had refused to name him, despite days and nights of teasing.

Finally, and alone, she breasted a rise in the road and saw in the distance the winding azure ribbon of the Mosella. It was almost three weeks since her journey commenced.

She remembered how she'd looked down over Nicomedia, while tied behind her master's cart at the beginning of the year. She felt very different now, hopeful, not despairing, a woman with a secret, not a slave girl with nothing. She was carrying important news for the son of an emperor. She felt a delicious anticipation and for a moment thought she might gallop to get to him faster, but she restrained herself. She didn't want to attract attention. She had to be careful. There were things to fear ahead, as well as things to hope for. Constantine's mother was in Treveris and she might see her as nothing more than a pregnant slave girl who Constantine needed to be rid of.

As she came nearer the river skiffs came into view. They were being punted along with long poles. Some were laden down, others moved swiftly, and some passed from bank to bank. They were unlike any vessel she'd ever seen before. As the road wound down close to the river the dark wooded hills became mirrored in its shimmering, glasslike surface. Then, through the thinning trees ahead, she saw the walls of Treveris.

After crossing at a great wooden bridge, she had to wait to pass through the crowded gate on the far side, and then wait again at a watch post to seek directions to the imperial palace.

She used two of Lucius' coins to buy a cloak in one of the busy shops that lined the road approaching the palace. The cloak was made from the softest silkiest wool she'd ever felt and had tiny flowers embroidered on its edges. It was the most perfect cloak she'd ever seen.

To her embarrassment, the old lady in the shop made a big fuss of her. She even twined a ribbon in her hair, when she said that she'd come all the way from Britannia to meet a special friend. She became nervous, and then suddenly convinced she looked a total fool compared to the sophisticated women walking by under the colonnade outside. Was she a fool? Maybe he'd forgotten her, or had found someone else? Her plans would come to nothing then. What would she do? She wanted to scream.

Slowly, she made her way to the slaves' entrance of the imperial palace, a large blank-walled villa near the forum. She walked past the door twice before summoning the courage to knock. As the door creaked open her breathing became shallow. A sour faced guard looked her up and down, grunted, then told her to go away. He closed the door. She thought for a moment that it was a joke. But the door stayed closed. He'd meant it. She banged again on the door, harder this time.

An officer was summoned to see her. He looked her up and down, sighed, then gave her permission to wait on a bench just inside the door, while Constantine was informed she was looking for him. All the guards stared at her with a mixture of curiosity and lechery, as if unknown females coming to their gate, claiming to know a member of the imperial family, meant only one thing. She shivered and clutched her arms around herself as she waited. Let him be true to his word, please, Heavenly Mother.

She closed her eyes. Was there any chance he'd be pleased to see her? Why had he never replied to Lucius? She'd enjoyed the journey. Her goal had been fixed. But now she'd arrived, all her fears re-emerged like worms erupting inside her. She felt ill. If he wouldn't see her, where would she go? Why hadn't he sent for her, or even sent a message?

And to cap it all, of course, Sybellina had been right. She was pregnant. The seed was growing and no amount of holding her breath could stop it. She'd tried to forget about it, but as each day went by without any sign of blood her fate became clearer.

But if he found out, he might well want no more to do with her. She'd heard about men like that. She closed her eyes, a surge of dread almost overwhelming her. No, she wouldn't tell him, she couldn't. Not yet. It was too risky. She had to know if he'd be true, treat her right, protect her.

A great clattering of hooves resounded on the cobbles beyond the door. She looked up. A voice issued an order. She knew his hard Danubian accent, though it sounded strange, cold. Her heart jumped. She stood, straightened herself, her hands clasped in front of her, her arms trembling, as if she'd gone mad. Through the arch of the doorway he came, far more handsome than she'd remembered, his black curls gleaming, tightly cut, clean shaven, wide-eyed, broad, so powerful, like a bull. His mouth opened when he saw her.

He rushed to her, lifted her high in the air. She laughed and hugged him tight, as if by pressing him to her he'd never be able to leave her again.

406

"It is you, Juliana. I was sure there'd been a mistake. I didn't expect to see you for months. My, you are as beautiful as ever." He stroked her hair.

"This place was getting boring and dull. Legal papers are all they let me play with. But now you're here the music has started." He leant forward, closed his eyes as if listening to some rhapsody.

Juliana sighed with relief. "I'm so happy to see you," was all she managed to say. Then she hugged him again, inhaling smells of leather and sweat, feeling his body against hers. Feeling his affection for her. A flood of desire almost overcame her. She groaned.

He laughed, swung her high in the air again. Then, as if suddenly remembering something, he put her down, placed a finger to his lips, and looked around. A guardsman waited beyond the doorway casting occasional glances in their direction. Constantine turned from him, raised an eyebrow, and cocked his head to one side as if to warn her. She stepped away from him and became once more the demure slave girl. He motioned her to follow him.

They walked at a brisk pace through the palace, looking to the entire world like favored slave and master. Her short brown tunic and rough woolen belt indicated her status. His soft purple tunic with its gold embroidered shoulder patches and his finger-thin belt fashioned from gold mesh indicated his. She listened as he complained about the empress' misuse of his father's treasury.

"The things I could tell him," he whispered indignantly.

She didn't care. The pleasure of being near him was enough. It felt unreal to be here, like a dream.

He apologized in advance for the state of his rooms. "The old witch likes us as far away from her as possible," he said. He reached towards her. Her fingers touched his.

A delicious prickling sensation passed right through her. She wanted to tell him everything in a rush, but her instincts stopped her. She had to be sure of him first.

He led the way along a corridor lined with aged stone pillars and lit by widely spaced oil lamps. Soot stains from the lamps marred the walls. At the end, double doors opened onto a small courtyard. It looked abandoned. Its wall frescoes were flaking, and its mosaic floor had been patched many times.

He crossed the courtyard and led her on through another set of doors into a spacious but gloomy room whose walls and high ceiling were also stained from generations of oil lamps. This was a forgotten part of the palace. She looked around. No slaves or guards waited on him. If he'd led her to a cave she'd have been happy, as long as they were alone. A flutter of anticipation ran through her.

But instead of falling into his arms, she paced up and down and described the difficulties she'd had getting here, then she sat on the edge of a long backless couch. She played with a ringlet of her hair while watching him intently. She told him Lucius had wondered why he hadn't responded to his letter. She tried to make it sound as if his answer was of little importance, but as soon as she finished speaking, she felt stupid. The way she'd put it was all wrong. She bit her lip and looked at the floor.

"But I got no letter. I'm still waiting for his stupid papers," Constantine shouted.

She looked up at him. Was he telling the truth?

"I've no way to prove this, Juliana, but I blame all such things on the empress. If anyone could interfere with the imperial post it's her, because if Lucius said he sent the papers, he must have. He's one man I trust completely."

She felt warm inside, and so glad to be with him.

He began pacing. "My mother warned me about plots against my life. You should be aware that you are in danger even being with me."

"I don't care." She reached towards him.

He stood in front of her, took her proffered hand, pulled her up to him, then stared at her for a very long time, his hands on hers, as if by holding on the moment might last.

She could smell him now. All polished leather, man sweat, warmth and power. They kissed. A terrible urgency grew inside her. She could barely control herself. Feelings, dammed for far too long, were bursting forth. Every moment of her journey she'd been nurturing daydreams of this moment, anticipating her desire. And now he was here she felt clumsy, as if afraid that she might make some terrible mistake, displease him. She pressed her body to him, as if she thought they might fall over.

And what about the life growing within her? That thought damped her desire fast.

"What is it?" he asked softly. Had he noticed? Panicking, she kissed him harder, but felt hollow, as if someone else was doing the kissing and she was only observing. She was right. She could not tell him she was pregnant. Not yet, anyway. She would please him first. And a great part of her yearned for him too. The part that needed someone. The part that'd do anything to have this be true and not taken away, ever.

Their bodies intertwined. She took a rasping breath, felt the hard thrust of his manhood against her tunic. She wanted him now, reached down, held it. Its firmness teased her. She'd dreamt many times of how hard it had been. Her tunic was up around her waist.

"I love you, Juliana. Never leave me." He sounded happy. His joy was infectious, a fierce brightness lifting her gloom. It was what she'd wanted and had prayed for. She kissed his lips, more softly this time. Their tongues touched. She felt his hands moving deliciously over her. He lifted her in the air and her legs curled instinctively round his waist.

Standing upright in the center of the room, he entered her. A rush of pain almost made her shout. But she stifled it, groaned and they stumbled to the bed.

He kept going until she was satisfied, and his own pleasure seemed heightened as he did so.

After they'd sated themselves, they lay quietly on his bed, like cubs curled together on top of the rough woolen blanket. It scratched, but it felt wonderful, a tingling sensation against her skin, reminding her that this was all real, not a dream. The air was warm too, and glittering shafts of sunlight from a window grille stirred in it. Distant sounds came to her from a broken part of the window, where there should have been a small square of glass; a horse neighing, and far off laughter, stopping abruptly. The smell of leather polish and pine scented oil from a cluster of oil lamps hanging on a stand nearby filled her nostrils. She'd been so long on the road the sounds and smells of a villa, which she used to take for granted, seemed odd.

Then she told him about finding her father and her family.

"He must come and visit," he said. She looked at him quizzically. He squeezed her hand. "To swear to your lineage, that you're a descendant of Brigantian royalty. Then you can become my wife. Our stupid succession rules cannot part us after that. You'll not be my slave girl concubine then. You will be my wife." He tickled her.

It was going to happen. He meant what he said. She could feel his certainty, the unsaid words of total commitment. A tingling of excitement and anticipation passed through her. Everything she hadn't dare dream about was coming to pass. Every risk she'd taken had been worth it.

"Well, concubine, are you hungry?"

She nodded.

He went off to the kitchens, leaving her in the room alone. She closed her eyes, tried to calm herself. She could not show too much joy. She had to be measured. She could sense no evil in Constantine's intentions, but there were others who were involved in this situation who would take his decision badly.

Constantine returned with two elderly male slaves. They carried a pot of steaming stew and bowls. They didn't appear to notice her. She knew the slaves would tell about her, but she didn't care, she was famished. The stew was lamb flavored with apricots and masses of tiny onions.

Constantine waved them away and served her a bowl of stew. She devoured it, as well as a good number of the thick bread squares the slaves had brought.

"Lovemaking is good for your appetite, I see," he said.

She glanced up at him, then back at the floor. She'd become anxious again, wondering what he would say when he found out she was pregnant. She'd heard that most men discard slave women soon after they heard such news.

"That'll auger well for our children, if we ever have any."

She stopped eating.

410

He laughed, as if that was some distant prospect.

She didn't dare look at him. Did he know? She waited until he spoke of something else, then set aside the remainder of her food.

What would it really mean to be his wife? All she had was a vague idea. She should have thought about it. There would be much more to being with him than she'd imagined. All she'd done was dream about being with him, being free, getting up whenever she desired and, especially, eating whenever she felt like it.

It felt as if she was at the edge of a dark forest. Her future would be very different. It was so much more than she'd hoped for even weeks before. But there were still things that could stop it all happening. First, she had to tell him about Sybellina. She put her goblet down.

"Sybellina tried to murder me."

Constantine sat up in his chair opposite her. "What happened?" His face was a picture of wide-eyed concern.

"It started when she asked me to tell her about your dreams. Do you remember, I read a dream of yours once? She didn't like it when I refused. She blames me for other things too." Her voice trailed away.

"What things?"

Juliana hesitated, but knowing it could all come out in a letter from Sybellina, she pressed on. "She believes I stole her magic charm."

"You didn't steal it, did you?" He looked intently at her.

She opened her mouth. No words came out. She was aware her hesitation had already answered his question. His expression was changing to concern. She had to tell him everything quickly. She brushed away a strand of hair at the side of her face. She had a sinking feeling that all she'd gained could now be lost.

She shrugged. "I threw away a stinking lump of flesh I found in a casket in her room." She curled her lip in a mockery of disgust. "It had been doused in perfumes and it stank. I went to the river in Londinium, and threw it in. It was horrible. I vomited afterwards. It was a heart. A human heart given to her by the governor of Massilia, I think. His slaves told me awful tales of young girls going missing

411

there, of human sacrifices, virgin's entrails being studied to foretell the future, hearts being used as love charms. It sounds too awful to repeat, but when I found that thing in her room, I knew those tales had been true. If you'd seen it, you'd have done the same. Such charms are abominations." She stuck her chin out.

"I agree," said Constantine. He held a hand towards her.

She ignored it.

"How did she try to harm you?"

"She poisoned me. She was going to sacrifice me, I'm sure. At dawn, most likely. My heart would replace her love charm."

A look of horror appeared on his face.

"She's well capable of it, you know. It was she who suggested Tiny castrate himself. She drank his blood too, before he did it. And she's having secret trysts with your father."

"I should have guessed she has strange appetites. I've heard stories about priestesses in Rome drinking the blood of young men to rejuvenate themselves." He made a growling noise, like an angry bear. "How did you get away from her?"

She told him about waking, listening to Sybellina's ranting, making her escape. She said nothing about Tiresias.

"You're brave." They hugged. It felt good to be in his arms. She could feel the muscles across his shoulders shifting as he held her tight. "You'll be safe now, Juliana."

"There's something else I must tell you," she said quickly, stepping back. "But first, I have a small gift for you." She took the two snakeskin bracelets from her pocket. She wound one around his wrist, the other round her own. She muttered a prayer. "Please, for me, wear this always."

"Now you're the one weaving a spell," he said playfully.

"All it means is that I'm close to you, wherever you are. Please promise me you'll wear it always."

He looked at her solemnly then nodded, kissed her on the cheek.

"So, what's this other thing?"

She told him that the emperor had agreed that Fausta would marry Delmatius, Constantine's half-brother, as soon as the boy came of age, to prepare him for becoming Caesar after his father.

"That makes our empress a two-faced bitch!" he said, vehemently. "She told me Sybellina would go back to Rome empty handed. She's gone too far with her scheming. She's trying to cut me from the succession, I know it. Soon she'll measure the cord to fit around my neck." He raised a fist.

"She'll not do it to me, Juliana. I'll be emperor long before her son. It's been foretold. She will not take what's mine." He slammed his fist forward, as if he wanted to punch someone.

That was when she told him that Lucius would meet him in Eboracum if he decided to confront his father.

"Lucius said you should demand your rights, appeal your father's decision."

He looked weary, his face grim. He stared straight past her.

"Delmatius is ten years old, Juliana. I can hear the sneers of her courtiers already." She didn't know what to say.

"I will tell Helena, my mother, about your news. Wait here. I'll be back soon."

LXIII

Treveris, Northern Gaul, 306 A.D.

When he told Helena what had happened she was furious. All her hopes, her position, and her livelihood were bound to his fate. Without him she could be cut off from the imperial household at a moment's notice. But there was more than bed and board at stake, whole families had lost their lives because they were close relatives of a losing contender for the imperial succession.

"Your father knows what will happen if he dies with multiple successors," said Helena, turning away from Constantine and returning to the embroidery she was working on. "Civil war is what will happen. Why should you stand aside while that ugly brat takes what belongs to you, what belongs to us? I'll not wait for favors from that ice-veined monster. You must fight for your place." She took a breath.

"She knows you are the rightful heir, the eldest, but she won't accept that your rule has been prophesized. She only thinks of her runt. This is the struggle that was foreseen. You must win. You must find a way to defeat her. Otherwise we are all doomed, believe me. Come, come with me." Helena spoke softly now, looking around like an animal in fear of the baying hunt just within earshot.

She led him out into the tiny walled courtyard of her villa, and spoke in a whisper, one hand entwined like ivy through his arm.

"You will confront him with justice on your side. If you are weak, as soon as your half-brother comes of age, they will destroy us all. We must destroy them first." She trembled with impotent rage and looked at him from the corner of her eye, as if searching for some sign that her frustration would be assuaged.

He'd heard her like this before, although her conviction had a note of intensity this time that he'd never previously seen. It made him uncomfortable to see his mother this way. He should have known how she'd react to the news.

They sat side by side on a marble bench in the garden. The air was scented from the roses that clung to the brick wall behind them. The roses clung in pink drifts around his mother's head as she stared at him.

"Your little slave girl came with the news, didn't she?" she said, as if she'd suddenly remembered Juliana.

"Juliana should never have been a slave, Mother. She's a descendant of Queen Arelldua, and from Royal lineage, from Britannia."

His mother sniffed incredulously.

"Her father's a free man. As a spoil of war, her freedom can be granted with no stain on her character. I want her as my wife, and I need your permission."

Her eyebrows rose further. "You want my blessing." She spat out the word, then turned away from him.

"You know if you take this girl as your wife, you'll be placing her life in danger too?" She looked at him. He nodded.

She began to smooth out some invisible creases in the pale blue wool robe that went all the way to her ankles. Her tone grew softer when she spoke again.

"If you succeed in changing your father's stupid decision about Delmatius, I'll bless your union with this slave girl, otherwise…" Her smile broadened. "No, I will not." She stood and looked down at him.

"I'd assumed the reason your father publicly adopted another as his successor was because you were a hostage at the time. I assumed he'd reinstate you to your rightful place as soon as you were released. Now, I see Theodora will not allow him to do this. Well, she must be stopped. She fights nature itself. The one god trusted his first born to do his work here on earth, didn't he?"

Constantine nodded.

"Why shouldn't you be emperor? You've earned it by your birthright and by surviving all that has been thrown at you." She
415

looked stern, like sculpted marble. "I pray you're strong enough to do what is necessary, Constantine, that's all, otherwise we'll all end up in a sack in the river." A shudder ran through her.

Constantine stood.

"It'll not come to that, Mother. I'm sure I can persuade Father to change his mind." He sounded more confident than he felt, but he had no choice now. This was his road.

"Put it about that I've gone off somewhere else, with my new slave girl. The matrons will love the gossip and we'll be out of Theodora's reach before she finds out any different."

*

That night he slept fitfully. Even Juliana's presence at his side didn't help. Twice he awoke and paced the cold mosaic floor, breathing in the heavy stillness of the palace.

The following morning, he, Juliana, and a small, two-man military escort, hastily assembled by a friendly officer, rode out of Treveris, across the wide bridge and up through the valley of the Mosella. As far as the escort were concerned they were on an excursion to visit friends. He didn't tell them until much later where these friends were.

LXIV

The dark-brown leather tents of Crocus' cavalry unit had been set up on the far side of the marshalling ground, at the edge of the bare heathlands to the west of the city of Eboracum. Banners and pennants cracked noisily in the breeze from the poles set along all four sides of the area where the cavalry would perform.

"This is how our young men are seduced into the legions, husband. Well, if you see our boy signing up, make bloody sure you drag him away, before he makes his mark," Juliana overheard a woman in front of her telling her husband.

They looked far too young to have a grown son. Juliana looked at the green pennants of the Alemanni, flapping in the distance. Through the heads of the spectators, they looked like the flags of a longed-for harbor. People strained their necks all around her, all together, as if they were connected, looking to see what was happening.

The last and most important events of the games of Apollo were about to begin. Anticipation swept through the crowd and infected her too, even though she was supposed to be looking for Lucius among the Alemanni, not paying attention to the games.

A little before, when they'd arrived at the main city gate, Constantine had been loudly informed that he would have to wait some time for an audience with the emperor. The gatekeepers seemed astonished that the son of their emperor would arrive without their being told in advance to expect him. Juliana had waited to one side as he'd announced himself and came here to look for Lucius as soon as Constantine was escorted away.

They'd been told by a member of Chlorus' cavalry that Lucius was to be found with the Alemanni by the marshalling ground. She'd assumed it'd be easy to find him. But she'd not expected these crowds.

Trumpet blasts rang out, rolling along the perimeter of the marshalling ground, one after the other, each building on the last as the clamoring of the crowd eased, then ceased, leaving only the trumpets echoing in her ears.

People were gesturing towards one corner of the marshalling ground, where Juliana spied cavalry cantering into the parade area. Four abreast, the rows of horsemen headed for the center of the earth-bare ground, their boiled-leather shields shining black, menacing in the sunlight, their scarlet cloaks flapping in the breeze behind them.

Each of the riders held a spear with silver tassels attached to its point. Their bronze helmets had a plume of silvered boar hair on top, except for every fourth man, whose plume was blue.

When the line of cavalry formed up, they turned and faced the crowd. A shout went up. A war horn blared. All went quiet.

Then, as one, the line of cavalry leapt forward. They were still quite a long way away, but Juliana could see a silver flash along the line as they lowered their spears in front of them. Everyone around her seemed mesmerized by the spectacle.

Underfoot came a rumbling. Just a tremble at first, as if it wasn't there. Then stronger, unmistakable. The cavalrymen let out a war cry. A menacing guttural roar, distant, but looming, inexorable. The horsemen thundered forward.

The spears could be clearly seen now, glinting, their points visible, as the wall of cavalry raced closer and closer. A delicious shiver ran through the crowd. A woman nearby stepped back, one hand raised to her mouth. She screamed.

A single horseman, at the center of the charge, carried a golden double-headed eagle standard, scarlet with green tassels flowing and jumping in its wake. The approaching wall of horsemen was inescapable now. An instinctive urge to run came upon her. A young boy wailed somewhere.

The approaching horses were frothing and shaking as they ran, straining every sinew. Closer. Closer. The pounding was in Juliana's ears. She looked around for somewhere to hide.

It would only be moments before they were all violently brushed aside or impaled on spears.

A war horn sounded. The cavalrymen raised their spears as one, and brought their horses to a rearing halt, dust billowing, their horses rocking on their haunches. So close were the horses to the crowd that dust swirled round those nearest the front, partly obscuring them from Juliana for a moment. The crowd shuddered. The cavalrymen, with a single roar, "Veni-I came," thrust their spears high into the air.

The crowd loved it. All around people were shouting and pointing; even the normally reserved toga-wearing officials, many of whom were locals trying to be more Roman than the Romans themselves, were chattering and laughing with relief.

The cavalrymen turned and rode slowly away. Juliana wiped dust from her face. The Alemanni were certainly well trained. She scanned the crowd.

They were mostly local farmers, or their slaves, but there were also traders from the other provinces of Britannia, and camp followers of the Legions, and others from every part of the empire, but no Lucius.

The trumpets blared again, and the crowd fell silent once more. The local tribesmen were about to parade their chariots.

Everyone watched attentively as a long line of chariots came across the field.

At that moment Juliana felt a tingle, a sense that someone was watching her, and she turned, quickly. Lucius was standing at the edge of the crowd, behind and to her left. Beside him stood Sybellina.

She didn't dare move. What was Lucius doing with her? The people around Juliana faded away, and all she could see was Sybellina. She wanted to find Constantine, but she couldn't. Sybellina looked directly at her, whispered something to Lucius, then turned away with a haughty swing of her tightly cut curls, and disappeared into the crowd.

Lucius motioned Juliana to him with his finger.

"We heard from the gate that you'd arrived," Lucius greeted her. He sounded annoyed. "We walked the whole length of the crowd looking for you. What's your news? He's here, I know that, but has he a plan?"

Juliana shook her head, looking past Lucius for Sybellina.

"Come." Lucius took her by the arm and led her towards the tents. They were surrounded by a palisade of thin stakes. They passed through a gate. The Alemanni guards saluted Lucius. Soon the hubbub of the crowd was behind them. They walked slowly along a picket line of mules and talked.

"Sybellina swore to me she meant you no harm, Juliana. She said she went to fetch a doctor and was amazed that you'd run off. She says if she wanted you dead she would have cut your throat when you were laid out in front of her." He paused, then turned to her. "Whatever the truth is, she's promised not to take any action against you for running away."

Juliana looked around, wondering if this was a ruse to stop her running off while the guards were called.

"Believe me, if Sybellina wasn't useful to us, I wouldn't have anything to do with her. Now tell me, where's Constantine?"

"Stop squeezing my arm and I'll tell you."

Lucius loosened his grip.

She didn't like the way this was turning out. She looked around as a gasp leapt from the crowd, as some performance came to its climax.

"Hail the Provincial cavalry." The cry went up and echoed round the heath.

"Come on, Juliana."

"He waits to see his father. He's expecting you."

Lucius made a fist with his hand, raised it, as if he'd won something, then called for two horses to be prepared. Soon afterwards they had skirted the crowd and were in the city. Children and beggars scampered after them as they rode. The gold medallion that Juliana had been given by Constantine secured their passage as far as the main doors to the governor's palace. There, their arrival was announced,

420

and after a short wait they were given permission to enter and escorted to a door at the end of a long corridor.

Beyond it, Constantine was sitting alone on a marble bench in a bare courtyard. It was crimson walled and had a small opening in the center of the high-beamed roof. A large empty shrine indent in the wall at one end of the courtyard showed that at one time this had been a place to worship family gods, perhaps before the city temples had been built. Constantine looked as serious as she'd ever seen him in his leather military tunic with his large silver and gold campaign medals spread across his chest, and good conduct bracelets in a thick band up his right forearm. Among them she spied the thin black line of the snakeskin bracelet she'd given him. She bit her lip, her gaze taking him all in, as if it was much longer than a few hours they'd been apart.

His gladius short sword hung in its scabbard from a jewel-studded belt, the one she'd told him to wear, and his black hair was now worn in the longer style popular in Gaul these days. His beard was thick too, like a Persian's. He looks more like an emperor now, thought Juliana. She walked briskly up to him and bowed.

Constantine came to his feet and opened his arms.

"Thank the gods, you made it. I've been ordered to wait for the emperor here. I'm sure he'll see me soon."

Juliana hugged him.

"You've become very friendly," said Lucius. "I wish you both well, I'm sure. And I must give Juliana to you as a gift, Constantine. She's taken to you in a way she never did with me."

"Juliana should never have been a slave," said Constantine. "She's the daughter of a Roman citizen and has the blood of the Brigantes royal line in her. You'll be compensated, but Juliana will no longer be treated as a slave. Her manumission documents are being prepared."

"Wonderful news!" Lucius lifted his hands in the air, in a show of jubilation that seemed insincere to Juliana.

"I expect because of this, Constantine," he continued, "that you aren't worried about your father passing that marriage offer from Maxentius to one of your half-brothers, now that you've Juliana to keep you warm at night." Lucius patted Constantine's shoulder.

"Lucius, stop." Constantine sounded angry. "I am the eldest. Any betrothal to Fausta should wait until my place in the succession is agreed. If I accept this, the next thing they do is find a way to kill me. I've been warned about such plots." He raised his fist. "They will not do this. I will not die so another can have my rightful place." He trembled with rage.

A bird trilled somewhere above their heads, as if it had trapped itself. She looked up. The trilling rose to an ugly pitch, then died. Was it a sign? She shivered. She'd spent too much time on the way here wondering what would happen after they arrived and how they could survive.

She didn't want to tell him how much she'd been thinking about it. She'd been hoping Constantine might have seen his father by the time she returned with Lucius, and that everything would be resolved about the succession. But it was clearly not going to be that easy.

"If you want my opinion, I think you'll have to stake your claim forcefully," said Lucius. His words came out softly, as if he'd been thinking about them for a long time.

It felt as if time was slowing as the meaning of his words became clear.

"I know you believe dreams show the future, Constantine, so listen to what I say, and you too, Juliana."

What was he doing? He'd said nothing about a dream on the way here.

Lucius stepped back. "In my dream you were dressed in purple, Constantine, standing at a great marble altar, surrounded by senators and priests. You were about to be crowned with the gold laurel. But the strange part was you were standing in a stream thick with fishes, and in front of you a crowd of white-garbed innocents offered their arms up in thanks, children they were, stretching on and on, as far as the eye could see, while behind your back, dressed in long gray shrouds, was another crowd. And a single shout echoed and was taken up by those at your back. "How long, master, dost though not avenge us?" Lucius paused. His fist went to his mouth.

"I was drenched with sweat when I awoke from this dream." His hand reached out, trembling slightly, towards Constantine. "I know it is a vision of what's to come. There can be no question of that. You're to be emperor, and you'll take up our cause, the cause of the one god. I am right, Juliana, don't you agree?"

Juliana looked at him.

Constantine could indeed help Lucius, especially if he became emperor, and if she became his wife her power would be tremendous. But was it right that Constantine would support Lucius and the Christians? She straightened her back and spoke.

"Lucius is right," she said. "To throw this moment away would be pissing in the wind of your destiny."

Constantine snorted.

Lucius put his hand out towards him, looked over his shoulder, then spoke in a low voice. "What I have to say now, Constantine, goes against everything I, and you, hold dear, but it must be said. There is a clear opportunity here to change the empire, and to ensure you survive. I hear your father is ill these past few days. All his bad decisions are coming back on him. He is far too long in his position. He is no longer capable. The empire cannot be run by a man who no longer makes the best choices for the people, and for his eldest son." He paused for a moment, then pressed on.

"It is your duty to get him to leave the stage, to press him to retire, as Diocletian has retired, and to do whatever is necessary to see this happen."

Juliana stared at Lucius. They were at the edge of treason. The consequences of treason started at having your eyes put out and your tongue cut off and ended at being burnt at the stake. She'd seen the charred embers of bodies at the gates to Nicomedia years before. Their mouths were wide in death, their final screams visible to all.

"Crocus, the cavalry commander will support you, Constantine, as will all the Christians across the empire who I and my father represent. We are ready, and we have a treasure of gold to encourage the support of all those you must win over. All we ask in exchange is toleration, and justice. Do you see the opportunity fate presents you? You must reach for it." Lucius sounded desperate, as if

423

he knew he'd gone a step too far. His right fist tightened and untightened as if he had a nervous twitch.

Constantine shook his head, like a dog throwing off water. "No. My father will listen to me, and when he retires, in ten or twenty years, I will be emperor, and then the support you offer will be appreciated, but not now. It is my duty to defend my father, my sworn duty, no matter how sick he may be or what decisions he makes. I will hear no more of this. No more." He was shouting by the time he'd finished.

His hand went to the hilt of his sword. He gripped it.

She'd never seen him so furious. He'd encouraged her to express her views during their journey from Treveris, and the bindings of her slavery had become loosened. Now she wanted to speak, and she wasn't afraid of him.

"Constantine." She said it louder than she'd planned. They both looked at her. "All the way from Treveris, you told me what you'd do if you were emperor. Well, now you have a chance, do not throw it away." Her voice was changing with each word she spoke, her anger rising. "Are you just full of talk like all the soft-cocked men after a gutful of wine?"

Constantine looked stunned. "What you're suggesting is that I raise a standard against my father. We'll end up at sword point."

"I'm not suggesting you take up a sword against him." She put her hand up, as if to grab him. "I'm suggesting you don't let him tease you if there is nothing to be gained."

The door at the far end of the courtyard rattled. Someone was there. A muffled voice called out.

"Open in the name of the emperor." A thud resounded through the air. Someone was about to break the door down.

"There is another way," said Lucius. He stood in front of Constantine and spoke quickly.

"A way that's guaranteed to secure your inheritance. I'll tell you later." He placed a hand on Constantine's bare arm. "Remember, I saved you the last time a sentence hung over you, so trust me, if I can save you from the wrath of one emperor, I can do it again. If

Theodora isn't exposed, we'll all have a sword point in our guts before her runt celebrates his wedding feast."

"That will not happen," said Constantine.

"Open the door, before the bastards break it down," said Juliana. The banging was louder, more determined.

Constantine walked across the courtyard. Juliana and Lucius followed him. He shouted he was on his way. The banging ceased.

"Honorable Constantine, why are you locked away? Anyone would think you'd been kidnapped." A centurion of the imperial bodyguard pushed through the door as soon as it was opened, followed by three guards.

"What do you want, centurion? Remember your place, or I'll have you flogged in front of your men," said Constantine.

"I beg your forgiveness, honorable Constantine. Your father has requested your presence, that is all, and I must carry out the emperor's orders at once." The man's expression was as fixed as a statue's.

"Escort me to my father," said Constantine. He turned to Juliana and Lucius. "Wait for me here."

But he looked to Juliana like a prisoner, being led away to his fate. She raised a hand to wave, but inside felt only a chill of foreboding.

LXV

Eboracum, Northern Britannia, 306 A.D.

As they hurried down the flag-stone corridor, Constantine's arms and feet felt heavy. He tried to pretend he'd nothing to fear, but Lucius' talk had unsettled him. Doors clanged as they were opened ahead of him, and then closed behind him. He took a deep breath. As he let it out his stomach shuddered. He would rather face a battle than this.

And then he was kneeling, bending his head low before his father in the grand basilica. Its black and white patterned mosaic floor, rows of red sandstone Corinthian columns on each side, and high coffered ceiling provided a very public backdrop for their encounter. High above, a row of square windows on each side of the building let in a pale haze of light, which enhanced the feeling of mystery and grandeur in the basilica.

The emperor, he'd been told, was preparing for a triumphal procession to the marshalling grounds outside the city walls. He'd returned only two days before from Hadrian's Wall and the fort at Corstopitum, where he'd supervised the execution of more than a hundred Pictish captives, men and women, who had refused to submit to Rome. Their heads were to be displayed along the wall.

Constantine lay face down on the floor as a dutiful emperor's son should. To one side a group of tribunes, legates, and other officials watched. Constantine awaited permission to rise.

"Father, I come to claim my place at your side, and to honor your victory," he said, his face turned to the floor. It annoyed him to be face down, but he had no choice. It would be seen as a public act of defiance if he didn't. But still it was hard to keep himself from standing and screaming defiance at his father. He was pushing him too far.

He heard the swish of someone approaching across the mosaic floor, then saw the leather and gold threaded sandals his father wore right in front of his head.

"You should have waited our order to return. You must follow my orders, Constantine, always. I will not say this again," his father shouted. It sounded as if he too was struggling to control himself. He certainly didn't sound sick.

"I don't know what habits you've picked up in the east, but they are not acceptable here."

A beetle crawled in front of Constantine. He watched it. Down here he was like that beetle, insignificant, easily crushed. The cold from the floor rose up through his bones. No matter how many braziers burned in such rooms, the floor was always cold. There was a faint smell of beeswax in the air down at floor level too, as if every officer had had his sandals polished recently.

He needed to stand, to raise his fist, to tell his father where to stick his stupid orders. He wished he'd never come to Eboracum. Every man in the room would be watching him, noting his humiliation.

"May I rise, Father?" Memories of other, older humiliations came to him, painful public rituals his father had subjected him to during his childhood. He'd hated those times of his father's spite-fueled rages. He could easily reach out and pull the bastard to his knees before any of his guards could reach them.

But reach them they would and a sword in his own belly would then be a real possibility if he struck his father now.

"Before you rise, Constantine, think on this. We will hear no complaints as to your role and orders. You will do what I say, until you display the gratitude required from one so fortunate, as you have been."

Constantine lifted his head a little. The emperor was bending down, looking at him. Constantine turned his face back to the floor.

"You know you look like a cockroach down there, Constantine." The emperor laughed. Laughter spread around the room.

Constantine trembled with rage, his brow furrowing. His father had gone too far. How could he mock him like this? A wave of fury passed through him.

The emperor bent down, his face near Constantine's, his wine filled breath pouring over Constantine. "You must be careful not to meet a cockroach's fate."

Constantine looked up, saw his father's head thrust forward, tightly trimmed beard bristling, flowing purple robe shimmering around him.

"Force, not affection, is the way all order in my empire is maintained. You of all people should know that. Obedience is the least of what I expect you to have been taught by Galerius." He leaned closer. "I have been informed that you left his domain in a hurry and killed some post horses in your haste."

"I did not." Constantine stared at the mosaic in front of him, his rage growing with each breath. He remembered what Juliana had said about controlling himself if he was teased. The mosaic depicted the choice of Hercules; a life of ease, or a dangerous voyage to recover his honor. He turned his head a little to look up at his father. Officials stood around, gazing down at him with scorn on their faces.

"Arise, Constantine."

His stomach had a stone in it, as if he'd eaten something rotten. He rose slowly to his knees, as if by delaying, he could mock his ill treatment. He reached down, kissed the embroidered hem of his father's robe, then his ring, quickly. As he did, he caught the reek of some disgusting ointment his father must have been using. It had the smell of decay, as if the maker had used some putrefying afterbirth in its concoction. He pulled away.

Constantine looked around. "It is unfortunate the empress isn't here," he said. "I am sure she would have enjoyed this." It was dangerous, he knew, to make any comment about the empress, but he couldn't resist. What had just happened was the type of will-breaking scheme she was capable of thinking up.

Like a snake uncoiling, the emperor hit Constantine with the back of a closed fist across the side of his face. The blow sent Constantine reeling.

Something wet ran down his neck. His cheekbone ached. He forced himself, with every muscle bulging, not to fling a fist up and strike back. Around him, a murmur of approval buzzed.

"No pup like you will ever speak in such a way about our empress. Join us at the gatehouse when you're ready, and make sure you find a clean cloak from somewhere."

The emperor turned and dismissed him with a flick of his hand. Constantine stood and walked out of the room, suppressing a terrible, trembling frustration. He'd been publicly humiliated. Like a child. The stone walls seemed to close in around him along the passageway as he walked.

His breath came heavily, his chest jerking as he fought to suppress his rising anger. Outside, at a small fountain, he used his cloak to wipe the blood from his face, then held the wool under the cold water and against his face for a long time, until the bleeding stopped, probably from a nick from one of his father's rings. He felt his jaw. It wasn't broken, but some teeth felt loose. And all the time he was thinking, what should he do?

His father had always been his ideal of a good ruler, courageous against his enemies, but fair in his dealings with friends. Years before, he'd taught him that there were only two types of men in the world, those who were for you, and those against you.

"Men are mostly ruled by fear," he remembered his father telling him. "They will make no move against you until you weaken. And, when you have a sworn enemy humiliated, you must destroy him, utterly, if you are ever to find peace."

I am that enemy, thought Constantine. Lucius is right. He could well have to return to Treveris empty handed. He shivered. Too much suffering makes a stone of a heart.

LXVI

Eboracum, Northern Britannia, 306 A.D.

"You can't stop me," said Juliana. "Constantine won't be back for ages. I must tell my father I'm here. His house is just across the bridge. I'll be there and back before you've even half-finished that flagon of wine." She walked to the door without looking back.

"You have certainly become even more willful," said Lucius. "Go, but make damn sure you come back soon."

She ran through the afternoon cart traffic. Off duty legionaries, officials and farmers, and hawkers selling everything from fried fish to hard sandals filled the streets. She had to dodge a dozen outstretched hands as beggars, seeing her fine tunic, tried to catch her attention.

At one point a clattering of hooves on the limestone cobbled street made her spin round. She half expected to see Sybellina pursuing her at the head of a troop of horsemen, but it was only some cavalrymen, probably off to join the procession everyone was talking about. All around her people were smiling. The emperor was going to finish off the Picts, and business was booming.

An army needed many types of diversions, and the city was obviously determined to provide them all. Every second doorway was a tavern and at many, a girl stood by the door to entice customers to share her delights. One of them even stared boldly at Juliana. There is a girl for every taste here, she thought, and, spying young boys in the doorways of some taverns, a boy for the others.

She reached her father's smithy. It faced onto the roadway between a tile shop and a small wine merchant. The door was barred, its shop front boarded up. Her mind raced. She had to get back soon.

No one answered when she knocked.

She was about to go around to the rear of the building when a voice called out, "Are you still looking for a good smith, girl?" She spun around.

Tiresias was sitting on a stool near the doorway of the wine shop. She gasped. She'd walked right past where he was sitting a moment before and hadn't recognized him. But he looked much younger now, more Roman, his scarred eye socket covered by a pale pigskin patch. He'd shorn his hair too and he must have dyed it, as the gray was gone, replaced by smooth black. He wore a faded blue, belted, Roman style tunic. She stared, dumbstruck.

"Don't just stand there like a fool. People will think you're a fly trap," said Tiresias. He waved her forward.

After speaking to the owner of the shop they went up a rickety wooden staircase to a private room above. Tiresias winked at the owner as he mounted the stairs. Juliana kept her head down.

"You know, we've waited a long time for someone like you to appear, someone we could trust inside the imperial household," said Tiresias, as he mounted the stairs.

"Is that all I am, Tiresias, a smooth skinned snake to infiltrate and find a soft ass to bite?" said Juliana as they entered a low-ceilinged room. A long, dark and roughly planed wooden table took up most of the room. A shuttered window kept the light from the street out.

She turned on him. "What's happened to my father?"

"You've become bossy since you went to Gaul," said Tiresias. "You are a real Brigantian princess now." He sat on a cushioned backless stool at the end of the table.

"But you're late too. Ten slippery wine-licked days I've waited, and as you're asking, your father and family are all well. They went south to avoid any complications, if all of this comes to the wrong ears. And now, before you ask any more questions, tell me what's happened. Is Constantine here in Eboracum?"

Juliana nodded.

He punched the air with a raised fist, then shook it above his head as if he'd won some great contest.

"Only the final ingredients to add now," he said. "And the great pot is nearly cooked. A quick stir and it'll be ready. Come, sit, I'll tell you what you must do." Juliana sat beside him on the bench.

*

She arrived back at the courtyard just in time. Constantine was sitting on the same marble bench, but with his head bowed, listening to Lucius, who looked to be berating him. He scowled at Juliana as she came forward. Then he told her what had happened.

"It's you or him, Constantine," hissed Lucius as she sat beside him. She took Constantine's hand and held it tight.

Lucius' voice went low as he continued. "This is it. You must decide! Will you fight all these agents of the empress when they come to get you, or will you fight now, while you still have a chance?" Lucius' fists were balled at his sides as he spoke.

"Stop, Lucius. I have something to say," she said.

Constantine looked at her, amusement on his face. Lucius was searching his tunic pockets for something. He waved for her to continue.

"I have spoken with a druid high priest," said Juliana. "He says that no man should be forced to give up his inheritance." She spoke softly, but unhesitatingly, unconcerned as to whether Constantine or Lucius might interrupt her. She was looking at Constantine's hands, at a scar from some old sword nick. She could smell his sweat. The day had warmed up. It was the hottest since she'd been here. There was barely a breeze.

Lucius let out a low, satisfied growl; he'd found what he'd been looking for, support. He waved something in his hand, brandishing it in the air. It was a small brown earthenware vial. She could see the Greek letter Alpha painted on its side.

"This potion causes the sleeping sickness, but not death."

Lucius held it forward for Constantine to see.

"Some Christians use it to numb the pain of torture." His eyes darted about, as if even talking about the vial had made him nervous. He looked from Constantine's face to hers, then over his shoulder.

432

"If this is used carefully, by tomorrow morning your father could be sunk in such an illness. And in his waking moments he will be consumed with worry as to who will protect his family, should he succumb to whatever is afflicting him," said Lucius. He sounded excited, like a little boy talking about some adventure he'd planned, not the poisoning of an emperor.

"He will know that no child of your stepmother, the empress, could possibly succeed him so soon, no matter what anyone says. Your presence will seem fortunate then, your experience and loyalty already proven. Sybellina will nurse him as we wish, I've seen to that. He trusts her, and with you, a newly appointed successor at his bedside, a speedy recovery will be imminent." Lucius laughed. It was grim laugh, showing clearly that he knew what he suggested was a path fraught with danger.

"This is your chance. By tomorrow you'll have all that you desire." Lucius turned to Juliana.

She was shocked, but hopeful. It felt as if a curtain had been thrown back, and a barely caged lion had been revealed, blocking their path. They could all be executed for thinking such thoughts.

"You are a lucky man, Constantine," continued Lucius.

Juliana shook her head.

Constantine shook his head too. "You are mad, Lucius. You know Sybellina tried to kill Juliana. She'd never help us. She's a plaything of my father's. You've fallen into one of her traps." He sounded exasperated.

"She's fallen into ours." Lucius' tone was angry now. "If your father finds out that Sybellina revealed the contents of his message to Maxentius, her fate will be sealed. He can press Maxentius to have her strangled after her return to Rome, for breaking the cardinal rule of her profession, trustworthiness. Others of her kind have met that fate before. You didn't tell the emperor everything about Sybellina yet, did you?"

Constantine shook his head. "No."

"Good. She'll say nothing of our little group, for now. As for her treatment of Juliana, she swears she meant no harm, that it was all a misunderstanding."

433

"Well, know this, if my father has me thrown in a river in a sack full of snakes because of her testimony, I'll see to it that you come with me, my friend. You are truly mad. Give me that vial!" He reached forward.

With a swift movement Lucius put the vial under his tunic. Then he pulled his short sword from its scabbard. He held its point to his own side, the handle towards Constantine.

Juliana took a step back. Was he serious?

"I call on you to repay your debt to me, or take my life," said Lucius. "I might as well be dead anyway, if you don't agree to this."

"Lucius, stop!" said Juliana. Her tone was more concerned than angry. "If Constantine doesn't wish to do this, you cannot change his mind this way."

Lucius looked at her, groaned as if a weight had dropped on him, then sheathed his sword, turned on his heel and walked out of the courtyard, slamming the door behind him. He was gone before either of them spoke.

"And now I have to choose," said Constantine. "And all my life I have dreamed of helping my father to win his battles, and then to sit by his side." He groaned, as if a knife was twisting inside him.

"He is clearly not the man you dreamed about," said Juliana.

LXVII

Eboracum, Northern Britannia, 306 A.D.

Constantine was still thinking about all the dreams he'd nurtured. Dreams of leading armies further than any emperor had ever done before, and of uniting the empire once more.

He'd hated his life as a hostage, being a token for his father's good conduct. When rumors came of disagreements his father had with Diocletian, he'd lived with a never-ending fear that he'd be executed the following morning as a punishment to his father. He couldn't live like that again.

But he still respected his father. Total respect and unquestioning loyalty had been bred into him from the moment he could swing a toy sword. How could he plot against him? But what would happen if he did nothing?

His thoughts circled like crows, each one alighting for a moment before another fluttered down behind, looking for a place to land. He remembered Helena, his mother, her ambitions for him, and Juliana, and hers, and his loyalty to Lucius, and above all, his memories of his years as a hostage.

The danger of battle is preferable to this, he thought.

He and Juliana made their way to his father's private quarters, where one of the ceremonials, highly embroidered purple silk cloaks encrusted with rubies, amethysts and topaz was brought to him. As they were waiting for adjustments to be made, Juliana closed the door of the robing room. Constantine was sitting on an elaborately carved wooden bench fitted to one wall. She paced nearby. Neither had said much since Lucius' outburst. Juliana spoke first.

"How can we hope to continue? The dream is over. I must go. You must forget me." Her face was composed, stern.

"No," said Constantine, angrily. How could she think such a thing? Where did she get the idea she could oppose him like this? Hadn't he enough to deal with?

She turned her face away, looked along the mosaic path into the middle distance.

"Lucius will never sell me to you after this," she said. "He will not sign the papers, and you have no power to force him. Your father will not support you in it. I have no choice. I must go." Her tone was resigned.

His anger faded, like snow on a brazier cover. She was right. She had no choice.

But he could choose. Choose to be weak, to accept his fate, to lose the woman he loved, or to seize the moment, and risk all for his future, their future. They'd spent every night since they'd left Treveris naked in each other's arms, their lovemaking the most fulfilling he'd ever known. She was one of the few women he'd ever wanted to keep repeating the act with, and that in itself was a sign, and there were more. The cold ache inside him he'd felt for so long, was gone when he was with her. He could remember the way he'd lived without her. He didn't want that back. Whatever the price.

He remembered what his father had done, how he'd humiliated him, treated him like a stray he'd let in from the street, the type you could break and have their tongue cut out if they became too troublesome. He saw the hollowness inside him, his disappointment, fear, and rage, all mixing together.

His rubbed his forehead, pressing in, as if by doing so he could rub away all feelings. He wanted to tell Juliana that he would do as she asked, but he couldn't speak the words. He looked at her and shook his head, slowly.

She sighed gently, came up close to him and kissed him on the lips, as if saying goodbye.

"Be careful of Sybellina," she said.

He pulled her towards him and kissed her again, more lustily this time, their tongues touching, stroking.

436

"I will," he said, when they finally came apart. His voice sounded oddly hoarse as he told her what he would do next.

He was sure that everyone could see his nervousness as he made his way back through the palace. His eyes met those of every man he passed. They all seemed to look at him suspiciously. Even talking about what they'd been talking about might be considered treachery, never mind doing anything about it.

He knew he could be arrested at any moment. If Sybellina had told his father of Lucius' plans, he would be implicated. And what would they do to Juliana? He shuddered. He should go to his father, tell him everything. Beg him for help.

A group of guards appeared to be whispering about him as he approached the doorway to his father's rooms.

LXVIII

Eboracum, Northern Britannia, 306 A.D.

Anxious shouts filled the corridor with a clamoring wave of noise as the emperor was carried towards his rooms, four, then five of his personal guards helping with the task. Other guards clearly wanted to be involved, as if every hand that helped him might possibly be due some reward when their emperor recovered. The emperor himself was tossing from side to side in their arms, groaning loudly, making their task exceedingly difficult.

"Clear the way. The emperor is ill. Clear the way," someone shouted, again and again, in a shrill tone, which added to the wave of urgency that engulfed the corridor.

A door banged open. Two old female slaves in dirty kitchen wear, clearly not the type to be seen in the dining room itself, stood gawping at the sight of the emperor's body jerking spasmodically as it passed.

Behind the emperor's guards came Constantine, his father's physician keeping pace by his side. Constantine shouted at the man as they turned the corner towards the emperor's private rooms.

"What's sickens him? What should we do?"

The physician looked worried, his lips pressed together, his brow furrowed. He didn't answer.

The double height door of the emperor's bedroom burst open with a bang that echoed down the corridor. The emperor's body sped headlong into the large, sparsely furnished room. A feeling of austerity rather than grandeur greeted them. The elderly physician fluttered around, as two tall shaven-headed eunuchs removed the emperor's embroidered ceremonial toga, and the guards who'd carried him there were waved away.

Underneath the toga, the emperor had on a yellow cotton tunic that came down only as far as his knees. A double width bed with an unpainted wooden headboard, carved into the shape of a double-headed eagle, stood in one corner of the room. Slaves pulled away the purple silk bed cover and laid the emperor onto the pale gray linen. His struggles had lessened into occasional jerks, and his head was lolling now, as if he were in a deep sleep.

Constantine turned to the crowd of officials that had filled the room behind him. Some were shouting suggestions as to a course of treatment, others were crying out for the gods to intercede, many were simply craning forward, as if at a freak show. Almost none of these people would have been allowed to come anywhere near this room, if the emperor had been well.

"Out, out, all of you out, all of you," he shouted. The slaves attending the emperor froze. Every face stared at Constantine.

"I'm the emperor's son. This is a matter only for our family. Clear the room. Clear. The. Room." His voice commanded attention. You had to be able to give orders if you wanted to lead a cohort or a century into battle. The head of the imperial guard, his purple helmet plume at right angles to his men's, presumably assuming he was excluded from Constantine's command, began herding people out.

Constantine thanked the man, waited until he'd almost finished his task, then told him he too should wait outside, but as a concession to his position, that he should guard the door against intruders.

Visibly bristling, his face stern and his step firm, the man left.

The physician, meanwhile, was listening to the emperor's breathing, tutting and hissing as he continued his examination.

Lucius and Sybellina had arrived moments after Juliana in the final rush of excited onlookers. Juliana had been lucky to get past the guards, and only her vigorous insistence that she'd been specifically called for by Constantine had allowed her, her blood thumping in her ears, to follow them in from the dining room. Constantine had pulled them all to his side when he saw them.

The governor and military prefect of the city stood, their hands together as if they were a matched pair of statues, at the end of the emperor's bed.

The military prefect, a tall bald man with wispy ridges of graying hair above each ear, spoke. His clipped disdainful manner marked him out as a true patrician.

"This is a matter for the army physicians, Constantine. I've sent for them. I'm sure you know the army takes precedence here, even over the emperor's family." His lips broke into a thin, fake smile.

Constantine looked at the man and took a deep breath. His father's physician turned, as if he was about to say something. Constantine put his hand up for the physician to be silent.

"You are wrong, Marcus, this is a family matter," said Constantine. "A troop of Alemanni cavalry has been sent for. Your men will not be needed. Now, let my father's physician get on with his duty. Crocus." He turned, looking for Crocus. "Are your men expected soon?"

Crocus was standing near the doorway, his hands on his hips, his face grim, one hand close to the handle of his sword.

"The imperial family has the full loyalty of the Alemanni cavalry, my lord Constantine. You may all rely and depend upon us for your lives. My troops will arrive before the start of the next watch."

"You see. We have no need for more men." Constantine turned to the military prefect. And then his father moaned, and all eyes went back to the emperor. Constantine's tone softened when he continued, but it was still firm. "Go now, both of you."

He waited. The military prefect of a province or a colony had a variety of duties, one of the most important of which was to protect the emperor's person. Constantine however had rights as the emperor's oldest son. The man hesitated, one hand pulling at an earlobe, in obvious indecision.

Crocus leaned forward as if he was about to do something. The temperature in the room rose. Constantine put his hand up as if to silence everyone.

"We cannot treat the emperor with so many by his bed. Do as I ask, leave. Come back in the morning when my father's recovered.

We'll tell him of your concerns as soon as he awakes." Constantine's tone was firm, persuasive. The atmosphere changed again.

The military prefect bowed slightly to Constantine, then turned and walked stiffly towards the door. The governor went with him, whispering to him and looking back fearfully over his shoulder as soon as they reached the doorway. Constantine followed them and closed the door behind them.

Now there was the emperor, Constantine, Crocus, Sybellina, Lucius, Juliana, and the physician in the room. The emperor groaned again. The physician looked expectantly at Constantine, as if he had been waiting for permission to speak.

"What's wrong with him?" said Constantine.

As if in reply, the emperor's eyes opened for the first time and then closed slowly, as if he was attempting to wake himself, but couldn't. A low moan escaped his lips.

"It appears he's been poisoned," said the physician softly. He emphasized the word poisoned. His eyes darted from face to face.

"Will he live?" asked Constantine flatly.

"If he wasn't killed by the first rush of poison there is a chance he'll flush it out by morning. I'll administer a purge. With luck he'll vomit much of it away."

The emperor's eyes opened halfway and then closed again.

"Droopy eyes and a rigid body are a sure sign," said the physician. "I'll have to get another physician to confirm it, but it looks to me like hemlock mixed with soma. A strong dose too. Plenty of water and a purge and he'll most likely survive. Without such help, he could well die." He looked wide-eyed, as if suddenly aware of what he'd just said. He rummaged through a small bag attached to his belt. His eyes darted occasionally towards the doorway.

Juliana's back was wet with sweat. Her worst fears had arrived, like in her most frightening dreams. This was something that could not be undone. Poisoning could not be taken back like words could. If he recovered, all their lives would end in some terrifying way if there was a hint that any of them could have been behind the poisoning. Multiple deaths invariably happened if emperors suspected anyone had tried to kill them.

Rain splattered against three high iron-grilled windows above. She looked up. The thick circles of glass made the windows look as if they had been stuffed with goblet bottoms. A summer storm was about to hit Eboracum. The first deluge had begun.

Soft golden light shone from two outsized glass oil lamps halfway up each side wall. The light made the room feel like a refuge.

A window rattled. The bronze brazier standing in one corner dimmed for a moment, as did the lamps. An eerie feeling came over her, as if people were listening, lots of people. A roaring wind pounded the window again, as if some frenzied animal was trying to break in.

Sybellina was staring wide-eyed at Constantine, fear coursing through her, as if she too had been poisoned.

Crocus walked to a large polished oak chest with brass corners. He unsheathed an ornamental sword lying on top of it. The sword had an elaborately carved ivory handle. As he pulled it free a slip of papyrus fell to the floor. He picked it up, looked at it, then at each of them.

His twisted grin made the hairs on Juliana's back stand up. She thought about all the men he must have killed and guessed that they'd have seen this grin just before they died.

"This is the sword of the emperor. Mars, the god of war, is released when it is unsheathed." All eyes were on him. No one spoke. Outside in the wind, a bird wailed.

"Deliver." Crocus looked at the sword, examining its edge. "An immediate recovery, physician, or your life will be forfeit. That'll encourage you to pick a speedy cure for our emperor's sickness, verein damut sheiserus." He spoke in guttural Germanic Latin, in a tone that resembled a spiky shard of ice cracking and dropping from a high temple colonnade on an icy winter morning.

The doctor drew his breath in sharply then glanced at the others around the bed, looking for a sympathetic face.

"This is poisoning, not a sickness," he said confidently. "There is no immediate cure."

Sybellina spoke. "Physician stop babbling." She circled the physician, then went to the bed and bent her ear close to the emperor's mouth.

"Do you want me to help, my emperor?"

The emperor's eyelids fluttered. Then he gurgled.

Sybellina wiped his brow, leaned in towards him and began making soothing noises.

Juliana felt uncomfortable, as if she shouldn't be watching this.

Sybellina looked up at Constantine. "Will you not soothe your father?" She spoke softly, while staring innocently at him.

Constantine stood still, his expression calm.

Juliana's mouth opened wide, as if she was about to say something. With a snake-like motion, Sybellina had pulled a thin silver-handled knife from inside the folds of her green gown. Juliana could see the three-faced symbol of Hecate, goddess of sacrifices and the cross-roads, emblazoned on a ball at the end of its handle.

Sybellina looked blankly at Constantine, as if the knife meant nothing, then waved its tip in small slow circles between them.

"You are so close to what you want, Constantine. So very close. Perhaps Hecate will finish the job for you? Remorse can be a thousand worms eating at your gut, but you might rather that, than to be burnt alive as a traitor."

Juliana wanted to shout at her, but that would spoil everything. The rebuke had to come from Constantine.

He glanced at Juliana. She nodded, almost imperceptibly. They might never have this chance again. Everything turned on this moment. Their futures and the future of the empire, and of the millions of people in its sway, were all finely balanced, waiting to be tipped one way or another. And afterwards there would be no going back.

"By all the gods, you'll not trick me so easily," Constantine said. "This is your doing." He pointed at Sybellina. "I know about your cures made from blood and the charms and dark spells you use."

The physician was staring at Sybellina. His face was contorted, as if he knew more than he should, but that nothing was working out as he'd expected. Sybellina looked surprised, her eyes wide and staring. She turned to Crocus.

"The emperor will decide who is behind this when he awakes." Her tone was matter of fact.

Constantine turned to Crocus. "She handed him his wine. She is the only one who could have poisoned him."

Juliana had edged closer to him and, having seen knives being thrown by disgruntled slaves, she flung her arm across Constantine's chest. Later they would call it a premonition, but at that moment it was instinct that made her do it, an instinct that cawed loudly in her ear.

Sybellina drew her hand back, and with a practiced motion hurled the knife at Constantine.

A sickening thud ran through Juliana's arm and up her shoulder. Her hand shook violently, as if it wasn't hers. Constantine's chest felt wet. He grabbed her hand. Before she had time to think about it, the knife was out and in his hand.

Blood spurted down her gown.

At the sight of all this, Crocus laughed uproariously.

"Your great mother has few powers this far from Rome, Sybellina. Your scheming has gone too far," he boomed. He slashed the emperor's sword through the air, as if testing it, then shook his head, as if already regretting what he was about to do.

Sybellina dodged the first sword thrust, but Crocus had experience in such matters. On its way through an arc the sword hissed as it sliced into Sybellina's thigh. She screamed in anger, staggered back as blood pumped down her leg, flowing onto the mosaic floor like spilled wine.

Juliana caught an acrid smell. It was a smell she remembered. A smell that lingered in your mouth if you went too close to the source. With Sybellina's blood she could smell it from across the room.

Sybellina did not go down on her knees and beg, as some might have done. She stood and faced her end. The second blow skewered her stomach. Her hands clawed angrily at the blade as it was jerked back out, until they too were bleeding. Then a screaming curse rang out, high pitched, enraged.

"Son of a whore, you'll lose everything you love. Everything!"

Constantine, seemingly oblivious, was cutting a strip from the sheet on the emperor's bed. He wound it tight around Juliana's hand, taking no notice whatsoever as Crocus impaled Sybellina again with a sword thrust deep into her chest. Constantine seemed well practiced in binding wounds. He reassured Juliana gently as he worked.

"It'll be over soon."

Sybellina flailed, her hands like claws. Crocus stepped out of her reach. Juliana's skin prickled. Sweat flowed as if she'd stumbled into the hot room at the baths. She'd assumed Sybellina's death would be quick. Something sharp and heavy pressed at the inside of her chest as she watched Sybellina die.

Pity bloomed inside her. Was this a just way for a priestess to die? But she kept her mouth clamped shut. A vision of Tiny's contorted face had filled her mind.

Sybellina crumpled to the floor. Her gown fell open to reveal full breasts, both of which were slick with blood.

Then, as blood bubbled from her mouth, Sybellina spoke, while glaring at Juliana.

"Witch." She coughed, then her eyes flared wide, animated, like a dying snake's.

Crocus grabbed the folds of Sybellina's gown and placed them over her face, as if blocking her eyes would diminish the power of her words. He pushed her down to the mosaic floor and stabbed her again, this time across the front of her neck, as if he was dispatching an injured animal.

A final jerk ran through Sybellina's body. Then she lay still.

Crocus pulled the covering from Sybellina's face, unsheathed his dagger, opened her mouth wide with his fingers, grabbed her tongue and pulled it up until her head came right off the floor. The tongue looked like the tail of a sea snake emerging from her mouth. He sliced it off. Sybellina's head hit the floor with a resounding thud. Blood flowed from it. Crocus placed the tongue into one of the braziers lighting the room. It flared and the smell of burning flesh filled the room. He grunted in satisfaction and looked around, as if for approval.

Juliana's stomach turned. She had never seen so much blood come from one body. But she could not object to what Crocus had done. Tiny's death and her awareness of how close she'd been to losing her own life, and any future for her baby, ensured that her lips were sealed.

The physician, meanwhile, was so startled by all this, his mouth was opening and closing, as if he wanted to scream but had decided attracting attention to himself was not a good idea.

Constantine picked up Sybellina's knife. He put it to his nose as if checking for poison, then put it down and hugged Juliana. She wrapped her arms around him. Relief ran through her. She closed her eyes again as a dream came to her. There was more of this to come.

A knock sounded at the door. Had someone been knocking for a while? Juliana couldn't tell. The corner of her mouth twitched.

Constantine shouted, "Wait!"

The banging stopped for a moment after Constantine's shout, but it resumed after a moment, this time with greater urgency. It seemed as if the door was being hammered by desperate hands.

Constantine walked to it and with Lucius by his side now, he yanked it open. The door flew inwards, and the head of the guards massing outside fell forward. He recovered, took in Sybellina's dead body with an impassive look and stood to attention. There was an array of grim faces behind him.

"Sir, a raiding party of Picts have overrun the North Gate. It was open late to let visitors in for your father's banquet. There're druids with them too. Setting fire to everything, they are, and they're headed this way. The city reserve has been called out, but. . . " As if to confirm what the man was saying a sudden clamor could be heard. Somewhere down the corridor swords were clashing and a great roar, like a hundred berserk warriors on the loose, was coming towards them.

"Hold your post," said Constantine. "I will join you!" he roared. The man fled. The physician, bowing, had positioned himself by the man's side as he was talking. Muttering about getting some things he needed, he followed the guard. Constantine closed the door and pulled across the wooden piece that locked it.

He turned back and gave a thumbs down signal to Crocus. His eyes had a look of doom in them, as if they'd been hollowed out by all the talking they had done about protecting those you loved, no matter what the price.

Juliana watched as Crocus bent over the emperor. One of his hands was covering the emperor's mouth and nose, pinching tight. Then he bent closer. His other hand was patting the emperor's brow. The emperor's body convulsed, noiselessly.

Juliana wanted to scream stop, but she couldn't. It was his life or theirs. And she couldn't look away. Time slowed as the emperor's body twitched on the edge of death. He was refusing to die. Juliana raised her fists, pressed them into the side of her face, distracting herself with pain.

A final convulsion came, like a shiver.

Crocus looked round, an expectant expression on his face as if he wanted to be congratulated. Constantine and Lucius were busy whispering.

Juliana remembered what Sybellina had called her. Witch. Was it true? Had she brought all this about? If she hadn't made Constantine fall for her, none of this might have happened.

No, he deserved this. Even without her being involved, plots would have formed against Constantine. He would have had to make a similar decision sooner or later. Her role had been to help him see what had to be done. Tiresias had also told her stories about how mothers and young children were being put to the sword in Caledonia by the emperor's legionaries and how it would be right and good to seek his death before more died that summer.

She looked around. Lucius was staring at her. His face was white. The windows rattled. A bloody stench had filled the room, whether it was from Sybellina's corpse or the emperor's was unclear. Most likely the guts had loosened for both.

She covered her nose. Her arm was throbbing terribly.

Crocus stepped back from the bed. "Your time has come, my lord," he said. He bowed towards Constantine.

Constantine went to his father's bedside, listened for breathing, his ear close to his father's mouth. Then he slapped his father's face and Juliana jumped, expecting the emperor to wake.

But he didn't.

Constantine shook the emperor's shoulder, pulled the body towards him, and hugged it, tenderly. The emperor's arms hung limp at his side. Then, as if an uncontrollable rage had overcome him, or he'd remembered some terrible injustice, he thumped his father's back with both hands as he held him, an animal howl emerging from him, part mourning, part anguish. He let his father fall back and he grabbed one of the dead emperor's hands and rubbed his forefinger on his forehead.

Then he wiped his hands on the bed sheet and stood.

His tone was sullen when he spoke. Everyone else was standing still, as if they were playing parts in some nightmare tableau.

"My father, the emperor . . ." His voice faltered. He looked lost, but only for a moment, and a moment later he looked composed, as if what they'd witnessed had never occurred.

Juliana's skin was tingling, and her breath was coming fast. Was this what that slave girl had meant all those years ago when she'd told her she was being saved for something?

"I will be the emperor now, as it was prophesized," he said. His tone lacked any note of rejoicing, as if he would simply take the prize offered him but had not enjoyed its winning. "Crocus, arrange for a proper funeral. One fit for a victorious emperor. A great emperor."

Crocus nodded in reply.

Juliana looked from Crocus to Lucius. In their eyes she could see only emptiness. Cruel, expressionless emptiness. She wondered was that how her own face looked.

She was suddenly overcome by a longing for her childhood home. She closed her eyes. Vivid memories came to her; the sweet scent of the olive orchards, the taste of figs at harvest time, the songs of the slaves as they worked in the fields. It all seemed so very far away now, unreachable.

There was a knock on the door. A single soft knock. Then once again, more softly. Crocus went to the door.

"My Alemanni guards have arrived," he said.

He unlocked the door, opened it a little and slipped outside. In a few moments he returned.

"My lord, we are ready. The Picts have disappeared into the darkness, as they promised." He stared straight ahead. "My men have relieved the remaining troops who were on guard outside." He jerked his thumb towards the corridor beyond the door.

Constantine nodded. He raised his hands and spoke.

"Quick justice was done tonight. My father was ill served by that wicked priestess. As far as the public is concerned, my father succumbed to an illness, an old illness. Sybellina poisoned him." He turned to Crocus. "Deal with the physician, tonight."

Crocus nodded.

Constantine continued. "All of you, tell me the name of anyone who presses you for more detail about what happened here, or who spreads wild rumors. Refer such troublemakers to me. Say nothing of what you have seen. Now come, we must announce the emperor's death."

Crocus opened the doors. Directly outside and arrayed down the corridor stood a double row of his troops. Further down the corridor a cluster of men waited, high imperial officials in spotless togas, leather-clad military officers from other legions, and the governor of the city, all standing close together, as if to support each other.

They were whispering frantically as Constantine took a step towards them and raised his hands above his head for silence.

An aura of command envelopes him, thought Juliana.

The officials surged forward but stopped within a sword's reach of Constantine.

"Friends, officers of my father. Dread news. The gods have looked aside tonight. Our glorious emperor is dead." He stopped, lowered his head. Around him a shocked silence settled. Someone moaned, softly.

"The witch who has been treating him for his illness for some time," he continued, his head lowered, as if in mourning. "She has paid for her failure with her life." He paused. There was a sudden babble of voices.

"You will all. . ." His tone was stern.

The crowd instantly hushed.

"Respect our grief in this period of mourning. I will inform the public and send the correct messages of condolence to the empress." He paused, looked from face to face of the men surrounding him.

"My father's dying wish was that I become emperor in his place. He made a sign with his blood on my forehead to prove this to you all."

There was a collective intake of breath.

Juliana stared, saw the sign for the first time. It was an X in blood on Constantine's forehead. She at once knew where the blood had come from. Constantine's hands were covered in it from the stream that had flowed from the wound on her arm. The mark on his forehead was her blood.

"I have decided, however, not to put myself forward for the succession. We will wait on word from the senior Emperor Galerius, as to who he will appoint over us. Now please, friends, go home, and pray to the gods for my beloved father."

Juliana couldn't believe what she'd just heard. He was turning it all down.

The military prefect, Marcus Scipio, stepped forward.

"I must be allowed access to the body, Constantine. I have a duty to report to the senate in Rome the exact circumstances of the emperor's death. Please, let me through." He lifted his hand, as if to move Constantine aside. All eyes gaped at the confrontation.

Constantine raised his hand equally high in reply. Crocus' men stiffened in anticipation.

Then Constantine put his hand on Marcus Scipio's shoulder.

"Come, Scipio, we have much to discuss. Crocus will assist you with your report later." He took a step, turning the tribune with him. Marcus Scipio resisted for a moment, then went along.

LXIX

Eboracum, Northern Britannia, 306 A.D.

"Augustus, Augustus, Augustus." The acclamation, reserved for the most senior of emperors, rolled over the crowd like giant waves, so loud the gods must surely have heard the roars. It was noon, and much of the vast assembly on the heath had been waiting since early that morning. Three times the ceremony had been arranged and three times it had been cancelled, on one occasion as late as the night before. Anticipation had grown with each delay and rumors had blossomed, but now at last, the ceremony was about to begin.

Even as the roars went up, the last of the plebeians were filling the spaces allocated them behind the tightly packed ranks of the legions in their full battle array, their spears glinting, lined up behind their standards, raised high against the pale midsummer sky.

At the rear of the crowd hawkers sold the last of their bead bracelets, cornbread, and long-lasting sandals as urchins raced through the crowd, like wild things released for the day, and proselytizers of every cult and persuasion worked the edge of the crowd, like wolves around a flock.

"He's coming, he's coming," people whispered, excitedly.

Two urchins stopped the fight they were having over a crust of bread and jumped up again and again, trying to see over the heads of the onlookers.

"Calm yourself, boys, our day will come," said a soft Pictish voice. The boys looked round. A tall, thin, aged figure of a man, wearing a long brown cloak stood behind them. The cloak looked new, being unstained, and having that soft look of a wool cloak that has yet to see the mud of a long winter. Around his neck hung a string of gray pebble beads, with a sickle moon-shaped emblem hanging from the center. The boys stared, their mouths wide open, as the man wagged a bony finger at them, then continued on his way, pushing straight through the crowd.

By the time the old man reached the lines of legionaries, the soldiers had begun to stamp their feet in mock impatience. It was ten days since the end of their beloved emperor's period of mourning. They needed a new leader. A new Caesar Augustus. The one that had been promised. An emperor of their own.

A braying cacophony of war horns could be heard now and the chink, chink, chink of body armor moving as the legionaries swayed while raising their fists in unison. Then all the war horns rang out together, as if they were announcing the arrival of a god.

The old man showed a freshly minted bronze pass to a disgruntled marshal, who reluctantly let him through. He walked slowly up a passage between the long rows of men. Behind him, a murmur ran through the crowd. How did such a lowly dressed man gain entry to a restricted area, he could almost hear them say.

As he walked through the lines, he could feel the power these men represented. The acclamations were still rolling from legion to legion, alternating from cohort to cohort, but what impressed him most was the cohorts that remained silent, while the others around them were shouting. Men stood like statues, their cloaks barely moving in the light breeze. Discipline, that's what made these Romans strong.

He could smell the torches now. A pungent mix of hazel wands, tallow and yew.

He walked on alone until he reached the open area at the front of the massed ranks. Skirting the open area, he headed for the large leather tent set up at the far end, with pennants flying from each of its four corners.

At the tent he was stopped again. After being searched and questioned, his pass examined and passed from one marshal to another, he was allowed entry. With a few more steps he was in the tent.

The crowd hushed as a troop of trumpeters blew a long signal. The dignitaries of the city, the board of ten councilors of Colonia Eboracum, stood to attention in their long white togas with the other high officials. They too had been waiting all morning. They too were getting restless. The praise singers had orated their endless panegyrics.

It was time.

A wooden stage had been set up on the crest of a low ridge. To each side of it a gold, double-headed eagle glared out at the crowd. A striped purple and white canopy provided shade. Beneath it, and alone on a raised dais, was a backless chair, whose golden arms were carved in the shape of sleeping lions.

The trumpets blew again. Then, to an audible sigh, a line of pale skinned virgins appeared from behind the imperial tent, hair running loose about their bare shoulders. They wore long yellow gowns and had green laurels perched on their heads. Each girl carried a wicker basket, and as they mounted the stage they sprinkled rose petals all about them. Then they waited in a line on either side of the throne, their heads bowed.

The crowd hushed, except for some distant nervous coughing. Somewhere, a horse neighed.

First out of the imperial tent came the priests and priestesses of every temple in Eboracum. Dressed in white, green, or sky blue they strode out two by two, and stood below the stage. Some wore elaborate headdresses of horn, and others wore wide gold bands, others were shaven headed, including two priestesses. At their rear, and alone, came that tall figure in a brown cloak. He had the appearance of a druid, but the large silver cross that now dangled from a chain around his neck made it clear he was a follower of the cult of Christ.

"Tiresias, has returned," whispered a local dignitary who stood behind his Roman overlords, to one side of the stage. "The one god's hand is in all this."

The flaps of the tent were held open by slave boys, and out came the man who almost everyone in Eboracum now wanted to be their new emperor. He wore a purple silk toga, and his head was bare.

453

Behind him came a young page in a short tunic, who held a cushion in front of him, on which a diamond-studded band, the imperial diadem gleamed.

A woman walked out of the tent after him. Her gaze was focused down onto the thin trampled grasses in front of her. Her hands hung stiffly by her sides. She was wearing a long black silk gown studded with precious stones; a stunning dress for one so humble, some women who saw it would later say.

The trumpets blew again. The woman looked up. Three long notes sounded as the claimant and his entourage mounted the stage. The commander of each legion present approached and greeted the claimant with a low bow. The pageboy stood behind the throne, the emperor-to-be stood in front of it.

The legion commanders kneeled. A cheer went up from the assembly. At last, the uncertainty was over. The most senior officers of the legions in Britannia lowered their heads, slowly, until their foreheads were touching the stage. The claimant raised his hands, for silence.

"I will accept what has been pressed on me. Remember this day, all of you, and that you were present when a new age began, and tell your children, and your grandchildren, when you wheeze by the fire, in your dotage, that you were there the day it all started." He paused. "I am ready." His voice was clear and loud as it rang out over the heads of the legionaries, towards the townspeople.

He sat. Behind him, Crocus, the most senior legion commander, lifted the diadem from its cushion.

He held it in the air for all to see, then placed it, slowly, on the new emperor's head. For a moment it looked as if he was about to take it away, because he lifted it up again. Someone in the crowd sniggered, nervously. Then Crocus placed the diadem more securely back among Constantine's thick black curls.

Constantine stood to bask in the acclaim of the crowd. "Augustus, Augustus, Augustus," was the cry, and wave after wave of cheering rolled over him, until the trees themselves seemed to bend to the cries.

454

Behind him, Juliana was beaming at Tiresias, who stood nearby at the end of the line of priests. He smiled back. No longer would he have to hide among his brothers. He led the priests, as they prostrated themselves in front of the new emperor.

Juliana moved forward and whispered in Constantine's ear, one hand resting on his shoulder. A thin snakeskin bracelet slid down her wrist.

"My lord, I'm sure I should be reminding you how quickly these cheers will die away, but I've other news for you, a surprise, and a present for your coronation." He made to turn his head. She touched his shoulder, leaned closer to him, was on the tips of her toes as she spoke. "Our first baby will be a boy, so Eborus predicts."

He pulled her towards him and kissed her, eagerly. A great roar went up from the crowd. And at that moment the sun broke from behind a cloud and lit their faces and the whole podium as if god was blessing their union. If anyone, a year before, had told her she'd be kissed like this, by an emperor in front of his troops, she'd have laughed at the idea. She could not be happier.

Epilogue

The official announcement of Constantine's succession was made throughout all of what had been his father's provinces. Many had heard rumors that the old emperor had died, but Constantine had refused to let the announcement of his father's death be officially proclaimed until the succession was agreed.

A period of toleration for all Christians was later proclaimed in all the western territories he ruled. The marriage of the Christian church to the state was entered into willingly. Lucius pointed out to Constantine that by controlling men's souls, a more permanent empire would be created than one that relied solely on physical force for control.

"We can make eternal temples of your governor's basilicas," was his way of putting it. And with his treasury overflowing from donations by Christians, Constantine could consolidate control on his father's provinces, and pay those who'd aided him.

When Constantine arrived in Treveris for the first time, as emperor at the head of his troops, he and Crocus went first to the Temple of Hercules, his father's namesake. It had been rumored that the priests there were agitating against him. The doors to the temple were forced open, and the high priest was found, cowering in the small inner sanctum. The man's face was so pox marked, the legionaries who caught him held him at arm's length as they brought him to Constantine, as if they thought they might catch something, and that it probably would have been better to leave him where he was.

When asked why he had refused to answer to their knocking, he said that an evil sign had occurred two nights before: a vase had fallen in the temple and had broken into smithereens. The vase had shown Hercules stealing the sacred tripod at Delphi. Since then he had refused to open the temple. Some of his acolytes had taken the sign as meaning an overturning of the order of things.

He said he could not himself determine what the sign meant but was planning to travel to Rome to have it interpreted at the great Temple of Hercules there. He would not read the augers anymore, he said, as the chance of a false reading under the present circumstances were too high.

Constantine laughed at that. He looked around at the numerous vases and statues, which stood in niches along all the walls. "You priests believe anything," he said. "You're lucky the whole lot wasn't broken."

While the priest cowered in front of him, Constantine made his demands.

"You will proclaim me Augustus tomorrow, at a special ceremony in front of this temple." His tone was cold. The priest nodded enthusiastically.

"My men will stay with you all day so that you do not change your mind and run away. As for your omen, it simply signified the arrival of a new emperor, that's all. There will be no need for you to go to Rome. Not until I say so."

After that, Constantine proclaimed a series of gladiatorial games to be held in honor of his father. They would be the best ever held in Treveris. A new arena and basilica were also planned, dedicated to his father.

He still had to ratify the position he'd been elevated to by his troops with Galerius, the emperor of the east. He knew his western army, if you included Crocus' cavalry, was the largest in his father's old provinces, Britannia, Gaul, Germania and Hispania, but he would still have to tread carefully. Galerius could decide to enforce the rights of the official successor to his father, whose position Constantine had usurped.

Galerius, as senior emperor, officially had the right to nominate the western emperor. Constantine still had a long way to go to consolidate the whole empire under him.

His father's wife, the ex-Empress Theodora, was permitted to keep her apartments in the old palace in Treveris. Constantine moved into the summer palace, downriver, on the opposite western bank.

The governor of Massilia was eventually brought before him for judgment, his sentence decided, and then he was charged. The man was returned to his city, crucified, and his body left to rot outside the gates as an example. The sight of such a once invincible man, so punished, would also be some recompense for the families of those he'd mistreated. The people of Massilia acclaimed Constantine as their savior after that and were loyal to his cause through all his subsequent campaigns.

He also gained the popularity of the plebs. He increased the bread distribution to the freed men of Treveris, and the guilds and colleges of trades were given new contracts throughout his provinces, all at favorable terms.

The day after his public acclamation at Eboracum, a messenger was sent with an image of him being crowned Augustus to Galerius. An accompanying letter informed Galerius of the sad event of his father's death and lamented the forceful nature of the acclamation that had compelled him to break from soliciting the purple in the constitutional manner.

The letter requested the title "Augusta" bestowed on him by his Legions, requesting the emperor to honor the will of the Legions in these exceptional circumstances. The title "Augusta" was claimed by Constantine, as he'd agreed not to claim the lesser title of Caesar when he had been released by Galerius.

Constantine also offered to act in concert with Galerius against the common enemies of Rome and reaffirmed his agreement not to raise a hand against his fellow Augusta. He did, however, assert his right to defend himself, if attacked.

The messenger arrived at Nicomedia in time for the festival of the Romani and was taken directly to the emperor. There he nervously prostrated himself, as a crowd of advisors and senior military officers looked on. Galerius read the letter in silence.

"Get up," he shouted when he'd finished.

The messenger rose slowly, then stumbled, overawed by his surroundings.

"Tell your master I have thrown his image in the fire! He must call himself Caesar, not Augustus. Now get out of here, before I throw you in the fire as well."

When Constantine heard the news, he was overjoyed. Galerius had given him what he needed, time and legitimacy. He'd granted a lower title than that he'd sought, but he'd ratified his position as his father's successor. For now, there would be no civil war.

Juliana had been asked by Constantine what she desired as her reward, and she'd agreed with Constantine's offer to bring her foster mother to Treveris. It took some time, but eventually Constantine's agents achieved their task.

Her mother arrived in Treveris not long before Juliana's baby was born. The old woman gazed from face to face when she arrived, trying to work out which was her foster daughter. Then, with a burst of surprise and joy, she recognized Juliana. She almost hadn't, due to Juliana's prosperous appearance, her sumptuous embroidered gown, coiffed hair and general well-fed air, and the confident look she now adopted. Juliana was overcome with joy that day. The emotion of all she'd endured burst through and she wept heavily on her mother's shoulder.

But news arrived the following day, which cast a long shadow over her joy. Advisors were recommending Constantine should marry Maxentius' sister Fausta, to seal a pact between the two imperial houses. Fausta's dowry would be substantial, it was said, and Constantine needed support for his treasury and the building program he'd planned.

A sense of foreboding dogged her for some time after that, and followed her for days until finally, one night, she saw Constantine's father in a dream, calling to her, pleading for his life. She woke in a slick sweat and felt the cold, clammy breath of evil all around. For a moment she wondered if it was coming from within her, so she picked up a hand mirror, and gazed at the face looking back at her. The ringlets she wore her hair in those days, in the new fashion, hung down like curtains on each side of a pale, gaunt face. She looked older than her twenty-two years. She threw away the mirror and with a shudder listened to it smash.

Had she encouraged murder, for selfish reasons? Was all the rest simply an excuse? Can you commit a terrible crime to achieve something good, and be forgiven? She went down on her knees.

When she was alone with him again, when he returned, she asked him what his plans were for his new son.

"We have broken the seal as was foretold. A crown has been given to me and I will conquer all," replied Constantine. "I will rebuild the empire, and our son will inherit it, as is right for a son. I promise you that."

She would always remember those words. One day they would come back to haunt her.

CPSIA information can be obtained
at www.ICGtesting.com
Printed in the USA
BVHW031721090620
581042BV00002B/73/J